TUMBLEDOWN MANOR

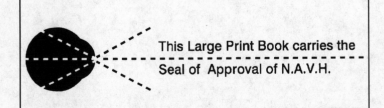

This Large Print Book carries the
Seal of Approval of N.A.V.H.

TUMBLEDOWN MANOR

HELEN BROWN

THORNDIKE PRESS
A part of Gale, Cengage Learning

GALE
CENGAGE Learning®

Farmington Hills, Mich • San Francisco • New York • Waterville, Maine
Meriden, Conn • Mason, Ohio • Chicago

GALE
CENGAGE Learning®

Copyright © 2014, 2016 by Helen Brown.
Thorndike Press, a part of Gale, Cengage Learning.

ALL RIGHTS RESERVED
Thorndike Press® Large Print Women's Fiction.
The text of this Large Print edition is unabridged.
Other aspects of the book may vary from the original edition.
Set in 16 pt. Plantin.

LIBRARY OF CONGRESS CATALOGING-IN-PUBLICATION DATA

Names: Brown, Helen, 1954– author.
Title: Tumbledown Manor / by Helen Brown.
Description: Large print edition. | Waterville, Maine : Thorndike Press, 2016. |
    Series: Thorndike Press large print women's fiction
Identifiers: LCCN 2016019249| ISBN 9781410492586 (hardcover) | ISBN 1410492583
    (hardcover)
Subjects: LCSH: Family secrets—Fiction. | Large type books. | Domestic fiction.
Classification: LCC PS3602.R69783 T86 2016 | DDC 813/.6—dc23
LC record available at https://lccn.loc.gov/2016019249

Published in 2016 by arrangement with Kensington Books, an imprint of Kensington Publishing Corp.

Printed in Mexico
1 2 3 4 5 6 7 20 19 18 17 16

To Michaela Hamilton with heartfelt thanks for her inspiration, guidance — and love of cats

A glass of prosecco at dawn is romantic. It fizzes with excitement while the morning yawns awake. As the day grows wiser, a flute of sparkling wine adds magic to a lazy afternoon.
But when the sky turns red over the hills and the evening star winks at the possibility of a kiss nothing surpasses champagne.

— Lisa Trumperton
Castlemaine, 2016

CHAPTER 1

A birthday ending in a zero was nothing to make a fuss about. There was enough to be grateful for — her health, a solid marriage, kids old enough to be off their hands (technically), a passable writing career. Why anyone would want to celebrate being another decade closer to filling a funeral urn was beyond Lisa Katz.

Nevertheless, she felt a prick of disappointment when, over breakfast at a diner near their apartment, she realized Jake had forgotten. But no wonder. Poor Jake was working crazy hours at the bank. His once lustrous tide of curls had receded to a charcoal reef, and the dark circles under his eyes had puffed out into pouches.

"You're still my best girl," he said, before draining his coffee and dabbing his lips with a paper napkin.

Standing, he bent over the table and brushed his lips against hers. It was one of their less awkward kissing positions, apart from when they were in bed together lying side by side.

As a teenager sprouting depressingly close to six feet, Lisa had imagined marrying someone as tall as — if not taller than — herself. But while she was getting her head around the idea of wearing flats for the rest of her life, she began to notice that most tall men were obsessed with women the size of dolls. Lisa, on the other hand, was a magnet to pint-sized Napoleons.

Still, what Jake lacked in stature he made up for with vigor. The height difference had only increased the inventiveness of their sex life in the early days. Back then, he'd stroked her large buttocks as if they were the foothills of heaven.

Now, Lisa felt a ripple of fondness combined with relief as Jake slid into his overcoat and disappeared into the gray fall morning. Pulling on her hat, cape, and fingerless gloves, she stepped outside into her own private birthday, a day of doing just what *she* wanted for a change.

After a couple of hours at MoMA, Lisa had a session of guilty gratification with Mark. It seemed vaguely immoral to pay for a stranger to rub oil into her back like that, but Jake was too tired these days — and

Mark's hands never wandered.

Then, flushed and gleaming with oil, she headed home to their apartment building on the Upper East Side. Set several blocks back from the park and surely the ugliest building in the entire neighborhood, it frowned down on a narrow, shaded street.

At the door, Pedro greeted her with his eternal smile — a miracle, considering he held down three jobs to keep himself and his family alive. "Lucky you missed the rain, Mrs. Trumperton." He beamed.

She'd stopped asking him to call her Lisa. It was typical Pedro to use her professional name. To most people she was just Mrs. Katz, Jake's gangly appendage.

As she opened the door to their apartment, Lisa stumbled backwards.

"Surprise!"

Jake stepped toward her, his dark eyes glowing in triumph. What was he doing home this early? He took her hand and guided her to the living room.

"Happy birthday, Mom!" Ted encircled her in his arms, sending her hat tumbling to the floor.

"Ted? You came all the way from Australia?" Lisa was suddenly aware that she was shaking. "When did you get here?"

"This morning." Her son picked up her

11

hat and dusted it off.

"How did you get time off?" She scraped her hands through her hair, hoping he wouldn't notice how oily it was from the massage.

"I've got a week before my next exam," he said.

The genetic slot machine had been kind to Ted. Not only had he inherited his father's Mediterranean coloring rather than her bloodshot, watery-eyed Nordic genes, but he was tall and well built. The shadow of a beard made his chin more pronounced and highlighted his eyes. Whatever he was up to besides architecture studies was doing him good.

Lisa was about to tease him about his Australian accent when the pantry door burst open. "Surprise!" Portia teetered toward Lisa in shoes that would qualify as stilts.

As her daughter bent to kiss her in a flurry of blond hair and blue fingernails, Lisa noticed a new Care Bear tattoo on Portia's neck. Had she lost weight? Either way, this wasn't the time to cause friction. Not when Portia had sacrificed hours of her glamorous Venice Beach lifestyle to show up.

Lisa's heart pounded in her ears. "How lovely," she quavered, wondering if they were expecting her to cook and, if so, what she could possibly feed them. Following her latest diet book's instructions, she'd gutted the fridge. From memory, the only thing in there was a half-dead bottle of Coke Zero. "I really had no idea. . . ."

"Surprise!"

A fresh surge of dread ran through Lisa. Kerry, her weekly lunch buddy, emerged from the hallway. Lisa relaxed a little. Armed with a potted peace lily, he was closely followed by Vanessa from the publishing house. Jake had chosen well. If he was going to startle her with anyone, these were the best possible . . .

"Surprise!"

Not another. Her system could take only so much. Lisa's blood drained to her feet as her older sister, Maxine, emerged from the bedroom with husband Gordon in her wake.

"We took the same flight as Ted," Maxine gushed, floating toward Lisa in a lurid caftan that made her resemble a psychedelic emu.

Most women of a certain age fade into blond. Maxine had opted for ginger, which had deepened to fiery purple. It was a shade that shouldn't have suited anyone, but it glowed against Maxine's pearly skin in a way that was strangely compelling. With intense emerald eyes beaming out from her round, freckled face, Maxine could've passed as an extra from *Lord of the Rings*. Smiling shyly over Maxine's shoulder was Gordon, his broom of white hair and podgy pink face resembling the features of a man-sized koala.

"But it's such a long way to come just for me," Lisa said.

"You always were the spoiled one," crooned Maxine, brushing Lisa's cheek with a kiss. "Just kidding." Maxine's smile flickered with complication, and Lisa wondered if her sister would ever let go of the endless list of evidence that proved Lisa was their father's favorite. High on the list, for example, was the time Lisa had allegedly tricked him into believing she needed to stay home from school because of a "tummy ache," while Maxine, who was the one coming down with authentic measles, was forced to go. Maxine needed therapy. She had nothing to complain about, not when she'd clearly been the center of their mother's universe. The moment Maxine drew her first breath, their mother, Ruby, had recognized a mini replica of herself. Everything about Maxine — from the red hair and compact build to the terrifying presence on any sports field — screamed MacNally.

In contrast, their father, William Trumperton, had been a sensitive man who avoided conflict. Lisa still clung to what he'd told her in a rare moment of unguardedness — that he found it hard to believe she and Maxine were from the same stable. Once or twice, she'd wondered if he'd been speaking literally and they had different fathers. She wouldn't have put anything past Ruby.

Now Maxine stood on tiptoe to help Lisa shed her cape. "Begging on the streets again, are we?" she said, casting an eye over Lisa's fingerless gloves.

Under normal circumstances, Lisa would've cracked back about purple hair and caftans covered in hideous fake rubies. Maxine had been born with appalling taste that no amount of private schooling could cure. But the ambush of family affection had thrown Lisa.

Maxine wandered over to the kitchen area, pulled a bottle out of the fridge and inspected the label. Her eyes narrowed. "You know it has to come from a special part of France to be the real thing."

Lisa assured her she was perfectly happy with sparkling wine from California. Jake had introduced it as part of their "post-global-financial-crisis" economy drive. It wasn't too sweet and had the same effect,

15

more or less.

Corks popped. Glasses foamed and were passed around. As Jake lifted a mosaic of hors d'oeuvres from the fridge, Lisa was reminded why she'd fallen in love with him. Jake Katz the romantic, the magician . . . "You *are* organized!" she said, giving him a peck on the cheek. She was amazed he even knew how to find a caterer.

"Well, my dear. It's not every day you turn f—"

"Hush!" She gently covered his mouth. "But darling, it's so thoughtful of you."

Jake cleared his throat and puffed his chest out, which was his way of making himself taller. The room settled expectantly. Poor darling — what hair he had left was graying at the temples. But he was aging well. Not just in looks. Even though their sex life was intermittent these days, Lisa took silent pride in the fact he took no interest in advertisements for Viagra.

"I'd like to thank you all for coming here today, some of you from a very long way," he said, raising a glass to Maxine and Gordon.

"Well, it was a convenient stop-off before our Alaskan cruise," Maxine chimed in — unnecessarily, Lisa thought.

"Those polar bears will be counting the

days till they see you." Jake chortled.

Lisa's smile froze. Jake and Maxine were too alike. Neither could stand the other's hogging the limelight. To Lisa's relief, Maxine lowered her eyes and took a swig from her glass.

"And we mustn't forget Ted," Jake continued.

Perched on the arm of the black leather sofa, Ted was engrossed in his phone. Hearing his name, he flipped out of whatever conversation he was having and aimed the gadget at his parents. Lisa hastily bent her knees so Jake could drape his arm over her shoulder and smile foolishly at the lens.

Portia stood cross-armed in a corner. She rolled her eyes as Jake asked to see the photo. "And you too, of course, Portia," he said, nodding approval and handing the phone back to Ted. "Venice Beach isn't exactly in the neighborhood. Anyway, I just wanted to take this opportunity to thank my wonderful wife of twenty-four years."

"Twenty-*three*!" Maxine corrected.

"Oh, is that right?" Jake said, looking to Lisa for rescue.

Lisa was hopeless at maths. She had no idea.

"Yes," Maxine said, pointing a glittering talon at him. "You two were married exactly two years after Gordon and me. Of course we had a *church* wedding. . . ."

As if nobody knew Maxine and Gordon Frogget's union had been sanctified by God and half the stockbrokers of Camberwell.

With rare composure, Jake loosened his tie and slid some notes from his breast pocket. "When we first met in Fiji all those years ago, I had no idea how deeply I was going to fall for this Aussie girl," he read.

"Oh, Jake," Lisa said, her eyes moistening.

"Lisa, I can't thank you enough for moving across oceans to make a life with me and raise our two kids here. You're my rock, my inspiration. . . ."

Lisa felt guilty for all the times she'd yelled at him for coming home late and going to those interminable conferences.

"You're the artist to my knuckleheaded bean counting," he went on. "The sunflower-covered straw hat to my suit. You remind me of what really matters in life. You're the —"

"Wind beneath your wings?" Portia said archly.

Honestly, there were times Lisa could have throttled her offspring. Temporarily, of course.

Jake composed himself and glanced down at his notes. He always liked his speeches to

18

have a serious core. Lisa could tell he was building up to a crescendo.

"When you were struck with breast cancer last year we all faced the terrible prospect of losing you. . . ."

Oh God. She'd packed all that away in a mental filing box labeled Forget About It. She was fine now, just fine.

There was a tap at the door. Ted moved silently across the room to open it while Jake continued. "And now, knowing you have the all-clear, we treasure you even more. . . ."

The room glowed with admiration as Ted reappeared with an enormous basket of red roses. Lisa had never seen anything like it. The arrangement was so huge it dwarfed her son.

"Oh Lord, Jake!" She reached for the small white envelope dangling from one of the stalks.

Jake suddenly turned pale. He lunged in front of her and tried to snatch the envelope. Smiling, she nudged him away.

Lisa could feel her cheeks reddening as she tore open the envelope and pulled out a heart-shaped card. Jake could be such a romantic devil. She blew him a kiss, but his eyes were blank, his mouth slightly open.

"To my darling . . . Belle," she read aloud.

There had to be a mistake. The handwriting was Jake's. Lisa's throat tightened. She tried to stop, but her voice kept reading the words aloud. "I cannot wait until we are together forever."

Lisa's body slowly turned to stone. She knew Belle, the blonde from HR at the bank. Belle of the enormous boobs and pipe-cleaner legs, who said she'd read every book Lisa had ever written and was her biggest fan.

"So I can bury my head in your thighs every night . . . All my love, Jake."

Silence.

Jake's face flushed with panic as the room's gaze swiveled from Lisa to him. "This is *outrageous*!" he declared, grappling for the phone in his suit pocket. Temples gleaming, he stabbed the numbers for Eva the florist.

Usually when Jake turned purple, Lisa tried to calm him down, because he loved cheese and didn't exercise enough. But the normal Lisa had vanished and been replaced by a hate-filled clone who was willing the arteries around his heart to explode.

"What do you *mean* you sent them to the usual address?!" Jake shouted at the plastic rectangle in his hand.

He should've known not to trust Eva. Ever

20

since her mother had died, she'd started talking to her carnations. Now Eva had sent the ridiculous arrangement to the usual address without thinking.

Lisa watched as a crazed woman roared across the room and walloped Jake across the face. Who was she? Oh, that's right. It was the other Lisa, the one so outraged and wounded she was about to commit murder. Or, on second thought, serious injury. Jake would be on life support for weeks. She'd enjoy the luxury of watching him suffer with tubes and probes sprouting from every orifice until she had the pleasure of switching off the machine.

Then she noticed Portia and Ted clinging to each other in the corner, as if they were watching a 3D version of *The Evil Dead.* Nice Lisa, their mother, wanted to protect them from the ugliness of this scene. But evil Lisa required them to witness the rawness of her pain, to know who the victim was.

She grabbed Jake by the shoulders and shook him savagely. Somewhere in the background, a door clicked. Vanessa and Kerry had made a discreet exit, leaving the peace lily as sole evidence of their presence.

Gordon lumbered over to the kitchen and stooped over the sink. He unraveled the rinse hose and studied it as if it might contain the solution to global warming.

Lisa the lunatic pummeled Jake's chest with her fists. Then a giant emu wafted over and peeled her off Jake and enveloped her in its wings.

Maxine's muscles were strong and tense as Lisa sobbed into her neck. Her earrings jangled. Lisa smelled Dior's Poison on Maxine's neck and champagne on her breath.

"Get out, you bastard!" Maxine yelled.

Lisa was suddenly six years old again, in the schoolyard. Big sister Maxine was shielding her, throwing sticks at Colin the bully from the butcher shop until he slunk around the corner of the bike sheds.

Jake stood frozen, wild-eyed, like a mouse about to be devoured by a snake.

"And take your lousy flowers with you!" screeched the crazed woman Lisa now recognized as herself as she tore roses out of the basket and hurled them in Jake's face. A sane part of her was grateful the roses were thornless — not that she would have minded making him bleed.

Jake scuttled into the bedroom.

"Liar!" she bellowed, clawing his back as he passed. *"I hate you!"*

Jake dragged a weekend bag from the closet and stuffed it frantically with socks and underpants.

"When did it start?" Lisa spat at his bald patch.

Jake pretended not to hear.

"When?"

"Dunno . . ." he mumbled. "Nine months ago or so."

She did the calculation. That would've been three months after her surgery, around the time of her last book launch. Belle had been all smiles as she waited in line for Lisa to sign a copy of *Charlotte,* the first in her trilogy called *Three Sisters.* "Such a brilliant idea to write historical romances based on the Brontë sisters," Belle had sniveled, all teeth and fake diamond earrings.

Hang on a minute. What if they *weren't* fake? Maybe Belle's earrings were the cause of Jake's latest economy drive restricting them each to one latte a day. Anyway, Cow Belle (*that*'s what Lisa was going to call her from now on) had sworn she couldn't wait to read about Emily Brontë in Lisa's next book, *Three Sisters: Emily.* Belle had then scurried off to screw the author's husband. Nice work, Cow Belle.

"Do you love her?" Lisa asked, her voice steeped in ice.

Jake stopped and stared at the carpet.

Soon after the book launch, Jake had gone

23

away for a two-week conference, which, come to think of it, was suspiciously long. Now Lisa scoffed at her own stupidity. She should've been savvy enough to check his e-mails. But she'd trusted him so naïvely, she hadn't even bothered to memorize his password.

Then there was the condom-packet-in-the-toiletry-bag incident. She'd been rummaging for dental floss one morning when the silvery little sachet had brushed her fingers. It was strange, because she hadn't had a period for months. When she had showed it to him, he had blushed before swearing it was leftover from ages ago and tossing it in the bin.

Why did she always believe him?

"I said, do you love her?" Her tone was dangerous now.

"I don't know," he replied quietly.

"You don't *know*?!"

"There are two sorts of loving," he said after a long silence. "Having and desiring. I have you . . . but . . ."

"You desire her!"

Lisa galloped to the living room, and grabbed what was left of the flower basket. Back in the bedroom, Jake was on his knees jamming T-shirts into his bag. With a rush of satisfaction, she emptied the remaining roses and the contents of the well-filled vase over his head.

Jake stood up and brushed the water off his suit. Then he picked up his bag, rearranged his hair, and ran. Lisa chased him as far as the living room, but he was too nimble on his feet. He slid out the door toward the elevator and was gone.

As she stood panting, gazing at her open-mouthed guests, Lisa understood exactly what she was having — a birthday ending with a zero.

CHAPTER 2

Lisa woke safe and warm inside a cocoon of sheets. Judging by the gray frame of light around the curtains, the sun — or what there was of it — had already dragged itself out of bed. Her tongue slid around the comforting shape of her mouth guard. According to the dentist, she'd been grinding her teeth at night. Lisa was pretty sure his insistence that she be fitted with a mouth guard had more to do with upgrading his Audi than her pummeling her teeth to powder. Lisa "teamed" the mouth guard with a pair of ear plugs — Jake's snoring wasn't getting any quieter. She'd put them in the night before out of habit — and to assure herself nothing was going to change.

She quietly fished out the mouth guard and earplugs and slid them into their boxes. Then she rolled over and reached for the familiar shape of Jake's head. But his pillow was as vacant as the wastelands of Antarctica. Lisa curled up in the fetal position and sobbed into her pillow — quietly, so as not to disturb Maxine and Gordon or the kids. It was her favorite pillow, so old it probably harbored superbugs. She'd tried to throw it out, but always stopped at the garbage chute and carried it back to bed. Stuffed with meager lumps of feathers and down, it was anorexic compared to Jake's anti-snoring plank. But it was a forgiving object, snuggling into the folds of her face without any attempt to improve her posture. Now tears drained into the feathers, reducing them to a soggy swamp.

When she could cry no more, she rolled on her back and ran her hand over the chasm her left breast had once inhabited. The surgeon had offered her reconstruction at the same time as the mastectomy. He said the mastectomy itself would take only forty minutes to perform, while the reconstruction would drag on for seven hours or more. After hours trawling the Internet and talking with friends who knew people who'd had reconstructions and those who hadn't, she'd decided to bide her time. It wouldn't be long before you could take a pill to grow a new breast.

Giving an excellent impersonation of a supportive husband, Jake had said he was happy to go along with whatever she wanted. She'd felt a surge of affection when he said appearances made no difference to him. And anyway, the surgeon had assured them she could have the reconstruction further down the track. She'd still not gotten around to it and now doubted she ever would. After all, Lisa had never been burdened with vanity. Her mother, Ruby, had made sure of that. ("Tidy yourself up, Lisa. . . . Cut back on the pastries, girl. They'll be calling you thunder thighs. . . . Run a comb through your hair!") The scar ran in a horizontal line across her torso like a ruler marking the end of a school essay.

Though Jake had claimed it didn't worry him, he'd never expressed interest in or even curiosity about her wound. During lovemaking, he'd lavished attention on her right breast, stroking and kissing (*never* sucking, because that would set her on a postcoital jag about the pathetic idea of grown men sucking breasts). He'd avoided her left side as if it were an abandoned neighborhood turned dangerous.

She couldn't believe how he'd lulled her into thinking their marriage was fine. For all his talk, he was just another primitively wired male who wanted a woman with two C cups. Clearly Jake was going through

28

some kind of man-opause. Surely it would just be a matter of time before he'd come to his senses and beg to come back.

A vacuum cleaner hummed on the other side of Lisa's bedroom door. The thought of facing up to her guests was almost unbearable. Still, how often did she get the chance to see her kids? So after showering and dressing, she padded out into the living room.

Maxine was hoovering up the previous night's wreckage. Ted was in the kitchen, wrangling a garbage bag. They both stopped and looked up at her as if she were a piece of crystal that might shatter at the slightest movement.

Gordon emerged from the guest room to fiddle with the coffee machine while Maxine assailed her bedroom with the vacuum cleaner. Lisa offered to help, but Maxine insisted she *sit down and relax.*

The black leather sofa squeaked as Lisa flopped onto it. The buttons dug into her backside. Everything about the apartment reeked of Jake. He used to go along with her love of what she called "soul objects." New Guinea masks and paint-peeled Buddhas took her back to the freedom of her traveling days. All that had changed when he started taking banking seriously and Jake readjusted his tastes. In the end it had been simpler to let him move "her stuff" into her study and succumb to his obsession with "clean lines." Now glass tabletops and piles of yachting magazines lent the apartment the air of a medical waiting room.

Lisa ran her eye over Jake's collection of second-tier Fauvists. Given the choice, she'd have preferred Ted and Portia's kindergarten daubs. Life-sized stainless-steel nudes stood in a corner, entwined in an outlandish position the sculptor had called the Lustful Leg. She'd tried to replicate the posture for Jake's pleasure a couple of times. Flinging her leg back over her shoulder had, however, made something in her hip lock in a sharp spasm of agony. As for the white baby grand piano that only Ted knew how to play, she pretended it wasn't there.

She wondered how she'd let herself slide into such an unlikely setting. Had she been too engrossed with the children, or working too much? She remembered feeling tired a lot of the time, perhaps even borderline depressed. She was a terrible banker's wife, anyway. Her hair wasn't blond-bobbish enough, her laugh too deep and brazen.

The coffee machine hissed and farted, enveloping Gordon in a cloud of steam. It was Jake's pride and joy, though it had never produced a decent cappuccino in its life. Gordon presented her with a pool of muddy liquid inside a mug emblazoned with a malevolent snowman. *Happy Holidays* curled in red letters around the rim. The mug usually lurked at the back of the top shelf. Christmas was more than two months away. Proof the dishwasher needed emptying.

To fill vacant air space, Gordon asked how her writing was going. Did people ask plumbers about their drains? Part One of her Brontë trilogy was selling okay, but she'd sunk into a boggy patch with *Three Sisters: Emily,* which was still not much more than a list of bullet points. She'd been a fool to sign a contract promising to have the manuscript in by March, and now the deadline was approaching with the menace of an asteroid about to collide with Earth.

Portia emerged ashen, her pale hair a mass of tangles. Lisa ached to scoop it into a tidy French plait the way she used to when Portia was six. Her own mother would've had no qualms about assailing her adult daughter with a comb. Lisa curled her fingers into fists. Every generation has to be an improvement on the last. If she was going to learn anything from Ruby's mistakes, it was to control the French-plait compulsion.

Maxine put on a pair of wooden earrings the size of Samoa and a gold vinyl jacket ("You New Yorkers call this *autumn*?" Ted reminded her the correct term was *fall.*). Then she spread a map of Manhattan over the piano lid.

Lisa knew what Maxine was up to. When they were little girls lying awake at night listening to their parents yelling down the hall, Maxine would play "Let's Pretend Nothing's Happening." As their mother's voice rose to a series of barks through the walls, Maxine would become a princess, or Dorothy in *The Wizard of Oz.* Lisa had to be the princess's servant, of course. Or the Scarecrow.

Tight-lipped with denial, Maxine set about organizing everyone's day. The girls would go on a retail-therapy binge while the boys walked the Brooklyn Bridge.

Gordon's face rose like the red planet from behind the coffee machine. He wasn't sure he'd brought the right shoes. Maxine patted his wine gut and assured him she'd packed his trainers.

After a mind-numbing morning traipsing through shops, the three women stopped at a French bakery. Before sinking her teeth into a croissant, Maxine offered to cancel the cruise so she and Gordon could stay on and "provide support." Lisa smiled at the image of Maxine as a giant brassiere.

When Lisa declined, Maxine's relief was palpable. "I talked to Ted this morning," she continued, dabbing her lips. "He's willing to change his flights and keep you company for a week or two."

Lisa felt like a starving bear presented with a plate of meat. To have Ted all to herself would be . . . But his exams!

"Never mind. I'll be fine," she said, patting her daughter's knee.

Portia stood up and flounced to the Ladies'. Heads turned as the gaunt goddess wafted past in a trail of golden hair. Lisa checked the menu for the number of calories in the three dandelion leaves Portia had chomped through (approximately seventeen). It was hard to imagine what was going through the child's brain. Maybe she was traumatized by her parents' behavior.

"Don't worry about *that* one," Maxine said, sinking her fork into a perfectly formed strawberry tart.

Lisa guessed from Maxine's tone that Portia had refused the opportunity to linger in New York to bathe her mother's wounds. Maybe through some distorted logic Portia had decided to side with Jake.

An unwelcome image of Jake sprang into Lisa's head. He was running his hands over Cow Belle's buttocks while he licked her pointy Chrysler Building nipples. His hand drifted to the mound between Cow Belle's legs, waxed bald as a newborn's. Jake had texted Portia saying that he was moving into a hotel, but everyone knew he was in that woman's Chelsea apartment asphyxiating himself between her legs.

Exhaustion washed over Lisa. She was desperate to go home, but Maxine had other ideas. With the compassion of a slave-ship captain, she urged them on to the Empire State Building and then to see the skaters at the Rockefeller Center.

When the family finally reassembled at the apartment, Lisa imagined Jake and Cow Belle knee to knee in a darkened restaurant. He'd be ordering champagne, the real French stuff. His hand would be gliding up Belle's thigh.

While Maxine corralled Gordon into the guest room to help squeeze Macy's shopping bags into their already overstuffed suitcases, Ted and Portia sat on the sofa like a pair of orphans. Portia wound her hair around her fingers and crossed her skinny legs. Someone, or thing, had taken a razor to her black jeans and slashed them to pieces. Ted made urgent little stabs at his phone.

"So when will I be seeing you two again?" Lisa asked in as breezy a tone as she could muster.

Portia picked at a thread dangling from one of the slashes in her pants. "I've got to get home to LA," she said.

LA was *home*?

"We've set up a theater group," Portia continued. "We're writing a play. They really need me."

And Lisa didn't? "What about Thanksgiving?" she asked.

"That's close to opening night," Portia whined. "I thought this visit could double as Thanksgiving."

Thanks a bundle, thought Lisa. She turned to Ted. "So I'll keep the spare room for you next year?"

Ted's dark hair draped over his forehead. She'd seen a photo of her father around the same age, and, with his long face and soulful eyes, Ted was almost an exact replica — apart from the darker coloring. The corner of his mouth twitched. "Actually, I'm thinking of staying on in Australia," he said.

A concrete ball settled in Lisa's stomach. "Oh. I guess you'll want to fit in a month

35

or two's surfing before you come back," she said.

Ted let his phone tumble nonchalantly out of his hand. The brown checks in his shirt brought out the color of his eyes. "I've had a job offer," he said.

"You mean you're going to stay on selling mushroom burgers at the market?"

Ted shook his head and smiled. "It's an architecture firm. They like my environmental approach."

He was staying in Australia? "That's great," Lisa lied. She wanted to weep at the thought of Ted stranded indefinitely on the other side of the world. Still, it was hard enough for graduates to find work anywhere these days. "You'll be based in Melbourne?"

Ted nodded, his color deepening. Lisa sensed something else going on. For all her disappointment about his decision to stay in Australia, her interest was piqued.

The next morning, Lisa's guests stood hunched against the cold, their bags scattered on the sidewalk while she tried to hail a cab. Pedro the doorman had seemed disappointed when she turned down his offer to do it. No doubt he would've been quicker at catching a driver's eye, but her Australian upbringing still left her uncomfortable when people performed menial tasks on her behalf. Cab after cab sailed past. They were either busy or ignoring her.

"Don't worry, Mom," Portia said when one finally pulled in. "I was the only one in my friendship group whose parents were still together. We're normal now." Portia always spoke of her "friendship group" with worshipful respect.

"Look after yourself," Lisa said, fighting the urge to pull Portia to her chest and never let go.

Portia flicked her hair and slid into the back of the cab with the effortless ease of youth. The child-woman hadn't heard a thing. White wires in her ears sealed her off in her own world. Inside her head Portia was already back among the hipsters of Venice Beach.

Maxine rested her hands on Lisa's shoulders and planted a kiss on each cheek. "You take care," she said in a big-sisterly tone before climbing into the front seat next to the driver.

Gordon flashed Lisa an awkward smile. He was limping from yesterday's walk. Brooklyn Bridge had turned out to be longer than it looked. Leaning forward, he aimed his lips at Lisa's cheek but collided with her chin. Blushing, he retreated into the shadows of the backseat.

Saying good-bye to Ted made Lisa's heart fray around the edges. She and he were carved from the same stone. They both had to fight the Trumperton tendency to sink into moroseness. They laughed at the same things and would finish each other's sentences. Australia was too far away. "See you at Christmas?" she asked, trying to eradicate hints of neediness.

"Sure. Come visit," he replied. "You can sleep on our sofa."

"Thanks, but the CIA should hire that thing out as an instrument of torture." So if she had any hope of seeing him in December she'd be the one climbing on a plane.

She kissed Ted and nudged him into the back of the cab next to Gordon.

Maxine's window glided down. She fixed Lisa with an emerald gaze. "I never liked that prick," she said.

As the cab dissolved into the traffic, Lisa caught a glimpse of Ted's profile in the shadows of the backseat. The unmistakable Trumperton nose. Gulping a buttery lump at the back of her throat, she waved good-bye.

Back in the apartment, Lisa was sucked into a vacuum of loneliness. She turned James Taylor up loud and plunged into a frenzy of housework. The kids had left her study a mess. She dredged one of Ted's socks out from under the sofa bed. For once it was hole-free. Someone was looking after him. As usual, Portia had stolen Lisa's shampoo and conditioner from the bathroom. Lisa wrote it off as a contribution to the starving artist of the family.

Once her study was looking half-civilized, she switched on her computer. The bullet points about *Three Sisters: Emily* glowered back at her. She had no hope of writing an entire book in four months. The first sentence was always the hardest. Her fingers hovered over the keyboard.

Then, in a cruel twist of what Portia would call irony, a deliveryman arrived with a sheath of freshly ironed shirts. Lisa didn't have the energy to refuse them. Instead, she carried them numbly to the bedroom. As she hung the shirts in Jake's side of the closet, she wondered whether they might herald his return. Perhaps he'd realized he'd made a terrible mistake, that he loved Lisa and wanted to come home. He'd promise to never see Cow Belle again.

She dug her phone out of her handbag. *Yr shirts r here,* she typed, her fingers trembling.

She made a mug of coffee. James Taylor

crooned "How Sweet It Is (to Be Loved by You)." He'd moved on to "Fire and Rain" by the time her phone buzzed to life. *Thx. Will come over.*

Sure enough, toward evening there was a tap on the door. Lisa opened it a crack. Jake peered through like a naughty schoolboy. Why was he knocking when he had a key? They examined each other in silence. Lisa would take him back after a decent interval of punishment, of course. They had too much shared history.

"Sorry," he muttered. "My shirts."

"Oh," she said, blood draining from her face.

"You okay?" he asked.

"Of course." Her voice was as cold as a surgeon's blade. "Just a minute." She left him fidgeting in the doorway while she collected the sheath.

"Let me know if you need anything," he said as she handed it to him.

What could she possibly need?

His forefinger was turning purple from the coat-hanger hooks cutting off the circulation.

Lisa knew what he wanted. If she exploded with rage again he could scurry away, confident she was a total witch. But she couldn't do it.

Instead, she watched as the boiled egg of his bald patch disappeared down the hall toward the elevator. She noticed a white thread on his shoulder. Jake had a neurotic loathing of imperfection, and she was about to call after him. But that wasn't her job. Not anymore. All Jake maintenance was over to Cow Belle. She could trim his ear hair, too.

The elevator doors sighed shut.

Lisa was officially and permanently alone.

CHAPTER 3

Over the following weeks, Jake negotiated times to visit the apartment as a legal thief. Once he and the removal men had taken the Katz family coffee pot, and his paintings, statues, and desk, there was hardly any evidence of Jake left.

Lisa played a game with herself, pretending he'd never lived there and she'd just happened to move into an apartment furnished by an obstetrician. But the king-sized bed still smelled of him. The dent in the mattress on his side stayed in his shape. When she opened the kitchen cupboards, ghosts of Jake and Lisa, the happy couple, hovered over remnants of the dinner service Aunt Caroline had given them as a wedding present.

Christmas came and went. Portia was too busy with her friendship group and the so-called play to put in an appearance. Ted sent a card featuring Santa wearing sunglasses on a golden beach. Lisa spent the day itself shrieking over Christmas-cracker jokes with Kerry and his friends. She went home and howled until her throat hurt. Her ribs ached. Abandoned, unwanted, unloved. Self-pity was exhausting.

The thought of Jake's treachery dried her tears into salt lakes of rage. Anger was invigorating, though only in short bursts.

After New Year's, she tried to settle at the computer, but the memories that clogged the apartment were cluttering her brain. Writer's block, she assumed. She'd been nuts to sign a three-book deal, especially in a genre that was new to her. All her other books had been safely anchored in nonfiction with a focus on real people and animals. Having witnessed Lisa's life implode, Vanessa had generously agreed to extend the deadline for *Three Sisters: Emily* until October. Though Lisa was grateful, she wished she'd given back the advance and abandoned the whole project. Still, it appeared the public had an appetite for feminist romantic twists on the Brontë sisters' lives. No doubt, the poor sisters were revolving in their graves at the cheerful, sexually empowered adventures Lisa was inventing for them. She was surprised by the enthusiastic reviews *Three Sisters: Charlotte* was getting on Amazon.

Lisa cast her eye around the study: In the rising sea of compromise her life had become, this room was the last vestige of who she really was. Apart from her desk and chair, bookshelves, and fold-down sofa, it was devoid of furniture. It was the other stuff — the so-called clutter — that mattered. Books spilled off shelves to form miniature skyscrapers on the floor. Tribal masks gazed down from the walls. She'd acquired them, along with the fighting stick from Fiji, long before people developed qualms about removing cultural relics from their homelands. On her desk, among photos of the kids, was a close-up of a black Persian cat. She'd met Bon Jovi at Bide-awee animal shelter, where she volunteered once a week. A refugee from Hurricane Sandy, Bon Jovi was the funniest, most affectionate feline. People adored him, but they turned away when they heard he'd been diagnosed with kidney failure. She'd longed to adopt him, but Jake was allergic to cats. Fortunately, Bon Jovi had found a home.

Lisa's computer sat on a piece of tapa cloth she'd been given by some Pacific Islanders before she was married. Stones and crystals she'd picked up from different parts of the world formed a rough circle around the screen. A sketchbook covered with scribbled story lines for *Three Sisters: Emily,* a desk lamp that had stopped working — in this jumble of books and memories she was never alone. She ran her eye across the photo albums on the second-to-top shelf. Only one had disappeared — the book of Jake's baby photos with the dates he'd first smiled and walked, meticulously recorded by his mother, Naomi.

On their first meeting Naomi had introduced herself as "Jewish but not religious." Lisa had been relieved, naïvely assuming it was the same as being a halfhearted Anglican. When Naomi and Sol said they couldn't make it to the wedding because of Sol's business commitments, Lisa had believed them. She took everything at face value back then. Naomi had gone berserk when Lisa refused to have Ted circumcised. Even when Jake and Lisa were middle-aged, Naomi never missed an opportunity to introduce Jake to a Hannah or a Miriam. Naomi had gone to her grave hoping Jake would come to his senses and run off with a nice Jewish girl. Well, only half of her wish had come true. Jake had gone, but Cow Belle didn't have a Jewish chromosome in her big-bosomed (those things had to be fake) frame.

Lisa dared herself to reach for the album she knew would hurt. The first page featured Jake the bearded radical, long hair rippling in the Fijian breeze, a tanned arm draped over her shoulder. Lisa was astonished at how beautiful she'd been, with her wispy hair and open smile, though probably only in the way young people always are. She wished she could fly back through time and tell her younger self that. Even then she knew what would happen. The compliment would get twisted in a ball of barbed wire and tossed back. No matter what people said, she'd always felt like a misfit.

She'd fallen into journalism then travel writing the way she did most things — by default. Travel writing wasn't the glamorous round of cocktails and cruises people assumed. Being dragged around resorts by self-important hotel managers was tedious. Writing gushing prose about sunsets and linen thread count was a semicolon short of prostitution. So she had had no idea how much the commission to write a feature on American student volunteers at a Fijian village would change her life.

The first time she saw Jake, he was cross-legged on a mat drinking kava with a circle of Fijian men. As he sipped from a hollowed-out coconut shell, he glanced up at her and smiled. That secretive, wicked grin had sent shudders through her groin. She was transfixed.

Jake's smooth olive skin and exotic American accent were only part of the attraction. Even when he stood up and she saw how short he was, she wasn't put off. She soon found out Jake possessed the ultimate aphrodisiac: He could make her laugh. She'd fallen deeply in lust.

On the next page was the wedding photo that made the kids snort with derision. What hippies, they said, getting married on the beach at Byron Bay. Okay, so her headband of frangipani flowers could be interpreted as alternative. The kids couldn't believe the bridal couple was barefoot by accident. But the tide was coming in — they'd *had* to take their shoes off.

A few pages on Jake shed his beard and exchanged his bandanna and most of his sense of humor for a cheap suit. They were living in New York, sporting the dark-circled eyes of new parents. She smiled at two-year-old Ted, bewildered at being supplanted, staring glumly down at his toy dinosaur while Lisa changed Portia's diaper.

Jake and Lisa then faded into the background while Ted and Portia laughed over birthday cakes, lined up for class photos, and posed at ballet classes and basketball games. Jake's suits upgraded to Armani for a while before reverting to post-global-financial-crisis no-name brands.

Toward the back of the album, Lisa and Jake appeared as middle-aged satellites, teeth yellower, hair thinner, waists thicker. Beaming proudly from the outer edges of graduation photos, they'd become unnervingly similar to their own parents.

During all those years, it had never occurred to Lisa to be unfaithful. Well, okay, perhaps once at a writers' festival in Berlin, with the only straight male publisher in a thirty-mile radius, a hand-kisser who was charming to the core of his Austrian bones. Oh, and the jazz pianist she had met through a friend of Kerry's . . . and maybe one or two others. She'd bathed in the glow of mutual attraction, but drawn the line at late-night scuffles in hotel rooms.

Now a pang of regret shot through her. She should've slept with *all* of them and more while she still had two breasts. Something strange had happened to her hormones over the past year or so. Any mention of the word *orgasm* gave her a mental image of a church organ. Orgasm, organ —

both were freakish remnants of the past.

Lisa slammed the photo album shut. So much had gone into raising children and trying to be a supportive wife she'd lost something essential — herself? Who the hell was that?

The computer screen glowed at her expectantly. She sank into her office chair and brought up the *Three Sisters: Emily* file. Writing about Charlotte had been a breeze, but Emily was more complicated. A recluse to the marrow of her bony frame, Emily "rarely crossed the threshold of home" to socialize in the village. Tall and frizzy-haired, she made no secret of the fact she preferred animals to people. Though she appeared fragile, she could be incredibly tough. Only the foolhardy tried to cross her. Emily reminded Lisa of Portia in many ways.

She flicked over to her e-mails. Maxine's name appeared in bold type. Lisa hesitated before reading her sister's latest missive. Maxine had been bragging about seeing so much of Ted and his friends: Lisa was frankly jealous. This time Maxine wrote to say that Aunt Caroline had been asking after her. According to Maxine, their aunt was swanning around the retirement village back in Melbourne, telling people she'd been engaged to a duke. It was sad to think of the old girl losing her marbles.

Lisa had always been fond of and intimidated by Aunt Caroline in equal measure. Maxine also said the old woman's ticker was on the blink. At some point, Lisa would have to make the effort to see her aunt before she went to the great bargain basement in the sky. Apparently, the retirement village had organized a bus trip to Castlemaine, where the former Trumperton family home still stood, but Aunt Caroline had refused to go; she seemed to have an irrational snitch against her ancestral dwelling. Maxine again mentioned how much she was enjoying Ted's visits before signing off with a bossy directive to Lisa to keep up her visits to the oncologist.

Lisa hadn't seen Trumperton Manor, as it was called, for decades. Her father, William, had seldom spoken of it, even though his father, Alexander — Aunt Caroline's father — had lived there as a young man in the 1890s. Now Lisa took her father's album down from the shelf and found the sepia image of the old country house. It was every bit as grand as she remembered, and its Georgian lines and portico supported by Doric columns would've been perfectly at home in the English countryside. Only the garden betrayed the fact that the house had been built in a much harsher, wilder place — rural Australia. Attempts to grow English oaks had been only partially successful, and the lawn was far from lush. The only plants thriving on the rim of the circular driveway were clumps of pampas grass with outlandish feather plumes.

Another photo showed a portly gentleman on horseback in front of imposing gates with posts topped by giant spheres. He wore a top hat and appeared to be in evening wear. Behind him stood a woman in a dark Victorian costume with a light-colored hat. Lisa supposed the old pair were Alexander's parents. They wore authority with ease.

A portrait of a handsome young man dressed in white tie slid out of the album into Lisa's hand. The young man's face was long and sensitive, with a carefully groomed mustache over full lips. He looked the perfect Victorian gentleman — apart from the fact that his eyes were immeasurably sad.

Lisa saw echoes of that face, Alexander's face, in the mirror and whenever she looked at Ted. Portia had inherited a more rounded, compact face from Jake. Strange things, genes.

A new e-mail announced its arrival with a

pleasant ping. It was from Jake.

Dear Lisa, I hope this finds you well. The tone was unusually formal. *Belle and I are great. . . .* Lisa's chest contracted at the sight of her rival's name. *As you can imagine, we're finding her apartment a little small for our requirements. . . .* How much space did they need for their sexual gymnastics — an Olympic stadium? *We're looking for a larger, more suitable place. So I think it makes sense to get on with divorce proceedings right away. Hope you don't mind. Best, J.*

Lisa's knees turned to blancmange. Kicking her shoes off, she stumbled over the herringbone parquet floor to the kitchen cupboard. Chocolate. *That's* what she needed. Preferably Green and Black's 70 percent cocoa.

Inside the shadowy depths of the larder her fingers trembled over a comforting shape. Rectangular, solid. But it turned out to be a protein bar. It was dipped in fake chocolate and was probably 100 percent carcinogenic.

She flicked the kettle on. Rinsing the *Happy Holidays* mug, she reached for the nearest tea towel. The crinkled face of a cockatoo unraveled in the linen. Only Maxine could leave such a garish gift.

The great white parrot's wings spread joyfully across the cloth, his yellow crest splayed like a hand. The bird seemed to be laughing, not at Lisa but at the ridiculousness of life in general.

Suddenly overcome, she buried her face in the bird's image, sank to the floor, and sobbed. She was sick of being alone. With Jake gone, she didn't even know who she was anymore. *Plus* she missed her kids and was worried about Portia. It was all too much. When Lisa could cry no more she stood up, rinsed the tea towel in cold water, and dabbed her face.

She tore the wrapping off the protein bar. Sinking her teeth into its plasticky flesh, she opened the door onto the balcony. A blast of cold air hit her face. Chomping mechanically, she stepped outside and gazed over the city. Nine floors up provided the ideal view — or diving board. Rows of buildings punctured the pale spring sky. Somewhere down in Central Park, daffodil spears would be pushing out of the soil in ridiculous acts of optimism.

Lisa loved New York and her friends. Unlike many people who'd been born there, she'd never taken it for granted. Having grown up in a culture-free zone, she adored the brooding architecture, the galleries, and the shows. For all its crowds and inconveniences, the city had every right to call itself the center of the universe. It pulsed with life. Lisa loved the crusty workmen and the cops. But even though she'd tried to feel at home among the carefully scrubbed faces of the Upper East Side, deep down she'd always been a big-boned Aussie girl.

Lisa twisted the ring on her left hand. It was tighter these days. She tugged it off. She was an "abandoned woman," tragic, though not quite so malnourished as a Brontë heroine. To climb over the rails and jump nine floors would be a considerate act.

She peered down at the street and reeled with nausea. She'd always wanted to fly. There'd be a few seconds of terrifying, exhilarating weightlessness. The thrill of it might make up for the inevitable splat.

But the mess would be unspeakable. Pedro would have to deal with it until the ambulance arrived. Or would it be a fire engine with high-pressure hoses? Either way, Pedro hardly deserved it. His wife was pregnant.

One thing was certain. The only thing worse than annihilation would be to continue living like this. Either she jumped or . . . Lisa tossed the ring in the air. It hovered over the city and winked in a shaft of light.

As gravity took hold and sucked the gold circle down to the street, she suddenly knew what she had to do. Lisa Katz was dead and gone. She was changing her name back to Lisa Trumperton. And she was moving home to Australia.

CHAPTER 4

The first tulips were blooming in their sidewalk tubs by the time Lisa was ready to leave New York. The whole business had turned out to be more draining than she'd imagined. The volunteers at the animal shelter put on a farewell coffee morning, but her closest friends seemed to go out of their way to be difficult.

Over lunch at the Oyster Bar in Grand Central, Vanessa had pretended to understand, but it was obvious she couldn't imagine why anyone would want to travel beyond the US for a holiday. The notion of leaving on a permanent basis was practically treason. She reminded Lisa how much effort she'd put into getting her colleagues to agree to the deadline extension. Vanessa wondered aloud if Lisa shouldn't stay in New York and finish the book before gallivanting around the globe.

Lisa had taken a gulp of sauvignon blanc

and steeled herself to tell Vanessa the truth — that she would need to move to Australia to have any chance of writing the book at all. When Vanessa saw how close Lisa was to breaking down, she softened and confessed that Lisa wasn't the craziest author she'd had to deal with. There was the guy who insisted on writing books with quill and ink on toilet paper. Nevertheless, after she'd settled the bill and kissed Lisa on the cheek, Vanessa promised to e-mail Lisa her shrink's details.

Kerry had played the guilt card. Tears blistered in his eyes as he wondered aloud if he'd ever see her again. She assured him she'd be back for visits, and there was always Skype. He claimed his knowledge of technology ended with the fax machine.

Others treated her like the doomed heroine of an Italian opera. She couldn't escape from them fast enough.

Jake made no attempt to hide his opinion that she was insane going to live with a bunch of kangaroos. Still, he didn't object when she suggested he move back into their apartment with Belle while the lawyers stepped into the wrestling ring.

Packing up was like deciding whom to save from the *Titanic.* Her wedding present from Aunt Caroline was rescued; the red negligee Jake had given her two Christmases ago was not. As Lisa encased Aunt Caroline's crockery in Bubble Wrap she admired the familiar art nouveau pattern of yellow tulips — or were they magnolias? It was typical of her aunt to have exquisite taste, even though Lisa suspected the old girl had picked the set up in a secondhand shop. Each cup was rimmed with gold, and the delicate vase shape rested lightly in her hand. The handle was angled in a way that insisted it be held elegantly, the little finger tucked away rather than poking out in a manner Aunt Caroline would have called vulgar. The set had survived this long because it had spent most of the past two decades roosting at the back of the top shelf. Only one cup was missing, along with the lid of the sugar bowl. The milk jug was cracked.

Lisa moved on to her study to shroud the masks and photographs in plastic. A copy of *Jane Eyre* tumbled off the shelves and landed at her feet. She opened a page at random and read the lines in which Jane asks herself what she wants. Her answer? She craves a new home, among new people and in different circumstances. Charlotte Brontë knew how Lisa felt.

Lisa's hand hovered over the photo of Bon

Jovi. Was it madness to send a photo of a cat she'd never owned across the world? His amber eyes flashed a swift reply, and she swaddled him up and added him to the box.

As a pair of removal men carried her possessions away, a strange sensation washed over her. She felt like a caterpillar nudging off the weight of the cocoon it'd been trapped in for years.

By the time she boarded the plane she was numb with exhaustion. At the door, she automatically veered left into business class. But champagne before takeoff was part of her old life. She turned around and fought a tide of Italian suits to the bowels of economy.

The flight was full. Her reward for forgetting to check in online the night before was a center seat next to the toilets. She squeezed herself between the Michelin man and a woman with a toddler straight out of *The Exorcist.* To divert anxiety, she slid her phone from her pocket and sent a text to Portia.

On my way xxx

No reply. Portia was probably too busy posting food porn on Facebook, perhaps chocolate gâteau and red velvet cupcakes that Lisa presumed would never pass her daughter's lips, if Portia's shrinking physique was anything to go by.

Lisa had hoped Portia might spend an hour with her during her two-hour stopover in LA. She'd already earmarked the airport café, where she planned to surreptitiously stuff Portia full of carbs. She felt guilty leaving behind a daughter who needed feeding so badly. But what was the point? Portia couldn't get far enough away from her.

As soon as Lisa landed, her phone buzzed in her handbag. *Soooo sorry, Mom! Last-minute audition. Safe travels. Love u heaps xxxxooooo*

On the long Pacific leg, Lisa managed to get some sleep. Somewhere over Hawaii, she hallucinated she was wedged in a whalebone corset serving burnt scones to the squire's wife. She woke with a jolt and decided *Three Sisters: Emily* was going to be an empowering read. Her fictional Emily was destined to be a rebel, not a victim. Like Cathy in *Wuthering Heights,* she'd be torn between two men. A local earl and a buffed-up stable hand would both fall desperately in love with her. She'd wander the moors and launch into physical relationships with them both.

Climbing over the snoring mountain beside her, she fumbled in the overhead locker for her handbag. For once it contained a notebook *and* a pen. She scribbled in it over the rest of the Pacific Ocean and then the giant dry biscuit of Australia.

When the pilot announced he was descending into Melbourne, where it was 8:35 a.m., Lisa was semi-delirious. She couldn't wait to see Ted. Lisa promised herself not to bring up the subject of his new boyfriend too soon. Then her mind turned to Portia. Had the child eaten anything since the plane left LA?

Just landed, she texted Portia.

xxxxxooo, Portia replied.

Red-eyed, stinking, and crazed from twenty-two hours in the air, Lisa staggered into the arrivals hall and scanned the crowd. "Ted!" she cried, hurling herself at her son.

Recoiling slightly, Ted planted a kiss on the hair above her right ear. He was wearing a red-checked shirt. His beard had filled out, but was neatly trimmed, and his dark eyes were twinkling.

"You look great!" she said.

He didn't return the compliment. Her red pashmina did nothing to conceal the crumples and stains on her charcoal track pants. Flying pajamas, she liked to think of them.

A young man with an orange-peel grin offered his hand and introduced himself as

61

Ted's flatmate. His calloused paw crushed her palm. Ted's last boyfriend had been a ponytailed cellist called Sebastian. This lad, with his unruly curls and sunburned cheeks was straight out of a Brueghel painting. Hardly Ted's type. She relaxed and let the flatmate's name sift through the mush that had become her brain.

Outside, Lisa blinked into the Melbourne morning. She'd forgotten the harshness of Australian light compared to the lived-in air of New York, and her eyes felt like apricot balls rolled in coconut.

"You're welcome to stay with us," Ted's flatmate said as he stashed her bags in the back of the Kombi van.

She assured him she'd be fine, thanks.

"Aunt Maxine's looking forward to seeing you," Ted hollered as they rumbled down the wrong side of roads lined with trees ablaze with color. New York's spring was Melbourne's autumn. It was going to take a while to adjust to being in Australia.

"Hope you're right."

As the van spun along the motorway toward glistening towers, she was struck by the sleek modernity of the city. New York's old skyscrapers and bridges seemed antique by comparison. Maybe this was the new New World.

The van dived into a tunnel under the river, then peeled off the motorway into the tree-lined streets of Camberwell. They jolted to a halt outside Maxine's house, crouched like a cat about to pounce. It hadn't changed in twenty years. Every clinker brick oozed stability and smugness, by-products of a successful Camberwell marriage.

A large autumn leaf fluttered down the path. As it drew closer Lisa realized it was actually Maxine in an orange poncho.

"How was the flight?" her sister asked as Lisa climbed stiffly out of the van.

"Fine," Lisa lied. Australians were immune to distance. They made a point of never complaining, whether they were driving across desert from one side of the country to the other or flying around the world.

Ted and the other boy heaved her bags up the path and deposited them in the hall before scurrying back to the central city.

CHAPTER 5

"What do you think?" Maxine opened the guest-room door onto a scene resembling something out of *Pirates of the Caribbean*. A stuffed seagull glared from the top of a crow's nest in the corner. Misshapen and cross-eyed, the bird had to be the work of an enthusiastic amateur. Shelves groaned with seashells enhanced with paint and glitter. Three ships were imprisoned in bottles. Maxine had been to night classes again.

"Fresh," Lisa said, smiling at two single beds with duvet covers featuring flurries of semaphore flags.

"Bit of fun." Maxine tossed a red lifebuoy cushion in the air.

Lisa wheeled her suitcase to rest under a tapestry portrait of a sea captain. She couldn't help smiling. Maxine's approach to kitsch was in no way ironic. She'd simply inherited their mother's appalling taste, along with the MacNally button nose. Yet for all their differences Lisa did love her sister.

"Come through to the family room," Maxine said. "We need to chat."

Lisa's surge of fondness waned. Maxine's chats always involved bossiness. Nevertheless, Lisa obediently followed her sister down the hall and settled warily in an armchair smothered with sunflowers. Red poppies clambered across the wallpaper until they ran out of space and fought for survival against giant hydrangeas on the curtains. French provincial, apparently.

"I'm so pleased you've come home for a little holiday," Maxine said, flourishing a tray laden with her signature white chocolate and raspberry muffins. "After all you've been through."

"It's not a holiday."

"Oh, you'll change your mind in a week or two," Maxine said, pouring tea into identical Portmeirion cups. Lisa marveled at her sister's ability to produce matching crockery. Maxine, on the other hand, was so bemused by Lisa's love of ethnic masks and brightly woven fabrics she had actually given her a subscription to *House Beautiful* one birthday. Lisa tried not to take it personally. If her sister had traveled more widely, read more books, and known a few more men when she was younger, she'd understand taste when she saw it.

"I'm back for good," Lisa said, reaching for a muffin and crumbling it on her plate to make it seem less fattening.

Maxine stirred her brew thoughtfully. "The thing is you can't come *back,*" she said in her primary-school teacher voice. "The Australia we grew up in doesn't exist. It's not all lamingtons and Hills hoist clotheslines anymore. You've changed since you moved to the States. Things here have changed, too."

"I know."

"We're more sophisticated. We have marvelous cafés in Melbourne now, but we're not all rich and famous like *some* people."

There was no point telling Maxine her finances were far from buoyant. Jake's reckless investments had taken a hammering through the double-dip recession. Now, thanks to Cow Belle, what was left was about to be halved. Lisa had a modest nest egg, but she needed to churn out at least one bestseller a year for the foreseeable future. And while *Three Sisters* had a Facebook fan page, she was hardly a celebrity.

"Don't worry. I'll find a place of my own in a week or two."

"That's not my point," Maxine said, waving her hand to display the colored flecks in her nail polish. "You can stay here as long as you like. Gordon won't mind."

It hadn't occurred to Lisa that Gordon would object to anything that had Maxine's seal of approval.

"The thing is, at *our* age . . ."

Lisa settled back in her chair and let the lecture wash over her. The whole house was a shrine to Maxine-ness. A photo of Maxine as a prefect at Methodist Ladies' College took pride of place on the bookcase. Everyone in the family had been thrilled when Maxine won a scholarship to such a posh school, largely due to her expertise with a hockey stick. Ruby was always encouraging Maxine to bring friends home, but the doctors' and lawyers' daughters avoided the shabby Trumperton house for more genteel company. The school directed Maxine's pent-up aggression to the netball court. Her goal attack terrified teams from public and private schools alike. In her final year she was made captain of the senior team.

Next to the prefect photo was an image of Maxine smiling coyly from under a bridal veil. Maxine had met Gordon, a good-looking though slightly plump Scotch College boy, at year-ten dance classes. It was the perfect Melbourne private school love story. They married after her first year out teaching.

Lisa was yin to Maxine's yang. Traipsing two years behind her, Lisa failed everywhere Maxine had triumphed, including at getting a scholarship to Methodist Ladies' College. Their mother said there was no way they could afford to send Lisa as a fee-paying student. Profoundly relieved, Lisa slouched along to Camberwell Secondary College, where she couldn't catch a ball of any size or make sense of anything the teachers droned on about, apart from English and art history.

One of the supposed advantages of Camberwell Secondary College was the presence of boys. Lisa's handful of male friends turned out camp as Christmas, the beginning of a lifetime trend. The few girls she managed to trick or bribe into alliances were unpopular freaks like her. Prefect status was out of the question.

Lisa's eyes strayed to the lower shelf where Maxine's children, Nina and Andrew, drifted from babyhood to goofy adolescence inside a series of elaborate frames. Andrew, a painful introvert, had taken off to Silicon Valley, where, according to Maxine, he was about to shove a rocket up Google's backside. Nina lived across the bay in William-stown with her "nice little Chinese" husband Dan and their small kids.

Lisa had no doubt Dan, a colorectal surgeon, had married down. The elder son from a family of Indonesian medical professionals, he had more sophistication inside his left nostril than the Frogget family put together. Maxine probably still shouted at him in her version of an Asian accent, while his expression settled in Buddha-like calm. The Froggets had never had a doctor in the family before, let alone a surgeon.

When Nina became pregnant the first time, Maxine had lain awake at night fretting the child might come out an unacceptable shade of yellow. As it happened, little Peaches was a cherub with almond eyes, olive skin, and tawny hair. By the time the other two came along, Maxine could see the bright side. With skin like that they'd get away with SPF15 instead of the standard MacNally SPF50.

Maxine hardly needed photos of her beautiful grandchildren when she saw them several times a week. They were always exquisitely turned out in French designer clothes from Dan's mother in Jakarta.

As Maxine droned on about the benefits of holidays versus immigration, Lisa felt a stab of envy. Maxine had a husband who brought her tea and toast in bed every morning and grown-up children and grandchildren in the same city. So what if Gordon was a tax accountant who doubled as a doormat? There wasn't a thing he wouldn't give Maxine, including the new lime-green Volkswagen Golf sitting in the driveway. Whether he operated from adoration or fear was beside the point. He was devoted. And he was there. Maxine had it all. Yet she'd had the nerve to say Lisa was spoiled.

If Lisa had been their dad William's favorite, it was only by default. They just happened to share the kind of nervous system that imploded when people yelled and threw things. William was the only person who understood Lisa's inability to tie shoelaces, whereas Ruby had quickly lost patience with her. Friends laughed when her laces collapsed into spaghetti in her hands. She simply couldn't get the hang of making a bow out of a single loop. Sensing her distress, William took her aside one day and helped her invent a new type of bow using two loops. While it didn't hold together as well as some people's bows, it saved Lisa's dignity. She still used the two-looped bow.

Like all MacNallys, Ruby had possessed a

wild beast of a temper. She had no qualms about letting the neighbors hear her screeching at William for being a snooty, good-for-nothing Trumperton. She let everyone know she'd have been better off marrying Ian Johnston the bricklayer instead of a man fifteen years older who was hardly cutting a dash at the Water Company.

"Never mind, Panda Bear," William would say, running his hand gently through Lisa's hair after one of Ruby's tirades. "She'll settle down soon." He didn't have pet names for anyone else. Lisa never found out why he called her Panda Bear. It was long before the debate about whether pandas were actually bears or not.

With his striking blue eyes and eagle-ish nose, William had once been handsome. Years with Ruby took their toll, however. The thick dark hair faded to silver, his shoulders stooped, and the once graceful stride slowed to a limp. After he retired, he took refuge in a fibro shed to make dolls' houses, most of them in a Georgian style not unlike Trumperton Manor. They were made so exquisitely and with such attention to detail the toy shop on Glenferrie Road couldn't get enough of them.

When he'd died of a stroke fifteen years ago, Lisa had felt part of her soul detach itself and float away. After booking flights for the funeral, she'd wandered around Central Park. The air was suddenly still. The city fell silent. Snowflakes caressed her face. She had felt her father's presence then, softly encompassing her before spiraling away with the snow. Now all she had left of him was Aunt Caroline. Lisa reminded herself to spend some time with the old lady.

Lisa tuned into her sister once again. Maxine's lecture was far from over. Lisa struggled to keep her mouth shut while she yawned. Admittedly, Maxine was the one who'd been stuck in Melbourne to ride out Ruby's later years. After a couple of incidents wandering the streets in her nightie, Ruby had been deposited in the Camberwell Palace retirement home. Maxine had no hesitation reminding Lisa she was the one who had visited every Sunday. And the one they called after Ruby dropped dead clutching the stuffed wombat she'd just won at bingo.

"I think I'll have a lie-down," Lisa said.

"You can't do *that!*" Maxine snapped. "The only way to get over jet lag is to stay awake and keep local time."

"But I'm exhausted."

"Let's not argue," Maxine said, which was her way of issuing a decree. "Country Victoria's beautiful this time of year. Pop in the shower. We'll get some fresh air in your lungs. I'll take you down the peninsula."

Lisa could think of nothing worse than rummaging through the so-called art galleries of Mornington for more nautically themed knickknacks.

"Wouldn't you rather go to Castlemaine?"

Maxine's eyes narrowed. "Why would we want to go *there*?" Her tone implied she'd been asked to drive overland to Kabul.

"It's closer, isn't it?"

"Castlemaine's a good ninety minutes away. With the new motorway we'll be on the peninsula in an hour."

"I'd like to see the ancestral home," Lisa said, attempting frivolity.

"That old dump our grandfather lived in? Even Aunt Caroline refuses to go there."

"Trumperton Manor looks lovely in the photos."

Maxine stared down at her cup.

Their father had been in his fifties when Maxine and Lisa were born. They'd never met their grandfather. "Aren't you curious about the Trumpertons?"

Maxine examined the contents of her cup. "Mum never liked them," she said, before draining her tea.

Maxine always sided with their mother

73

and the MacNallys. Ruby's tribe were vague about exactly when and how they had arrived in Australia. Lisa suspected a prison ship was involved. Regardless, the moment they set foot on the dusty continent, they proceeded to mate like cane toads and punch anyone who looked at them twice.

Lisa had lost count of how many cousins she had, but she could spot the red hair and MacNally freckles anywhere from Antwerp to Alaska. Their alabaster skin forced them to avoid the tropics and beaches in general, unless covered from head to toe like *Star Wars* characters.

The MacNallys were always squabbling among themselves. The moment anyone outside the family offered a word of criticism — or even a suggestion for improvement — the clan instinct took over, and they became a human fortress. You could never argue with a MacNally.

The Trumpertons, on the other hand, were softer and more complex, if their father was anything to go by. He loved classical music and art, and indulged his daughters with books. A gentle man with impeccable manners, he was the last male twig on the Trumperton family tree. The Trumpertons were officially sawdust, although, now Lisa had claimed her name back, a tentative new shoot had sprung from the mulch.

"They were stuck-up wannabes," Maxine muttered.

"You're starting to sound like our mother."

"She had an awful life married to Dad, you know." Maxine gazed melodramatically out the window.

"I always thought it was the other way round," Lisa said after a pause.

Maxine shot her a wounded look.

"They were poles apart; that's all," Lisa added, trying to smooth things over. "I guess these days they would've gotten divorced."

Maxine swept her hair off her forehead. "I don't see why we should go out there, anyway. Aunt Caroline's right. What's the point of wallowing in the past?"

As Maxine packed the cups and plates on the tray, a spear of anger ran through Lisa. What was wrong with Maxine and Aunt Caroline? They were behaving as if they had something to be ashamed of.

"Why are Australians so phobic about delving into their family histories?" Lisa said. "Are they scared they might find out they're descended from Jack the Ripper?"

"He was never caught," Maxine said, brushing the crumbs off her poncho.

75

"Most of them were hardly criminals, anyway," Lisa continued. They were sent out here for next to nothing. I'd be proud if we had a shoe thief in our background."

"Speak for yourself," replied the former prefect of Methodist Ladies' College.

Lisa held her ground. She longed to connect with something tangible, something that wouldn't run off and sleep with the head of HR. There were no guidebooks for how to live this next phase of life. "I hear Castlemaine's awash with knickknack shops these days," she said, having no idea if it was true.

Maxine stopped in the doorway to the kitchen. She could never resist a collectable. "Oh well. If you insist."

CHAPTER 6

Maxine's Golf hummed through Melbourne's gray suburbs to the tones of Michael Bublé. Until recently, Lisa had despised him for being just another outlet for hormonally challenged women, but she'd changed her mind when she saw him in a television interview. Michael Bublé had worked pubs in his early days and had to put up with louts throwing beer at him. She respected him for surviving that. Humiliation was an essential ingredient for maturity. Besides, he had thick eyelashes.

McMansions huddled together behind high fences on land that had been covered with sheep the last time Lisa had been there. "If you're going to live in a house like that, wouldn't you want a garden?" she said, yawning.

"They're maintenance free," Maxine replied. "Besides, who wants to be outside in forty-degree heat? They're better off inside with air-con and flat-screen tele-visions."

Lisa dropped into an abyss of sleep. When she woke the suburbs had made way for parched hills under a giant basin of sky. The dramas of recent weeks seemed to evaporate in endless space.

Maxine turned off the motorway. A flock of galahs rose in a pink cloud from the roadside. Maxine and Lisa approached a yellow road sign featuring the black shape of a kangaroo.

"Isn't that cute?" Lisa said.

"Not really." Maxine pointed to a furry mound lying on the side on the road.

"Shouldn't we stop?"

"He's long gone. Bloated," Maxine said. "Probably got hit a few nights ago."

Two decades in New York had reduced Lisa's ability to assess the condition of road-kill.

The road narrowed and twisted through archways of eucalyptus trees. Lisa lowered her window and gulped air so crisp it made her lungs sting. It carried the mentholated tang she'd yearned for — eucalyptus, the smell of disinfectant, cough drops, and home.

They meandered past burnished oaks and poplars that blazed like Roman candles. She felt a flush of childish excitement as they hurtled past old gold-digging sites and rows of miners' cottages. A woman stood on a veranda fringed with elaborate ironwork. A man leaned on a rake beside a pile of leaves and raised his hand.

"When did the gold rush start?" Lisa asked. Sometimes having a primary-school teacher for a sister came in handy.

"July 1851," Maxine replied. "A shepherd found gold in a creek near here. He showed it to his mates in the men's quarters. They told him it was fool's gold, so he chucked it out.

"Then his mates snuck off and started panning. They found humungous gold nuggets. Word got out, of course. Before long the area was swarming with hopefuls, thirty thousand of them. Turned out to be the richest gold mine in the world."

Castlemaine was prettier than Lisa remembered. Colonial houses were sprinkled across hills that yielded to the grid-like layout of the town center. Shops peered out from under roofs that stretched across the pavements. As in all pioneering towns, God had continued his ongoing war with the devil, and there was a church for every pub. Lisa didn't waste time wondering which side of the churchyard gates the Trumpertons would've been on. They were decent stock. The town had been built for an opulent future. Wide streets and grand buildings had been designed to last centuries.

Maxine pointed out the Theatre Royal. "The oldest continuously running theater in mainland Australia," she said with noticeable pride.

"Why can't you just say the oldest theater in Australia?" Lisa asked.

"There's an older one in Tasmania."

"People came here with big dreams," Lisa mused as they turned onto the main street.

"Yes, and most of them turned to cactus."

The Golf purred to a halt outside the town hall. Two stories high, it was an Italianate confection of brick and stone. A tower and flagpole topped Renaissance arches with 1898 etched on the front.

"Do you think our grandfather saw it built?" asked Lisa.

"No idea," Maxine said, sliding into her fake-fur jacket and swooping toward Togs café.

Lisa savored the air — apple-crisp and colder than in Melbourne. The streets were empty apart from the occasional ute lumbering past. Time had decelerated to half its pace. Even Lisa's heart seemed to have

slowed to a leisurely plod. Her ears buzzed
with an unfamiliar sensation. In New York
there was always a taxi honking, a whistle
blowing, the thrum of wheels over tarmac.
On the streets of Castlemaine there was no
background noise, apart from the breeze
rippling a pile of yellow leaves.

A mother pushed a stroller of pink-
cheeked twins toward her and said hello.

"Did you see what those kids were wearing?" Lisa said as they hurried into the
warmth of the café. "It was all hand-knitted
— jackets, beanies, the lot."

"Not everyone puts their kids in sweatshop
chic," Maxine said, settling into a seat at a
corner table.

"But that stuff would've taken hours to
make," Lisa said. "And she'd have to hand-
wash it. I haven't seen anything like it
since . . ."

"Since we were kids?" Maxine said. "Be-
ware of nostalgia, little sister. There's plenty
of time for it when we're dead."

Logs crackled in a central fireplace, lacing
the air with a tang of smoke and pine. Old
wooden tables and bentwood chairs were
scattered casually over rustic floorboards.
The work of a local textile artist glowed
against white brick walls.

"Let's see," Maxine said, running her eye

down the menu. "Organic pumpkin soup . . ."

Three men, roughly shaven and dressed for the weather, sat at a nearby table and discussed the merits of farm machinery. Though each belonged to a different generation, they shared the same complexion and rugged jawline — grandfather, son, and grandson.

Lisa ordered quiche and salad.

A small group of thirty-something women in track pants and puffy vests chatted at another table, coats and scarves draped over their chairs. They were most likely a walking group taking time out from motherhood.

Lisa was surprised she could taste the individual ingredients in her quiche — eggs, cheese, onion. Each one seemed to have sprung fresh from the earth onto her plate. The café latte warmed her insides and sharpened the fuzziness in her brain.

After she'd settled the bill, Lisa examined advertisements on the cork bulletin board — seasonal organic vegetables delivered to your doorstep, singing for pleasure. "Oh, look, there's bush dancing in the town hall on Saturday," she said. "What *is* bush dancing?"

"Sounds feral to me," Maxine replied.

"Come on. There's an antique shop round the corner."

Maxine's definition of "antique" was different from anyone else's. She liked her antiques fresh off a container ship — shiny and in good working order. Anything older than 1990 was written off as "old junk." Maxine's regal French tables invariably had MADE IN INDONESIA stamped on the underside. She preferred the craftwork of artisans like herself, who had been to night classes and learned to fashion garden ornaments out of driftwood. Though Lisa tried to be tactful about their differences, Maxine made it clear it was just a matter of time before Lisa gave up her quirky interest in mixing old colonial furniture with ethnic pieces and bright minimalist art.

Letting Maxine loose among aisles of distressed coffee tables and headboards was like setting a golden retriever free on a beach. Maxine salivated over reproduction fireplaces, a so-called oil lamp that ran on electricity, and a family of faux Edwardian dolls dressed in cheap, flashy fabrics.

Meanwhile, Lisa's body clock was hovering like a ghost in the early hours of a New York morning. She collapsed on a bench under a heater and stared up at a faded print surrounded by a frame perforated with fake worm holes. It was a portrait of Lord Byron. The Brontë sisters had been crazy about the bad-boy poet.

About an hour later Maxine was triumphantly carrying armfuls of booty back to the car. "You'd never think we'd find a foghorn this far from the sea," she beamed, wielding a large red tube. She'd always had a weakness for phallic symbols.

They climbed into the front seats. "Oh well, back to the city," Maxine said, resting her hands on the steering wheel.

Lisa grabbed her elbow. It was typical Maxine to trick Lisa out of her end of a bargain. "Aren't we going to see the old house?"

"No idea how to get there," Maxine said, glancing at her watch.

Suddenly irrational, Lisa felt on the brink of tears. "There's an Information Centre sign outside the old Market Building," she said. "Wait here."

Another fine example of gold-rush confidence, the Market Building was like a nineteenth-century Parthenon. Lisa climbed the steps to discover a vast hall inside. It was largely empty apart from a wall covered with brochures and postcards.

"Do I detect an accent?" the old man behind the counter inquired.

Lisa bottled her frustration. Having spent the past two decades being teased for her Australian accent, she was now accused of having an American one. If only she could be in a place where she had no accent.

When she mentioned Trumperton Manor, the old man's eyes clouded. "It's seen better days," he said. "Some say it's haunted."

Lisa felt a chill run down her neck, though it was probably just a bug she'd picked up on the plane.

"People say it hasn't been the same since the scandal."

"What scandal?" Lisa's voice echoed off the marble columns.

"It was a long time ago."

"What happened?" Her voice sharpened.

The old man smiled. "Oh, you know what small towns are like," he said, scribbling directions on a map.

Lisa nodded, not that she had any experience of small towns. She tried to probe him further.

"How would you like some of our Castlemaine Rock?" he asked, waving a red and yellow tin. "It's world-famous."

Tempted as she was by the retro rock candy, Lisa remembered her diet and declined. She tried to steer the conversation back to Trumperton Manor, but a German couple appeared, wanting to know about vineyards. The old man made it clear his interaction with Lisa was over.

She could hardly wait to get back to the car to share the gossip. A scandal *and* a ghost!

As she nestled into the passenger seat, she was about to tell all when she suddenly had a vision of Maxine at about eight years old, arms crossed in typical pose, announcing that the Easter Bunny didn't exist. Maxine had delighted in watching six-year-old Lisa crumple into tears, so much so that Maxine had added that the daisy Lisa was holding was poisonous and she would be dead by four o'clock. Maxine still took pleasure in snuffing out what she perceived to be Lisa's fantasies. And for someone who was an expert in just about everything, Maxine had been unusually cagey about Trumperton Manor and the Trumperton family.

For once, Lisa shed the role of gullible baby sister. If Maxine could keep a secret, then so could she. "Second on the left, then over the railway line," she said, deciphering the old man's scrawl.

They drove in silence up a hill and through a subdivision of newish houses. Castlemaine was getting its version of suburban sprawl. Beyond the subdivision the road undulated across pastureland before turning into a broad valley. A twinkling creek coiled along the roadside and disappeared behind a stand of wattle trees. Ancient hills were etched against limitless sky.

As the car rounded a bend, a flurry of white hurtled toward the windscreen. Maxine stamped on the brakes, but collision was inevitable. Powerful wings thudded against the glass, followed by the sound of claws scraping across the paintwork above their heads.

"What was *that*?" Lisa asked, swiveling to look out the rear window.

Maxine stopped and switched off the engine. A mess of feathers writhed on the road behind them. The poor creature had to be mortally wounded. But defying all logic, the bird clambered to its feet, ran its beak over its feathers, and shook its wings. It waddled to the side of the road and stared at them from the shelter of the long grass.

"Is he all right?" Lisa asked.

"He was just about cockatoo stew, but he'll be fine."

"Oh my God, look!" Lisa said, pointing out a pair of decrepit gateposts across the road. "They're the ones in Dad's old photo."

One of the gateposts had lost its sphere, and the ornate gates had disappeared. The gravel drive had reverted to weeds, but there was no mistaking the entrance to Trumperton Manor. It was exactly the spot where Alexander Trumperton's father had sat on his horse and posed for the photo.

Lisa strode across the road and peered into the shadows. The driveway curved and vanished frustratingly into a cavern of pines. Going by the old photo, the house would be just around that bend. She stepped forward.

"No!" called Maxine. "It's private property."

"Let's knock on the door and say who we are," Lisa said, sounding like a six-year-old again. "They might ask us in."

"Another time," Maxine said firmly. "I need to get home to put the tea on."

As they were about to drive off, Lisa spotted a side road a few meters behind them, near where the cockatoo had almost met his fate. "Let's go down there," she pleaded. "We might be able to see the house."

With the enthusiasm of Mata Hari being marched to the firing squad, Maxine turned onto the gravel road. Lisa craned her neck, but it seemed Trumperton Manor had been devoured by bush. Just as she was about to concede defeat, two elegantly shaped chimneys and a slate roof rose above the canopy.

"There it is!"

They rounded a corner, and the house suddenly appeared. Lisa made Maxine stop the car. Heart thumping, she climbed over a grass-filled gutter and stood at a wire fence.

Basking in the afternoon light, Trumperton Manor seemed larger and more imposing than in the photos. Two stories high, it was the archetypal redbrick manor, worthy of a BBC costume drama. With its handsome portico and wraparound veranda, the house was a splendid example of Georgian architecture at its height. The decorated eaves and columns offered hints of grandeur. Large shuttered windows whispered of rustling gowns and gavottes. Lisa could almost hear horses clopping up the driveway and gliding to a halt outside the entrance while the strains of a string quartet wafted from inside. Half-closing her eyes, she imagined the scent of honeysuckle mingled with freshly poured champagne on a warm summer's evening.

"Stunning!" she breathed.

"It's a wreck," Maxine said. "Just look at that roof. It's a sieve. And the brickwork's wobbly. The place needs a demolition ball."

The manor certainly had been neglected for years, if not decades. Paintwork blistered on window frames and eaves. In some places it was peeled back to the wood. On the upper level, two shutters hung at drunken angles, perilously close to plummeting to the ground. Large cracks glistened in the windowpanes. Curtains hung in rags. Two of the downstairs windows were boarded up with wood. A dilapidated wooden add-on slouched against the back of the main house.

Across a yard around the side of the house, Lisa could see another building. It was even more disheveled than the main residence, and some of the slates in its pitched roof were missing. Lisa had spent enough time with her fictional heroines to know any establishment like Trumperton would have needed stables. These ones were larger than a modern family home.

The garden had reverted to scruffy paddock. Not even the pampas grass had survived. From where Lisa was standing, she could make out a tangle of overgrown fruit trees behind the house. Trumperton Manor was as unloved as Lisa had felt since Jake walked out.

A squawk pierced the autumn air. "Look who's here!" Lisa said.

A tiny white figure waddled down the driveway. With his crest waving like a yellow glove, the cockatoo looked like a small circus clown. When he saw Lisa, he stopped and put his head to one side, raised his wings and flapped furiously, affording a glimpse of the pastel yellow feathers on the underside of his wings. Lisa willed him to take flight. But for all his efforts the bird stayed earthbound.

"He can't fly!" she cried. "Oh, Maxine, did we do that to him?"

"He'll be fine," Maxine answered. "He's probably still in shock."

The bird gave up flapping and hopped across the paddock to peck at the grass.

The house tugged Lisa's attention back to the front door. She longed to climb the front steps, walk through the rooms, and drink in the aromas that Alexander had known. She felt an immediate attachment to the crumbling ruin. Trumperton Manor needed healing as much as she did.

"Don't you feel a connection to this place?" she asked her sister.

"Not a bit," Maxine said, shooing a fly off her shoulder. "You always were the fanciful one."

Maxine escorted Lisa back to the car and firmly shut her in the passenger seat.

They drove off in a plume of dust.

CHAPTER 7

Morning light filtered through the net curtains in Maxine's spare room. The red foghorn leered down at Lisa from a corner shelf. She removed her mouth guard and snapped it in its box. Her teeth must've known something was wrong with her life before she did.

Sleeping in a single bed was like returning to childhood. Even after several weeks at Maxine's, Lisa was still falling onto the floor in the middle of the night. The pillow was hard and high. She'd tried to bring her special pillow with her, but her suitcases had been overflowing.

Rolling onto her back, she fingered the ridge of scar tissue across her chest. The tapestried sea captain stared down with prurient interest. The bitter charade of her marriage paraded through her mind. The week before Jake had walked out on her, he'd had the nerve to hold her hand in the

Central Park Zoo. She should've guessed something was up. He hated the zoo with its swarms of tourists and screaming kids. He'd only taken her there out of guilt.

Japanese snow monkeys had scrambled over their artificial island. Leaves sailed off branches and landed gently on the lake. Suddenly overcome with gratitude for being alive, she'd turned to him and told him how much she loved him. She felt comfortable being older and no longer slave to her hormones. He'd nodded agreement and said he felt the same way. The reptile.

They'd made love that night, slotting comfortably into each other's bodies. With the lights out, Lisa's self-consciousness about her lopsidedness dissolved. She swam in a private lake of bliss before returning to the familiar warmth that was Jake. He'd stroked her hair, the outline of her hip. As usual, he had avoided the chasm in her chest. She had reminded herself to change the sheets the next morning. Washing the bed linen the morning after they'd made love had become a routine. As they were guaranteed to make love once a week, she didn't need to count the days. It usually happened Saturday nights. Except in recent months, it'd stretched out to ten days — and once even two weeks.

Jake was wasted in banking. He should've starred in B-grade movies. His affection for her was as artificial as an island for Japanese monkeys in the middle of New York.

Now hot with anger, she reached for her phone on the bedside sea chest. She checked the time. It would be midafternoon in LA. Texting was hardly communication, but it was the only hope she had of getting a response from her daughter.

How r u?

The screen flashed a reply. Lisa's pulse quickened.

Gr8! U???

When baby Portia had slipped out of her thighs into the world Lisa had been overcome with a golden concoction of sensations. Triumph melted into relief when she heard her daughter's first sputtering cry. And when Lisa had looked down at the little creature — slimy, indignant, and perfect — every pang of agony she'd endured had dissolved. Happy tears had tumbled down her face. She'd looped her hands under the baby's armpits and, with the rope of pulsing umbilical cord still attached, raised Portia to her breast.

Right from the start, the infant had known who she was. She'd gazed up at Lisa with an appraising stare, and a fierce maternal flame was ignited. Lisa had adored her laughing, chubby toddler with a tangle of fair curls that framed aquamarine eyes. Portia had grown into a tall, clever, outgoing girl who devoured books, music, and theater with equal fervor. Having had her own confidence battered by Ruby, Lisa knew how, for a young woman, self-esteem was vital. So she often told Portia she was beautiful — and meant it — but Portia always looked away.

Lisa loved her daughter with every cell in her body, her devotion huge and constant as the stars. Lately, though, the thought of Portia jagged her with all-consuming anxiety. Lisa tried to pinpoint when things had gone wrong. Although she'd been disappointed when Portia dropped out of college, Lisa had tried not to let it show, instead encouraging her daughter to pursue the acting career she so desperately wanted. Perhaps it was the day she made Portia her favorite waffles and the offering remained untouched on the plate. Or was it the time she told Portia she was beautiful and Portia spat "No, I'm not! I'm fat."

Portia had never been overweight, but she was wholesome by the standard of the pipe cleaners on magazine covers. Portia's height more than compensated for any extra waffles. Nevertheless, she began eschewing cakes and fries for bottles of water, shedding pounds to become a Botticelli beauty. Perfect in anyone's book. But Portia hadn't stopped there. Her arms and legs had become more spidery, her torso stooped over the stalk that had been her waistline. The eyes that had once been hauntingly beautiful were now sinking into their sockets.

The thinner Portia became, the more violently she pulled away from Lisa. On the few occasions Lisa had confronted her, regrettable screaming matches had ensued: "You don't understand! I want to be beautiful!"

"But you *are*!"

Most of their communication was now reduced to butchered type.

Fine. What r u up to?

Just chillingxxxxx.

The *X*'s were the equivalent of a nod from Queen Elizabeth I declaring the conversation finished.

Lisa Xed Portia back and let the phone tumble out of her hand. It landed with a thud on the turquoise carpet.

A chill of sadness crept over Lisa. At least the sleepless nights had allowed some privacy to rough out a few early chapters of the book. Emily had accepted an invitation to a ball at the earl's mansion. Frederick the stable hand had gone into a sulk while he got the horses ready.

Lisa waited for the next scene to appear in her head. The sea captain leered down at her. She desperately needed her own space if she was to make any real progress. Her chest shook with sobs.

"Lisa?" Maxine called from the room next door. "Are you all right?"

Lisa had to move out. Soon.

Maxine and Ted were open-home junkies, and they cheerfully sacrificed their Saturdays to trudge through properties. The flatmate friend, who had nothing better to do, tagged along with them. Wary of the smell of freshly brewed coffee wafting through hastily painted hallways, Lisa wasn't so keen. The salesmen's fake smiles, aftershave, and bright-eyed lies made her innards shrivel. But there was no choice. If she stayed with Maxine much longer there was going to be a case of double "sistercide." Fortunately, Jake had been sufficiently crippled by guilt to agree to a reasonable divorce settlement, but with half of a shrunken nest egg, the Palace of Versailles was out of the question.

Maxine had urged Lisa to rent a studio, but Lisa thought of that as lack of commitment. Instead, Lisa warmed to a cottage in downtown Carlton. Ted and his flatmate approved, too. Ted ran an architectural eye over its century-old ceilings and deemed it structurally sound. Tastefully renovated with exposed brick walls and scrubbed floorboards, the cottage had French doors opening onto a tiny paved garden. With an outdoor table it would be the perfect setting for Sunday lunches. Ted lived just a few blocks away — close enough to be cozy without her presence being overbearing.

Around the corner on Lygon Street, cafés bustled with university staff and students. An art-house movie complex advertised live screenings from the Metropolitan Opera. Across the road from the movie house stood a thrilling example of an endangered species — an actual bookshop. Ted dived into the back of the fiction section and waved the two copies of *Three Sisters: Charlotte* they had in stock. He assured her they must've sold the rest, and arranged them on top of the number-one bestseller pile.

Maxine drew attention to the fact the cottage had no off-street parking, but Lisa was unconcerned. She could see herself putting in an herb garden. And now Jake and his allergies were out of the picture, she might take on a rescue cat or two.

Maxine pointed out the house was jammed up against a large student accommodation block. "Do you really want kids keeping you awake all night?" she said. "Young people don't sleep anymore. It's the drugs. Which reminds me, isn't there a rehab clinic around here somewhere, Ted?"

They walked around the corner to the local café and ordered coffee and cake.

"I could see you in that cottage, Mrs. Trumperton," Ted's flatmate said.

"Oh, call me Lisa."

This habit Lisa had of not registering the names of young people was appalling. In an effort to at least dredge up the boy's first name, she asked about his background.

His pale eyes shone with amusement under the froth of dark-gold curls. He'd grown up on a sheep farm on the South Island of New Zealand. There was evidence of an outdoorsy youth in his square shoulders and the sprinkling of freckles on his nose and cheeks. His father had wanted him to take over the farm, but he had "zero interest," he said. He'd moved to Melbourne and worked his way up to chef in a restaurant specializing in modern Australian cuisine.

"You like living here?" Lisa asked, trying not to sound patronizing. She willed Ted to give her a clue about the boy's name, but he was engrossed with the real estate brochure.

"It was hard to begin with," the young man said, digging into a trembling tiramisu. "But now it's sweet."

Either sweet was a Kiwi colloquialism, or he was referring to the confection. Watching enviously, Lisa swilled her sparkling mineral water and hoped the bubbles would fill her up.

"I suppose you two are out on the town tonight?" she asked, sounding like a creature that observed life from under a stone.

"Why don't you join us?" Ted's flatmate said. "Stella and Heidi are coming. One more won't hurt."

He was joking. Obviously.

"No, I mean it. You'd enjoy it."

The prospect of being included in Ted's social circle was alluring. But she assured them she'd be tucked up in bed well before they set out for the clubs.

The next place they looked at was an apartment on St. Kilda Road. German appliances gleamed so ferociously they hurt her eyes. The en suite bathroom shone with Italian marble. Standing in the living room, she gazed over the botanical gardens. There didn't seem much point moving all the way from New York to live in another tower block.

"I have a feeling this next one's going to be you," Maxine said, aiming her Golf back toward Camberwell. Bare branches clawed the gray sky. Winter had claimed all but a few of the suburb's leaves.

"You can't go past brand new," Maxine said, pulling up outside a construction site. Two recently completed townhouses stared across the street. "There's one more out the back," Maxine called, already out of the car and halfway down the drive. "It's more private."

The smell of fresh concrete tickled Lisa's nostrils. The single-story townhouse was solidly built in a Tuscany-meets-Camberwell mode.

A woman stood at the door holding a clipboard. Glossy as a seal in a dark satin suit, she bared her teeth through scarlet lipstick. "The builder won an award," she recited, handing them each a brochure. "The other two are sold. I've got an offer coming in for this one later on today. You'll have to be quick."

They stepped into a featureless living room overlooking a small rectangle of rubble. The carpet, walls, and fittings were so neutral they were practically invisible.

"You'll be able to make it your own," Maxine muttered out of the agent's earshot. With a nod of approval Ted pointed out the solar-heating panels on the tiled roof. His flatmate, the chef, said the kitchen was extremely workable. "And look at the way the sun's pouring in," Maxine said with a flourish of her fake-fur sleeve.

The townhouse ticked many boxes. It was spacious, private, and sunny. Most of the rooms opened onto the rubble that would someday be a patio lined with rosemary and lemon trees in tubs. Lisa's imagination was in overdrive. There was a guest room for Portia, Vanessa, or Kerry, if any of them deigned to visit. Next to it was a smaller room. Lined with her books and masks and painted an interesting color it could make a study.

Lisa thanked the agent and wandered back to the car.

"What do you think?" Maxine said, hurrying after her.

"Bland."

Maxine drew a breath and took lipstick and a powder compact out of her handbag. "The thing is, when you get to *our* age . . ." she said, circling her mouth in orange lipstick, "you have to be practical."

Not another lecture.

"You'll be just a few streets away from us here. I'll keep an eye on you. Our doctor, Ross, isn't taking any new patients, but I'll put a word in. And you'll like our dentist, Evan. He's very good."

"Thanks, but . . ."

Maxine put her hand on Lisa's shoulder. "You need to look to the future," she said, gazing into Lisa's eyes. "Single-story's ideal. When your knees give out you won't have to climb stairs. . . ."

Oh Lord!

"And the Meals on Wheels people will be able to drive straight to your doorstep." Ted chuckled.

"I'm not dead yet!"

"Seriously, it's solid. You should think about it," Ted added. "There's a train station at the end of the street."

"And a good café on the corner," the chef chimed in.

Lisa was confused.

"I reckon it's a good investment," Ted said. "You could lock it up and leave it anytime you want to travel."

Lisa knew they were right. The townhouse was logical to the core of its concrete-pad foundation. Besides which, a month with

Maxine had been more than enough. A force-fed diet of Maxine's muffins was taking its toll on Lisa's waistline. More important, Maxine didn't understand the quirky rhythms of a writer's life. The moment Lisa got into a flow with *Three Sisters: Emily,* her hostess would burst in on her with mugs of tea, while working at night led to pointed remarks about lights being on at all hours.

The agent tapped down the driveway and was about to climb into her BMW.

"How soon is it available?" Lisa called.

"Pretty much immediately," the agent replied.

"How do I make an offer?"

The agent flicked her ponytail and flashed her teeth. She slithered into the BMW and trailed the Golf back to Maxine's house.

They arrived to find Gordon in his dressing gown reading the newspaper at the kitchen table. Maxine told the agent not to mind him. He'd been sick with a cold lately, she said, which wasn't true. Gordon scraped his chair back and shuffled amiably down the hall to their bedroom.

The group arranged themselves around the table as the agent explained how the contract was quite straightforward. It was just a matter of initialing every page and . . .

Lisa didn't hear the rest of the sentence.

Gordon had left the newspaper open at the property section. Her attention zoomed in on an advertisement halfway down the left-hand page.

She recognized the shabby brick house in the photo. It was Trumperton Manor. Printed above it in large bold type were the words FOR SALE.

If anyone understood how it felt to be torn between worlds it was Emily Brontë. In *Wuthering Heights* she'd penned one of the most powerfully frustrating love stories ever written. Unable to choose between respectable Edgar Linton and her wild soul mate, Heathcliff, Emily's heroine was destined to make a mess of things. Now, with pen poised over the land agent's offer, Lisa was about to opt for an Edgar Linton life. Growing old in the comfort of Camberwell, she'd join a garden society and torment her unmathematical brain with the rigors of bridge. Then, after a decade or two, she and Maxine would be wheeled off in matching coffins to Springvale cemetery. No doubt Maxine would order their plots in advance, quietly earmarking the sunnier one for herself.

But the moment Lisa saw the advertisement for Trumperton Manor, she was inflamed with longing for something more dangerous. Trumperton was the architectural equivalent of life with Heathcliff. She wasn't *that* old, anyway. With any luck she'd have at least two decades before she needed a walking stick. After a lifetime of enabling others, surely she'd earned the right to make her own choices, no matter how outlandish?

Maxine, the agent, Ted, and his flatmate focused expectantly on the pen in Lisa's hand, but it refused to lower itself to the dotted line.

Lisa could feel her face turn hot-flush red. "Sorry," she said. "I need to think."

Maxine looked mortified.

"If that's how you feel," the agent said coldly. "Don't forget the Johnsons will be placing their offer this afternoon, and they're cash buyers."

Lisa waited for a jolt of competitiveness to stir the pen into action.

"Don't do something you'll regret later," Maxine warned.

"It's a big decision," Ted said, trying to smooth things over.

Flustered, Maxine offered white-chocolate muffins all round. The agent slammed her briefcase. She had another open home to go to. Flashing a hostile grin at Lisa, she stood up and left.

Lisa apologized and hurried down the hall to shut herself in with the sea captain. The computer screen offered a welcoming glow. Her hands trembling, she drew up the captain's chair and took three deep breaths.

Thank God for the Brontë sisters. Lisa was developing maternal concern for the most highly strung sister, in particular. The middle child invariably finds a way to stand out, and Emily had made a point of it. Determinedly antisocial, she'd spent hours wandering the moors. Emily had quit her first teaching job, reputedly telling her students she preferred the school dog to any of them. A visitor to the parsonage, Ellen Nussey, had observed that Emily had a "lithesome, graceful figure . . . her hair, which was naturally as beautiful as Charlotte's, was in the same unbecoming tight curl and frizz . . . She had very beautiful eyes — kind, kindling, liquid eyes; but she did not often look at you . . . dark gray, at other times dark blue, they varied so." Every time Lisa tried to picture Emily, she saw Portia's face.

The bedroom door creaked open.

"You okay?" Ted asked.

She adjusted her pashmina.

"You did the right thing," he said. "That townhouse wasn't you. I'm sorry if it looked like I was pushing you into it."

"You weren't."

Ted pulled the newspaper from his back pocket and unfurled the advertisement for Trumperton Manor. "Maybe you need a drive in the country," he said.

CHAPTER 8

Lisa was hoping to sneak back to Castlemaine with just the boys, but Maxine had a
sixth sense whenever people tried to arrange
things behind her back. She insisted they
wouldn't want to be going out there in that
old Kombi van. So early next morning, the
boys squeezed into the Golf's backseat.

Winter had dusted the landscape with
frost. Trees stood bare, their branches
spreading latticework patterns against a
defiant blue sky. Livestock were scattered
sparsely over the land.

"Does it ever rain out here?" Lisa asked.

"Not enough," Maxine said.

Lisa warned the boys the house was a
dump. Nevertheless, her heart pulsed in her
ears as they pulled up outside the gates.

A "For Sale" sign had been hammered to
the post that still had its sphere. "Renovate
or Detonate!" it read. "Tired old lady on
five acres. Five bedrooms plus stables. Call

Beverley Green at Hogan & Hogan."

"Whoever wrote that flunked Marketing 101," the Kiwi flatmate mumbled.

Lisa was beginning to like him. "What *is* his name again?" Lisa whispered, drawing Ted aside.

"M-um!" Ted groaned, rolling his eyes. "It's James."

Lisa scanned the area for the cockatoo, hoping he was still alive. The boys were already halfway down the driveway. She grabbed her handbag and followed.

"We should call the agent first!" Maxine barked after them.

Lisa caught up with the boys, panting, as they plunged into the shadows of the pines and rounded the bend.

"I'm not going down there until we have permission!" Maxine's voice echoed off the tree trunks.

Whoever had designed the manor had arranged it to be seen from this spot just past the curve in the driveway. At a slight angle, it was more welcoming than imposing. The portico reached over the entrance, offering shelter to visiting carriages. Engraved on a central panel above the front door was TRUMPERTON MANOR 1860.

No effort had gone into dolling up the house for sale. In fact, it seemed to have deteriorated since the last time Lisa saw it. Dust caked the windows. Cobwebs shimmered in the eaves. An old gas lamp lay in a clump of grass like a fallen soldier.

"My God!" whispered Ted.

"You're right," Lisa said. "It's a disaster."

"It's fantastic!"

She felt a rush of delight. Ted had enough Trumperton blood in his veins to connect with the place. She snapped a photo with her phone and sent it to Portia with the message *Yr g/gfather's house. Like 2 spend Xmas here?* Lisa was joking . . . sort of.

Defs!!! Portia replied immediately.

"Do you think anyone's home?" Ted asked.

They scanned windows that were blank as the eyes of the dead. The stables were silent. There was no sign of life in the garden, either. They crept through patches of wild grass and up the front steps. Lisa hesitated at the front door. They were being cheeky. Maybe Maxine was right and they should call the agent.

Lisa turned and gasped at the view from the veranda. Eucalyptus trees rustled on either side of the front paddock, silvery threads of vapor rose from the creek as it snaked across the valley, and folds of golden grass rolled toward blue hills in the distance.

"Imagine waking up to that every morning!" she said.

"The soil's not bad, either," James said. "Volcanic, by the look of it. Good enough for an organic vegetable garden. Looks like there's an orchard out the back. With this amount of land, you could grow enough to sell at market."

"I thought you'd gone off farming?" Lisa teased.

James blushed. "Just sheep shit I've had a gutful of," he muttered.

"I reckon you could get irrigation from that creek," Ted added.

"The house needs a lot of work," Lisa said, glancing up at the sagging roof.

"It's doable," Ted said.

Doable was one of Ted's architect words. It sounded so capable.

"You wouldn't have to do it all at once," James chimed in.

"It could happen in stages," Ted added.

"Wouldn't it be expensive to heat?" Lisa asked, trying to sound practical.

"Dunno," Ted said. "With insulation and a few discreet solar panels about the place it could end up contributing energy to the grid. You could reach the point of getting money from the power company instead of the other way around."

So Ted could imagine her living here, too.

Lisa glanced up at the front door. Two panels of stained glass refused to offer a glimpse of what lay behind. Bubbles of gray paint revealed handsome old-fashioned wood underneath — oak, mahogany, or some other timber sent from the old country by sailing ship. A large circular door knocker, rusted with age, dared them to reach up and touch it.

"C'mon, you townies," James said, stretching a freckled hand over Lisa's head and seizing the hoop. "They're not going to bite our heads off."

To everyone's horror, the metal ring dislodged from the door and came off in the young man's hand.

"Crikey!"

James tried to shove it back in position, but the metal pins were exhausted with age. He laid the door knocker reverently beside the front step.

Lisa wanted to flee, but Ted was emboldened by the mini disaster. He strode across the veranda to a nearby window. Shading his eyes, he peered through the murk and beckoned her over.

Though much of the room was concealed in shadow, it appeared quite spacious. Apart from a lavishly tiled fireplace, it was boardinghouse plain, with tired beige walls and bare floorboards. The room was empty except for a single piece of furniture — a decrepit sofa.

Lisa thrilled at the thought of Alexander, dressed in evening attire, strolling across that floor before pausing to warm his hands at a crackling fire. Who knows? Perhaps he had even sat on that sofa? She could almost see him raising a crystal glass to his lips and looking at her with those sad, pale eyes, confusion flickering across his face as if he'd seen a ghost from the future gazing through the window at him. She smiled. Perhaps the real Alexander had experienced an eerie moment countless years ago. Or was it him doing the haunting? She raised her hand, and the vision evaporated.

"There's something I'd like to show you," James said, jolting her into the present.

She followed him around the side of the house to the orchard. Rows of fruit trees radiated from an old apple tree in the center, like the spokes of a bicycle wheel.

"Must be a hundred years old," James said, patting the old tree's twisted trunk. "It'll produce great apples. You know, the old-fashioned sort that are bittersweet."

It was good of him to drag her out, but it

was just a tree. She turned to go back to the house.

"Hang on!" he called. James wedged his boot in a cleft between the trunk and a lower branch and, with the ease of a jungle primate, swung himself upward. She averted her gaze from the flash of underpants only just covering his buttocks.

"Look here," he said, pointing out a shape in the silvery bark.

Someone had carved a heart in the trunk a long time ago. A couple had stood under these branches and been very much in love. Though the air was cold, a wave of warmth washed through Lisa.

CHAPTER 9

"You're nuts," Maxine said.

Hogan & Hogan's window was a patchwork of yellowing photos. Most of the properties seemed to have been on the market since the year David Bowie discovered hair gel. Trumperton Manor was at the center of the bottom row with NEW! scrawled in bright-red letters across one corner. Underneath, a large fly lay on its back on the window ledge. It wriggled its legs as if receiving intermittent electrical shocks. A small white dog, its feathery tail tied up in a red ribbon, placed its front paws on the ledge. The dog put its head to one side, rolled out its tongue, and with a flash of its diamanté collar devoured the fly.

"That place was built for an army of servants," Maxine added. "You need a low-maintenance property, especially after your health scare."

That was a low blow. "You mean I should

buy a hospital?"

Ted and James excused themselves to explore Castlemaine's café scene.

"You don't want this old dump," Maxine grumbled. "There's nothing wrong with that townhouse. Remember Lucy Jordan?"

"Who?"

"You know. The Marianne Faithfull song. She reaches thirty-seven and realizes she'll never ride through Paris in a sports car?"

"Castlemaine's hardly Paris."

"All I'm saying is, every woman gets to a point when she's done everything she's going to do. You can't take risks anymore."

"Didn't she commit suicide?"

"Who, Marianne Faithfull?"

"No, Lucy Jordan. Doesn't she throw herself off a building at the end of the song?"

"God, I don't know! My point is . . ."

"*My* point is, I don't have the luxury of not taking risks," Lisa shot back. "My kids took off to different corners of the world, and my husband walked out on me."

A vision of pink and rhinestone appeared in the property agent's doorway. "Can I help you two ladies?"

The agent — if that was what she was — wore a Barbie-pink jacket squeezed over a sequined top. It was difficult to tell if the strip of fabric over her thighs was a skirt or a belt. Her cleavage was deep enough to be seen from Google Earth. The heels of her matching pink boots were so high she was practically standing on tiptoe.

The sisters regained composure.

"We're just wondering about this property," Lisa said.

"Trumpington Manor?"

"Trump*er*ton," Lisa corrected.

The agent ran a hand through her mane of blond hair extensions. "Yes, well, it's as pooped as my uncle's prostate. The owners have already accepted an offer from a developer. He's going to knock it down and put in a subdivision of new houses."

Lisa flushed with rage. How could anyone get away with such vandalism?

"But the contract's not signed yet," the agent said, clearly tuning in to Lisa's reaction. "You could always put in a better offer."

Offering a hand of glittering rings and beaming from under a canopy of false eyelashes, the agent introduced herself as Beverley Hogan. "Want to take a look, anyway?" she asked. "It's nothing a demolition ball won't cure. You could put in one of those lovely kit homes."

"I'd *never* knock it down," Lisa replied. "It's a magnificent building."

"Oh, you could fix the outside up all right," Beverley said, changing course. "My ex could help with that. But, really, the place is a knockdown."

"So you set up this business with your second husband?" Maxine asked.

"Hell no! I only married Bob, the younger Hogan, a couple of months ago."

The sisters offered restrained congratulations.

"Anyway, Scottie could fix the outside in a lizard's blink," Beverley said, fumbling in a tiny silver shoulder bag before pressing a card into Lisa's hand. "I'll get the keys and meet you there."

Lisa glanced at the card in her hand. It read: SCOTT GREEN LANDSCAPING, PROJECT MANAGEMENT, AND GARDEN MAINTENANCE — SPECIAL RATES FOR PENSIONERS!

When they pulled up outside the manor's front gates, Maxine consented to venture onto the property — providing everyone understood she was driven by curiosity, not approval.

Beverley cursed when she saw the door knocker lying on the step. "Hooligans," she said with a shrug. "I'll send Bob to the hardware store to get a new one."

Ted grimaced at the prospect of exchanging a historical relic for a cheap imitation.

Beverley produced an ancient metal rod almost as long as her hand. "Guess they never lost their keys in those days," she said, rattling it in the reluctant lock.

Lisa held her breath as the door creaked open on a large entrance hall. Though paneled in dark wood, the space was bathed in shafts of color. She glanced up to see the source of the light — above a central stairway was a huge stained-glass window glowing with images of roses gleaming against writhing green foliage.

The hallway might've been welcoming once, but now the air smelled moldy, and it was festooned with spiderwebs. Though Australia's arachnids had a fearsome reputation, they barely registered with Lisa. Anything that could be sucked up by a vacuum cleaner didn't warrant attention, as far as she was concerned. And anyway, she figured people weren't entitled to more than one phobia each, and her personal nemesis was snakes.

"How come it's on the market?" she asked.

"The current owners had lived here since Moses was in nappies." Beverley's voice bounced off walls fissured with age. "The old woman inherited the old dump from her mum. The maintenance got too much for them. They moved to the cottage across the road."

Lisa hadn't noticed any other houses in the neighborhood.

She turned left into a room that overlooked the driveway. There, the floor was a patchwork of shabby linoleum, and a sheet of stained plywood covered what was probably a fireplace. Curtains hung like dishcloths, and the walls were cracked and painted snot green.

"The old couple slept in here," Beverley explained. "It used to be the library." She led them back to the hallway and into the room with the sofa. The settee was an old rollback, and resembled an abandoned animal with its seat sagging to the floor and stuffing vomiting out of its arms.

"Bet they had a few booze-ups in here." Beverley winked.

Ted crouched beside the fireplace and rubbed his hands in front of an imaginary blaze. For a moment, Lisa saw Alexander again.

Beverley escorted them past the stairs to a large kitchen at the back of the house. "Reckon they had to squeeze a few servants in here," Beverley said.

Taps leaned at drunken angles, and the

121

walk-in pantry smelled of vinegar and damp.

An ancient wood-burning stove sulked in an alcove. "We used to have one of these on the farm," James said, smiling. He bent to turn the handle of the heavy metal door. An avalanche of black grit spilled onto the floor. "Looks like there's been a cremation. I reckon I could get it going."

Lisa rattled the lock of a back door that must have opened onto the yard between the kitchen and the stables, but Beverley said the key was back at the office.

A narrow passageway led from the kitchen to a set of small rooms, including a utilitarian lavatory with a wooden seat and chain flush. "Scullery and servants' quarters," Beverley said.

Lisa wondered what life had been like for servants at Trumperton Manor. She hoped her ancestors had treated them fairly.

"That was put up after the original servants' quarters burned down years ago," Beverley explained. "Those weatherboards have got white ants, I reckon."

Either country land agents were more honest than their urban colleagues, or Beverley was still in training.

"What about the stables?"

"Nothing much there," Beverley said quickly.

"Is there room to park a car under cover?"

"Let's concentrate on the house."

Lisa wondered why Beverley was unwilling to open the stables. Maybe they housed a dynasty of rats or worse. Lisa had never recovered from the time her cousin Trevor from Bendigo had chased her with a snake. It had probably been harmless, but she was only six or seven at the time.

"I've saved the best for last," Beverley said, clattering up the staircase.

Lisa ran her hand over the smooth balustrade and tingled at the thought of Alexander's doing exactly the same thing.

"Great for sliding down," James said.

Honestly. How old was this kid, twenty-six? No generation had been better educated or taken so long to grow up.

"Four bedrooms and a bathroom," Beverley said, pausing at a small landing under the leadlight window. They followed her up a dogleg twist to a foyer on the upper floor. Lisa smiled at the different-sized doors leading off to the left and right. She felt like Alice in Wonderland.

Most of the doors were standard-size bedrooms, Lisa assumed. She longed to uncover the secrets behind every one of them. Even more compelling was the set of impressive double doors standing directly in front of them. Lisa held her breath as Beverley reached for the tarnished brass handles. The creak of ancient hinges revealed tall windows draped with curtains so ragged they were practically translucent. The fireplace was handsomely carved, the built-in mirror above it speckled with age. Lisa tried to imagine the scenes that mirror had reflected.

"The old ballroom," Beverley said, opening French doors onto a generous balcony formed by the portico beneath. "I reckon you could make it the master bedroom."

Stepping outside and gazing across the valley, the group inhaled a single breath. The mist had lifted, and the hills were drenched in amber. A tinge of lemon outlined the hills before dissolving into limitless blue sky.

"Spectacular," breathed Ted.

The air exploded with husky screeches. A flock of cockatoos spiraled off a gum tree to regroup on the paddock below.

"Greedy buggers," Beverley said. "They scoff all the crops."

Lisa craned her neck to identify the parrot from the other day. Maybe he'd learned to fly again. But the rowdy skydivers all looked the same.

"Doesn't the house have a heritage order?"

Lisa asked.

"Not that anyone talks about. If I were you I'd flatten it and subdivide. People are flooding into Castlemaine these days. All the city slickers are wanting a tree change. Pick the best bit of land and put up a nice place for yourself, throw in six or seven houses around it, and you'll be set for life. I'll sell them off the plan for you."

Lisa glanced toward the gum trees opposite the driveway entrance. A spiral of smoke rose from a chimney in the depths of the silvery forest. So that's where the manor's current owners lived. She wondered if they might be open to some creative negotiation.

A hunched figure hobbled toward the roadside letterbox. Lisa raised a hand. The old woman looked up, but didn't respond.

"They're keen to sell," Beverley added. "If you can top the other offer, it's yours."

Lisa sensed it was time to play her trump card.

"We have family connections to this place, you know."

"Really?" Beverley's interest was piqued.

"Yes, my grandfather, I mean *our* grandfather" — she nodded toward Maxine, who'd wandered off to the other end of the balcony — "was a Trumperton."

Lisa waited for Beverley's reaction. It wasn't the warm recognition she'd expected. "I thought they died out," Beverley said, inspecting the heel of her boot.

"Who, the Trumpertons? Well, I suppose technically the name died with Dad. But we're still here."

"Oh."

"I thought it'd be great to bring the house back into the family. . . ."

The agent eased the ridiculous piece of footwear off her leg. She turned it upside down and shook it. A pebble flew out and rolled across the mosaic tiles. "You were thinking of living here alone?" she asked.

"I write for a living and . . ."

"Wouldn't you rattle around in it? I mean, for one person . . . I sure as hell wouldn't do it. They reckon the place is haunted. And in any case, the other offer's a very good one. It's already underway, so technically the house isn't really for sale at all. . . ."

What was wrong with the woman? "But you said the deal's not signed," Lisa said. "Isn't it your job to get the best price?"

"Your ideas just seem a little fanciful, that's all," Beverley replied.

"Thank God someone's talking sense!" Maxine flounced past and strode inside. "It's freezing out here."

126

"I can't believe you think it's okay to pull this magnificent place down," Lisa said, aware her tone was becoming strident.

Beverley's lip curled with amusement. "I don't know if you realize it, coming from — where did you say?"

"New York . . . but I'm from here, really. Well, not *here.* I was born in Melbourne."

Beverley gazed glumly down at her clipboard. She drew a line of frowning faces on her clipboard with her diamanté-encrusted pen. "We've been in drought for years. The land's drier than a lizard's dick."

"But you said your ex could help?"

"Actually he's flat-out landscaping the new medical center."

The change in Beverley's mood was extraordinary.

"Is it true there was a scandal here?" Lisa asked quietly.

Beverley turned pinker than her jacket. "Every house has stories," she said, clicking her pen.

"What happened?"

Across the valley a kookaburra cackled like a lunatic.

"I don't know the details."

The woman was frustrating beyond words. Lisa walked over to Ted and James, who were locked in conversation.

"A developer's going to tear it down and cover the land in McMansions," she said, her heart thudding.

Ted's mouth dropped open.

"We can't let it happen," she said. "This house is our heritage."

Ted and James looked at each other. "If you buy it, we'll help fix it up," Ted said.

"Really?"

"Weekends, holidays, that sort of thing . . ."

"You mean it?"

"Yeah, we'll fling a few paintbrushes around." James nodded in agreement.

Lisa felt a frisson of excitement.

"We'll help you move in. Your stuff will fit in the Kombi."

Lisa willed her thoughts into slow motion. Her mathematical calculations always erred on the optimistic. The asking price for Trumperton Manor couldn't be much more than that of the townhouse. The renovations would cost a bomb, but she could just about live in the old house as it stood. Maybe she could enroll in DIY night classes. The mortgage would be a stretch. On the other hand, *Three Sisters: Charlotte* had been sold to Germany.

Setting her jaw, she strode back to Beverley. "What's the offer you have on the table?"

CHAPTER 10

The developer was unwilling to lose the battle for Trumperton Manor. Every time Beverley phoned, the price went up another five thousand dollars. Just when Lisa couldn't go any higher and had prepared herself for the worst, her opposition slunk away. Apparently his backer had suddenly become a "person of interest" to the federal police, and he'd taken himself and his bank account off to Asia.

Lisa couldn't wait to visit Aunt Caroline in the nursing home to share the wonderful news. But the old woman spent most of the time nattering about cruising "the Med" on the royal yacht *Britannia* with Queen Elizabeth and that handsome Prince Philip. When Lisa interrupted Aunt Caroline to shout for the third time that she'd bought Trumperton Manor, the old girl finally fixed Lisa with a vivid blue eye. "Why on earth would you want to do *that*?" Aunt Caroline said, before changing the subject.

The day after the owners, the Wrights, finally accepted her offer, Lisa bought a battered green station wagon. It had belonged to a friend of Ted's who was moving to Berlin to do a PhD in immunology. The brakes were soft, but Ted assured her it was in good nick.

The Camry smelled of dog and old socks. The back third of the vehicle looked particularly worn. Maybe it had doubled as a meth lab. But with the back seats down, there were heaps of space for whatever country people stowed in their vehicles. Pitchforks?

Once Lisa got the hang of the hand-shift gears, she rattled through the streets of Camberwell with an irrational sense of freedom. She'd always pitied people who gave their cars names, but the rust bucket was screaming to be christened, so secretly she named it Dino, after the Flintstones' pet dinosaur.

Maxine was far from overjoyed to have "that thing" parked outside her house. She was in an almost permanent grump these days, though she was kind enough to offer up an assortment of cobwebby kitchen chairs, an old wardrobe, and a twenty-year-old fridge. She also threw in the old oak table that'd languished in the shed for decades.

Lisa melted at the sight of the furniture she'd grown up with. Its borer-ridden surface had witnessed countless family rows. She found the extension boards nestled in the shadows behind Gordon's workbench. With the boards in place, the table could seat ten or twelve.

For the remaining month, Lisa did her best to make herself invisible. She shut herself away with the sea captain for hours on end, hunched over her computer, tapping away. Even though she was behind schedule with the book, sentences were starting to trickle. Buying the manor had somehow knocked the edges off her writer's block.

Much as Lisa worshipped the Brontë sisters, one aspect of their work wore her down — the men. From Heathcliff to Mr. Rochester, the men were mostly brutes who were kinder to their dogs than to women. They bathed in the power that went with their wealth and could brood and take off with floozies as they pleased. Meanwhile, the female characters' piercing intelligence did little to rescue the women from their horrific lives.

Lisa wanted to make the male characters

in *Three Sisters* more appealing to the twenty-first-century reader. Emily's earl was turning out to be more of a metrosexual. Frederick the stable hand had the sort of well-sculpted body Lisa had seen in gyms.

"Someone's here to see you," Maxine announced, sweeping into the room and pulling back the Jolly Roger curtains. Lisa checked the calendar on her phone. Twenty-three days to go.

"Who?"

"That bastard."

"Jake?" Lisa said, incredulous. Wasn't Australia far enough away to avoid seeing him?

Maxine crossed her arms, as though confirming the death of a family pet. "Thinks he can turn up out of nowhere. I'm not having him on the property."

Lisa peered through the netting. Her heart melted momentarily at the sight of Jake standing in the driveway. Rugged up in a black parka, he was barking into his phone. Same old Jake. Physically in one place, mentally somewhere else.

"He refuses to leave," Maxine says.

Lisa glanced in the mirror and scrunched her hair. Her eyes were amphibious from hours of computer time. In the hallway were Maxine's UGG boots, lying like a pair of discarded pups. Lisa dived into them before walking down the frost-lined path.

Jake slid his phone into his pocket and flashed a smile designed to turn babies and little old ladies to mush. "You've gone native," he said. "Never thought I'd see you in those things."

"Not mine," she said, glancing down at the UGG boots. "What are you doing here?"

"I was in the neighborhood. Singapore, to be exact. Thought I might as well drop by." Jake treated airplanes like country buses. He was immune to jet lag.

"Have you seen Portia?"

"Last week. She's getting heaps of work in animal costumes."

"Like *The Lion King*?"

"No. Kids' parties."

"Is she eating?"

"Dunno. She ate *some*thing when I saw her last week. . . . It was green, I think."

Clearly Jake was too focused on his own life to worry about his daughter's health. He'd certainly been looking after himself. His teeth had an unnatural glow, and his hair seemed darker. The distinguished gray around his temples had vanished.

"How's . . . Belle?"

"Amazing!" He hugged his chest and scuffed his feet in imaginary snow. "Every-

134

thing's great. I feel so . . . *energized.* We've started jogging."

Jake hated running.

"We're thinking of doing a half-marathon."

"Good for you."

"She took me to hot yoga. It's spiritual, all that sweating, you know. They wouldn't let me out till I fainted."

Jake was talking to her as if she were his mother. She played along and gave him the approval he hungered for. "Looks like you've lost weight, too," Lisa said.

"High-protein diet."

He used to make fun of her protein bars.

"Works wonders," he added. "Apart from the constipation."

"That's what the kids would call TMI," Lisa said.

"What?"

"Too much information to share with an ex-wife."

"Oh. I guess you are now. What's this I hear about your buying a dump in the country?"

He'd been talking to Ted.

"You should've rented first. I mean, how long is Ted going to stay in Australia, *really*? I know he says *now* that he wants to stay, but it won't last."

Lisa looked up at a bird shivering on a wire. She'd had enough of other people's advice. Besides, Jake had relinquished his right to offer any. "How's work?"

"Oh, the usual," he said. "No fun being an old bull in a paddock of ambitious calves."

"Maybe it's time to leave the farm."

"Seems I've been banned from the dragon's lair," he said. Jake gazed up at the curtains twitching in Maxine's window. "There's a good-looking café on the corner. Don't suppose you're free for lunch?"

To drink coffee with Jake, to laugh with him and talk about the kids . . . Her brain kicked in just in time. "No thanks. I'm working." She turned and scurried up the path.

Maxine greeted her at the door.

"What did he want?"

"Nothing."

"How long's he here for?"

"Forgot to ask."

Once she settled back at the computer, a fresh plotline flashed into Lisa's brain. An older man, a parson from a nearby parish, would take a shine to Emily. She would quickly see him for what he was — vain and insecure, his hair oily with black shoe polish in a futile attempt to camouflage the gray.

136

CHAPTER 11

The receptionist at Hogan & Hogan handed Lisa an orange envelope. She fumbled for the outline of the key inside. It was hard to believe the scrap of ancient metal was hers. She asked to see Beverley in person, but the receptionist said the agent was away on important business at a spa in Daylesford.

Clutching the envelope, Lisa hurried outside. Sharp morning air caught the back of her throat. A truck lumbered past. The black-and-white sheepdog on the back gave her a casual bark. Rush hour in Castle-maine.

Dino was sprouting mops and brooms. With his knees jammed against the dash-board, Ted looked like a grasshopper about to be crushed. "That was quick," he said.

Lisa glanced across the street to where James had double-parked the Kombi. It was a miracle the trailer and its contents were still attached. The wardrobe and fridge stood to attention alongside her boxes from New York and a battered microwave oven Maxine had thrown in as a parting gift. Leaning against them was a queen-sized bed Lisa had picked up from a wholesale outlet. Behind it the legs of the old dining table threw themselves up in horror.

The lens of a video camera gleamed from inside the Kombi's back window. She pulled her beanie over her ears and climbed into Dino. Though it was heartening Ted had brought friends, she was hardly ecstatic about being filmed. Still, she couldn't say no to poor Zack (she was getting better at remembering their names). A film student, he had the deranged idea of making a documentary on what he called her "life-style change."

The Kombi followed them down familiar roads until they reached the gates of the manor.

"Wait!" Ted said, peering up at the "sold" sticker slapped across the sign.

Lisa was still adjusting to the eccentricities of Dino's brakes. As the car glided to a standstill, Ted leaped out and beckoned his mates. James and Zack emerged from the Kombi with a couple of laughing girls.

Heidi wore red-framed glasses and polka-dot tights. Partway through a vet-science degree, she had a wonderfully zany style. Heidi leaped and demanded to be piggybacked.

Stella's vibe was softer, more self-contained. Her curls were tied up in a bright yellow scarf. She was training to be an occupational therapist. Lisa was grateful they'd shown up for the modest hourly rate she could afford.

Wielding his camera, Zack arranged the group under the sign, placing Lisa in the center. "Action!" he called.

Did anyone say "action" anymore? She scrunched her eyes to examine the cameraman. His poetic face was framed with flaxen hair twisted up in a bun. The big, soft eyes could've been stolen from a seal. There was more than a touch of Sebastian the cellist about him. Though Ted hadn't introduced Zack as his boyfriend yet, he was obviously The One. James was too much of a country boy for her son's taste. Besides, James and Heidi were almost certainly an item.

Lisa brandished the key and bared her teeth at the camera. Ted and James shimmied up the fence post and dismantled the sign — the muscle strength of the under thirties really was awe-inspiring.

Zack then jogged ahead and stood at the bend in the driveway to film the convoy's arrival. He was wearing purple corduroy trousers and an orange paisley shirt. The pinstriped waistcoat looked as if it had seen better days in the members' stand at the Melbourne Cup. Strands of hair had struggled free of his man bun to float on the breeze. Maybe amateur scientists were right when they claimed all the estrogen in the water systems was obliterating the male species.

"I hope he isn't using that camera as an excuse to get out of heavy lifting," Ted muttered as they crept past splashes of yellow wattle.

The house suddenly loomed over them against a steely sky. The boarded-up windows stared out like empty eye sockets. A cold ripple of dread washed over her. Trumperton was every bit as disheveled and impractical as Maxine claimed. And what if it really *was* haunted?

Dino rattled to a halt under the portico.

"Tell me I'm not crazy," she whispered.

Ted latched his arm around her and gave her a squeeze.

Lisa's knees trembled as she climbed the front steps. She tore the envelope open and jiggled the key in the lock. It swiveled half-heartedly. She tensed her arm and employed brute force, but the key seized in the lock and refused to budge. Heat flared up on her neck. The girls offered to help. But it was *her* house, dammit.

A gust of wind set gum trees quivering. Lisa heard a tentative squawk. Surfing the lowest branch of a bottlebrush was a white parrot. It gazed up at them.

"Oh, look!" she said. "It's the cockatoo Maxine and I nearly killed."

The others exchanged glances. Didn't she know all cockatoos looked the same?

Lisa stopped wrestling with the key and tried to remember what her yoga teacher always said: *"Breathe . . ."*

"Good thing that agent didn't get to Bunnings," James said, inspecting the door knocker in his hand.

Relaxing her wrist, Lisa applied gentle pressure to the lock. She felt arthritic movement inside the mechanism. The metal innards finally yielded. She wondered if this was the manor's way of telling her that whatever she had in mind, the house would always be in charge.

As the door creaked open, acrid air piqued her nostrils. She stepped into the entrance hall. A beam of sunlight played across the leadlights and filled the hall with soft pinks and greens.

"Amazing!" Stella exclaimed breathily. A

serpent of vacuum-cleaner hose was coiled over her shoulders.

"Where's the kitchen?" Heidi's voice echoed against the paneling and floorboards.

Lisa reached for a light switch beside the door. Black and circular, it was set in a round of wood. She'd arranged to have the power connected, but most of the light sockets were bare. The switch was stiff. It'd be a miracle if . . . A naked bulb flickered to life above their heads. The group let out a cry of jubilation.

They heaved up the few sash windows that would budge to set cross-breezes through the rooms. Ted and Stella unloaded the trailer while Lisa and Heidi attacked the kitchen's mushroom-colored matchboard walls with scrubbing brushes.

After investigating a leak under the sink and tightening the taps, James laid the front page of the *Herald Sun* in front of the wood-burning stove.

"How else are you going to cook?" he asked, creating a volcano of ash on the floor.

Lisa had been thinking microwave and takeaways.

"You're lucky the place hasn't been done up," he said, tugging at a patch of old lino. "I reckon . . . hey!"

Lisa emerged from the pantry.

"You've got flagstones!" James said, scraping away decades of grease. "We'll have to pull this old flooring up. Not today, though."

Though the floor was uneven, it was soon mopped and semi-clean. While the girls unpacked crockery and pots, Lisa sorted cutlery into drawers. As she stood at the sink gulping a glass of water, the boys brought in the old oak table. Once the extension boards were slid into place, the table fit in the kitchen as though it had always been there. Lisa brushed spiderwebs off Maxine's chairs, which were mismatched enough to pass for vintage chic.

The girls oohed and aahed as they unraveled Aunt Caroline's dinner set from cocoons of Bubble Wrap. Its swirling floral design seemed more at home here than it ever had in New York.

As they shared a picnic lunch around the table, Lisa conjured up images of the people who'd sat in that same spot more than a century ago — a cook resting her feet after rising before dawn to bake bread; a lady's maid primping her bonnet; maybe a butler presiding over the spot where Zack was fiddling absentmindedly with his left nostril.

She watched her son talking animatedly with his friends. As a little boy, Ted would refuse to be left at kindergarten. He'd grip her hand and bellow until she conceded to sit with him and build Lego castles. But the moment she thought he was absorbed enough for her to attempt escape, he'd grab her hand. The teacher would urge her to go, assuring her that Ted was always fine after she left. Lisa would creep around the side of the building and peer through a window. Ted would be sitting alone, weeping quietly into the colored blocks, causing her heart to implode.

At school Ted had been a loner with a talent for drawing cartoons. Lisa had kept some, but had thrown out the one of Jake dressed as Darth Vader with Lisa and the kids as his storm troopers. Ted had a better sense of the family dynamics than she did.

Much to his father's disappointment, the only sport Ted ever liked was swimming. Jake said it didn't count because there was no team spirit. Instead, Ted preferred tinkering out tunes from *The Phantom of the Opera* on the piano. Lisa had found him a teacher and he had practiced diligently. Soon he was in demand as an accompanist for the extroverts who wanted to prance around onstage in school musicals. That was typical Ted — to make others shine.

Heidi exploded with laughter and rustled

James's hair. Ted smiled across the table at Zack. Australia had been good for him.

After lunch, Lisa and the girls set to work dusting, vacuuming, and cleaning the master bedroom while the boys heaved the bed, wardrobe, bedside table, and countless cardboard boxes upstairs.

The carpet in the bedroom had faded to a color that reminded Lisa of the time she'd thrown up in a doctor's waiting room. The floor-to-ceiling curtains were crisp with mold, their floral pattern all but invisible. Still, she declined the girls' offer to pull them down. Even in their disgusting state they might provide temporary protection against the early morning sun.

Sixteen-foot-high walls gave the room an airy feel, and light streamed through the French doors. Though the pressed metal ceiling was cracked, it had attractive edging that resembled piped icing. An empty light socket dangled from a cord in the center.

"Smells damp," Ted said. "Sure you want to sleep here?"

Heidi and Stella brushed cobwebs off the fireplace while Lisa took a breadknife to her boxes. She was overjoyed to unearth her pillow.

The boys exchanged looks as she patted it, cooing. She smoothed the sheets and tossed a red angora rug over the covers.

Stella brought in a branch of fluorescent yellow wattle in a jar and set it on the mantelpiece. Such a thoughtful girl.

Lisa's New York clothes seemed to belong to another person. It was unlikely anyone in Castlemaine wore heels and a little black dress, or the floral dress from JCPenney that was Scarlett O'Hara on steroids. Lisa snorted at the dark suit she'd bought for library talks and interviews. Out here, the only thing likely to ask questions about her modest literary pursuits was a wombat. Still, she had to put *something* in the wardrobe, so she hung up the suit, alongside the secondhand Japanese wedding kimono that doubled as a dressing gown and the dark tailored coat she wore to the theater when it snowed.

The rest of her New York clothes were shoved back in the box and kicked in a corner. Her new Aussie look consisted of things that didn't need to be hung in wardrobes — check shirts, an assortment of beanies, a polar-fleece jacket. She was particularly proud of the butch elastic-sided boots from Aussie Disposals. Then there was the old-fashioned flannelette winter nightie she'd bought at Target. . . .

The girls gathered up their buckets and

moved on to the bathroom down the hall. The bedroom still smelled like a mushroom farm — Lisa would have to pick up a bottle of lavender oil next time she was in town. With her nightie stuffed under her pillow and the mouth guard tucked discreetly away in the bedside table, the room felt almost homey.

Ted climbed a ladder to fix an energy-efficient lightbulb into the socket.

"How are you feeling?" Lisa asked, polishing the mirror above the fireplace. The specks of age refused to budge.

"Right now my fingers are a little numb," he replied carefully. Her son could smell an interrogation a mile off. "That's because the blood has flowed downward because my hand is raised," he added.

"I mean about Dad and me. It must be upsetting for you. I worry about Portia, too. . . ."

"She's okay," he said. "We Skype a lot."

"Is she really? Don't you think she's lost weight?"

"Yeah, but you know what girls are like these days," he said.

Lisa couldn't tell if Ted was trying to calm her down or disguise serious concern. Maybe both.

"I just hope the divorce didn't trigger

something. It must've been a shock for you both."

Ted lowered his arm and looked down at her. His eyes were flat with sorrow. Sympathy, too. "We always knew it would happen," he said.

"What?"

"C'mon, Mom. Dad was away all the time. And when he came home he was a stranger."

The duster fell to her side. "I thought we were happy."

Ted fixed her with a gaze that made him look a thousand years old. "The only difference is, we always thought you'd leave *him,*" he said.

"Really?" The duster dropped to the floor. She scooped it up and attacked the mirror with renewed vigor. She needed fresh energy, something to lift her mood. "Is there someone special in your life?" she asked, watching for his reaction in the mirror's reflection.

Ted froze.

"You seemed so happy today, I was just thinking . . ."

His brow settled in a line.

"He's great," she said, applying a squirt of Windex.

"Who?"

"Zack . . ."

Ted studied the lightbulb in his hand. "Yeah, he's great."

"He adores you."

They listened to Zack tapping away with a hammer in the adjacent room. He'd been so fascinated by the Fijian fighting stick, she'd put him in charge of arranging it and the masks on her soon-to-be-study wall.

Ted rolled his eyes.

Typical of her son to be bashful in love. "I know," she continued. "It's never easy."

The tapping stopped. A balloon of silence filled the room. Zack must've been eavesdropping.

Lisa wished she'd kept her mouth shut. She'd overstepped the mother-son privacy line.

Ted twisted the lightbulb in place. She watched him climb down the ladder. He seemed tired all of a sudden. Her energy was flagging, too. By the time they assailed the downstairs reception room she wasn't up to anything more than wiping the crimson and blue tiles around the fireplace. Their condition was good. Not one was cracked.

She picked at a bubble in the cream wallpaper near the mantelpiece. The hole revealed diagonal patterns of dark-blue fleur-de-lis that marched in crisscross lines across an eggshell-colored background. The original wall covering was beautiful, and she felt a prickle of excitement. This was the backdrop against which Alexander had acted out his life.

Lisa lifted Alexander's photo from one of the boxes and placed it on the mantelpiece. If only those mournful eyes would flicker to life and she could hear his voice. Handsome in his white tie, Alexander was finally home. And quite the gentleman.

"It's a beautiful sunset," Heidi said. "Do you mind if we take the sofa out onto the veranda?"

"Go for it," Lisa said.

The girls tried to lift the old rollback, but it was heavier than it looked. They called for Zack, Ted, and James to help lug it outside and position it under the window.

Lisa stood up and tore off her rubber gloves. Every joint ached. She hadn't felt this tired since giving birth. It was a satisfying weariness, though. The walls assumed a golden glow. Young people's laughter drew her outside into the twilight. James stood up from the sofa to make room for her. Claiming he had something important to do, he disappeared back inside the house. The sofa groaned as she sandwiched herself in with the others. The firm warmth of their bodies was reassuring.

Stella pointed out a white bird picking its way through the scruffy grass below them.

"That's our cockatoo," Lisa said. "He's limping."

Nobody bothered arguing.

Above the valley, the sky melted from gold to apricot. Lisa remembered her father saying high wisps of cloud usually meant rain.

"Do you think this will be your happiest house?" Zack asked, focusing his camera on her.

"What do you mean?" she asked, scraping cobwebs from her hair.

"If I could move back to the place my grandparents lived, I'd go there like a shot," he said.

She glanced up at Zack. He was too young to be nostalgic. Maybe some other ache of the soul lingered under those pale eyelashes and his baby-fresh skin.

"I love it here."

"Reconnecting with your roots?"

"Yes, but my sister hates the house. . . ."

Lisa was disturbed by the vehemence in her tone. The spectacle of a middle-aged woman fretting over her big sister's opinion was undignified. "There's beer in the fridge," she said, snapping out of it. "Any volunteers to get takeaway?"

"No need for that." James was standing in the doorway wielding a large tray. "I finally got the better of that chimney."

"And I've brought something better than beer," Stella said, flourishing a bottle of prosecco.

The aroma of wood-fired pizza inspired a whoop from the team. An orange moon rose over the horizon as they fell upon the feast.

The wine tickled the back of Lisa's throat, and her cheeks glowed with warmth. "What is it about sparkling wine?" she asked.

"The bubbles," Stella said. "They send alcohol into your system much faster."

As the alcohol surged through her veins, Lisa's fears faded. Ted leaned toward Zack, cupped his hand over his ear and whispered. They exploded with laughter. The chemistry between them was palpable.

Lisa swallowed a small lump of sadness when Stella announced it was time to leave. Another student friend was having a birthday party back in Melbourne and they didn't want to be late. Of course they had their own lives to be getting on with. It was up to Lisa to invent one for herself. They hugged her and promised to be back the following weekend with buckets of paint.

Ted pressed a packet into Lisa's hand.

"Housewarming gift," he said.

Lisa tore the wrapping to find a headband with a tiny light attached. It was the sort of thing people wore for exploring caves.

"Gee, thanks!" she said with mock enthusiasm.

He adjusted the straps and showed her how to operate the torch. It had the beam of a small lighthouse. "The wiring can be dodgy in these old places," he said. "Keep it by your bed."

They piled into the Kombi and drove off down the driveway. Lisa suddenly felt catatonic, her face muscles locked in an unfamiliar shape. It took her a while to realize she was actually smiling. Trumperton Manor was much more than the house of her dreams. Her chromosomes were soaked into every brick and creaking floorboard. It was hers.

On top of that, she'd met Ted's new love.

CHAPTER 12

A good hot bath was in order. Lisa staggered upstairs, filled the old claw-footed tub and immersed herself in its comforting depths. Her aquatic ballet was interrupted by a thump over her head. Something of considerable size had landed on the roof. She turned the taps off and listened.

The steady beat of the cold tap dripping into the bathwater was all she could hear. Maybe a branch had fallen on the roof. "Silly fool," she said aloud to herself. She was bound to be jumpy on her first night. The house was going to have all sorts of noises she'd have to get used to.

She reached for the hot tap. Suddenly, every muscle in her body went rigid — footsteps. Someone — or thing — was walking on the slate tiles above her.

She leaped out of the bath and gathered up her clothes. Sprinting down the hall to her study, she flicked on the light. Mercifully, Zack had done a lousy job attaching the Fijian fighting stick to the wall. She pulled it down. She'd seen Fijian warriors wield the things with fearsome vigor, but in her hands it looked as intimidating as a toothpick.

The steady thuds grew louder. Whoever was prowling on the roof wasn't shy about announcing his or her presence. She ran to the bedroom and grabbed her phone. Ted would be halfway back to Melbourne. She was about to call 911, but then remembered that the emergency number for Australia was different. Triple 9? That was the UK, surely. She couldn't remember. . . .

Lisa froze with dread. The thumping over her head had been joined by another set of feet. *Two* assailants! She didn't stand a chance. They were moving faster now, sprinting toward the front of the house.

Numb with adrenaline, she ran to her bedroom and tugged her nightie out from under her pillow. If she was about to meet her murderers, she was going to do it with dignity. She pulled on the nightie and slipped Ted's torch over her head. Reassured by the powerful white beam, she raised the fighting stick and nudged one of the French doors open a crack.

The neighbors' window glowed through

the gum trees at the end of the drive. It looked like something out of a tale by the Brothers Grimm. If she screamed they wouldn't hear a thing. There was no option but to confront her foes. Heart pulsing in her throat, she clutched the stick and stepped outside. The icy mosaic floor made her bare feet tingle.

There was no one on the balcony. She sensed she was being watched. Whirling the fighting stick over her shoulders, she spun around and looked up at the roof.

A pair of red eyes stared down at her. They were joined by a slightly smaller pair of eyes. A bushy tail draped over the guttering. The larger brush-tailed possum scampered away toward the chimney. The smaller one put his head to one side and studied her. The end of his nose was pink as fairy floss. She called out to him, but he turned and galloped after his companion.

Trembling with relief, she waited for her breathing to return to normal. The sky was so dark compared to that of New York, where it was never more than serge gray. Stars glittered with universal indifference. A terrified woman in her grandfather's house meant nothing in the life cycles of solar systems. Looking up at the stars, she could almost smell the tang of tobacco in her father's jacket. He had been a man who could turn an ordinary activity, like walking home through the dark, into something magical. She remembered the warmth of his breath as he put his arm around her and pointed out the line of three bright stars that made Orion's Belt. They were easy to find, but when he tried to show her the ones that made up the rest of the hunter, she sank into confusion. It was the first time she'd realized a lot of things would never make sense to her. She was destined to spend the rest of her life either bluffing her way through or being exposed as an ignorant fraud.

She hurried back inside and pulled on a purple beanie left over from a short-lived knitting craze. Like most of her knitting, she never wore it in public. The orange daisy she'd sewn on it flopped like a victim of chronic fatigue. The thermal socks and polar-fleece jacket looked sane by comparison. She lowered the fighting stick onto the floor beside her bed and placed the head torch on the table next to her phone and the dog-eared paperback of *Wuthering Heights.*

Tucked in bed with blankets up to her chin, she tried to ignore the loneliness gnawing away at the soft tissue inside her ribcage. She reached for her phone. *Guess wot?* she texted Portia. *Just met Ted's new bfriend.*

?????!!! The reply was almost instant. Presumably, it was a question.

Zack. Has he told u? Lisa typed.

No! Howz house?

Lisa wondered what level of truth was appropriate. Portia probably didn't want to know Lisa was frightened, exhilarated, and exhausted all at once.

Gr8

A row of *XXX*'s and a smiley face flashed on her screen, signaling the conclusion of the royal audience.

A sad lump formed in Lisa's throat. Children have no hope of knowing how much their parents love them until they become parents themselves. Portia had been the most affectionate, easygoing baby. She'd hardly ever cried. In the mornings, she'd cooed in her cot until Lisa opened her bedroom door, Portia raising her chubby arms to be picked up. Her smile was pure sunshine.

Lisa had delighted in watching her baby daughter devour bowls of custard, and smear the remains over her face. The child had reveled in the textures, flavors, and colors of food. Sure, she'd grown perhaps a little chubbier than some of her friends, but Lisa was never concerned. Portia was prettier and cuddlier than all of them put together.

Portia had never been short of passions besides food. She adored acting and singing, and was always near the top of her class. As Lisa's friends' daughters became spiky adolescents, Lisa took pride in the fact Portia remained soft and open. They'd gone to galleries and concerts together and read the same books. Though they were inseparable, Lisa refused to become one of those women who wore her daughter's jeans.

The change had happened so abruptly, Lisa was still trying to absorb the shock. The second Portia left home for college, she'd built an impenetrable wall around herself. Lisa was frozen out. She no longer knew what books Portia was reading or whom her friends were. Now Lisa grieved for the closeness they'd had.

Portia's first vacation break had coincided with the appearance of a pink Care Bear tattoo on her left ankle. Lisa had tried not to express alarm. It was nothing a decent plastic surgeon couldn't erase in a decade or so.

The next time they met, a green Care Bear grinned malevolently from Portia's forearm.

159

Lisa couldn't hold her tongue any longer. She had suggested to Portia that by the time she reached thirty or forty she might wish she'd chosen a more general theme for her body art. Portia had erupted. Lisa obviously had no idea that Care Bears were ironic.

Lisa had retreated into silence. Soon after, a yellow Care Bear beamed defiantly from Portia's right calf. It was as the army of Care Bears trotted over her limbs that Portia herself started shrinking. Boys fell for her haunted beauty. Portia was understandably flattered.

For a while, Lisa had to agree: Her daughter's new looks were startling. Then Portia won a Most Promising Actress award for her portrayal of Polly in the Venice Beach Players' production of *The Boy Friend.* Lisa had been dismayed by how much the flattery went to Portia's head. Portia dropped out of college and waitressed between auditioning for bit parts in movies. Portia, it seemed, had yet to understand an acting career was a license to serve coffee for the rest of her life.

Lisa had visited whenever she could, which wasn't often due to Portia's "busyness." She had a terrible shock the night she saw Portia slipping into a flimsy jacket with no warmth in it. Portia's shoulder blades jutted out like angel's wings waiting to lift her off the ground and spirit her away.

Anxiety had clawed at Lisa's stomach. On the few occasions they dined together, Portia eyed the food on her plate as if it were laced with poison. She stopped eating meat, then dairy products. It was only a matter of time before she refused lettuces because of the trauma they experienced being torn out of the ground. At the same time, Lisa had seen Portia knock back cocktails containing enough alcohol to render a cow senseless.

Lisa had tried coaxing, then begging Portia to eat, but it only made her daughter distance herself more. When Lisa had the mastectomy, she'd hoped Portia might resurrect their closeness, but her visits were short and dutiful. In darker moments, Lisa wondered if Portia had inherited some of her father's coldness.

Lisa's anxiety had finally exploded over a plate of spaghetti in a diner one day. Portia had scraped her chair back and flounced out into the street, leaving the food untouched. The invitations to California dried up after that. Conversations were reduced to interrogative phone calls, which had then been downgraded to texts.

Was it the child's reaction to family tensions? Or maybe they'd been too close. Deep down, Lisa had to admit that Portia's behavior was beyond the realms of normal rebelliousness. Portia was stubborn, difficult, and far too thin. Just like Emily Brontë.

Lisa went to the bathroom and riffled through her toiletries bag. The earplugs glowed like plump little friends in their plastic bag next to the moisturizer she hardly ever used. Thank God she'd kept them. She squished them between her fingers and shoved them in her ears.

Back in her room, she slid between the sheets, pulled the beanie over her ears, and flicked the bedside lamp off. Weariness enveloped her, but something was missing from her blocking-out-the-world routine. She rolled over, opened the bedside drawer, and felt for the smooth surface of the mouth guard case. Satisfactorily barricaded, she was safe. Not even a ghost could wake her.

Something roared across the roof above her. The noise was relentless, oppressive, and Lisa's earplugs did little to stifle it. Half-asleep, she thought she saw a ghost bearing down on her, but after a few moments she realized it was just a draft moving one of the curtains, and the source of the noise wasn't unworldly. It was rain.

Lightning flashed blue phantoms across the walls. A burst of thunder shook the roof. Wind wailed down the fireplace. She'd always claimed to enjoy thunderstorms. But this was more primal than anything she'd experienced.

She burrowed under the sheets and squeezed her eyes shut. She'd sat through dreadful concerts before, and tried to picture herself at Lincoln Center, where Kerry had procured free tickets to a discordant orchestral piece by one of those postmodern composers he adored. The percussion section had been in overdrive, flutes and oboes were wildly out of synch, and strings whined out of tune.

Lying on her back now, Lisa waited for the thunderstorm to finish, but a steady pinging sound was an ominous addition. From deep in the percussion section, a triangle was emitting the regular plunk of water dripping onto carpet.

A gust of freezing air rushed across the bed. She fumbled for the bedside lamp and flicked the switch. It refused to work. Thank God for Ted's torch. It cast a dispassionate beam at the curtains, billowing like towering specters. She ran across the room and wrestled the French doors shut. Shivering, she hurried back to bed and pulled the mohair rug up to her chin, but it was cold and wet. She shone the torch up at the ceiling. A silver waterfall trickled through a crack down onto her bed.

She glanced at her phone. 2:07. Maxine would be sound asleep in Camberwell, dreaming of perfect little grandchildren (a brain surgeon here, a start-up computer billionaire there . . .). Ted would be engrossed in an intimate stage of his night with Zack.

Lightning again flashed across the room. She tried to think of what her father would say: "It's only Nature doing her thing, Panda Bear. It'll blow over. Make yourself a cup of tea."

The only thing worse than almost drowning on her first night would be owning up to it. In the flick of a false eyelash, Maxine would be in her Golf and flying down the motorway. Lisa could see her bursting through the front door in a flurry of orange and green, demanding Lisa return to the suburbs.

She took two Panadol, in the hope her body might mistake them for sedatives, and willed herself back to sleep. Just before dawn, she dreamed of a hooded ghost chasing her across the roof and trying to push her off. As she fell, she managed to grab the ghost's hood and reveal its face. It was Aunt Caroline, cackling at her. "Why on earth would you want to buy Trumperton Manor?"

CHAPTER 13

Charlotte Brontë was eight years old when her father sent her to the world's worst boarding school. Charlotte later exacted revenge by recording, in the early chapters of *Jane Eyre,* the cruelties she and her sisters suffered. As well as suffering starvation and physical punishment, the Brontë girls had been expected to survive on very little sleep.

Now, having woken painfully just after dawn, Lisa wondered how long a person could stay awake without going insane. She couldn't have dozed off for more than twenty minutes through the night.

The air was still and silent. She pulled out her earplugs. The rain must've stopped. She wandered through the quagmire that was her bedroom in the direction of the French doors. Stepping onto the balcony, she was startled by the scene before her. Overnight, the valley had become a vast, serene lake.

Trees admired their reflections in the water. A mob of kangaroos preened themselves on a hillock as galahs squawked across a pale-blue sky. This unpredictable country with its outlandish animals hardly belonged to humans.

Lisa straightened her beanie, zipped her polar fleece over her nightie, and went downstairs to the kitchen. She stepped through the doorway and was ankle deep in water. The table, where she and the kids had sat so happily yesterday, resembled Noah's Ark, floating in a brown sea.

A weight settled in her stomach. She tried to think what a Brontë heroine would do. A minor flood was nothing compared to their deprivations. They would dig into their reserves and deal with it. Emboldened, she strode down the entrance hall and grabbed a broom. When she returned, she was astonished to see a pair of muscular brown legs wading toward her.

The legs rose into a pair of khaki shorts, above which was the sort of rustic jacket favored by Portia's hipster friends. Except this particular jacket wasn't an ironic nod in the direction of classic masculinity. Lisa could tell from the shape of the shoulders, the large sun-bronzed hands, that this was the genuine article. Some kind of outdoor god had wandered into her kitchen. She raised the broom.

"Welcome to the district," the bronzed deity said, raising his hands in mock surrender.

Lisa was suddenly aware that she was dressed like an escapee from a home for the bewildered. "How'd you get in?" she snapped. Her words came out thick and clunky. She'd developed a lisp. Blushing, she turned her head, spat the mouth guard into her hand, and buried it in her pocket.

"Back door," the man said with a twinkle of amusement. "It was jammed."

She pointed the broom handle at him and steadied it, ninja style. His eyes widened. Either he was telling the truth, or he was one of those insane outback killers movies are made about. "It was *locked*!"

"Oh, was it?" He seemed apologetic. "I didn't realize. . . . I gave it a shove. Get your husband to take a look at the lock." He seemed genuinely upset by her alarm. Serial killers probably did the same with their victims — cajoled them into a state of trust. With his height and strength, there was no doubt who'd win if she tried to force him out.

"You can put your teeth back in if you like," he said, eager to be helpful.

168

"It's not my *teeth*!" She excavated the mouth guard and flashed it at him.

"Oh. A sportswoman. I used to wear one of those when I played footie."

His age was difficult to assess — somewhere between thirty-five and fifty. Probably older than the average testosterone-crazed sex criminal, though Lisa realized she was flattering herself to imagine her beanie-nightie ensemble could inflame anyone. On the other hand, he could have escaped prison after years of deprivation. . . . His dark hair was cropped, but not convict-short. Boots of sideburns dug their heels into the day or two's growth shadowing his jaw. A scar meandered over his left eyebrow. One of his eyeteeth was crooked. He had the air of an action hero who'd yet to develop full confidence in his jet pack. Yet behind the boyish grin was a kind of sadness. She couldn't work out if it was resignation, disappointment, or something more complicated. Whatever, the man had no right to be there.

"Scott Green," he said, sloshing toward her with a dazzling smile. "Scottie to you. Creek's up. Been a fair bit of flooding overnight. Just checking up on the neighborhood."

The name was familiar. "The gardener

169

with special rates for pensioners?" she asked.

"Why, you up for a senior's concession? Matter of fact I'm a landscape designer. But I do pretty much anything these days. What part of the States are you from?"

Damn. The accent again.

"I was born in Melbourne."

"So what possessed you to buy Tumbledown Manor?" he asked.

"It's Trumperton Manor, actually."

The intruder grinned. She couldn't tell if he was teasing.

"My grandfather lived in this house," she added defensively. "I'm Lisa Trumperton."

Scott seemed to look at her for the first time. He ran an amused eye over her beanie, polar fleece, and nightie. She felt ridiculous. "So you're an Aussie after all?"

They stared at each other across the shallow ocean at their feet.

"I've got another one of those things in the ute," he said, nodding at her broom. "Want a hand?"

Lisa wanted to weep with gratitude. Instead, she waded across the pond and flung open the back door with its now broken lock. Side by side, they worked with broad, even strokes, sloshing the torrent out of the kitchen and down the back steps. Scott moved with animal ease, achieving more in

170

a single swoop than Lisa could with three.

He assured her she was better off than her neighbors, who were thigh-deep in water. He'd had to lend them his pump. "Lucky the sky's cleared," he said, opening the windows. "It might stink in here for a couple of days. The forecast's good, though. Should dry out pretty fast." His optimism was impressive.

After tossing the broom in the back of his ute, he asked if there was anything else she needed. She told him about the power cut. He reached for a toolbox and assailed the fuse box in the back porch. Ten minutes later the lights flickered, and the fridge grumbled back to life.

Scott achieved so much with so little apparent effort she wanted to hug him. But it wasn't proper behavior for a woman in a nightie and a beanie. Instead, she went to find her purse. He shook his head, embarrassed. Instant coffee with milk and three sugars was all the payment he wanted.

"How's the roof?" he asked, slurping from his mug.

"Are you psychic?"

"No." He chuckled. "I've known this house since I was a kid. Those slates have always been fun and games."

She took him upstairs to inspect the bedroom.

He stared glumly at the saturated bedding. "So there's no Mr. Trumperton?"

Lisa flushed with annoyance. He was a nosey creep. She should never have let him upstairs.

"The slates'll need shifting around," he said, diverting his attention away from her bed. "You'll need someone to fix the shutters and windows, too."

"Actually, I have an adult son," she said, sounding snooty.

"You do?" he said with a disarming smile. "Maybe he could give you a hand."

She bit her lip. Ted and his friends were wonderful, but they were up to their necks in their city lives. She was clearly going to need more help than the odd weekend visit.

"Or you could get hold of the Gray Army," he added. "Real craftsmen. Ron wouldn't rip you off. I'll text you his number."

As he pressed her digits into his machine, she could hear Maxine wailing: "You gave your phone number to a strange man?! Why don't you just go ahead and offer your services in the sex offenders' wing?"

He helped her heave the bed onto the balcony. She spread the blankets over the balcony rails while he laid the mattress in a patch of sun.

"Should be dry by this afternoon," he said, gazing across the valley. "Water's down already."

The lake did seem to be shrinking. She'd never known a landscape that could change so quickly.

She sent him downstairs so she could change into jeans and a sweatshirt. While she was at it she flung on some foundation and neutral lipstick.

When she returned, Scott was crouching on the floor, investigating the place where James had unearthed flagstones. She offered him a slice of cold pizza. He devoured it in seconds. She placed two more slices on a plate and watched them meet the same fate.

"Never seen the creek so high," he said, repressing a burp.

"And they call it a drought."

"We've just had the hottest summer on record. Not that it means much. Ron only bought a weather gauge last year."

She giggled. Oh God, surely he wouldn't mistake it for flirting? She straightened her mouth and poured two more mugs of coffee.

"Have you always lived here?" she asked.

"Grew up down the road. Wasn't too flash at school. I liked being outside so I did a course in architectural landscaping in the city. Set up my own business. It went gang-busters for a while. Some sheila from *Vogue Living* did a story about me."

"So why did you come back?" Her mug seared her hand. She poured extra milk in to cool it down.

"To see more of my boy," he said after a silence.

She hadn't thought of him as a father. "Oh, how old is he?"

"Sixteen. My ex dragged him here when she shacked up with the real estate dude."

"Hogan the younger?"

He put his hands in his lap and studied his thumbs. "She reckons I'm a useless dad."

Lisa nudged the sugar bowl toward him. He shoveled spoonfuls into his mug.

"I bet you're not. What's his name?"

"Todd. He's just a regular kid. You know what they're like at that age."

"Fast cars and girls . . ."

His gaze lowered to the floor. Maybe the boy was in trouble.

"They don't have drugs out here, do they?" she asked.

"Nothing serious."

"How long have you been back?"

"Nearly two years. I love the area. It's part of me."

Lisa felt a jab of envy. She longed to claim the land was in her blood, too.

Scott ran his hand over the table.

"Nice old oak. I've gone for Australian hardwoods at my place."

"Did you get flooded?"

"No way. I'm on a ridge up the valley."

"A house?" She didn't mean to sound rude, but he seemed the sort of bloke who'd live up a tree.

"Man cave," he said, grinning. "Open fire, Keith Jarrett on the sound system, and a glass of Australian red. Simple pleasures."

"Sounds perfect," Lisa said, meaning perfect for him — not necessarily for anyone else.

"So what brought you to the land of Oz?" he asked, assaulting his fourth slice of pizza.

He was a good listener. As she unraveled her story (minus the mastectomy and the pathetic aspects of her divorce), he nodded encouragement and was serious in the right places.

"You're one gutsy lady," he said, standing up and rubbing the back of his neck.

"Why, because the house is haunted?" she asked.

"You don't believe that stuff, do you?" he

said. "If you're going to believe in fairy tales, you might as well get it right. The house isn't haunted."

"I knew that," she said, crossing her arms with satisfaction.

"But the stables are."

The hair on Lisa's arms prickled. She felt a sudden chill. "What do you mean? Did something bad happen there?"

"So they say," Scott said, examining his fingernails.

"What was it, a suicide?"

"Something like that," he said breezily. "I wouldn't worry. It probably never happened."

She wanted to ask more, but Scott was halfway out the door. She'd forgotten how it felt to walk beside a man taller than herself — he was almost overbearing. Outside, they blinked in the sunlight. The gum trees gleamed silver.

He swung his equipment into the back of his ute. "I'll be back first thing in the morning to take a look at that roof," he said.

They hadn't discussed payment. Besides, he had yet to prove he wasn't a murderer. Just as she was about to say no, her phone buzzed with a text message from Ted. He and his friends were going to a music festival and wouldn't be able to make it to

Castlemaine the following weekend after all.

"That'd be great, thanks," she said.

Scott drove off, leaving a trail of pheromones in his wake.

CHAPTER 14

Derisive laughter echoed inside Lisa's head.
Scott was perched on a barstool, relishing
his role as center of attention at the pub.
Throwing back his handsome head, he
spread his giant hands in imitation of the
crazy Yank with false teeth who'd attacked
him with a broomstick. The cackling grew
louder, hysterical. Lisa was the laughing-
stock of Castlemaine. Sweating with embar-
rassment, she jolted awake. Shafts of gray
light filtered through the curtains. She ran a
finger over her mouth guard and coaxed it
out into its case. As she excavated the
earplugs, the laughter started up again.
Kookaburras.

It hadn't been a bad night. With a chair
jammed under the back door, she'd felt
passably safe. Her bedding smelled of fresh
grass after being aired all day. The stale
smell of her bedroom was more comforting
than off-putting. And the ghost, if there was

one, had found better things to do.

Scott had promised to show up first thing. That could mean six a.m. in country terms. Lisa sprang out of bed and pushed the curtains open with the backs of her hands. New curtains were high on the agenda. Flinging open the French doors, she stepped onto the balcony. The sun was still dozing in the hills under a clear lavender sky. The valley sprawled before her like some prehistoric landscape waiting to stir with life.

But there was no time to linger. This time, Scott wasn't going to catch her out. She hurried back inside to shower and put on khaki trousers and a blue-and-white-check shirt. Her hair was combed, makeup minimal. Elastic-sided boots completed the look: She was only an Akubra hat away from being Crocodile Dundee.

By five forty-five she was downstairs shaking muesli into a bowl. It crunched like gravel against her teeth. She'd need to find a dentist soon, and a doctor to keep up her annual checks.

An hour later he hadn't showed. It was still early and there was plenty to do, opening boxes and arranging the kitchen chairs at tasteful angles. She was seriously short of furniture. Now the sofa was on the veranda, there was nowhere to sit in Alexander's room except the floor. Part of her was dreading seeing Scott again. The other part, in fact most of her, was looking forward to it.

At eight thirty, she checked her phone. Maybe he'd been held up. Or, at nine thirty, had an accident. Around ten, a cloud of dust hurtled down the road. Her jaw tensed. The truck went straight past her gate. By ten thirty, she was annoyed. The least he could do was come back and fix the lock he'd broken. By noon she was furious, not because he was obliged to turn up, but because he'd just proved himself to be like every other man on earth.

Hot chocolate wasn't part of Lisa's latest diet, but not everyone said it was bad for you. Chocolate could be mood-enhancing and an antioxidant, which had to be good for a woman in her situation. After heating a mug of full-cream milk, she shoveled in a mountain of what claimed to be the finest Belgian chocolate powder. Then she toasted two slices of bread, suffocated them with raspberry jam, and carried it all upstairs to her study.

She switched on her computer. The screen emitted its lifeless glow. She tried to tap into Emily Brontë's world, but her heroine refused to respond. The toast vanished with depressing speed. So did the hot chocolate. Just as she was reminding herself to be one of those people who stop for lunch instead of eating at their desks, the door knocker crashed against the front door.

So, he'd finally deigned to show his face. She checked Portia's Facebook page. Portia had been to, and Liked, a zombie musical.

Scott deserved to wait. The knocker hammered again.

She adjusted the collar of her shirt and strolled downstairs.

"You took your time," she said, opening the door.

A turtle in white overalls looked up at her through rheumy eyes. "Ron Sotheby, Gray Army," he whistled through ill-fitting teeth. "Scottie told us to drop by. He said you needed a quote."

Behind Ron were two other men in paint-spotted overalls. Though the years had put their bodies through the wringer, their eyes were bright with curiosity.

So sending this motley crew was Scott's way of apologizing for not showing up.

"Oh! Come in."

"This is Ken." Ron waved a hand at a man with a mane of white hair and a nose like a turnip. "Electrics and plumbing. He's got a dodgy knee, but he's pretty good."

181

"And I'm Doug." Ron and Ken's bearded accomplice was a dead ringer for Santa Claus. "Retired carpenter, emphysema."

"And there's nothing wrong with me long as I remember my heart pills," Ron added.

She beckoned them into the kitchen and settled them around the table. Ron peered hopefully at the cupboards as she put on the kettle.

"Sorry," she said, taking out a packet of Anzac biscuits. "This is all I've got." She shook the contents onto a plate.

Ron accepted a biscuit with the dignity of an athlete who'd won silver when he really deserved gold. "So what can we do you for?"

"I'd like to start with painting the kitchen," she said. "Then maybe expose the flagstone floor."

The air was heavy with caution. It was a trial marriage of sorts. If both sides assumed the best of each other, the relationship might work. Alternatively, it could end up in resentment and tears.

Tempting as it was to mention the awful upstairs bathroom, the floorboards that needed sanding, and every other surface in the house thirsting for three coats of paint (not to mention broken windows and shutters), she said nothing more. She didn't want to give them simultaneous heart attacks.

The Gray Army dunked their biscuits and rolled appraising eyes over the kitchen. Like a trio of magistrates, they assessed its less admirable attributes. After two more biscuits and a lot of small talk, Ron announced their hourly rate, not counting lunch and morning-tea breaks. It seemed reasonable.

"Oh, and if you could take a look at the roof slates and the back-door lock, I'd be grateful," she added.

Ken said that shouldn't be a problem. They agreed to start work the day after next. That, Ron said, would give her time to get some color cards from the paint shop and do some baking.

The next morning, the sky was bright and plastic blue. After showering and brushing her teeth, Lisa checked her e-mails and the weather forecast. A row of suns yellow as egg yolks ran across her screen. If the weatherman knew anything, her bedding was safe for the next few nights.

The prospect of going to town was almost exciting. But what to wear? Her shirt from yesterday was in the wash, along with most of her other Aussie outfits. She rummaged through her New York clothes and pulled out a navy polo and skirt. Standing in front of the mirror, she stabbed pearl studs in her lobes. She was overdressed by local standards, but she had no choice. After raking a comb through her hair, she collected her handbag and wandered downstairs.

When she opened the front door, she was startled to encounter Atlas in work shorts, his hand raised to reach the knocker. The hairs on his copper legs gleamed in the sunlight, and the sunglasses he wore shoved back on his head glinted.

Scott flashed a row of near-perfect teeth. "Off to the CWA?" he asked.

"What's that?"

"Country Women's Association. They dress like that. And they do good works."

Rude. Sexist, too.

He offered no explanation for his disappearance. Instead, he scratched his coarse green jumper, scuffed his boots, and waited to be asked inside. She wasn't going to let him get away with it.

"What happened?"

He blinked like a stag caught in headlights. "Oh, you mean *yesterday*?" His face lit up with a tender smile. "I took Todd river rafting. It was a great day for it."

Lisa stifled annoyance. He'd gone gallivanting off with his kid when, for all he knew, burglars could have been strolling through her back door, and her roof was collapsing on top of her.

"I'll get my gear from the ute," he said, ambling away.

Now he'd decided to show up, she felt obliged to stay in the house. She climbed the stairs to her study, and opened the *Emily* file.

Anxious to impress the talented young author, the earl put on a magnificent feast in his dining hall. . . .

An electric drill buzzed to life in the kitchen.

The earl's complexion deepened with concern when he noticed that Emily hadn't touched the pheasant on her plate. He'd shot it with his own gun, and Cook had spent hours preparing and roasting it to perfection. Yet when he inquired after her health, Emily snapped back that she was perfectly well, thank you. . . .

Lisa's concentration was interrupted by the thud of boots stomping across the roof over her head. She logged off and went downstairs to make instant coffee. He probably expected her to call out and invite him to join her.

She laid out a tray with the *Happy Holidays* mug, a jug of milk, and a bowl of sugar. Taking a pencil from the window ledge, she scribbled a note on a scrap of paper:

Gone to town. Back late. Help yourself. Please leave your invoice. Thanks, L.

The tray seemed a miserly offering — especially with the note slid under the coffee jar. She hunted through the cupboards and discovered the packet of chocolate macaroons she'd hidden from herself. She tore it open at one end and laid it next to the sugar bowl.

It was a relief to get away from him. After the supermarket and the paint shop, she went to Togs for quiche and a latte. It seemed a lifetime since she and Maxine had sat at the same table over lunch.

When she arrived back at the old house, there was no sign of Scott or his ute. The kitchen tray seemed untouched. On closer inspection, the milk jug and sugar bowl were empty. The mug had been rinsed and put back where she'd left it. The packet of macaroons appeared pristine — until she peered inside. A solitary biscuit was left.

Under the coffee jar, large, childlike letters had been scrawled on the back of her note.

Roof will need replacing one day but OK for now. Call if you need anything. S.

A shiny brass key lay next to the note. She took it to the back door. It slid neatly into the new lock he'd fitted.

There was no need to see him again, thank goodness.

CHAPTER 15

Days melted into one another, and Lisa grew accustomed to the house's eccentricities. The third tread on the stairs always squeaked. Her study windows rattled. The toilet in the servants' quarters had to be flushed twice. She grew fond of these peculiarities the way a person warms to the mole on a child's nose. At night, the walls closed in and wrapped themselves around her like the paws of a friendly bear.

Lisa was beginning to understand that Trumperton was a house to live *with* rather than *in.* She seldom felt alone or frightened, though since her conversation with Scott, she'd avoided the stables. The big old doors were too heavy, and it was dark and smelly in there. Besides, Dino was perfectly happy parked outside, and she found it far more convenient to store gardening equipment in the servants' quarters.

Though she loved the house, part of her

knew it wouldn't be truly hers until she'd brought the grounds back to life. Magnificent water features and gazebos swirled through her head. They were all too ambitious. Much as she ached to get started, her pocket and energy levels insisted on patience.

There was plenty going on inside the house, anyway. The Gray Army transformed the kitchen to the color of sunshine with surprising speed, though Ron grumbled about her taste. He was an off-white man himself.

The old boys were an easygoing presence about the place. Unable to work the wood burner to bake for them, she fussed over egg sandwiches. In return, they told stories of Castlemaine in the old days. Whenever she asked about the Trumpertons, however, the Gray Army became vague and said it was before their time. Their offhandedness was strange. She needed to find out more about her family's connection to the house.

Ron claimed to have an expert nose. According to him, every house had a particular odor. He could tell everything about the people who lived in it by the smell. Babies saturated a place with a sour milkiness. He could tell the cat lovers from the dog owners, smokers from the drinkers. Houses owned by couples smelled different from those lived in by single men.

When Lisa asked what Trumperton Manor's signature perfume was, he sank his teeth into his sandwich and chewed slowly. "It smells like it belongs to someone who's obsessed with the past," he said after a long pause.

She didn't know how to respond.

With the Gray Army on the job, Lisa had no reason to call Scott. She thought she saw his ute in town a couple of times, and when an unidentified number flashed on her phone one morning she assumed it was him, but it turned out to be Maxine using her landline. Her sister rang to say that Aunt Caroline had finally deigned to visit the manor, though only for afternoon tea. Lisa was pleased — at last she'd get a chance to interrogate the old girl about the house. She just hoped her aunt would be willing to tell her something — no one else seemed to want to.

In the meantime, up in her study, *Three Sisters: Emily* limped along. Trumperton Manor was great for Lisa's creative energy, and each morning she woke with a fresh flood of ideas. But the minute she settled at her computer, a Gray Army foot soldier would tap at her study door to ask if she wanted matte or semigloss paint on the shutters, or plain or nonreflective glass in the windows. With rising panic, she realized she had no hope of handing the manuscript in on time. Yet if she didn't meet the deadline she'd be eating grass.

Eventually, Ted, Zack, and James reappeared one Saturday morning. Lisa was disappointed they hadn't brought the girls.

"Hey! What happened?" Ted said, peering up at the gleaming windows and straightened shutters. "Did you find a man?"

"Several."

"Heathcliffs to your Cathy?"

"Where's Stella?"

"Her sister had a baby."

"Come inside. I'll put the kettle on."

It was good to see the boys again. James declined the offer of day-old egg sandwiches and presented her with a tin of melting moments he'd baked that morning. She hardly noticed Zack's movie camera anymore. He'd become an amiable sci-fi figure with a face that was half machinery.

Ted and James collected a couple of ride-on mowers from the hire center and assailed the front "garden" and orchard. The grounds looked half-civilized by the time they'd finished.

191

As shadows lengthened, Lisa opened a bottle of ginger ale and beckoned the boys onto the veranda. James asked what was on the menu for dinner. Steak and salad, she said.

"Simple's good," he assured her. "Can I help out?"

Did Jane Eyre wear gray?

James lifted a portable barbecue from the back of the Kombi and set it up on the driveway.

"He thinks of everything," Lisa said as musky smoke coiled into the sky.

"He does," Ted said. "Who's that?" He nodded at a shabby figure shuffling around the bend in the driveway. The old man's white hair stood out in Einstein spikes.

"Looks like Mr. Wright, the previous owner," Lisa whispered to Zack and his camera. "They moved to the cottage across the road."

The old man paused and leaned on his stick. He swayed as if on high seas.

"Hello!" Lisa called.

Mr. Wright's mouth set in a downturned line.

"Would you like to come and have a drink with us?"

He fixed her with a bloodshot glare. Anyone would have thought she was hurling insults, not an invitation.

Mr. Wright drew a handkerchief from his pocket and snorted into it. He then turned and hobbled back down the drive.

"What was *that* about?" Zack said.

Gum trees rustled. A chorus of frogs cleared their throats down by the creek.

"Maybe he's confused," she said. "Never mind. Let's eat."

After dinner, the boys shooed Lisa out of the kitchen. She grabbed a woolen shawl from the coat hook in the hall and nestled on the veranda. Ted brought out a freshly opened bottle of sparkling white from the Yarra Valley.

"What did Alexander do, anyway?" he asked, sitting beside her.

Lisa watched the bubbles spiral inside her glass. "Your great-grandfather? I don't know much, apart from what my father told me. Alexander was an only child. His parents moved here during the gold rush. They were in the jewelry business. Apparently they moved in high society — well, what there was of it in Castlemaine. They had fabulous parties here."

"What went wrong?"

"They got caught up in the financial crash of the 1890s and moved to New Zealand.

That's where Alexander met Gran."

Ted rested his hands behind his head and smiled. "They had a global financial crisis back then?"

"Something like that. There was a lot of hardship, starvation even."

Down by the river, frogs croaked companionably. A broken biscuit moon hung in the sky.

Ted's orientation had never worried Lisa. As a preschooler, he used to sneak into her jewelry box and raid her earring collection. He adored piano lessons and developed a passion for Sondheim musicals. What little sport he played was to please Jake.

Ted had always been open with her about his boyfriends. She invariably became attached to them and started thinking of them as surrogate sons. It had been quite a wrench when Ted and Sebastian the cellist split up, and before that Jasper the artist. She'd try to protect herself this time.

"Where did you meet Zack?" she asked.

Ted stroked the stem of his wineglass and gazed at the outline of the darkening hills.

"We shared a shift together at the market. Why?"

She saw a flash of white in the trees. "Oh, look," she said. "The cockatoo."

A tiny smile rippled across his lips.

"I'm so pleased you've found someone special," she added under her breath.

Not for the first time, she was dazzled by the natural perfection of his teeth. No wonder young people kept falling in love with each other.

"At least you're right about something," he said good-naturedly. "I have found someone."

Ted took a gulp of wine and nodded at a silhouette standing in the frame of the doorway.

"To the love of my life," Ted said, raising his glass.

Lisa felt blood rush to her cheeks as the figure stepped out of the shadows and wrapped his arms around Ted.

"I know." Ted laughed over James's shoulder. "You thought it was Zack."

"Well, I . . ."

"Your gaydar needs an overhaul, Mom. Zack's straight."

Lisa stood up and adjusted her pashmina. Her assumptions about Ted's taste in men had been naïve.

"I always wanted a chef in the family," she said once she'd regained her composure.

James extended an arm and curled her into a three-way hug.

A flash of a camera lens peered over the

balustrade.

"Oh, Zack!" she groaned. "Not now!"

Lisa placed her frozen Skinnymeal on the kitchen bench top. Neon green peas glowed up at her from the chicken masala. It seemed unlikely peas originated in India.

The old microwave refused to heat things up properly. It did a better job if she took the meal out of the freezer an hour or two early and defrosted it first. Not that she was looking forward to dinner. Whoever made Skinnymeals lacked a natural affinity for food. Either that or the ingredients lost their flavor in the freezing and transportation.

Evening shadows stretched across the lino. The kitchen was beginning to look as if someone cared about it — even if Ron was right and her choice of marigold was a little strident.

The smell of paint threatened to bring on a headache. She opened the back door to a welcome waft of night air, then trailed up the stairs to her study. Lisa wondered how Emily Brontë would have handled a gay son. Homosexuality had been illegal back then. He'd have been slammed in jail and made to crush rocks like Oscar Wilde. But if Emily had been half the woman Lisa knew she was, her love for her son would've won out.

Sitting at her computer, she opened her *Three Sisters: Emily* file and straightened her spine to start a new chapter. She reached for her phone instead and scrolled to Portia.

Do u know about Ted & James?

Gr8!!! He finally told u!!!

She glanced at the computer clock.

Have u had breakfast? she typed.

Portia signed off in a fence line of *x*'s.

Lisa pressed Shut Down and tramped downstairs.

The moment she entered the kitchen she sensed the atmosphere had changed. Another presence was in the room. A shadow shifted under the table. It was the wrong time of year for snakes, and they hardly went out at night. Still . . .

"Hello?" Her voice sounded weak and girlish. She waited for the snake/rapist to return her greeting.

Fingers of orange goo stretched across the floor under the table. Blood? Chunks of flesh floated on its surface. And peas. Her chicken marsala!

The upturned container lay under the chair nearby. Whatever was under the table made a shuffling sound. She was relieved to hear it had feet rather than scales. If it was a possum she could deal with it, possibly.

Cool air wafted through the open door. If

only she'd closed it before she'd gone upstairs. She hadn't adjusted to how quickly darkness fell in country Australia. Her instinct was to tiptoe across the room and close the door. But then whatever it was would be trapped inside with her.

She drew a breath and peered under the table. An amber orb glowered back at her. Except it wasn't an orb. It was an eye hovering asymmetrically over a downturned mouth.

The Halloween mask emitted a discordant yowl. She ran a quick scan through her mental checklist of Wild Animals of Australia. With its tattered ears, it was too disheveled to be a potoroo, and too small to be a wombat. The shaggy coat was too furry for a lizard or any other kind of reptile. Instead, it resembled a miniature one-eyed hyena, except she was pretty sure they didn't exist in Australia. Or a Tasmanian devil, though presumably the whole point of them was they stayed in Tasmania.

Lisa took a closer look. The creature crouched and exposed palisades of teeth. Its ginger and white fur hung in clumps. The tail was matted with twigs. It was a cat, feral most likely. Back at Bideawee, she and the other volunteers had dealt with similar feline fugitives who had survived on their wits.

"So you're a Skinnymeals fan?"

The ugliest, most bad-tempered-looking cat in the world glared back at her through his single eye.

"Hardly gourmet, is it?"

The cat flattened its ears and hissed.

"Don't be scared," she said, offering a hand.

The creature lashed out. A sudden sting made her withdraw with a jerk.

The cat spun on its tail and hurtled out the door.

She looked down at her hand. Blood bubbled up from two parallel lines.

A hostile neighbor and a killer cat. Life wasn't dull.

CHAPTER 16

Australia had no concept of winter. The thermometer had barely dropped before buds started sprouting on bare branches. A magnolia burst into a flurry of pink and white near the front gates.

While the outside of Trumperton Manor was hardly grand, the interior was responding to attention with heartwarming speed. Several rooms were now sparkling with new paint (after her marigold binge, Lisa restrained herself to bisque, not that Ron liked that color much, either). The entire house instantly smelled fresher when the moldy curtains were replaced. And after the Gray Army finished sanding and polishing the floorboards, the manor took on new life. Lisa had inherited her father's love of Persian carpets, but the real deal was out of her budget. Secondhand rugs of dubious heritage did the job, providing splashes of color on top of the bare boards.

Her ramblings through the countryside unearthed treasure troves of colonial furniture, which she loaded into Dino's hatch and ferried back to the house. The chunky armchairs she bought from a retired farmer for the living room were delivered on the back of a truck. She was grateful the old boys were on hand to help her unload them. Covered in maroon linen, each chair was large enough for a tiger to curl up in — though they were a little firm on the backside.

An old traveling chest made an ideal coffee table. The Edwardian clock with its hands frozen at three thirty seemed at home on the mantelpiece alongside Alexander's photo. Standard lamps and bookshelves made the room inviting.

Stacking pyramids of logs in the fireplace and watching them flare to life became a meditation. As the flames crackled and released musky aroma through the room, Lisa could hardly resent the prospect of cleaning up next morning. Other women went to the gym. She swept cinders.

The bedrooms were still stark, but at least the upstairs bathroom was no longer spooky. The only time she'd come close to having a real argument with the Gray Army was over the bathtub. Ron and Ken had shaken their heads when she'd announced she wanted the old one resurfaced. Ken told her she'd be better off with a new plastic bath from Bunnings. She argued some people would kill for a genuine claw-foot. He walked away muttering "crazy Yank."

Now even Ken had to admit the revamped bath looked good. She'd emitted a yip of delight when the shiny new taps gushed instead of dribbled. A new mirror gleamed against fresh white tiles. The heated towel rail was the ultimate luxury.

The wood-burning stove still lurked in the kitchen like a medieval weapon. It sprang to life on weekends when James set it alight and produced delicious meals from its belly. His efforts to teach her how to feed the fire while keeping an even temperature all ended in failure. To Lisa, the relationship between the firebox and the vents was advanced physics, with the added risk of burning the house down, so she was still eating Skinnymeals.

Lisa continued to steer clear of the stables. She was almost disappointed by the ghost's refusal to show up. Every time a curtain fluttered or a door creaked, there was always a logical cause.

Her jaw clicked the morning Maxine called to say she and Aunt Caroline were on their way. Maxine warned her again that the old girl was losing her marbles. Aunt Caroline was keeping the nursing home in stitches with more invented stories about her past, including horse riding with Princess Elizabeth and having an affair with a duke. But no matter how nutty Aunt Caroline might become, Lisa knew egg sandwiches wouldn't cut it. The duchess of Camberwell would expect home baking.

She creaked the wood stove's door open and peered into its belly. How James produced melt-in-the-mouth lamb fillets from the thing was a mystery. Still, if she didn't try . . . She snapped a few kindling sticks and set them ablaze in the firebox. Once they were crackling away, she added a block of wood. To her surprise, it actually caught fire. She added another, closed the door, and wondered what to bake. Her collection of recipe books was risible. Scones from the yellowing pages of the *Camberwell High Cookbook* were too plain, Julia Child's Queen of Sheba cake too ambitious.

She mixed the batter for an old carrot cake recipe. Once she'd grated the carrots and beaten in the eggs, she folded the mixture into a tin. According to the temperature dial, the oven was about right. With a silent prayer, she slid the cake tin inside and sealed the door shut.

As she was melting butter for the icing on the stove top, she was startled by the appearance of a video camera at her elbow.

"We let ourselves in," Maxine said. "Zack wanted to come too."

"Hello, Zack."

"Hi, Mrs. Trumperton. I need another multigenerational scene."

What was he making, *Gone with the Wind*?

"It certainly is bright in here," Maxine said, surveying the walls. "I'd never have picked you as a bright-yellow person."

"Marigold," Lisa corrected.

Aunt Caroline's walking stick tapped across the lino. A stately woman with white hair and the Trumperton nose, she resembled a Roman emperor in drag.

"Never liked the old dump," she said, sweeping a lilac shawl over her shoulder and offering a corrugated cheek to kiss.

Lisa resisted the temptation to suggest that, if that was the case, Aunt Caroline could have stayed away. "Did you visit here as a little girl?" she asked instead as she took the pan off the stove top.

"Your grandfather wouldn't come near the place. Not as long as I knew him," she replied.

"Didn't he live here as a young man?" Lisa

asked, filling a kettle and placing it on the hob.

"That doesn't mean he liked it."

Lisa was getting nowhere. She'd have to tackle her aunt head-on. "What do you know about the ghost story, Aunt Caroline?"

The old woman turned her walking stick in her hand. "Where's the lavatory?" she snapped.

Lisa pointed at the door to the servants' quarters.

"Oh, still there, is it?" Aunt Caroline said, before toddling out of the kitchen.

Lisa set up a tray with Aunt Caroline's teacups. She shook her head. The old woman was incorrigible.

"I think we can safely say *that* subject's closed," Maxine said, casting an appraising eye over her surroundings. "Why did you paint everything else brown?"

"Bisque," Lisa said, drawing a breath.

"Oh, those silly people in the paint factory dreaming up names. I'd call it Cow Poo," Maxine said under her breath so Aunt Caroline wouldn't hear her saying a naughty word.

It went without saying that Aunt Caroline would die of horror if afternoon tea were served at the kitchen table. So Lisa escorted the old lady to Alexander's room and settled her in a maroon chair while Zack filmed. Hoping to dislodge an avalanche of memories, Lisa pointed out the photo of Alexander on the mantelpiece.

"Who's that?" Aunt Caroline asked, squeezing her eyes to the size of raisins.

"Your father."

"Is it?" she said, waving a dismissive hand. "I suppose he was young once."

Encouraged by the presence of Zack's camera, Maxine recited a list of her offspring's latest accomplishments. Andrew was on the brink of selling some kind of app to a company in Silicon Valley; she'd just found out her grandchildren were in the genius percentile; and Dan was likely to win a Nobel Prize for his services to colons.

An alarming spiral of smoke meandered through the hallway. Lisa leaped to her feet and bustled back to the kitchen. Black clouds billowed from the wood stove.

Lisa fought her way through until she reached the oven door. Pulling the cake pan out, she dumped it on the bench before filling a pot with water and dousing the flames in the firebox.

"Everything all right?" Maxine asked from the doorway.

Lisa opened the windows and examined

the cake. The top was blackened. "Fine," she replied. "You take the tea tray through. I'll sort this out."

Lisa emptied the cake on a wire tray, let it cool for a bit, then sawed the top off with a bread knife. She smothered what was left with icing, which immediately dribbled down the sides.

Back in Alexander's room, Aunt Caroline was delivering a monologue at Zack's camera about the time she danced with Charles de Gaulle in the glory days after World War II. She really was away with the pixies.

"Tea?" Lisa said, kneeling at her aunt's elbow.

"No need to shout." Aunt Caroline watched warily as Lisa remembered to pour tea first and *then* the milk. The old woman peered at the slice of cake on her plate. "Is that a scone or a biscuit?"

"Carrot cake."

"It remains a mystery to me how anyone can make cake from anything as humble as a carrot," Aunt Caroline said, prodding the cake with a fork. The delicacy snapped under pressure and lumps of charred carrot flew across the room.

"Don't you remember you gave us this lovely dinner service for a wedding present?" Diversion tactics were all Lisa had left.

Aunt Caroline snorted. "Fat lot of good it did you." The old girl was sane enough when it suited her.

Maxine announced she and Zack were keen to do the grand tour. Lisa assured her the house wasn't as big as it looked from the outside.

"Hardly a budgie cage, though, is it?" Maxine said as she sailed up the stairs. "Remember that townhouse you nearly bought? Eugene Drummond, the magistrate, and his wife, Madeline, snapped it up. She says it's perfect for two people to downsize into."

Zack zoomed in on each of their faces. Lisa wished he weren't so keen on close-ups.

Though Maxine approved of the new bathroom, she appeared underwhelmed by everything else. She was particularly unimpressed that Lisa had followed Beverley's suggestion and transformed the ballroom into her bedroom. A pretentious notion, she said. The inspection was interrupted by the thud of the door knocker echoing up the stairs.

Lisa hurried downstairs, but Aunt Caroline's arthritic hips had miraculously flown her across the hall to open the door. "You have a visitor," she decreed.

Standing in a halo of sunlight was the unmistakable silhouette of Scott Green. Tanned and as well-defined as a Rodin sculpture, he nodded at Lisa before beaming at Maxine and Aunt Caroline, who responded by blushing and fawning like a pair of geishas.

"Just thought I'd drop by to see how things are going," he said, sliding his boots off as if the invitation to come inside had already been issued. He introduced himself to Maxine and Aunt Caroline, who then bustled him into Alexander's room.

Hot with annoyance, Lisa collected another cup from the kitchen. She returned to find Aunt Caroline insisting Maxine cut a large slice of cake for Scott to "fill up those legs." Maxine asked if anyone had a chainsaw.

"Things have certainly picked up round here," Scott said.

Zack adjusted a standard lamp to throw light on Scott's face.

"So you're the gardener?" Maxine asked, pouring lukewarm liquid into his cup.

"More of a consultant," Scott said with a grin as wide as the Nullarbor Plain.

"Aren't you the land agent's husband?" Maxine would qualify as a terrier if she had a tail.

209

"Ex," Scott replied, crunching through the cake. The teacup resembled a toy in the paw of his hand. His huge gray socks were spread out in front of the fireplace in a way that was far too familiar.

"Looks like the boys have done a passable job," he said. "Floors have come up good."

Lisa fought the urge to correct his grammar.

"His tea's gone cold!" Aunt Caroline gushed. "Run along and make another pot."

Relieved to have an excuse, Lisa grabbed the teapot and scurried to the kitchen. The kettle was still steaming on the stovetop. Thank heavens it hadn't run dry and set the place on fire.

Maxine suddenly appeared at her side. "A bit of rough trade?"

Lisa's cheeks sizzled. "No way. He's only been here a couple of times."

"What did Shakespeare say about the lady protesting too much?"

Water bubbled furiously into the teapot. Lisa pushed past Maxine and swept back into Alexander's room to drown their cups.

Silence settled over them.

"How's the family?" Maxine asked.

"Fine," Lisa replied. "Portia's borderline anorexic, possibly bulimic, but you knew that."

Maxine's mouth dropped.

"As if you haven't got enough on your plate with a gay son," Maxine said.

"*What* did she say?" Aunt Caroline snapped.

Suddenly aware Zack was doing another of his dreaded close-ups, Lisa felt her face redden.

"She said Ted's gay," Lisa explained.

"Oh, there's nothing wrong with *that,*" Aunt Caroline mused. "People are far too dismal these days. When I think of what our generation went through in the wars . . . night raids, those poor boys who never came home . . ."

Scott seemed to have discovered a thistle in his sock that required a great deal of attention.

"Not *that* sort of gay!" Maxine hissed. "She means homosexual."

Aunt Caroline's mouth formed the shape of a gothic arch. "You don't mean *Artistic*?"

Maxine nodded.

Aunt Caroline turned purple. She gasped for breath and her eyes bulged. Lisa tried to remember what she'd seen on posters about the choking hold.

Aunt Caroline seized her walking stick and propelled herself to her feet. Scott towered over her and took her hand.

211

"Thank you, young man," she snapped. "I'm quite all right." Her skin reverted to its normal waxy color. "Is that the time?" Aunt Caroline pointed her stick at the broken clock. "Come along, Maxine. I'll be late for bridge."

With uncharacteristic tact, Scott decided to see if the apple tree needed pruning while Lisa packed Aunt Caroline, Zack, and Maxine into the Golf.

As Lisa waved them good-bye, she felt a watershed of relief. She turned to go back inside. At that moment, Scott appeared around the side of the house.

"That wasn't my fault, was it?" he asked.

He'd had no right to barge in on a family occasion. The man had the sensitivity of a termite mound. And to think the whole thing had been recorded for future generations to chortle over.

"Anything I can do?" he asked.

"Just go."

CHAPTER 17

Three Sisters: Emily was still way behind schedule. Unfortunately, the more Lisa learned about Emily Brontë, the more Lisa fretted. The poor child had a raft of emotional problems, including what could only have been a tendency to self-harm.

Out on the moors one day, Emily had been bitten by a wild dog. She strode back to the parsonage, took a red-hot iron from the fire, and cauterized the wound herself. Emily would've carried that scar for the rest of her life.

More worrying was Emily's attitude to food. When things weren't going her way, she punished those around her by refusing to eat. Portia and Emily had more in common than Lisa could bear to think about. Young people think they're immortal, but Emily died at the age of thirty, just a year after *Wuthering Heights* was published. The coffin maker said it was the narrowest box he'd ever made for an adult.

At night, Lisa lay in bed almost willing a ghost to show up just to take her mind off things. It'd be great material for a new book, she decided. Writing about a haunted house would be a walk in the park compared to exhuming Emily Brontë. Sooner or later, Lisa would have to take a look inside the stables. In fact, next time she saw Scott, she'd ask him if the person who committed suicide in there had been a Trumperton. Except she refused to bother with him anymore.

One evening she found a dead rat on the back doorstep. It was large and plumpish. The mouth was frozen in a grin, as if someone had just told a wicked joke. If this was death, she wondered why people made such a fuss.

She squinted into the sharp night air — surely the rodent hadn't gotten there under its own steam. A single eye beamed back. He — or she — had deposited the thing as an offering, possibly even an apology for stealing her food and scratching her.

"Tastes better than my chicken masala, does it?" she called. "Indian cooking's not for everyone."

The eye blinked.

"Want to come inside? Here, puss!"

The bushes rustled and enveloped the tip of a tail. The cat had more important things to do.

Lisa closed the door and went to bed, hoping her feline friend would get hungry enough overnight to take the rat away. But when she opened the door next morning, the rodent was still there. It looked slightly rounder and happier, as if it were sunbathing at some tropical resort. She would need to dispose of the thing before she created a personality for it.

"Puss!?"

Nothing. The corpse would have to be buried. She strode into the servants' quarters, grabbed a shovel, and chose a spot under a withered camellia bush along the side of the house.

She raised the implement over her shoulder and thrust it at the ground. The effect on the drought-hardened soil was minimal. She tried again, emitting a grunt. But the earth barely moved.

She was interrupted by the sound of tires crunching cautiously over the driveway. A silver sedan slid into the shade of the portico. She wondered what sort of people arrived unannounced at a house in the middle of nowhere. Did Mormons hire rental cars?

A combination of nausea, hatred, and longing washed over her when she saw who was struggling out of the driver's seat. What was *he* doing here?

Jake stared up at the house as if he'd left something inside, but couldn't remember what it was.

Lisa strode toward him, giving the shovel a menacing swing with each step. "Another conference in Singapore?"

"Consulting," Jake said, clearing his throat in a way he always did when nervous. "Sydney."

His blue shirt and Clintonesque tie looked wildly out of place. "Wow!" he said, attempting charm. "Downton Down Under."

"Have you seen Portia?"

"Yeah, I dropped by Venice Beach on the way here."

"How is she?"

"Her feet starred in a shoe advertisement. And she said to tell you she ate a plate of ice cream in front of me."

"And did she?"

"What are you, the diet police?"

He was clearly aching to be asked inside so he could snoop around. She offered him the veranda sofa instead.

"Mind the springs," she said.

"That was quite a drive," he said. "You

wouldn't have a glass of water, would you?"

He wanted hospitality as well?

"Where's Belle?" she asked, leaning the shovel against the balustrade. She wouldn't hit him with it — just yet.

"Meditation retreat in Thailand. Cleaning her chakras or something." He rearranged his weight on the sofa. "What is this? Some kind of acupuncture machine?"

She stifled amusement.

"Look, Ted phoned the other night," he said, taking a handkerchief from his pocket and dabbing his brow. "I had no idea."

"About what?"

"Why are you always so flippant, Lisa? Our son's GAY for Chrissakes!"

Jake twisted the handkerchief in his hands. He'd spent so many years rushing out the door to catch planes, he hadn't noticed the impeccably groomed young men gathered around the piano singing Sondheim.

"But he always has been, Jake. I thought you knew."

"Stop." Jake sounded weary. He rested his head in his hands. "Where did we go wrong?" he said, his voice cracked with emotion.

"It's not a disease."

"Did I spend too much time at work?"

"Did Elvis eat too many hamburgers?"

Jake's eyes became moist. He hardly ever cried. Surely he wasn't expecting her to *hug* him? "I should've taken him fishing."

"Fishing?!"

"Or football. Male bonding, that sort of thing." Jake must've picked up a self-help book in some airport.

"It wouldn't have changed anything. Have you met James? He's lovely. A Kiwi boy."

"I can't believe it."

"You should be happy for Ted."

"My son the fruitcake."

Lisa was losing patience.

"It's not genetic, is it?" he asked.

Why couldn't Jake sift through his turmoil in the privacy of his own head? "What does Belle say?"

"It's a silent retreat. I can't call till Thursday."

The skin around his eyes seemed taut. He had a vaguely Japanese air.

"You look so young, Jake. Is that the kiss of the plastic surgeon's blade?"

"No! Oh *God,* no! I wouldn't do that in a million years. . . ." He cast a longing gaze at the front door. "Do you have a tap inside or do I go find a well?"

Much as he'd hurt her, he was the father of her children, so she allowed him to trail after her through the sun-dappled hallway.

"Quite a place," he said.

She led him to the kitchen and shook a couple of biscuits onto a plate.

"When we were over the Pacific Ocean this time, a guy had a heart attack in the row in front of me."

"Was he okay?"

"No, they put this oxygen mask on him. . . ."

"Poor guy."

The fridge hummed in sympathy. Jake shook his head. "I don't want to die on a plane," he said quietly.

"At least it would be in business class."

He shot her a rueful look. "What's that thing?" he said, changing the subject. He pointed.

"Wood-burning stove."

"You cook on *that*? Isn't that taking your punishment in the desert a bit far? Jesus, Lisa, where's your bed of nails?"

He asked if she needed help with anything. He was obviously feeling sorry for her now. She took him outside and handed him the shovel.

Then, standing in the shade of the veranda, Lisa folded her arms and watched with satisfaction as one rat buried another.

CHAPTER 18

The Gray Army did a stalwart job of tearing up the kitchen lino. It was tough, physical work. Doug turned purple and breathless a couple of times. He insisted he'd be right after a sit-down in the sun and an egg sandwich.

The stone floor revealed itself in handsome slabs. Though it was gray, Ken insisted it was blue, mined from a local quarry. She shrugged his color blindness off as an example of Lucky Country optimism.

After the floor was scrubbed and sealed, Lisa and her trio of handymen stood in silence, admiring the work of the craftsmen who'd laid the stone more than a century earlier. They would have arrived on claustrophobic wooden boats propelled by canvas, possibly even in chains. Exiled by Queen Victoria, they'd brought little more with them than their skills.

Lisa could hardly contain her excitement

the day a new oven was installed alongside the old wood burner. A name she couldn't pronounce was etched into its stainless-steel front. It would have to be her last big expenditure until the next royalty check. Pale blue flames rose from the hob with breathtaking obedience while the oven fan whirred.

The next day she baked a brilliant carrot cake and smothered it with cream-cheese icing. In an uncharacteristic act of frivolity, she dribbled a chocolate heart shape on top. Then she lowered it onto one of Aunt Caroline's plates and ferried it across the road to the neighbors' gate. She hesitated beside the Wrights' letterbox. NO JUNK MAIL was scrawled across it in red paint.

Gathering her nerve she made her way down the dirt driveway. A weatherboard cottage crouched in a grotto of pines. The bones of an old Holden rusted under a makeshift carport.

As she climbed the steps to the front veranda, Aunt Caroline's voice boomed inside her head: *Never appear unannounced at a front door. People will think you're presumptuous. On a casual visit it's more polite to announce your presence at the back.*

Lisa turned, tiptoed back down the front veranda, and walked along the side of the house. A shadow moved inside a window. She sidestepped an empty birdbath, a cactus plant, and a poinsettia shriveling in a pot. A row of large women's knickers drooped from the clothesline.

She tapped on the frosted glass of the back door. Silence. The old couple's hearing was probably off. She rapped more assertively. "Are you there, Mr. and Mrs. Wright?"

There was a furtive thud on the other side of the door.

"It's Lisa Trumperton from across the road. I just thought I'd drop by."

Nothing. She coughed. The pine trees shooshed. A breeze set a shirt moving on the clothesline. Its sleeves seemed to be warding her off.

"Oh well," Lisa said loudly enough to be heard through the door. "I'll just leave this here." She lowered the cake onto the concrete step. As she hurried back up the driveway, she could have sworn she was being watched.

She arrived back at Trumperton feeling spooked. An urge to get away overcame her. She climbed into Dino and drove into town. She needed to go to the supermarket anyway.

As she was wheeling her trolley down the aisle, ahead of her, a couple in their midfifties bickered. "When I said corn I meant *fresh* corn, not this frozen muck!" the woman snarled.

The man scurried back to the freezer like an obliging retriever.

It made Lisa think: Had Jake done her a favor? Maybe people weren't designed to stay married for a lifetime.

She turned into the pet-food aisle. Supreme Imperial Kitty Treats were on special. She turned a can of tuna and prawn in her hand. It looked appetizing enough to spread on crackers and serve to her nonexistent friends. But the manufacturer was ahead of her — NOT FOR HUMAN CONSUMPTION. She placed the can back on the shelf.

Although her relationship with Skinnymeals was officially over, thanks to the new oven, she tossed one last Boeuf Wellington de Luxe into the trolley just in case, followed by toilet paper, protein bars (she'd half-hoped they hadn't made it to Australia), biscuits, eggs, and special treats to hide from herself when she got home. As she was about to head for the checkout, something drew her back to the pet-food aisle. A can of Supreme Imperial Kitty Treats tumbled into her trolley. She added three more.

After she'd loaded the supermarket bags into the back of Dino, she wandered over to

Togs for a latte.

There she noticed a new addition to the community bulletin board. The Women's Monthly Book Club was looking for new members. While a few people had started recognizing her and saying hello, she was a long way from being embedded. Perhaps joining the local book club would help. She tapped the number into her phone contact list.

On the drive home, she felt the magnetic pull of the garden center. Her groceries would surely last another five minutes in the back of the car. Hundreds of plants would be needed to make any impact on the front paddock. Still, there was no harm looking. . . .

A pretty woman, probably in her early thirties, with a crest of purple hair and a nose stud, was aiming a hose at a forest of camellias. "Can I help you?" the woman asked.

Lisa noticed the woman's alabaster skin and eyes the color of Sri Lankan sapphires. "Just looking."

"You're new to the district, aren't you?" the woman said, lowering her hose and offering a hand. "I'm Juliet Fry. Sing out if you need me."

Lisa thanked her and wandered down an

aisle of gardenias. But any attempt to create the English garden that Trumperton's first owners longed for would be futile. So Lisa made a beeline for the drought-resistant section, where coppery succulents spilled out of their tubs, and green rosettes tipped with purple clustered alongside vivid yellow fingers. The colors were astonishing.

"Wait till you see them in flower." The voice emanated from a giant cactus.

Lisa peered around the spikes.

Teeth white as pumice glowed back at her. "I wouldn't shop here," Scott said. "Not at these prices. I buy wholesale."

"So what are you doing here?"

"Keeping an eye on trends," he said. "Not that Juliet's going to set the world on fire with these things." He stepped through a cluster of tiny imitation Swiss chalets with perches for front doors. "These'd look good at your place," he said, lifting a pot of fleshy leaves, each ending in a point. "Agaves do well here. They're from Mexico." He turned the plant in his large bronze hands.

"Is it a cactus?" she asked.

"More of an aloe. No prickles. Good for the grandchil . . ."

Lisa wondered why Scott's mouth wasn't stretched from the number of times he'd put his boot in it. He was too tanned for her to tell if he was blushing.

"Oh, don't worry," she said. "Gay people can have kids these days."

His eyes crinkled into a smile. "I've been thinking about that front paddock of yours. You could do great things with mass planting."

"It would have to be low-maintenance. I don't want to spend the next twenty years chained to a lawn mower."

"Goes without saying." He scratched his chin. "We could bring in some boulders to give it structure, then create avenues of native trees and grasses. Have you got a pen?"

Lisa fumbled in her handbag, but it was a writer's curse to never have a pen.

Scott loped over to Juliet watering the camellias and returned beaming. "Paper?"

Lisa handed him the supermarket receipt.

"Anything bigger?"

She dug out a fresh tissue.

"Here's the house," he said, drawing a line at the edge of the tissue. "We'd arrange the boulders around the edge of the property like this. The effect would be informal, very Australian. We'd hang onto most of the trees and natives to keep the local wildlife happy — clumps of kangaroo paw here along this path. . . ." He etched a line curved from the front of the house to form a rough circle

226

inside the ring of boulders. "Every garden needs a secret," he said, drawing a branch off the main path into the top right-hand corner. "From the house and the road, it would look like just a clump of trees. But if you were in the garden, this little path would curve off here, into the bush, see? It would draw you in. You'd turn this corner and find — I dunno . . . an outdoor spa tucked away under a pergola."

The man was a genius.

"You mean *per*gola," Lisa said.

"That's what I said."

"No, you didn't. You said per*go*la. You're confusing it with pagoda, which is pronounced the way you were saying pergola."

"What are you, a schoolteacher?"

"Sorry, no. I write books."

"Like Dan Brown?"

"Not exactly."

Their conversation had meandered off on a side path of its own, not nearly as magical as the one he'd just described.

"And the paths? What are they made of?" she asked, trying to claw back his vision.

"Just gravel with weed mats underneath."

Whatever controlled her body heat had lost its switch-off mechanism.

"Good time of year for planting," he added offhandedly.

Lisa shook herself into reality. "Yes, but the cost."

"No pressure," he said, squinting into the sun. "I could leave equipment in your stables and do it in stages, if you like."

"Which reminds me. You didn't leave an invoice."

He blinked. "For the other day?" he said after a pause. "Just think of it as a welcome present."

She thanked him. Her temperature was starting to return to normal. "Your ideas are great," she said.

"Yeah, I like cactus plants the way I like women." He grinned. "Prickly on the outside, but squishy on the inside." He nudged his boot against a fountain into which a concrete cherub was peeing. "Have you heard about the fundraiser at the town hall next Saturday? It's for spinal injuries. . . ."

A charity event. Turning it down would risk being ostracized.

"Want to come along and meet some locals?"

"I'd love to," Lisa lied. "Is it a trivia night?"

"Bush dance."

Oh God. Happy couples, drunken strangers, some weird form of dancing. "You mean line dancing?"

"Easier than that. There's a caller who tells you what to do. Everyone muddles through."

Lisa cast around desperately for an excuse. Oven cleaning? Too soon. Besides, her new stove had some kind of self-cleaning thingie. Work? Only a tragic would slave over a computer on a Saturday night.

"No need to be shy. I'll pick you up. Say around seven?"

"What should I wear?"

"Something comfortable."

As she gripped the steering wheel on her way home, Lisa's head spun with visions of the paddock transformed into a blaze of color. She imagined following the secret path to a pool shimmering under a pergola dripping with grapes. Her conscious mind wanted it to stop there, but the reptilian quarter went into overdrive. It envisaged a semi-naked Scott rising from the water and shaking his torso in the sunshine.

As she turned into her driveway, she laughed at her stupidity. Still, it was good to know her hormones hadn't shriveled up completely. The other business was altogether more worrying. Had he tricked her into what could be a date? Surely not. She was at least five years his senior. He was just offering country hospitality.

She parked Dino outside the stables, and spotted a familiar shape on the doorstep. With his back to her, the cat was bent in concentration, his tail pointed skyward. She prayed he hadn't brought another rat.

She opened the driver's door and called gently.

He swiveled and stared unblinkingly at her through the eye. Then he tensed and raised his front paw, preparing to make a run.

"It's okay, puss." She stood still while the cat assessed her sincerity.

She needed a friend. So, from the look of it, did he.

The cat put his head down and reverted to his previous task of licking the icing heart off the carrot cake. Someone had returned it and left it on her back doorstep without even a note.

Chapter 19

Lisa wriggled her toes inside her UGG boots. She squared her shoulders in front of the computer screen. It was about time Emily Brontë got down and dirty with Frederick the stable hand.

Writing about squelching, writhing bodies used to be pleasurable, if not — as some critics had pointed out — her forte. Lately, it had become a chore. She could barely remember the mechanics of it, let alone the out-of-body highs she used to experience when she was younger. Every time she tried to conjure up a sexy man he ended up wearing enormous work boots and a goofy smile. Readers had also become hardened, lately. Even literary writers were churning out porn to give their sales a boost. Depravities that were barely legal were now in demand. She'd heard throttling was in vogue.

The computer screen fixed her with its empty eye.

"Anal?" she typed tentatively.

"Not disturbing you, are we?" Ron said, peering over her shoulder.

He'd been startling her in all sorts of places since he'd bought a pair of trainers. She quickly typed a *C* in front of the *A*.

"We thought we'd start in here today," he said, lowering a paint tin onto the floor. "Are you sure you want Racing Green?"

Ken swung into the room and with matador flair flourished a paint-speckled dustsheet. Doug appeared with a stepladder. Next to it he placed a ghetto blaster permanently tuned in to a talk-back station favored by racist homophobes who believed in alien abductions.

"What? Oh, yes."

"The color's a bit dark, if you ask me," Ron grumbled. "Turn that thing down, Ken. She's writing about boating in Europe."

Lisa made her excuses and moved her laptop downstairs to the kitchen table. She usually needed chocolate for sex scenes. Protein bars didn't cut it. Green and Black's white chocolate was good for extramarital affairs; 80 percent cocoa for enduring passion. Warm feet were also essential, hence the UGG boots. Happily, they doubled as insulation against the bluestone floor.

She opened her laptop and glanced over her shoulder.

> Frederick thrust her against the hay bales. . . .

Emily was about to get spikes of straw digging into her backside.

Lisa stood up and opened the back door. A shaft of sunlight stretched suggestively across the floor. She stirred two heaped teaspoons of instant coffee into a mug and waited for the caffeine kick.

> Her knot of hair unraveled against the straw. . . .

Lisa scanned her abdomen for erotic sensation. The only identifiable pressure was from her bladder. Lisa wasn't up to it. Glancing over her shoulder to ensure Ron was safely upstairs, she Googled "How to Write a Sex Scene." A tidal wave of advice poured onto her screen.

Never use the word penis. Lisa agreed it was an ugly noun. She ran through some alternatives — cock, dick, manhood, prick, schlong. Penis didn't seem so bad in comparison.

She flicked to Portia's Facebook page.

There were three new photos — two of Portia laughing maniacally with two young men, the veins in her neck standing out. The third photo was of a meringue cake drowning in berries and cream. Portia had typed "Yum!" for a caption. As if the child would allow that number of calories anywhere near her lips.

Sighing, Lisa returned to "How to Write a Sex Scene." *Attention to detail is essential. Let the reader know if buttons and/or zips are involved.* Frederick probably had buttons.

Make sure the man removes his socks.

Good point.

Don't forget contraception. Maybe Frederick could be expert at coitus interruptus.

A battalion of black ants marched in single file across the floor toward the pantry. Lisa gnawed her thumbnail and checked her e-mails. There were two new messages. One was from a reader in Germany who wanted to know her shoe size. He claimed the sensuality of the female foot, the toes in particular, was overlooked by the mass media. A woman's foot was nothing to be ashamed of, especially when the toenails were painted bright red.

Frederick, a foot fetishist? It would solve the contraception problem.

The second e-mail was from Vanessa, asking if the manuscript was on track for delivery the following month.

Lisa drew a breath and settled her mouth in a line. The deadline had come around too fast. She flicked back to "How to Write a Sex Scene."

Couples seldom climax simultaneously in real life. Decide who's going to come first and why.

Frederick would be first over the finishing line because he was so masculine and physical. But that would leave Emily stranded. Lisa decided to make him a kind of tantric master. She willed sentences to straggle across the screen.

She could feel his throbbing member . . .

How could she sink to such a creaky cliché? The folds of her brain pleated in on themselves as she hammered the Delete button. There was no option but to raid her stash of liqueur-flavored chocolate.

She went to the pantry and stood on tiptoe. As she ran her hand along the top shelf, she could hear her laptop making underwater noises — the unmistakable sound of a Skype request.

Jake's face flickered into view.

"Where are you?" she asked, fingering a

brandy cream.

"Bangkok airport."

"Has Belle finished the retreat?"

"Tomorrow."

Jake ran a hand through his blue-black hair. If Belle felt an ounce of kindness toward him she'd explain how older skin requires softer tones.

"I've been thinking about Ted," he said, clearing his throat. "It can't be easy for him."

Lisa slid the brandy cream between her lips while pretending to wipe her mouth thoughtfully.

"And you're right about love. It's not easy to find."

Was this a coded message? She let the brandy cream slide to the back of her mouth. "How's Belle?" Why did Lisa always ask that, when all she really wanted was for Belle to climb onto the roof of a Thai temple and impale herself on the spiky bit?

"She wants to go to Provence as well as Tahiti next year to keep up her French."

"*Magnifique,*" Lisa said, swallowing the chocolate.

"How are you?" he asked.

"Fine. Just fine."

"Still wearing those UGG boots?"

"They weren't mine. They were Maxine's.

236

I bought a new pair."

"Are you wearing them now?"

She glanced down at her feet.

"Let me see."

"No, Jake."

"Go on."

"Don't be ridiculous." Giggling, she lifted the laptop and pointed it at her boots.

"They're kind of sexy." Clearly Jake wanted to eat his cake and have yesterday's bagel as well.

She placed the laptop firmly back on the table.

"I miss you," he said.

He was toying with her. In truth she missed him, too. Not the cheating, lying Jake, but the Jake who'd hire a horse and buggy in Central Park just for the hell of it, the Jake who tap-danced down Broadway after they'd been to a revival of *Singin' in the Rain.*

Fall was her favorite time in New York. Central Park would be draped in curtains of red and gold right now. It wouldn't be long till the Thanksgiving Day Parade and the first snowfall. A dull pain nestled in her rib cage. Did she belong nowhere?

"Remember that time we took Ted to the movies and there was that terrible stink? We thought the kid next to us had farted. Then

Ted turned to me, looking angelic, and said: 'Dad, I just breathed through my bottom.' "

"What about the time we took Portia to the child psychologist because we were having trouble potty training her?" Lisa said. "He asked her why she refused to give up nappies, and she said because they were advertised on TV."

They smiled fondly, not at each other but into the pool of memories they shared.

"Twenty-three years is nothing to sneeze at, Lisa."

But Lisa no longer trusted nostalgia and the way it wrapped the past up in gift boxes festooned with paper flowers. As she grappled for a reply, a shape appeared on the doorstep. It threw a monstrous shadow across the floor.

"What's the matter?" asked Jake.

"Oh, nothing. Just a cat that's been hanging around."

"New friend?"

"More of a frenemy."

Her visitor sailed lightly over the threshold. Crouching close to the ground, he glowered up at her, every muscle tensed to turn and run. He was waiting for her to shoo him out.

"Are you hungry?" she asked gently.

"Nah, I had a good meal on the plane . . .

but I could do with a snack," Jake said, warming to her maternal tone.

"I was talking to the cat."

"Oh."

The feline cruised the perimeter of the kitchen like a shark.

"I'd better go," Lisa said.

"So had I," Jake said, suddenly faking busyness. "I've got a meeting. See ya." Jake's image melted into the screen.

The cat sniffed the cupboards. Their encounter over the carrot cake had been brief. He'd scurried away when she'd approached.

"So you've come for another visit?" Her voice echoed across the kitchen. The cat became rigid and flattened his ears. She needed to adjust her tendency to boom. "Don't be shy," she crooned in an überfeminine tone that didn't sound like her. It was the first time he'd stayed still and close enough for her to have a good look at him.

His coat was flat and mostly ginger. Grubby cream chunks dangled from his throat. Dirty white socks rose over his feet. He was a mess of a cat.

She rubbed the scar on the back of her hand. Those claws were daggers, potential harbingers of disease. She searched for his good points. The nose was rose pink. There were tiger stripes on his forehead. But the tail was a disaster. A disheveled duster, it was home to an assortment of twigs and leaves. As for the permanent wink, her heart turned to olive oil. Maybe he'd lost the eye in a fight. Back at the shelter she'd met felines who'd developed eye ulcers as a result of cat flu. A few unlucky ones ended up blind.

The animal was filthy. And yes, ugly. Yet there was something mesmerizing about him. She itched to reach out and touch the matted fur. She leaned forward.

The cat cowered.

"It's okay," she said, leaning back in a less aggressive pose. "Do you like kitty treats?" She might as well have been speaking Vulcan. "See those cans on the windowsill?"

The lighthouse beam of his eye followed her sightline to the cat food. Maybe he'd had a home once.

She stood up slowly, trying not to make a noise scraping her chair.

The cat hurtled to the no-man's land of the doorway.

She trod noiselessly across the room like an underwater diver.

The utensil drawer rattled when she reached for the can opener. The cat darted outside.

Damn. He could've trusted her a little. Still, she'd come this far. . . . She latched the can opener onto the tin and felt it sink through the lid. As it chomped the tin with a satisfying rhythm, she sensed a presence in the doorway. The cat was back. She scraped the food onto a saucer and laid it at her feet.

The cat stared longingly at the food, then up at her.

She was too close. She stepped backwards and leaned against the new stove.

The cat skittered toward the saucer and buried his face in kitty treats.

"What shall I call you?"

Giving him a name was lining herself up for heartache. Still, what else was new?

"Cyclops?"

He appeared to have no interest in the classics.

"Marmaduke," she said, edging toward him.

He continued hoovering up the food.

"Okay, how about something simple like Mojo?"

The cat stopped and gazed up at her. "Meow." His voice was quieter and more high-pitched than she'd expected.

"Mojo?"

The cat winked.

"Okay. Mojo it is." She bent and reached out to his shaggy coat.

As though her touch connected him to the electricity grid, Mojo jumped. Tail down, he turned and scurried out the back door.

CHAPTER 20

It wasn't a date. Obviously. The only reason he'd asked was because he felt sorry for her. And because she couldn't say no.

He'd said to wear something comfortable. She interpreted that to mean layers of deodorant, concealer under her eyes, an African-print skirt and a dark top. Dangly red earrings made from bottle tops added devil-may-care festivity. Footwear was problematic. She settled for a pair of black, orthopedic-looking Mary Janes.

Thirty minutes after he had said he'd pick her up, Scott still hadn't arrived. He'd probably forgotten. Unreliable. No wonder Bev had dumped him.

A glass of wine seemed a good idea. On the other hand, it might make her talkative. She cast about for a diversion. There'd been no sign of Mojo since he'd run out on her. She opened the back door and called. No answer. The kitty treats had done nothing to seal their friendship.

The only good thing about the dance was that it'd be over in a few hours. It wasn't too late to flick him a text. Better to be the rejecter than the rejectee. She reached for her phone.

Hi there, Scott. So sorry . . .

Headlights flashed across the paneling in the entrance hall. Seconds later the door knocker emitted a series of thumps. Damn.

His eyes flashed with boyish charm as she opened the door.

"You're late," she snapped.

"Yeah, I know," he said, looking sideways. "Todd and I were horse riding. Took a while to clean up."

For someone who'd been dumped because he was a lousy dad, Scott seemed to be the patron saint of fatherhood. Maybe he was trying to get Beverley back.

"You look nice," he said, breathing peppermint in her face.

Of all the words in the English language, "nice" was her least favorite. Still, it wasn't a date.

"So do you." It was the first time she'd seen him in long trousers. He looked surprisingly grown up — apart from the ear-to-ear grin he was now dazzling her with.

"Gee, thanks," he said, shifting the weight

244

in his elastic-sided boots. Thank God she hadn't worn hers. His skin glowed in the half-light. Some men looked less attractive freshly shaven, especially if the usual stubble camouflaged a disappointing chin. Scott was even better looking without a day's growth. He smelled of cinnamon and soap.

She offered to take Dino. He insisted on the ute, opening the passenger door with a flourish. The interior smelled of dry dust. It was pleasingly utilitarian, apart from the pine-tree deodorizer dangling from the rearview mirror.

As they rattled into town, a jazz trumpet oozed from the radio.

"Been practicing your dance steps?" he asked. In profile, his face resembled that of a warrior in a Grecian frieze.

"Can't I just sit on the sidelines and watch?"

"Relax."

Easy for him to say when his attitude was permanently horizontal.

"A bush dance sounds like something that should happen under the stars around an open fire with boomerangs."

"Not quite," he said, shifting the gear stick. "Try to imagine how you'd feel after a day's harvesting somewhere in England in the 1800s."

"Who'll be there?" she asked.

"Just about everyone," he replied.

"The Wrights?"

"They don't go out much these days. Why do you ask?"

She told him about the carrot cake. He said not to worry about old Aunty May.

"You're *related*?"

"You know what it's like in the country. Everyone's your aunty, even when they're not."

Another Aussie peculiarity.

"I've been meaning to ask you about the stables at my place. Who was it that committed suicide there?"

Scott swerved to avoid a human-sized shadow bouncing across the road.

"Kangaroo," he explained. "The stables? It's old stuff. I wouldn't worry."

A boulder weighed on her abdomen. But at the moment, far worse than her stables' having a sinister history was the prospect of appearing in front of the entire town of Castlemaine with Scott. Tongues would wag, assumptions be made. If he hadn't already ruined her reputation spreading laughable stories around town, he was about to make things worse.

They reached the center of town. Everything was quiet, the windows of the town hall reassuringly dark.

"Must be the wrong night," she said hopefully.

"Nah," he said, yanking the hand brake. "The girls have been making soup all afternoon."

Soup? At a dance? She followed him past the main entrance and down an alley along the side of the building. A rectangle of light shone from a doorway.

"I've changed my mind," Lisa said, grabbing his elbow.

"What?"

"I can't dance."

"C'mon." He seized her shoulder and steered her through the doorway into a brightly lit foyer.

A group of women sat at a table. They raised their heads simultaneously, their eyes flashing from Scott to Lisa and back again.

"Evening, ladies," Scott said, oblivious to the undercurrent. "This is Lisa Trumperton. She's new in town."

The women's smiles were wide but shallow. Lisa recognized Juliet from the garden center. She was wearing black lace and a Frida Kahlo headband made of imitation roses.

"Where do I pay?" Lisa asked.

"All sorted," Scott said, taking two small

cards from his pocket and pressing them in her palm.

Juliet asked if Lisa would like a two-dollar raffle ticket. Desperate for approval, Lisa bought ten.

Scott wandered off to talk with an elderly couple. He towered over them, smiling and chatting. The old man laughed, and his wife's eyes shone. Scott could certainly pump out the charm.

Lisa handed their tickets to a man guarding a set of double doors. As the doors swung open, a wave of heat and folksy violin music washed through. She peered anxiously into the soup of moving bodies.

"Let's get started," Scott said, backing into the doors and ushering her through.

Couples stood in a large circle around the perimeter of the hall.

"And now for the bush polka," a voice drawled through the sound system. "Gentlemen on the inside, ladies on the outside." A Gandalf lookalike in a red-check shirt was directing proceedings from the stage. He surveyed the crowd the way Julius Caesar might inspect his troops. A violin dangled from his gnarled hand. A morose guitarist with lank dark hair stood next to him. A woman in a bright-green dress raised her violin and nodded amiably to a man nestled behind a set of drums. A flautist in a tan Akubra moistened his lips.

"Face your partners!"

"I'll sit this one out," she muttered, casting a longing gaze at the kids and old people seated around tables at the back of the hall.

Scott grabbed her elbow and nudged her into the circle.

"Right, ladies and gentlemen," the caller announced. "I'll walk you through, then you're on your own."

The violins started up a reedy whine. It was the sort of music an Irish granny would knit to in her rocking chair. The drummer set a sedate pace.

Scott latched his arm around her waist and enveloped her hand in his. As she rested her left hand on his shoulder, she could feel solid muscle through his shirt. She floated almost doll-like in his arms, but there was enough distance between them to keep a nun happy.

"Heel-and-toe, heel-and-toe . . ." droned the caller. "Four steps to the right, four steps to the left . . ."

For a solid guy, Scott was nimble in his boots.

"Clap right hands together . . ."

Scott swept his arm diagonally across his body and nodded at her to do the same.

Their hands collided.

"Now the left."

She was coping.

"Clap both hands together."

She raised her hands in surrender. Scott's double-handed clap almost knocked her backwards.

"Now slap your knees. . . . Swing your partner."

He twirled her on his elbow.

"And change."

She was suddenly in the grip of a man with an orange mustache.

Lisa glanced over her shoulder at Scott. "What do I do now?" she shouted.

The music accelerated to the beat of a slow jog. No wonder most of the dancers looked lean and fit. If they were going to keep this up for more than one song, someone would have to scrape her off the floor.

Orange mustache flung her into the arms of a man with sweaty palms. She tripped over his shoe. "Sorry. I'm not much good . . ." Before she could finish her sentence she was heel-and-toeing with a young woman in a floor-length gown.

As the music sped up to a dizzying pace, the woman fitted in an extra twirl, delivering herself to a man and Lisa into the arms of another woman.

Lisa looked behind and craned to see who was in front of her. She'd been manipulated into a line of men. Her next partner was a teenage girl, who didn't hide her disappointment at dancing with a woman.

"I've had a sex change!" Lisa shouted.

A middle-aged woman in a floral skirt adjusted her arms to ensure Lisa took the masculine hold. None of them wanted to dance with another woman — except maybe for the young lady with cropped hair and dungarees.

Heel-and-toe, heel-and-toe . . .

Lisa wondered if she could spin out of the dance altogether and head for the tables at the next partner change. But that would leave some poor woman stranded on the floor. She twirled again to find herself chest to chest with a jacket of pink sequins. "Beverley!" she cried.

The estate agent shot her a snaky smile. Her hair was up in a beehive bedecked with crystal beads. A tiny pink skirt clung to her buttocks. How she could heel-and-toe in six-inch heels was beyond Lisa.

Beverley swung off to the following man, scraping Lisa's arm with her fingernail extensions.

Lisa's next partner was a teenage boy, thin and translucent as a prawn. His hand lay damp in hers. Somehow or other, he too had been the victim of gender exchange.

"Do you want to be a man?" Lisa bellowed over the music.

The boy looked startled, as if she'd made an indecent proposal. But this was no time for political correctness.

"Are you READY TO BE A MAN?!"

He nodded earnestly.

With the next spin, Lisa and the boy completed an extra half-turn and threw themselves gratefully at the opposite sex.

Lisa glanced across the circle. Scott and Beverley were slapping hands. Lisa whirled into the arms of Ron from the Gray Army. With a natty sense of rhythm, he passed her on to Ken, who danced lopsidedly because of his knee. Doug was outside having a smoke.

A moist strip formed over her spine. Her lungs pumped. Blisters erupted between her toes. She stopped caring about the steps. The challenge was to stay vertical. As the dance took on a power of its own, she became a particle in a swirling universe. She was compelled to keep spinning till the music stopped. Just when it seemed the band was slowing down, the fiddlers raised their chins to begin another cycle.

No wonder this sort of dancing had been

popular in the old days. It was preindustrial speed dating. In societies where physical contact was formalized to the point of extinction, dances supplied huge quantities of nonverbal information. Each encounter was sex in a trial package under controlled conditions. The pompous man who told her off for not knowing the steps would have no idea how to please a woman in bed. The handsome laborer who stepped forward, offering himself as a gift to womankind, then crushed her toes, had the hallmarks of a premature ejaculator. Talent was tucked away in unpredictable packages. A short fellow with purplish-red eyes guided her gently through the steps. His touch was firm yet appreciative. With impeccable rhythm and tolerance, he made her a better dancer. A man in a blue shirt pressed against her abdomen, introducing more anatomy than necessary. She almost choked in a cloud of aftershave she recognized as Brut.

"Well, hello there! What's your name, young lady?"

"Lisa."

"Charmed to meet you. Bob Hogan."

"Of Hogan & Hogan?" she said, panting.

"That's right." He gripped her to his body and almost spun her off her feet. "The Younger." As he moved on he squeezed her hand, as if saying farewell after an intimate act.

Two schoolboys, one potential heart attack victim, and a farmer later, the music stopped. The circle collapsed as dancers returned to their tables. Lisa waited for her breath to return to normal. The whole town had shown up for the dance — from babies and schoolkids to old folks in wheelchairs. She looked for Scott. He was standing in a circle of blokes, apparently oblivious to her presence. She wandered over to a table where Juliet was serving drinks and asked for a wine.

"You're out of luck," Juliet said, handing her a plastic cup. "We've only got cordial. Lime or orange."

Lisa opted for lime.

Juliet eyed her for a moment. "So are you and Scott an item?" she said, before turning to pour bright-green fluid into a paper cup.

The cordial burned the back of Lisa's throat. She coughed extravagantly. "God, no!" she said, before scuttling away to take refuge in a group of women gathering outside the ladies'.

When the band packed up around nine thirty, everyone was ready to go — the dance-floor workout had taken its toll. Scott was suddenly at her side, but quickly disappeared again to issue drawn-out, hearty farewells. Lisa befriended the local osteopath while she waited. The osteopath had moved to Castlemaine as a solo mother a few years ago. People were friendly and welcoming, she said. She'd found new love in the form of a local electrician. Lisa had noticed them on the dance floor, a handsome couple emitting sparks of mutual attraction.

At last Scott tapped her on the shoulder. She trailed after him like a sheepdog, back to the ute, and they drove home in silence.

"You certainly know how to dance, Ms. Trumperton," Scott said as they shuddered to a halt under the portico.

"Thanks." She fumbled for the door handle.

"Allow me," he said, leaning across the gear stick.

She savored his woody smell. His breath landed on her face in little puffs of cinnamon. Surely he wasn't about to kiss her? His right hand was drifting dangerously close to her breasts.

"The pleasure was all mine, Ms. Trumperton," he added, lowering his face toward hers.

She recoiled against the passenger door and assumed the posture of Queen Victoria with a bad case of hemorrhoids.

Innocent hurt flashed across his face.

She scooped her handbag off the floor and bolted, hobbling across the gravel to her front door. When she reached the top of the steps she turned and waved. But he was already back behind the wheel and careering toward the gates.

Chapter 21

It was insane to expect him to call the next day. Especially after a non-date. However, he had mentioned he might come over and measure the garden.

It didn't matter. She was on a roll with her book.

Erotic images of Emily and her stable hand were pouring into her laptop on the kitchen table.

Frederick feigned shock when Emily refused to ride sidesaddle. Galloping through the forest, she reveled in each thrust of the black stallion between her thighs. Keeping pace on the white horse she'd lent him, he was mesmerized by the rhythm of her breath exploding in gasps. At one with her mount, she sailed a ditch. Her hair struggled loose of its net and tumbled over her shoulders.

"You certainly know how to ride, Miss

Brontë," Frederick said, flashing his crooked canine tooth.

Lisa checked her phone. Not even a text.

Their horses stopped at a stream and dipped their noses in the pool. Frederick dismounted and caught Emily in his arms as she slid to the ground. She took his hand, so large in hers, and led him into a stand of pines. The trees were perfectly formed, their sturdy trunks prodding the sky. . . .

Lisa wondered if she should call Scott. Basic manners, some would say.

Trees kaleidoscoped through her head as they kissed. Her thighs oozed desire. Frederick pressed her onto a bed of pine needles, his warm spicy breath . . .

Or just text. But then he might think she was chasing him.

Lava flows of desire coursed through Emily, stirring parts of her body that had been dormant for years.

Lisa kicked off her UGG boots. Her feet were in agony.

Frederick dug into her corset and fished her breasts out into the dappled light. Perfect breasts, the nipples compact and brown . . .

"But, my dearest," Frederick said, recoiling with alarm. "You are fading away! Could you not eat more?"

Something damp nudged Lisa's toe. A fly must've wafted in through the back door. She flicked her foot. The creature withdrew. Breasts.

If she'd granted Scott an opportunity in that department, he would've recoiled in revulsion. Or worse, pretended it was okay.

A strip of sandpaper rubbed her big toe. She peered under the table. A single eye gazed at her through a mess of orange fur.

"Mojo!" she cried, offering her hand.

He flinched and studied her fingers with suspicion.

"Come on; I'm not going to hurt you."

Maybe it was the tone of her voice, but the cat moved toward her and nudged her knuckles with his forehead. She couldn't believe it. He was inviting contact.

She tickled his chin, carefully avoiding the matted lumps. She'd never dreamed they'd get this far. To her amazement, he took another step forward and let her run her hand over his back. Lifting his tail, he turned around and let her stroke him again — and again.

Mojo was starting to trust her.

"There's a boy."

The cat emitted a soft, melodic purr. The patting was going so well, she reached over and tried to pick him up. Mojo yowled. He tensed, wriggled out of her grasp, and scurried toward the door. Biting her lip, she tried to imagine how it must feel living inside that shaggy coat. Having someone pick you up would be like having your hair pulled in different directions at the same time.

She waited for him to leave. He sat beside the door, arranged his broom of a tail over his front feet, and considered the situation.

Keeping well clear of him, she stood up and moved like a mime artist to the bench top. He watched as she opened a can of kitty treats and spooned the contents into a saucer.

She returned to her seat and pretended not to take any notice of him. After what seemed a very long time, he padded across the bluestone and ate ravenously.

She was beginning to understand Mojo. He was a cat who operated on his own terms. When he wasn't initiating contact, he preferred to be ignored.

She turned her attention back to Emily Brontë's nipples.

"You did *what*?"

Lisa leaned into the computer screen. She couldn't tell if the patches on Portia's neck were shadows or love bites.

"I went to a dance with someone. It was a social thing."

"Oh my God, Mom!" Portia was reacting as if Lisa had just announced a post-menopausal pregnancy. "Is he hot?"

Lisa had a vision of Scott striding godlike through the garden center. It was quickly erased by his chimp-at-a-tea-party performance with Aunt Caroline.

"An acquired taste."

"Did you hook up with him?"

Lisa had no idea what the term meant. Portia and her friends were always "hooking up" with people. They referred to it as though it were just cuddling, but *hooking* had a biological intonation.

"Heavens no!"

Portia flicked her hair. She was clearly bored. Any moment she'd change the subject back to her failed audition for Blanche in *Streetcar*.

"But there was a moment in his ute after-ward."

"You didn't try to kiss him?"

"No!"

"Thank God. Kissing's political. Some girls I know make the first move, but that's giving their power away. I prefer things to happen more . . . organically."

This was the same little girl who'd run to her room and slammed the door when Lisa had tried to explain the mechanics of menstruation?

"You can't get up to much in the front seat of a ute, anyway. Those things are damned uncomfortable. Did he put his arm across the back of the seat?"

Lisa had long suspected her daughter's sexual experience surpassed her own. "I don't think so."

"Did he put his arm around your waist and try to work it up to your boobs?" Portia was warming to her subject.

"God *no*!"

"So what *did* he do?"

"He . . . breathed on me."

Portia was deflated. "Some old dude in a ute *breathed* on you?"

Lisa couldn't take the humiliation any longer. "Are you coming to Australia for Christmas?"

CHAPTER 22

Mojo didn't seem to mind being chased around the kitchen. On his second circuit, he slowed down and let her catch him. He didn't even try to scratch. Flattered, she slid him into a picnic basket and closed the lid.

The cat emitted a couple of resigned mews. He seemed to understand that if their relationship had any future he'd have to meet the vet.

Once she'd dropped him off at the clinic, she hurried home to prepare for the onslaught of the Women's Monthly Book Club. Her plan to get to know some locals had gotten off to a rocky start. When she'd called the book-club number, the gravelly voice at the other end of the line had seemed vaguely familiar.

"You're looking for new members?"

"Sure are. Want to sign up?"

Every chromosome in Lisa's body had screamed *No!* "Yes."

"Great! We have a little tradition where the new member hosts her first book-club meeting at her place."

"Okay."

"That'll be next Tuesday at two thirty. Oh, and you'd better get hold of a copy of this month's book."

"What's the title?"

"You'll laugh your tits off at this. A fancy writer's moved into the district. I sold her a house, an overpriced heap of rubble. Anyway, we thought we'd take a look at her stuff. It's called . . . Hang on. I've got a copy of it here somewhere. That's right, *Three Sisters: Charlotte.*"

The phone had sizzled against Lisa's cheek.

"Oh, and I forgot to ask your name," Beverley Hogan had added.

The only thing worse than hosting a book club at her house would be a group of strange women — neighbors and potential friends — reviewing *Three Sisters: Charlotte* in front of her.

Lisa flung herself into a frenzy of vacuuming. There wouldn't be any genuine fans among them, so she could relax about that. She often perceived disappointment when fans showed up at book signings, especially from those who'd driven miles. The less tactful ones commented on how different she looked from her Web site photos. They didn't understand *recent* meant anything taken in the last twenty years.

Maybe the book-club members would be the type of aggressively competitive house-keepers who expected to find flowers in the bathroom. Lisa bustled down the drive to pull wattle blossom off a tree. The Gray Army, who were painting window frames, watched on, bemused. Then she slapped together a mountain of egg sandwiches — half for the Gray Army and half for her guests. It didn't seem enough for country appetites.

Carrot cakes brought bad luck, so she threw together her own version of white chocolate and raspberry muffins. They emerged from the oven flat and anemic compared to Maxine's.

Lisa glanced at her watch. There was just enough time to zip into town and collect Mojo from the clinic. She didn't want to extend his suffering more than necessary.

The vet approached her with a cautious smile. He soothed her alarm by saying her cat was fine, if somewhat underweight for his size. The neutering operation had gone well, though the vet had never seen so many fleas in his professional life. Mojo's teeth had been cleaned, his claws trimmed, and he was now inoculated against every disease known to the feline world. The vet estimated Mojo was about three years old. He encouraged Lisa to keep Mojo inside at night to help preserve native wildlife.

Mojo had been upgraded to a proper carry case with breathing holes in the sides. As the vet handed her the case, he prepared her for what he called a change in her pet's appearance. "His fur was so matted I had to shave him," the vet said.

She peered through the holes and perceived a cattish silhouette. A sleepy eye winked back. "You mean he's bald?"

"No, not at all," the vet said with a little laugh that could've been a cough. He went on to explain it was the best that could be done for a cat in Mojo's condition. Besides, his fur would grow out in a month or two.

The carry case was silent.

A hairdresser had told Lisa the same thing after he'd given her a mullet. But Lisa didn't have time to interrogate further. After handing over half the deposit for the vet's next holiday in Thailand, she slid Mojo's case into the back of the car. Then, on the drive home, she tried to avoid bumps in the road, remembering how much her stitches had hurt when Jake had driven her home from the hospital.

Dino puttered through an archway of gnarled gum trees. In her younger days, she'd dismissed the Australian landscape as ugly and barren, having seen nothing lovely in dry red soil crumpled into ancient hills, or trees with peeling bark and gray leaves as tough as leather. Even the freakish animals had offended her Eurocentric pretentions. Crippled with cultural insecurities, she couldn't have been further off the mark.

As she rounded the curve in the driveway she was horrified to see half-a-dozen figures assembled outside her front door. The Women's Monthly had arrived early. A flash of a camera lens glinted in the sun. Zack had begged to film the book-club event. Her heart sank.

Lisa parked Dino outside the stables, gathered up Mojo's carry case, and hurried toward the visitors. "So sorry, ladies! Please come inside."

Familiar spikes of purple hair approached. Juliet from the garden center presented Lisa with yellow pansies in a pot.

"How lovely!" Lisa crooned. She'd been nervous around Juliet since the young woman had asked whether she and Scott were an item. "You must have a green thumb."

"Oh, she dabbles in all sorts," Beverley said. "Handcrafts, *and* she runs the wildlife shelter."

Lisa's interest was piqued. "You rescue animals?"

"When there's a need." Juliet smiled, stepping over the threshold. "Come visit some time."

In a rare casual mood, Beverley was decked out in a black velour tracksuit with a pink logo across her breast. Diamantés twinkled from the brim of her cap. "Sharky and I have just been for a little walk, haven't we, darling?" she said, addressing a shaggy white glove puppet in the crook of her arm.

Lisa leaned forward to examine the creation. It lurched toward her and bared its teeth. "Oh! It's real!"

"He's not an it! Sharky's just an itty-bitty Chihuahua-Maltese cross, aren't you, babypie?" Beverley's tone was unrecognizable.

Lisa remembered the little dog from the fly-eating episode in Hogan & Hogan's window.

"He's named after Greg Norman the golfer," Juliet said in a nonjudgmental tone.

Zack's camera drifted across the Women's Monthly. Some faces were familiar. Lisa had danced with June from the medical center during her man phase. A trim, older woman in gold-rimmed spectacles introduced herself as Dorothy Thatcher, the local historian.

Another face stood out because it belonged to a man. His hair was slicked back in the manner of Fred Astaire. Spilling from the breast pocket of his tweed jacket was a paisley handkerchief of the same fabric as his cravat. The last time Lisa had seen corduroy trousers had been when one of Ted's friends had worn them ironically.

"Dexter's our token male," Beverley said. "He's a brain box, too, aren't you, Dex?"

"Retired English professor," he announced, bobbing his head in pseudo modesty. "I'm leading today's session."

Lisa quailed. Academics tended to regard her books with scorn. It was hard to know if they were jealous of her sales figures, or her writing really was crap.

She led the visitors into Alexander's room. They studied the furniture with the curiosity of creatures introduced to a new enclosure. Dorothy made a beeline for the fireplace and studied the photo of Alexander. Zack trailed in her wake.

"My grandfather," Lisa said.

Dorothy turned and examined her over the rims of her glasses. "I know."

"Really?" Lisa gasped. "I'd love to learn

more about him. And the house too, of course."

Dorothy didn't seem enthused. "Well, you've heard about the terrible so-called accident in the stables. . . ."

"Not really . . ."

Dorothy glanced sideways. "If you want to know about your family history, you should talk to your neighbors," she said.

"The Wrights?"

"You two can have a chinwag later," Beverley interrupted. "Let's get started."

The Women's Monthly settled themselves in a circle and produced their copies of *Three Sisters: Charlotte.* Beverley nestled Sharky between her breasts and zipped him into her tracksuit top. He wrestled his face into the daylight and growled softly at the carry case on the coffee table.

"I'll put the kettle on," Lisa announced, grabbing the pet container and whisking it down the hall. "Never mind, Mojo," she whispered, placing the container and its dozy inmate on the kitchen table.

When she returned, Dexter had already launched into a diatribe. "As a Brontë scholar at Bond University for many years, I have to confess I'm uncomfortable with the concept of fictionalizing these young women's tragic lives, let alone turning them into Disneyfied soft porn. . . ."

Lisa stood at the doorway and crossed her arms. She thought she heard another vehicle pulling up outside the house. Unless it was the sound of impotent rage coursing through her veins.

Juliet doodled on the inside back cover of her copy of *Three Sisters: Charlotte*. Dorothy Thatcher studied the patch of ceiling the Gray Army had forgotten to give a second coat. Lisa heard the clatter of a ladder being shifted in the hallway. The old boys had found an excuse to work within earshot.

"I suppose it was bound to happen," Dexter continued. "Wasn't there some author who mutated Jane Austen into a zombie?"

Sooner or later he was going to mention the *C* word.

"Honestly, to have Charlotte Brontë toying with lesbianism. It strikes me as blatantly . . . *commercial.*"

Lisa mouthed the word in unison with him. "You'd rather I wrote books nobody wanted to read?" she countered.

Dexter inflated like a puffer fish. "Without meaning to offend our hostess, I would be grateful if Ms. Trumperton would tell us exactly what her motives *are.*"

Zack's camera swiveled back to her.

"People need cheering up."

"How could you be so frivolous?" Dexter retorted, rising to his full five feet, two inches.

"I'm not! Life's so grim these days. The news is unwatchable. Everyone's on medication for something. People are tired. And sad."

"Poking fun at three of the world's great writers is a cheap trick."

She'd had enough. The Women's Monthly watched enthralled as Lisa assumed a dominant position in front of the fireplace. "I'm not the first author who felt compelled to reshape the Brontës' miserable lives, actually, Dexter. You're no doubt familiar with Elizabeth Gaskell?"

"Yes." He nodded. "She knew Charlotte Brontë. Gaskell wrote the famous biography of her."

"Well, Elizabeth Gaskell said that Charlotte, in her novel *Shirley,* based the main character on the person whom Emily Brontë would have been, had she enjoyed blooming health and wealth."

Dexter said nothing.

"I'm no Charlotte Brontë," Lisa continued. "But . . ."

Beverley's breasts emitted a series of hostile yaps. Sharky snarled and bared his teeth at the doorway.

The Women's Monthly followed Sharky's line of sight. They let out a collective screech. A bizarre creature was crouched on the floorboards. It had a lion's mane, fluffy boots, and a feather duster of a tail. The rest of its body was devoid of hair. Though it was the shape of a lion, it was the size of a domestic feline. It had a crumpled ear and one eye.

"Mojo! How did you get out?"

A pair of size-thirteen workmen's boots appeared behind the cat.

Scott's brow rippled with confusion as he surveyed the room. "Sorry, I knocked, but . . ."

"You let yourself in?!"

"I was loading some gear in the stables when I heard cries for help," he said.

"So you barged in and opened the pet carrier on the kitchen table?"

Mojo's good ear twitched approval. But his eye was focused on the enemy lurking in Beverley's bosom.

"How come you're always breaking into peoples' houses?" Lisa said.

"He was an expert in his teenage years." Beverley chuckled. "Hello, Scottie. Looking for business?"

Sharky curled his lips and growled.

"He certainly is not," Lisa snapped. "The job's cancelled."

Mojo crouched low and hissed.

"What?" Scott was bemused. "I've ordered a front-end loader."

"I thought we were just at the planning stage," Lisa said.

"So did I. That's why I ordered the front-end loader, to get an idea of the out-lines. . . ."

Yapping, Sharky shook his head and wriggled. Two white paws appeared over the top of Beverley's zipper.

"Well, go ahead and un-order it."

Dexter took his handkerchief from his pocket and dabbed his forehead. "Now the formalities are sorted, I'd like to discuss Chapter One. . . ."

Sharky sprang into the air, forming a perfect arc. He landed a few inches in front of Mojo and drew back in momentary alarm. It was Sharky's first encounter with a one-eyed, half bald, lion cat.

"Scottie, you'd better pick that thing up before it gets shredded," Beverley said in a measured tone. "Sharky hates cats."

The two animals sized each other up. Mojo was taller than the snarling ball of wool. His muscles rippled under his skin. Sharky emitted a falsetto growl and lunged.

Scott bent to grab Mojo, but the cat slid through his hands and charged at the dog. Yipping pitifully, Sharky turned on his tail. A white streak zigzagged through the chairs and tables. The small ginger lion was gaining on him.

"Mojo, *stop*!" Lisa yelled.

But after years in the wild, her new pet wasn't about to be humiliated by a wad of yapping cotton wool. Gathering speed, Sharky executed another circuit of the room and dived into the comforting depths of Beverley's cleavage.

Mojo sailed after him, colliding midair with Beverley's hardback copy of *Three Sisters: Charlotte.*

"Get that thing out of here!" Beverley commanded, replacing the book on the table and zipping up her top. Sharky squirmed and settled in a lump, giving Beverley the appearance of having three breasts.

Momentarily stunned from the impact, Mojo crumpled on the floor. Lisa gathered him up and shut him in the library.

When she returned, the Women's Monthly had regained composure. Scott had mercifully shoved off.

"Anyone for tea?" she asked.

"Actually . . ." Beverley said.

Lisa set her jaw. She'd had enough of Beverley to last several lifetimes.

"I think you're wrong about the book, Dexter," Beverley continued. "It's hilarious."

"You liked it?" Lisa asked, astounded.

"Hell yeah. And the sex is a hoot."

Beverley wasn't a monster in pink sequins after all.

The Women's Monthly squirmed in silence.

"She's right," Juliet finally chimed in. "Maybe you're not the target market, Dexter. I loved it, too."

CHAPTER 23

Lisa woke next morning with a powder puff in her face. She tried to blow it away, but it pressed against her nose. She pushed it off and rolled over. Something brushed her lips. Whatever it was had moved to the other side of the pillow. It padded each of her eyelids, urging them to open. A mane of scraggy fur came into focus. An amber eye glowed like an off-center sun. She removed the earplugs. They were useless against the insomniac kookaburra colony, anyway.

Mojo gave a gentle meow.

"Hello there," she said, stroking his forehead. She was pleased he wasn't a person she had to be careful not to breathe on in case she had bad breath. Jake always winced and closed his mouth when she kissed him in the mornings.

Mojo's purr reverberated up her arm into her chest. He looked more like a circus animal than a pet, but she was grateful for his presence. The business of finding hu-man friends was too complicated. While Lisa hadn't warmed to the Brontës' father, Patrick, she was beginning to understand him better. Soon after his wife's death he told a friend, "In this place I have received civilities, and have, I trust, been civil to all, but I have not tried to make any friends, nor have I met with any whose mind was congenial with my own." The Brontë sisters had also been famously antisocial. A modern psychiatrist would have had a field day with them. Emily muttered. Anne was "reserved even with her nearest of kin" (social anxiety disorder?). Charlotte swiveled her chair and hid her face while she spoke (Asperger's?). Severed from the outside world since birth, the Brontë sisters had minimal interest in anyone beyond family. Ordinary life was dull compared to the wild universes they shared in their imaginations. If they'd been medicated into chattier, more "normal" young women, they would never have penned masterpieces.

Usually by this time of day the Gray Army would be scraping away in the guest bed-room. Ted and James had chosen the décor, being her most regular visitors. Flocked gold wallpaper and a king-sized four-poster bed from the Restorers Barn wasn't her usual style, but the boys were excited. But today, the old boys were taking the day off from wallpapering to go to a funeral in Daylesford. Twenty-four hours of glorious solitude spread out before Lisa.

Mojo bounced off the bedcovers and asked to be let out onto the balcony. As she opened the doors, a sharp eucalyptus scent tickled her nose. Sunlight tipped the trees with 24-karat gold. Cool air filled her lungs. The resident cockatoo waddled through the long grass where Scott had talked of putting a pergola.

Mojo pranced toward her and wove a figure eight around her legs. He arched his back and shivered with delight as she stroked his spine. As she stooped to pick him up, he squirmed out of her grasp. She was a little hurt he still refused to let her pick him up, even without the burden of his matted coat. He was doing it either from habit or because he refused to relinquish independence. Still, dancing across the floorboards as if he couldn't believe he was loved, the cat was clearly heartbreakingly grateful to have a home.

She threw an old cardigan over her nightgown and headed downstairs. Mojo trotted after her, then sat mesmerized while she sliced a piece of chicken breast. When she put it in front of him, he hesitated, as if unworthy of such a banquet.

"Go on," she said, chomping through a leftover egg sandwich.

The cat devoured the chicken with appreciative wet noises before licking the bowl clean. Then he sprang onto her lap and purred prettily. Mojo placed his paw on her hand and gazed up at her as if she were the moon and the stars combined.

She'd read that blinking is the way cats express love. She blinked at him. He winked in return.

"I love you, too, Mojo." People were impossible. Thank God for cats.

They were interrupted by a tap at the back door. Lisa ran a hand through her hair. If the caller was selling anything, one glimpse of her would scare him or her off.

She opened the door. Her breath froze. Scott stood on the step looking solemn and well scrubbed.

"Don't worry," he said, studiously avoiding looking at her attire. "I parked on the road. I've just come to get my stuff from the stables, if that's okay."

"Sure," she said. "What's in there?"

"Just a couple of spades and a rake."

"Okay. Wait. I'll get them." The last thing she wanted to do was go near the stables, let alone *inside* them, but Scott had done enough snooping around her property.

"Cute cat you've got there," Scott said, crouching and clicking his fingers. "It *is* a cat?"

To her annoyance, Mojo raised his lion's tail and trotted over to Scott, then, purring loudly, butted his head into Scott's hand.

Lisa stepped into her UGG boots, strode across the yard, and pushed open the stable door. Inside, the air was dark and dry like an Egyptian tomb. The smell of ancient timber mingled with rotting hay, creating an earthy perfume. As her eyes adjusted to the darkness, she could make out hefty beams running across the ceiling. Lisa wondered what "terrible accident" could've happened there. A row of three chest-high doors drifted on their hinges. Shivers ran across her shoulders as she walked past the stalls. She could almost hear the neighs of ghostly stallions.

Where had Scott left his damned spades? Lisa made out the shape of a wheelbarrow and some tools leaning against the back wall. She shuffled toward them, but her foot collided with a bucket. There was a clunk. For a moment, she thought nothing was going to happen. She'd simply continue her journey to the wheelbarrow. Then she felt a crunching sensation as her foot rolled sideways. The bucket flew forward. She extended an arm, not to catch it, but because she was falling. The instinct to reach out and break a fall was natural, but hadn't she read somewhere that it was the wrong thing to do? That people broke their wrists or caused other dire injuries when they landed on their hands? But what, she thought, as she succumbed to gravity's force, were the alternatives? Landing on her head or shoulders? Surely concussion or shoulder surgery would be worse than a broken wrist? Then again, wasn't she supposed to curl up like a caterpillar and roll?

As she crashed to the stable floor, her wrist twanged like a guitar string. The soil was hard and unforgiving after years of being trampled by horses' hooves. Her knees felt raw. Her ankle throbbed. A burning sensation ran up her right arm.

She'd landed in this ridiculous position with speed and efficiency. Getting out of it was going to be more complicated. One thing was sure. She wasn't going to do the "helpless woman" thing and cry out for Scott.

A ladder reared up in front of her, lit by a cone of light admitted through a hole in the roof. It was missing several rungs and looked as fragile as an old woman's spine, but with any luck it would be solid enough for Lisa to pull herself up on. But as she reached for the ladder with her good arm, she felt something soft ripple across her lower leg. It moved with the delicate touch of a masseur.

Lisa glanced down. A shape resembling one of Aunt Caroline's draft stoppers was slithering over her calf. Reptilian scales glistened in the half-light.

She screamed. The guttural yells she'd barked at Jake were nothing compared to this. It was pure, distilled terror.

The door burst open, and the stables were flooded with light. Scott ran toward her. She pointed to the snake's tail sliding under the wheelbarrow.

Scott put his hands on his hips and smiled. "*That's* all?!" He laughed. "It's just an old brown snake."

"Only the second most venomous snake in the world." Lisa had been indulging in bedtime reading of *Australia's Deadliest Animals.*

"Yeah. I've been handling these things since I was a kid. This hot weather makes them more active. Here . . ." He reached for her good arm and helped her to her feet.

She pulled her nightgown over her knees.

"Anything broken?"

She didn't think so.

"He'll be in here looking for mice and stuff." Scott strode over to the corner and grabbed a spade.

"No!" Lisa was horrified.

"I'm not going to *kill* him! I'll just take him outside."

Who did he think he was — Steve Irwin? She hobbled across the floor to the horse stalls and nursed her wrist.

"Now, where are you, old fella?" Scott chirped as he moved the wheelbarrow away from the wall. "Time to come out."

The snake had arranged itself in a straight line and was gliding discreetly across the floor toward the ladder.

"Wow! He's a big fella," Scott called. "Nearly six foot long, I reckon." He stood with his legs apart, knees bent in what seemed to Lisa a vulnerable pose. "The trick is to get them by the tail." Scott's voice was higher than usual, his breathing shallow with excitement.

The snake undulated swiftly across the floor. Scott grabbed the tip of its tail and raised his arm. "Look at that!" he called.

Lisa pretended not to be impressed by this display of macho exhibitionism.

The reptile coiled back and with an elegant swoop tried to strike his captor.

"He's cranky with me," Scott said, dropping the snake onto the floor.

The snake coiled into an *S* shape. Raising its head, it opened the red diamond of its mouth and confronted Scott.

"See? See that? That's what they do when they're going to . . . *OWWWW!*" Scott doubled over.

The snake put its head down and slithered out the door.

"My God! Are you all right?" Lisa hurried over. Scott was cringing over two small puncture wounds just below the line of his shorts. "Lucky it didn't go any higher," he whimpered.

According to *Australia's Deadliest Animals*, victims of the brown snake can collapse within minutes. Lisa's wrist wasn't hurting anymore. Nor was anything else. "What should I do?" she asked. "Aren't I supposed to suck it?"

"Not this time," he said. Pain hadn't deadened his irony-laced sense of humor. "Have you got a bandage?"

"What sort of bandage?"

"A *bandage* bandage. A tourniquet."

She tore off her cardigan and wrapped the arms around his thigh and knotted them together as tightly as possible.

"Is that a new nightie?" He had to be delirious. He needed an ambulance. But she had no idea how far away the nearest hospital was. Scott could be dead by the time paramedics arrived.

Lisa grabbed Scott's elbow, hurried him out to Dino, and bundled him into the passenger seat. There was no time to change. She dashed inside and threw a parka over her nightie. Hands trembling, she grabbed her handbag and fumbled for the keys. For once they were where she thought she'd left them. She galloped outside and drove a whining, moaning Scott to the medical center.

She recognized the receptionist from the book club. "Your timing's good." June cast an eye over Lisa's attire. "We've just opened."

"He wasn't staying over," Lisa explained. "He was just collecting his stuff. And I went into the stables. . . ."

June twisted her mouth. She wanted to know the color and the size of the snake. Scott said it was brown and at least two meters. She escorted them to a small room. It had a bed, a steel chair, and an array of tubes and boxes.

Lisa's mistrust of the medical profession stemmed back to childhood, when the doctor had promised that having her tonsils out would be fun because there'd be ice cream afterward.

The nurse told Scott to sit on the bed rather than lie, to keep the bite below his heart. "Take his boots and socks off," she said. "Keep him calm. Don't let him move. The doctor will be here in a tick."

Lisa knelt on the floor and untied Scott's boots. He watched as she slipped the laces out of their holes. She loosened the heels and placed the boots under the bed. He asked how her wrist was. It was fine. She asked if there was anyone he wanted her to call.

He shook his head. "I made a dick of myself," he muttered.

She told him he hadn't and rolled his big woolly socks down his legs. She'd never touched them before. The muscles were hard under the surface of skin and hair. She asked how he was feeling.

"Like I'm on one of those rides at Luna Park." His breathing was shallow. His forehead gleamed. "Look, I'm sorry about this," he said. "I didn't mean . . ."

"It's okay, Scott," she soothed. "Have you ever done yoga breathing?"

"What's that?"

"Keep nice and still; that's it. Breathe

through your nose. Take it deep into your diaphragm . . . in, two, three, four . . ."

His eyes flashed wildly over the ceiling. "There're spots in front of my eyes!"

She looked up. "Those are *real* spots, Scott. The ceiling tiles have little holes in them."

He rubbed the back of his hand across his nose. "I might be going to snuff it, and there're a couple of things you should know."

His strength seemed to be waning. She wondered if she should press the red button on the wall behind his bed.

"Don't worry about ghosts and stuff," he said. "Some bloke shot himself in the stables once, that's all. It was years ago. . . . It's how they dealt with depression in those days."

"Really? What about the Wrights?"

"They're just old and nutty." His voice trailed off.

"The other thing is . . ." He drew a jagged breath. "I think . . ."

Lisa leaned forward to catch what he was saying.

"You're spunky."

She sprang back.

"And beautiful," he whispered.

He latched his hand over her shoulder and

drew her toward him. To her astonishment, he pressed his lips to hers. The room, with all its stainless steel surgical feel, melted around her. Erotic syrups coursed through her and blossomed in places that had been asleep for years. He was hallucinating because of the snakebite, obviously. But the sensations were so unfamiliar and delicious she was overcome by the urge to reciprocate. She closed her eyes, latched her arms around his tree-trunk neck, and let her mouth move softly against his. Relishing the sensations of desire, she thought that this must be how astronauts feel when, after long journeys through space, their feet finally touch earth again. Or how a desert feels in a deluge, after years of drought. She was alive. Her teeth scraped against his. Clumsy. She was out of practice.

He pretended not to notice.

"Excuse me." The voice was cold, disapproving.

Lisa tried to disentangle herself. Scott held on.

A man with the face of a boxer dog peered around the door. "The patient needs complete rest," the doctor said. "Could you wait outside, please?"

Scott groaned and released his grip.

Lisa rearranged her parka and clumped

down the corridor to the waiting room. Thumbing through a March 2007 issue of *Women's Weekly,* she went cold with panic. If Scott really was dying, she needed to tell him a few things, too:

- For all his issues, he had a good heart.
- She would've been stranded in the flood if he hadn't shown up.
- If it hadn't been for him she'd never have met the Gray Army. Well, she might have, ultimately, but it would've taken longer.
- That she'd probably overreacted about his letting himself into the house a few times.
- His ideas for the garden were inspired. She'd been mean to correct his pronunciation of *pergola.*
- She'd also been stupid to fire him.

Lisa promised herself that, if he survived and things went any further, she'd tell him about the mastectomy. Which would scare him off permanently.

An old woman shuffled into the waiting room. First patient of the day, she eyed Lisa's outlandish getup.

"Emergency," Lisa explained.

The woman slid an iPhone from her

pocket and started playing Candy Crush.

Target would be open by now. Lisa wondered if there was time to drive over and pick up a sweatshirt and track pants. It'd only take ten minutes. But just as Lisa stood to leave, the doctor emerged, holding a clipboard. She scanned his body language for signs of triumph or defeat.

"Is he going to be okay?"

The doctor scribbled something on his clipboard.

"It was a dry bite."

"What does that mean?"

"He's lucky. The snake didn't inject any venom. Still, I'd like to keep him here for the rest of the day."

CHAPTER 24

Lisa pulled up the driveway and stepped out of Dino with caution. A cockatoo screeched. There was no sign of the snake. She wondered how Mojo had survived in the wild so long, and exactly how he'd lost that eye.

After a shower, she slipped into a summer dress festooned with roses, the Scarlett O'Hara one she had thought she'd never wear. It suited her mood somehow.

Scott's ute was still on the side of the road. She'd bring him back from the clinic later. And who knows? He might not be going home tonight.

She made a cup of instant coffee and settled at the kitchen table to work. Sunlight bore through the windows. The room was heating up. Normally, she'd open the back door, but it was hotter outside than in. Besides which, she didn't want impromptu visits from the snake. She set up a table fan and pointed it at her face.

Mojo padded across the bluestone, and put his head to one side.

"Scott's fine, if that's what you're asking."

The cat sprang onto the table and tried to sit on her keyboard. She lifted him onto the floor. He jumped back on the table, this time knocking the fan. She lowered him down. He jumped back. . . .

"If this doesn't stop, you'll have to go outside."

Mojo sprang up onto her lap, turned around three times, and nestled in. Lisa rubbed his ears. He was learning to be a writer's cat.

The Brontë parsonage had never been short of pets. Though the whole family had adored animals, nobody had loved them more than Emily. Her portrait of Grasper, one of the parsonage dogs, was full of loving detail, each hair and whisker defined. Grasper's bright-eyed expectancy leaped off the page, even today.

Emily's favorite had been a bullmastiff called Keeper. She had painted him lying on a tuft of grass, his globe of a head resting on his front paws, apparently transfixed by something just off the page. The power in his shoulders was palpable; Keeper was not a dog to mess with. The adoration had been mutual. After poor Emily died, Keeper had lain at the feet of the mourners in church and listened to the service. Keeper's sorrow had run deep — with that sense of knowing some dogs have, he had moaned outside her empty bedroom for nights on end.

Lisa tapped away, and for a couple of hours the words flowed. Emily dumped the earl, who was so heartbroken he sold everything and up and moved to America. After his lovemaking sessions with Emily, Frederick cooked superb broths, dumplings, and stews. Emily stopped using food as a psychological weapon against those who loved her, instead filling out a little and taking on a healthy glow.

Lisa carried her phone and a plate of stale egg sandwiches outside onto the veranda. Mojo followed and sat on the sofa beside her. The wind was like the inside of a clothes drier. New York could be unbearable in summer, when warmth radiated off the streets and buildings, but this Australian heat rushed in straight from the desert.

She called the medical center. June informed her Scott was doing well and would be ready to go home around five o'clock. Putting the phone aside, she had another go at the sandwiches. They were inedible. She tossed a crust into the long grass. A flash of white shot after it.

"Hello there!"

A yellow crest fanned above the blades. She tossed another crust. The cockatoo gobbled it up. Meanwhile, Mojo sat watching the parrot with the intensity of a judge of *Australia's Got Talent.* To Lisa's alarm, the bird waddled toward them and hopped up the step. She rested her hand on Mojo's back in case he was getting ideas about Thanksgiving's arriving early.

The parrot fixed them with a brilliant gaze. He wasn't afraid. Lisa wondered whether the cat knew the bird from his previous life in the wild. The bird was no pushover, if his claws and beak were anything to go by.

"Well, I'm pleased someone likes my egg sandwiches," she said, emptying the rest of her plate over the step.

The cockatoo relished the egg as much as the bread, putting its beak to one side to hoover up the last crumb. Then, satisfied there was no more food on offer, it hopped down the step and waddled back toward the grass.

"See you again!"

The bird stopped, turned, and spread its

wings in what looked like a gesture of thanks.

"You're welcome."

She waited for it to take flight. The wings flapped in a glorious display of pastel yellow feathers, but the bird didn't take to the air. This had to be the same cockatoo that had been hanging around the property ever since she'd moved in. It was always alone. The flock it belonged to had probably rejected it when it couldn't keep up with them. The parrot must've been fighting for survival since it was first injured.

Lisa went inside and tried to settle into the next chapter, but the hot wind made her restless. Besides, she couldn't wait to tell Scott about the cockatoo. Finally, she turned off her computer, circled her mouth with regulation neutral lipstick, fired up Dino, and spun into town.

At the clinic, June greeted her with a sardonic smile. "He's not here. Discharged himself an hour ago."

When Lisa arrived back at the house, the only evidence of his ute was tire marks in the dust. She reached for her phone. Her finger hesitated over his number. Portia's voice lectured inside her head: *It's political, Mom.* Lisa's thumb scrolled down from Scott to Takeaway Pizza. She ordered mush-

296

room and cheese and, with Mojo on her knee, resigned herself to a night of BBC costume dramas.

CHAPTER 25

Lisa was in bed with Mr. Rochester when Beverley showed up wielding a flaming torch. "I was lying when I said I liked your book," Beverley said before setting fire to the sheets. "It's bloody rubbish." Lisa woke yelling at Mr. Rochester to find a chamber pot to douse the flames.

A miniature lion came into focus on the pillow next to hers. Mojo seemed curious rather than frightened by her shouting. Human behavior was clearly crazier than anything he'd seen in the bush. She stroked his spine. His fur was beginning to grow back in the form of handsome ginger fuzz. "Honestly, Mojo. The sooner I finish this trilogy, the better. These women are driving me crazy."

As the dream faded, the smell of smoke refused to dissipate. She rolled out of bed, stood at the top of the stairs, and sniffed. Maybe she'd left the oven on. To her relief, the smoke didn't seem to be coming from downstairs. Yet it hung heavy in the air. Her eyes prickled. She'd closed the balcony shutters the previous night because of the wind. Mojo jumped off the bed and trotted after her. She opened the latch and stepped onto another planet.

A red blister of sun glowered in a charcoal haze that engulfed the valley. Lisa could see no farther than the silhouettes of gum trees at the end of the paddock. Flocks of birds squealed overhead. A mob of kangaroos bolted across the grass. The animals were all headed in one direction — away from the Wrights' property and past hers. She worried for the cockatoo. How would he escape without wings?

She coughed. The smoke was laced with eucalyptus and getting thicker. She stood on tiptoe and peered over the trees along her driveway. Tongues of fire rose from the pine trees behind the Wrights' house. They crackled brilliant reds and yellows into a shroud of dense black smoke. Cinders surfed the wind toward her house.

Running inside, she grabbed her phone from the bedside table. The charger was hanging half out of the wall socket. It was out of juice. She fought the urge to scream and curl up in a ball. A cool logic settled

over her, and she tried to remember everything she'd heard or read about bush fires.
She was in no position to defend her property alone, she realized. Her best bet was to
flee.

She threw on a coat and the purple beanie.
Somewhere she'd read that for all the high-
tech fabrics around, wool was still one of
the safest in a fire. She slid into her elastic-
sided boots. Swooping Mojo into her arms,
she ran downstairs. The pet container was
still on the kitchen table. She slid him into
it and whisked her keys off the window
ledge.

As she opened the back door, the hot wind
blasted her face, roasting her cheeks and
searing the back of her mouth. She
squinted, scanning the garden for the cockatoo. There was no sign of him.

She closed the door and filled a water
bottle. While the tap was on, she doused a
tea towel in cold water and tied it under her
eyes. The bank-robber look could be the
next big thing in Milan, for all she knew.

Her hand rested on the tap. If she was
about to lose her worldly possessions, the
choices weren't difficult. On the laptop, she
summoned the manuscript for *Three Sisters:
Emily* and saved it onto a memory stick.
Then, with two-thirds of her next book

dangling around her neck, she hurried to Alexander's room and lifted his photo from the mantelpiece. Grabbing Mojo's carry case, she rushed from the house and clambered into Dino.

The car grumbled to life. She spun out onto the main road. To her horror, the fire had already crossed the road. Several trees at the entrance to her driveway were flaring like candles. The Wrights' drive was an avenue of flames. Though their house seemed intact, clouds of smoke were wafting from the guttering. Surely the old couple had left for a safe haven? She pressed the accelerator to roar into town. Then she saw the Holden in their driveway. She peered at the cottage. Something moved in one of the windows. It was almost certainly a hand.

Crouching over Dino's steering wheel, she stamped the accelerator and roared toward the cottage.

The car skidded to a halt outside the Wrights' back door. Lisa leaped out and ran up the steps. The door was locked. She ran into the garden and seized a gnome from under the birdbath. Immune to the drama of the situation, the statue grinned back at her. Wielding the concrete ornament, she ran up to the back door and hurled it through the glass. It shattered with a satisfying clash. Lisa slithered her forearm through the remaining glass daggers and turned the lock.

The air inside the house was heavy with smoke. "Mrs. Wright?" she called.

No response. A siren wailed in the distance.

Lisa strode down the hallway to the living room. A photo of a dark-haired child smiled from the wall. An unfinished crochet rug sprawled over a chair.

"Help! Please! Help me!" It was a woman's voice.

Lisa sprinted across the hall to the bedroom.

Mr. Wright lay unconscious on the floor. A frail old woman was kneeling at his side, holding his hand. They were surrounded by piles of old newspapers, boxes, and broken furniture — perfect fuel for an inferno. It appeared the Wrights were hoarders. A single spark would barbecue them all.

"We were trying to get out, but he fell," the old woman wailed. "It's his hip."

"Come with me!"

"I'm not going without him!" the old woman shouted, clinging to her husband.

Lisa's forehead drowned in sweat. The house seemed on the brink of explosion.

Lisa assessed the old man's body weight. He wasn't heavily built, and much of his muscle had shriveled with age. She bent down and raised his torso off the floor. It felt doable, as Ted would say. But as she heaved Mr. Wright over her shoulder and tried to stand up, his dead weight was too much. She wobbled, then flopped him onto the bed.

"Leave us here!" the old woman sobbed. "Just *go!*"

Desperate, Lisa cast about the room. An old-fashioned stroller with fat rubber wheels groaned under a pile of newspapers in the corner. She jettisoned the newspapers and dragged Mr. Wright off the bed before draping his limp frame over the stroller. Then she threw a blanket over him.

"Come with us *now!*" she urged, wrapping the old woman in another blanket and bundling her down the hallway.

Once she'd helped Mrs. Wright down the steps and into Dino's front seat, Lisa sprinted back inside for the stroller. As she negotiated it down the first step, Mr. Wright's limp form slid forward. He was in danger of toppling off the pram and straight onto the concrete path below. Summoning all her strength, she heaved the front wheels up and eased the stroller down step by step.

When they reached the path, she turned and looked back at the cottage. Flames were shooting through the roof.

She opened Dino's rear door, seized Mr. Wright under his armpits, and dragged him into the back of the car. Uncertain if he was alive, she curled him on his side like a fetus and placed the blanket over him.

She stamped on the accelerator, and they roared back up the driveway to the main road.

When two fire engines whined to a halt in front of them, she almost collapsed with relief. The first engine swerved and zoomed down the Wrights' drive. Yellow-clad firemen leaped out of the second fire engine and started dousing the trees on the manor's side of the road.

A sturdy fireman swaggered toward Lisa and rested his elbow on Dino's roof. She wound her window down and tore the tea towel off her face. It was no longer damp.

"Bit early in the fire season for this sort of thing," he said, grinning.

CHAPTER 26

When Charlotte Brontë wrote about fire in
Jane Eyre, she had the luxury of symbol-
ism. To Charlotte, fire represented sex and
passion, cleansing and renewal. For Lisa,
when she was finally able to return home, it
was heartache. While she'd been over at the
Wrights' cottage, the inferno had raged
down her driveway and engulfed the stables.
The stables' roof had collapsed, leaving a
smoldering ruin. The blaze had then arced
across to the servants' quarters at the back
of the manor. Another fire truck had arrived
just in time to stop the flames from spreading to the kitchen in the main house.

In the meantime, embers had rained down
on the front paddock, causing the dry grass
to explode into flames. Firefighters had
done what they could, but the fire had run
rampant until it reached the natural barrier
of the river.

With the main house out of danger, the

team had turned their attention to the spot fires on the other side of the river, but just as it seemed the conflagration might leap the water and roar through the valley toward town, the wind had changed direction and dropped.

By Australian standards, it was a small fire covering just a few acres and had been quickly extinguished. Yet the devastation was going to take months, possibly even years, to recover from.

News was back from the hospital that Mr. Wright's condition was serious due to smoke inhalation. Mrs. Wright was in shock and dehydrated, but would probably be okay. Their house had been checked out, too. Though it was badly damaged, it was repairable.

Now the firefighters finished packing up their equipment. Humbled by their courage and cheerful pragmatism, Lisa hugged them one after the other. They waved as they drove off to check properties on the other side of the ridge.

After they'd gone, Lisa took Mojo's carry case from the car and stood on the veranda. The air was hazy and heavy. Her front paddock was a blackened desert. Ravaged trees were etched against a tangerine sky. The cockatoo wouldn't have stood a chance. The stables and servants' quarters were destroyed. Her front garden was razed. She'd nearly lost the house she could hardly afford in the first place.

Sobs jagged from her lungs and echoed across the valley. Somewhere in her head she heard Aunt Caroline's voice. *Pull yourself together, girl.* Where was Scott when Lisa needed him?

She crouched and flicked the latches on Mojo's carry case. He stepped onto the veranda and lifted his nose. With tail looped close to the ground, the cat padded down the steps and sniffed the smoking grass. Head to one side, he extended a cautious paw and dabbed the blackened soil. Then the lion cat shook himself, as if this changed world were beyond comprehension, and crept back up the steps and inside the house.

Lisa walked around the side of the manor. Charred beams jutted like ribs from what was left of the stables. Amid the smoldering wreckage, a door to a horse stall swung from the outline of a frame. The servants' quarters were a blackened skeleton. Empty windows stared back at her. The extension would've fared better if it'd been made of brick like the rest of the house.

To her amazement, the firefighters had managed to save the orchard. The apple tree spread its fresh green branches in astonishment.

Numb to the core, she walked to the end of the driveway. All her favorite trees — the magnolia, the wattles, and the gums — had been reduced to charred sticks. The fire had ripped through at breathtaking speed. Leaves, scrub, everything that had been green was now gray. Lisa felt like a character in a children's book who'd stepped through a portal into a black and silver world. Charcoal tree trunks rose from ashen earth. Maxine had been right all along. People who came to Castlemaine with big dreams were destined to fail.

Lisa hugged herself. Her skin was black and sticky — she needed a shower. As she turned to go back to the house she noticed a shape huddled near the base of a burnt-out tree trunk. It looked like some sort of animal. She tramped through the ash toward it.

To her astonishment, it was a human form, crouched on the ground with its back to her. It was a man wearing a dark-brown hoodie.

Scott turned and looked up at her. He put his finger to his lips and beckoned her over. Branches crackled under her feet. As she drew closer, she saw the focus of his attention. Sitting on the bush floor in front of him was a bewildered koala.

"You okay?" he said under his breath.

She nodded.

"Sorry I didn't get here sooner, but I had to check on Todd. They live out this way."

She should've guessed.

"Is he all right?"

"He's fine. They saved your house."

She glanced back at the silhouette of the manor. Standing proud in the gritty air, it reminded her of photos of the blitz of London in World War II. "Only just."

"I parked on the road. I know you have a thing about my barging in. . . ."

"No," she said softly. "Not anymore."

"I heard what you did for the old people. That's incredible."

She ached for him to stand up and encircle her in his arms. But that would just make her howl her eyes out. It was a good thing at least half his attention was on the koala.

The animal gazed up at them through black button eyes. With his furry, rounded ears he was as cute as a gray teddy bear. The white fur on the underside of his chin extended down his chest, giving him a sort of baby's bib. His leathery nose had a painful raw patch.

The koala turned and plodded away in a

bandy-legged waddle.

"He's disoriented," Scott said as the koala stopped beside a blackened tree trunk and sat down. Scott slid a bottle of water from his pocket, and stepped slowly toward the animal. The koala didn't move. Scott crouched beside him and ran his hand over the koala's sloping forehead. "You're thirsty, boy, aren't you?" he said, unscrewing the lid and tilting the bottle against the animal's mouth.

Understanding what was being offered, the creature raised its head and gulped the liquid.

"There you go," Scott crooned with tenderness Lisa hadn't heard before. "He's dehydrated."

The water level sank in steady chugs. Lisa's heart turned to butter when the koala raised his paw and rested it on Scott's hand. This was a different Scott. His voice was soft, every movement gentle and considered. He seemed to have tuned in to the koala on a level beyond words.

"We need to take him into the shelter," Scott said. "The pads of his paws are burned."

"Does that mean he'll spend the rest of his life in a zoo?"

"No way! He's lost his habitat, but we'll

find him another home close by. Won't we, boy?"

The bottle was nearly drained. "Can you grab me another one?" he asked quietly. "And a towel."

Lisa sprinted back to the house and refilled her own water bottle. She ran upstairs and snatched her towel from the bathroom. The house reeked of smoke, but she thanked God most of it was still intact.

"How did you know he needed water?" Lisa asked as the koala started on the second bottle.

"I've done a bit of wildlife rescue — not that you'd know from the business with the snake."

"Really? I worked in a shelter in New York. Nothing glamorous. Cats, dogs . . . the occasional crocodile."

"There's an orphaned wallaby in the back of the ute," he said. "His hind legs need dressing."

"Can I see him?"

She watched in awe as Scott wrapped the towel around the koala with the gentleness of a midwife handling a newborn. He stood up with liquid ease and, cradling the koala, crunched across the smoking earth.

"Come over here," he called.

The back of the ute was covered with a

silvery tarpaulin. Scott lifted a corner of the cover. Two large ears and liquid eyes appeared from under a blanket. "I've brought you a mate," he said, lowering the koala into a cardboard box next to the kangaroo.

Lisa noticed a dome-shaped blanket on the passenger seat and asked what it was.

Scott replaced the tarp. "You'll like that one." He strode around to the ute door and lifted the blanket. Inside the cage sat a cockatoo, its yellow crest flattened against its head. "I found her waddling around the orchard," he said. "At least, I *think* it's a she."

"How can you tell?"

"Females have dark red eyes. The males' eyes are blacker. Hard to tell with cockatoos, though. Only way to be sure is to take them to McDonald's and see which toilet they go into."

The parrot tilted her head and blinked at Lisa. She offered a tentative hand. The parrot bowed and rubbed her scalp against Lisa's finger.

"She's okay," he added. "But I reckon one of her wings is damaged. She can't fly."

Lisa broke into smiles. Tears of gratitude streamed down her blackened cheeks. "I know this bird!"

■ ■ ■ ■

Later that night Lisa took a long shower. The water turned charcoal gray as it poured off her body. Her throat felt burned. She shampooed twice. It was going to take forever to get rid of the smell of smoke. After the shower, she filled the bath with lukewarm water. Sinking into the depths, she thought of Scott. Maybe she'd been too quick to jump to conclusions about him. Perhaps his ravings at the medical center meant something. Dipping her head under the water, she hoped she'd done the right thing accepting his invitation to visit the animal shelter in the morning. Whatever happened, she was going to need his help with the garden.

She rose early the next day. Relieved to have an excuse to leave her decimated property, she climbed into Dino and rattled down what was left of her driveway. Scott's concept of "a couple of kilometers" along the road to Maldon turned out to be closer to ten. If Lisa hadn't been so anxious about missing the turnoff, she might've enjoyed resting her eyes on the green-gray country-side, the hum of the road unraveling under the tires.

She knew she'd reached the right place when she saw Scott's ute roughly parked in the gravel. The house was what she'd expected of Juliet — a wooden Edwardian villa nestled behind a tall hedge.

The gate opened with a gracious creak. Lisa made her way up a brick path lined with lavender bushes. A dream catcher swayed in the breeze. Scott's boots lay like a pair of drunken sailors under the step. She tapped on the door.

Juliet's shape appeared in a shaft of light beaming from the end of a woody corridor. "Is that you, Lisa? Come on in."

Lisa hesitated. Was it one of those quasi-spiritual shoeless houses? To be safe, she shook off her Mary Janes, the same ones she'd worn to the dance, and padded past sepia photos interspersed with splashes of modern art.

There was nothing fussy about the room at the end of the hall. Plates and babies' bottles were scattered over the workbench, waiting to be washed. A pile of laundry lay slumped in a basket on one of the chairs. A calendar from the Castlemaine Arts Fair hung above the toaster. Almost every day had a name scribbled on it.

"That's the volunteer roster," Juliet said. "Would you like to sign up?"

Lisa said she'd love to, once she'd finished her book, which would be soon. She asked after the koala. Juliet said she'd dressed the burns on his feet the night before. He was sedated and on a drip now. They were hoping for the best.

"Impressive work you do here," Lisa said.

"Oh, there are hundreds of shelters like this all over Australia," Juliet said, spooning instant coffee into mugs. "They're all run by trained volunteers like us." She smiled. "I hear you're a bit of a hero yourself."

Lisa's earlobes tingled. "You mean the Wrights? Oh, that was nothing. I just acted on instinct."

"I don't know what they would've done without you."

Lisa shrugged the compliment off. She was more interested in hearing about Juliet's shelter and the animals they rescued. Bush fires and road accidents were only part of the problem for native wildlife, Juliet explained. With every new subdivision, animal habitats were destroyed. As people built new homes for themselves, native animals lost theirs. "We do what we can to get them back on their feet and into the wild again," Juliet said, absentmindedly spiking up her hair. She was one of those women who could wear a sack and gum boots and still look like she was going to a fashion show.

Due to her time at Bideawee animal shelter, Lisa was no stranger to people doing great things for animals. But Juliet's dedication was awe-inspiring. Thanks to the roster system, when Juliet was working at the garden center, someone else would oversee the furry patients. Some baby animals needed feeding around the clock. Juliet's helpers often stayed over and set their alarms to make sure their wards didn't miss a feed.

"You have to be psychologically tough to do this work," Juliet said. "Some of the injuries are terrible. We lose a lot of animals. It can be devastating."

"Make mine a skinny soy latte." Scott grinned from a doorway.

Juliet laughed and handed him a steaming mug. He swamped it with four sugars. The teaspoon looked like a toothpick in his fingers as he clattered it about.

Lisa's gaze wandered to Juliet. Her pretty face glowed with affection as she watched Scott drown his coffee in milk. Then Scott caught Juliet's eye and gave her a knowing smile.

Heat prickled on Lisa's neck as she remembered the kiss in the doctor's surgery. Was there something between Scott and Juliet? How could she have been so stupid!

Lisa wasn't in love with Scott, anyway. She had no claim on him. He was hardly her type.

The words of Mr. Rochester echoed in her head. *You never felt jealousy, did you, Miss Eyre? Of course not: I need not ask you; because you never felt love.*

"By the way," Scott said after a loud slurp, "someone's waiting to see you." He clattered his mug on the bench and lifted a blanket-covered cage from under the table. "The vet took a look at her this morning. Her wing's damaged, but it's not too bad," Scott said, lifting the cover. "She might even learn to fly again."

The cockatoo dipped her head at Lisa and raised a claw in salute.

"If she can survive a fire and that cat of yours she'll get through anything," he added. "Take her home and see how she goes."

"You can come through and see the other animals, if you like," Juliet said. "Try to keep quiet. Noise startles them. And don't make any sudden movements."

Lisa followed Juliet and Scott to what would've been the back porch in the old days. The space had been enlarged and enclosed, and the windows shaded. Mattresses and boxes were arranged around the perimeter of the floor.

As Lisa's eyes adjusted to the dim light, she saw the outline of a wheelchair. In it sat a young man with long dark curls and looks that belonged on a movie screen. The teenager was cradling a wallaby and feeding it with a baby's bottle. The tender expression on his face was worthy of St. Francis.

"This is my son, Todd," Scott said, clearing his throat.

Todd looked up at Lisa with dark brown eyes and smiled.

CHAPTER 27

Later that night, Lisa stood on a chair and felt along the top shelf for the packet of Tim Tams she'd bought the other day. There was no point watching her figure anymore. She ripped the packet open, shoved two biscuits in her mouth, and eased herself back to ground level.

The cockatoo watched from her cage on the kitchen bench. Lisa broke a Tim Tam in half and poked a piece through the wire. The bird accepted the gift with a gracious claw. Lisa had grown fond of the parrot. It was a wild animal, though. She'd have to set it free to find a new home soon.

Mojo pounced on her lap as she sat in front of the computer. Running a hand through his mane, she reached for another biscuit. His tail flicked languidly. Tomorrow she would face the horrendous task of cleaning up after the fire. Tonight she needed to focus her attention elsewhere.

Emily knew it was over the day she found Frederick in the arms of Amy, the village barmaid.

"Farewell, Frederick," Emily said, concealing the ache in her heart.

"How can I live without you?" he cried.

"I imagine you and Amy will manage perfectly well."

His eyes turned dark as Guinness.

"And you, my love?" he asked, his eyes swimming with tears.

Emily straightened her shawl, turned away from him, and strode back across the moors. She went home to drown her hurt and rage in her inkpot. Man-free and in the prime of health, she produced the first of many great novels.

The End

Lisa thought she'd feel triumphant typing those last two words. She should've been overjoyed at finishing the book — a week before deadline, too. Instead, she felt like a dishrag wrung of its last drop of water. Now a week or two of redrafting weighed down on her. She couldn't face the thought of wading back through the manuscript, eyeballing the inadequacy of her writing on every page. Simpler to delete the whole file and send it whirling into cyberspace.

The biscuit packet was empty. She sank into a pool of guilt and made a cup of peppermint tea. It was hard to imagine why Scott had kept Todd hidden away from her like some shameful secret. He had every reason to be proud of his son. Wise and funny, Todd was a fantastic kid. She'd never seen a young person with such empathy with animals.

She could see Scott was fiercely protective of and devoted to Todd, though Scott had clearly been stretching the truth when he had spoken about taking Todd white-water rafting and horse riding. But that was hardly surprising. Her relationship with Scott — not that there was one — had been based on a series of lies from the start. Since seeing Scott and Juliet at the animal shelter that morning, Lisa had been piecing things together. No wonder Scott had shown up to work at her place when it suited him. All the stories about his son's needing him had been convenient excuses. He was in love with Juliet, who was an amazing woman. He had to be. He'd probably stayed countless nights at her place. No wonder Juliet had been on edge about Scott's taking Lisa to the bush dance. Obviously there was something going on between them.

It was past midnight by the time Lisa put a towel over the cockatoo's cage and climbed the stairs in Mojo's wake. Her heart was as heavy as one of the flagstones on her kitchen floor. The Brontë sisters knew how it felt to run away from a place with their tails between their legs. Charlotte hadn't been able to hack more than a few months as a governess. Emily had given up her teaching job in Halifax after six months. They had scuttled gratefully back to the moors.

Lisa had been nuts to move to this harsh country. She could barely afford to buy Trumperton Manor, let alone renovate it. The damage was going to cost a fortune to clean up. Her insurance didn't extend to bush fires. Now the stables were gone, she'd never find out what had happened there, because no one would talk to her as she had no friends anyway.

There was no option but to cut her losses and put the house on the market. Once it was sold, she'd buy a discount economy fare back to New York, where she'd probably spend the rest of her life as a bag lady. And to top it off, tomorrow was her birthday. Again.

She'd been so desperate to finish *Three*

Sisters: Emily, she'd told Maxine and Ted to keep away. Just as well: Lisa needed to conserve her energy more than ever now. Besides, there was no reason to celebrate the anniversary of Jake's walking out on her.

Collapsing into bed, Lisa fitted her mouth guard and earplugs, then lay on her side, waiting for the comforting *plonk* of Mojo's landing on the covers. As the cat snuggled into the bend of her knees, she dropped into a chasm of sleep.

Lisa was woken by Mojo's meowing and clawing at the curtains. She checked her phone and fought off disappointment: With California so many hours behind Australia, she couldn't expect a message from Portia this early. Lisa slipped into her kimono and opened the balcony doors. If only something magical had happened overnight. But the air smelled like the day after a cannibal feast, and the view that had once sent her soul soaring was now a source of dread.

Lisa's throat tightened at the sight of Maxine's Golf shimmering in the driveway. She relaxed a little when she saw the Kombi van parked behind it. Ted's alkali always neutralized Maxine's acid. To her surprise, Doug's old blue Honda now rattled down the drive. What was the Gray Army doing

323

there on their day off? A silver car glided in behind it, then another. She rubbed her eyes. It was some kind of invasion.

"Yoohoo!" Maxine called, waving up at her. "I've brought muffins."

Lisa waved a finger in return. She could see Ted and his friends at work gathering burned branches and dragging them down the driveway toward the road. A man she recognized from the bush dance lifted a chainsaw from the back of his truck. Doug directed him to the remains of a burned pine that was on the brink of toppling.

Lisa climbed into her bushwhacking pants and green check shirt from Target's menswear section. Her blue Cancer Council hat with a brim as wide as a coral reef completed the look. Hurrying downstairs to the kitchen, she stepped into her lace-up boots. She could hear the sound of more vehicles arriving.

The cockatoo squawked from under her towel. Lisa flicked the towel off. Agitated, the bird clawed the cage door. The poor creature craved freedom. As soon as Lisa pried the cage door open, the bird pushed her way out and flapped onto the floor.

Dexter from the Women's Monthly sailed through the back door, brandishing a bottle of whiskey. The cockatoo took the opportunity to waddle through his legs and hop down the steps.

"I think a peace offering's called for," Dexter said. "Single malt."

Whiskey made Lisa gag, but she appreciated the gesture. She took a glass from the cupboard.

"Heavens no! *Far* too early in the day for me," Dexter said. "I mean, what is it, ten o'clock?"

"10:37, to be precise." Maxine swooshed in and spread her arms like someone parking a plane. "Happy birthday!"

"Let's save it for another year," Lisa said, allowing herself to be crushed into Maxine's bosom. She waited for the inevitable tirade of "I told you so's."

"I'm so glad you're safe," Maxine whispered. "I'll put the kettle on. Gordon's organizing the traffic, telling them where to park and whatnot. Go outside and meet your people."

Her people? Mojo led Lisa out the back door. Dexter decided to stay inside and check that the whiskey hadn't gone off. A semicircle of figures stood around the blackened ruins of the servants' quarters.

A man with a face like a storm-ravaged cliff stepped forward to envelop her hand in his calloused paw. "I'm John from the hardware store," he said. "We'll tidy this up for you in a jiff. And this is Lawrie the electrician."

A man in his midthirties wearing what appeared to be a sock on his head gave her a friendly nod.

She glanced over their shoulders to the twenty or more men, women, and children raking ashes and wheeling barrows of burned wood out to the road. "You're very kind, but I can't afford . . ."

"This is nothing to do with money," Juliet interrupted. Juliet had tucked her hair into a red beret, and Lisa hadn't noticed her among the crowd. "We all know what you did for the Wrights," Juliet said. "We just want to say thanks."

"Yeah," added the man with the ginger mustache from the bush dance. "We're here to help."

Ted jogged down the drive, his feet flying at wild angles the way they always did. James was close on his heels, followed by Heidi and Stella. They wrapped her in their arms.

"Happy birthday!" Ted said, kissing her on both cheeks.

"Sssshhh!" Lisa said, glancing down at her boots.

"We've just about filled up a whole skip.

Another's on its way," Ted said. "These people are *amazing*!"

Lisa pulled up the edge of her collar and dabbed her tears.

"Snot alert!" Ted announced, handing her a crisp paper tissue from his pocket. "Seriously, Mom, this fire damage is a great opportunity."

"You sound like Oprah."

"The servants' wing was creepy, anyway. We'll pull down what's left and tidy up that area. Maybe someday we'll build a glamorous kitchen extension there. Meantime, James wants to put in an herb garden."

Ted offered to design a new building where the stables had been. Based on the original structure, it would be fully insulated and built to the highest environmental standards. Solar panels would be placed out of sight on the pitched roof. Tucked in the space where the hayloft once was would be what Ted called the honeymoon suite — a spacious guest room with its own bathroom. New plumbing would be part of a graywater system for the entire house. Used water from the kitchen and laundry would be treated and filtered, to be used on the garden. The ground floor of the new stables would provide generous storage for cars and equipment. It would be sealed to modern standards, a no-snake zone.

"It sounds wonderful but —"

Juliet interrupted. "All the tradesmen here are offering their services for free. And we're getting the materials at wholesale cost."

Lisa scrabbled for words. These people's hearts were wider than the desert.

"Think of it as a birthday present," Juliet added.

"Yeah, happy birthday!" John chimed in.

"Thanks. Just another day," Lisa said, blushing.

With Mojo leading the way, she walked down the driveway. At the roadside a group of people were working near a skip. Lisa's smile grew broader as they waved and called happy birthday. Dorothy Thatcher from the Women's Monthly was barely recognizable in walk shorts, a Hawaiian shirt, and a hat that looked like a UFO. She strode through the burned forest with the chainsaw man, pointing out branches that needed chopping.

"She's a qualified botanist," Juliet explained.

"You'll be able to keep a lot of these trees," Dorothy called as Lisa approached. "The Australian bush is extremely resilient. It's designed to catch fire every so often. You'll see regrowth on this trunk in a matter of weeks."

Aware that Dorothy was a friend of the Wrights, Lisa asked how they were getting on. Mr. Wright was out of danger, but still in serious condition, Dorothy informed her. Mrs. Wright was making steady progress. Though repairs to their cottage were already underway, it would be some time before they could move back in.

"Could I visit them in the hospital?" Lisa asked.

Dorothy reacted as if Lisa had asked to wear the crown jewels for a day. "Oh, they're swamped with visitors," Dorothy said quickly, before marching off in the direction of a large, blackened tree that was leaning perilously toward the ground. Producing an aerosol can, Dorothy sprayed a large white *X* on its trunk.

Lisa's attention was diverted by a wheelchair near the front of the house. She made excuses and hurried toward it, Mojo leading the charge. To her disappointment, it wasn't Scott hovering near Todd's wheelchair, but Beverley and an older woman.

When Todd saw Mojo, his face beamed. The boy seemed to carry the sun around with him. "Is that your cat, Mrs. Trumperton?"

"Yes, that's Mojo."

The cat circled the wheelchair, sniffing with interest.

"It's all right," Beverley said. "Sharky's in the car."

Mojo sprang onto Todd's lap and arched his back under the young man's hand.

"You should change his name to Leo," Todd said. "Shouldn't she, Nan?"

"Looks more like a pirate to me," the older woman remarked. "I'd call him Long John."

"Have you seen the cockatoo?" Lisa asked.

"She's round the back doing laps of an apple tree," Todd replied.

"You're the talk of the town," Todd's grandmother said to Lisa. "Usually takes three generations to get accepted around here."

"Yes, but my grandfather —"

"She writes a good yarn too." Beverley shaded her eyes and shot Lisa a brisk smile.

"I don't think Dexter agrees," Lisa said.

"Oh, don't worry about him. He's a nutty old wino."

A yellow bulldozer rumbled down the drive. "Bloody good thing you had that fire," Scott called over the purr of the motor. "Saved a fortune clearing the paddock. I'll go ahead and level it now. Still happy with that plan we drew up?"

"Yes, but . . ."

"Happy birthday, by the way." He winked. "What's your number?"

"Nothing you should know about," she replied.

"I was never any good at math, anyway," he said, gunning the motor. "I'll do an outline of the paths and the spa pool. We can change it as we go along."

He rattled off over the paddock, chewing up ash and stones under the caterpillar tread.

"You're putting in a spa pool?" Beverley asked.

CHAPTER 28

The volunteers finally packed up and went home. Scott parked the bulldozer in the paddock and left with Juliet in his ute. They looked happy together.

"Count your blessings," Maxine said as she arranged a picnic dinner in the orchard.

It was the sort of platitude that usually set Lisa's teeth on edge. But as rugs and cushions were spread under the apple tree, she knew Maxine was right. The generosity of her Castlemaine friends and her family had saved her. As her family and Ted's friends toasted her birthday, Lisa gulped back emotion. This birthday had been a considerable improvement on the one ending with a zero.

Gordon's hip was playing up again, so he went back to the car and produced a fold-out chair. Perched on it, he gazed over everyone's heads like a Shakespearian monarch bereft of a kingdom. Stella and

Heidi shook out another rug. Lisa was pleased when they asked Zack to join them. She worried about the boy. He seemed to use his camera as a shield against the world.

As they basked in shafts of late afternoon sun, James brought out trays of chicken pie and salad. "Those women left enough food to last a year," he said, pouring wine into glasses. "I won't have to cook another thing for you."

"Tell me that's not true," Lisa said, thinking of James's chocolate mousse.

Ted interrupted. "Look who's here!"

The cockatoo emerged from under a gorse bush and lumbered toward them. She stopped at the edge of Lisa's blanket and ogled her plate. Lisa tore off a corner of pastry and held out her hand.

The bird extended her neck, opened the great weapon of her beak, and swept the crust from Lisa's grasp.

"Strange pet," Maxine said. "What's its name?"

"She doesn't have one."

"If she can't fly we should call her Kiwi," Ted said, "in honor of our New Zealand friend."

The bird cawed approval.

Ted raised his glass. "While we're at it, I'd like to make an announcement."

"Watch out!" Lisa pointed to a shadow slinking through the trees. It was Mojo doing a commando crawl. He hid behind the trunk of a pear tree and focused his telescopic vision on the parrot.

"Those two are natural enemies," Heidi said under her breath.

Lisa was about to shoo Kiwi away when Mojo charged across the grass at the bird. Kiwi screeched, spread her wings, and eyeballed her assailant. Mojo skidded to a halt in front of her.

The human audience watched openmouthed as the two creatures circled each other, Mojo sliding close to the ground like a panther, Kiwi tall and haughty.

"The cat doesn't stand a chance," Heidi said, nudging her friends aside and quietly gathering up the blanket they'd been sitting on. "Have you seen the claws on that bird?"

Lisa's odds were on Mojo. He was one tough cat. Either way, it was inevitable: If something wasn't done about it, feathers or fur would fly.

Heidi crept toward the rivals and raised the rug. Her plan seemed to involve smothering the parrot and whisking her away to a safe haven — though exactly where that might be, Lisa had no idea. Besides which, a blanket of clawing, biting cockatoo could present its own problems.

Mojo and Kiwi continued their cautious dance around each other, their moves stately, almost formal. The atmosphere was charged. Any moment now . . .

Heidi prepared to dive.

The cockatoo suddenly stood still and faced the cat. Mojo froze and sank to his haunches. Kiwi lifted a terrifying claw and took a slow-motion step toward the cat.

Heidi wielded the blanket.

"Not just yet!" Lisa called.

Mojo shuffled on his belly toward the parrot. To everyone's astonishment, Kiwi then dipped her head in a gracious arc and nestled it behind the cat's ear. Mojo lifted his chin to let the parrot groom him gently with her beak. He raised a paw and rested it across her back.

Ted laughed. "They're friends!"

The pair had probably known each other from their days in the wild. Both were loners with significant injuries. They must've helped each other out or, at the very least, enjoyed a companionship.

Lisa was relieved she wouldn't have to act as policeman between her two pets. If anything, she was the newcomer in the relationship.

Heidi was now brandishing her phone

instead of a blanket, taking photos of Mojo and Kiwi to show her vet-science friends.

As the light faded, the animals took turns chasing each other through the trees. The humans lay on their backs, watching midges perform aerial acrobatics.

When Maxine started making noises about going inside, Ted stood up and cleared his throat. He beckoned James to his side. "In case you have all forgotten, I was about to make an announcement."

Oh, yes, thought Lisa. Ted always had an exaggerated sense of drama.

Glasses were thrust into hands. Sparkling wine from New Zealand's South Island was poured.

"As most of you are aware, James and I took a trip to New Zealand last week. While we were there we did some bungee jumping and saw some beautiful scenery. . . ."

Lisa's attention wandered. Ted must've had a few too many.

"And we got married."

Lisa sprang to her feet. "What?!"

"James and I were legally married in a beautiful stone chapel on the shores of Lake Tekapo."

Gordon turned purple and sputtered into his glass. Heidi and Stella performed an impromptu circle dance. Zack reached for his camera.

"Good grief!" Maxine cried. "Can people *do* that?"

"It's legal over there," James said.

"Wonderful!" Lisa quavered. Her sincerity was in doubt until she saw the faces of her son and . . . his husband. Who could argue with love? "Congratulations!" she said, hugging them both. "Why didn't you tell me?"

"We are now. Anyway, that was a private ceremony. If it's okay with you, Mom, we'd love to have a proper celebration here at the manor."

"With an exchange of gold rings," James added. "We were so excited we forgot to have them at our first wedding."

"Fine, but . . ."

A circle of faces looked up at her expectantly.

"When were you thinking of having it?" she asked.

"We can tidy the place up by November," Ted said.

"Next *month*?!"

"Why wait? It'll be great. We want everyone we love most to be here."

Lisa's inner Machiavelli kicked in. Though Portia might be able to wangle her way out of coming to Australia for Christmas, no way could she miss her brother's wedding.

The manor's walls were already steeped with history. It would do no harm to add another generation's layer of happiness before she had to pack up and put the place on the market.

"Will there be bridesmaids?" Maxine asked.

"Flotillas of them," James replied.

"Do you think Aunt Caroline will accept her invitation?" Ted said.

Laughter echoed across the orchard. They drained their glasses and wandered back to the house. A great orange moon rose over the apple tree.

CHAPTER 29

Green blades had sliced miraculously through the charred earth. Kiwi was becoming bolder. The parrot waited outside the back door most mornings, and with Mojo's encouragement, she was soon hopping over the doorstep and waddling about the kitchen. It was a friendship of equals. Meanwhile, Mojo's tummy was getting rounder by the day.

Lisa loved watching the unlikely allies preen and take turns chasing each other. There was only one source of tension. The moment Mojo was out of sight, or diverted by a fly in the window, Kiwi made a beeline for his food bowl. Kiwi devoured anything from kitty treats to fresh chicken slices. The self-appointed artful dodger soon widened her territory to pinching bananas from the fruit bowl. One morning Lisa caught the parrot on the pantry floor, rustling through a toppled packet of muesli. The bird looked up at her and squawked defiantly. Bags of sunflower seeds became part of the weekly shop.

Lisa began to feel guilty sending the cockatoo outside at night. Kiwi had proved herself a survivor, but her damaged wing made her vulnerable. The first night Kiwi was allowed to stay inside, she seemed grateful. Perched on the back of her favorite kitchen chair, she tucked her head in her wing and closed her eyes. Lisa slid sheets of newspaper on the floor underneath the chair legs, closed the door, and followed Mojo upstairs.

The Gray Army abandoned painting the upstairs study and focused their energies on tidying up what was left of the stables and servants' wing. Lisa spent her days at the kitchen table with Mojo on her lap and Kiwi perched on the back of a chair, wading through *Three Sisters: Emily,* tweaking and reworking. She finally sent it off to Vanessa just hours before the deadline. Now Lisa was free to concentrate on the upcoming celebration, and researching gay weddings became her new hobby.

Lisa was puzzled when the boys sent most of their wedding invitations by Facebook, but James assured her it was logical, considering the timeframe. Still, the boys hadn't forgotten the computer illiterate. James bought a small stack of invitation cards that he filled in using a calligraphy pen before posting them to the elderly and "just plain weird" who refused to own phones or computers. To everyone's amazement, Aunt Caroline sent a note of acceptance by return.

Ted insisted on inviting the Gray Army, along with all the locals who'd helped with the fire cleanup — and "that gardening dude."

Lisa was overjoyed that Portia was among the first to accept. Lisa booked a flight for Portia to arrive a few days before the wedding and stay on for two weeks. Not that Lisa was holding out much hope — Portia would probably invent an audition or a vegan festival to rush back early for.

Then Jake and Cow Belle had the gall to announce they were arriving a week early and would be staying at the manor. Lisa was ready to book them into a motel, but Ted begged her to let them stay. He seemed to have romantic notions of his parents' sleeping under the same roof on the eve of his wedding.

In the end, acceptances numbered close to 150, including James's New Zealand relatives.

Scott showed up to work on the landscaping most days. His snakebite bandage had been replaced with a modest Band-Aid. No doubt Juliet had seen to that. Lisa limited their discussions to garden planning. Truckloads of boulders, some the size of small caravans, arrived and were unloaded by crane. Scott oversaw the placement of each one, and they formed an imposing backdrop in harmony with the valley and hills. Toward the end of each day, the stones took on a reddish glow, and Lisa couldn't resist going outside to stroke them. Smooth and sandy, they seemed to hum with ancient energy.

Outlines of paths meandered in studied nonchalance toward the stream and back. The shapes and curves Scott had carved with the bulldozer were the work of an artist. The only eyesore was the ridiculous hole he'd made for the spa pool, which was at least three meters deep and the size of a mass grave. Scott showed Lisa a plan he'd drawn up for the garden and assured her it would look just fine once it was lined with concrete, filled with water, and nestled under the *per*gola.

She hated to think how much it was all costing. With luck, her royalties from *Three Sisters: Emily* would cover it and she'd get the money back when the house was sold.

With the wedding only a couple of weeks away, Lisa encouraged Scott to charge ahead with planting. Most of the seedlings were small, but they already provided softness and color. The front paddock was rapidly being transformed into a breathtaking landscape.

The boys visited more frequently as the wedding drew closer. A chef friend of James was organizing catering with an impressive Australian theme. First course would be sustainable seafood such as whiting and blue mussels, followed by an amuse-bouche of walnut puree topped with shavings of pine mushrooms and a cabbage flower. Main course was to be steak fillet sprinkled with native pepper berries. There would also be a vegetarian option. For dessert, wattleseed and honey custard would be surrounded by desert limes and emu apples. The menu sounded so outlandish, Lisa would've tried to veto it if the creator hadn't been voted best chef in Australia.

Whenever she stressed out about flowers or seating arrangements, the boys told her to relax. Everything was under control. The day after she fretted over what to wear to her son's wedding, James arrived with Terence, a stylist friend from the city. Terence threw open Lisa's wardrobe doors and emitted cries of dismay. Lisa recoiled. She hated clothes shopping, especially since the mastectomy, let alone the thought of schlepping down Collins Street with an impeccably groomed young man in an Italian suit.

To her relief, Terence was a mind reader. He told her he'd pop into the city and bring out a few garments for her to try on later in the week. It was only fair to tell him about her prosthesis. He waved it aside and said there was nothing he liked more than a challenge. She could've kissed his handmade shoes.

According to the boys, another friend, Damien, was dying to do her hair and makeup on the wedding day. When she started to fret about the devastated-looking driveway, they booked her a massage.

There were no bridezillas, no tears over tiaras. The boys networked with the best. Their taste was impeccable as always. She was beginning to think nothing could be easier than being mother of one of the grooms at a gay wedding.

An avalanche of luggage clattered into the hallway. The bags were all matching brown with pale trim. Lisa bent to examine them. The marks she'd mistaken for bird droppings were carefully formed LVs. She could never tell the difference between the real deal and stuff from the back streets of Bangkok. She wondered if there was a collective noun for designer luggage — an ostentation?

To say she was dreading having her ex-husband and his lover to stay was an understatement. The thought of sharing her upstairs bathroom with them, perhaps even having to dredge Cow Belle's flaxen hair out of the plug hole, made her skin crawl.

"Great to see you!" Jake chirped, heaving a wheelie bag up the steps. No doubt Belle had talked him into the tightly fitted shirt. It made him look six months pregnant. Gray never was a good color for him. Belle was a wardrobe satirist.

Bright desperation shining in his eyes, Jake put his hands on Lisa's shoulders. She resisted as he drew her down into his neck. His smell, a stale concoction of offices and planes, was so familiar she felt a stab of loss.

It was quickly replaced with resentment. Belle, hiding behind huge sunglasses, glided toward them. "It's quite small for a manor, isn't it?" she said. "I guess you do things differently in Australia. I mean, I've been to beach houses in the Hamptons bigger than this. How do you put up with the heat?"

Lisa and Jake lugged the bags upstairs

while Belle fanned herself on the front porch.

"It's not easy for her coming here," Jake whispered. "She feels an outsider already."

"Your towels are on your bed," Lisa said, escorting him to the guest room.

It'd been quite a performance getting their room ready. She'd stripped the bed and made it up with fresh linen, filled a water jug, and placed glasses on the bedside tables. Not to mention a vase of bottle-brush, a book entitled *Picturesque Drives of Victoria,* and copies of *Vogue Living.* She'd even dragged the vacuum cleaner up the stairs and scraped it around the floor. The towels were just an afterthought. Resisting the urge to dip them in poison, she'd crowned them with a little square of guest soap each (an inexplicable birthday present from Maxine).

Not only that, Lisa had shoveled all her makeup and old towels out of the bathroom, and scrubbed the toilet with lemony stuff that made her hands sting.

"That's one helluva fire you had," Jake said, pulling back the curtain. "Are you okay?"

Why did he always ask that? Did he think she couldn't breathe without him?

"I'm fine."

"Who's *that*?"

Lisa joined him at the window. Scott, wearing nothing but boots, shorts, and a sunhat, was strolling down the driveway looking like a *Cosmo* centerfold.

"Oh, he helps with the garden."

"Guess he costs more than a Mexican."

Scott shaded his eyes, looked up at them, and waved. His tan heightened the spectacular curve of his chest muscles. She focused on a tantalizing valley running through the center of his torso down to his belly button. Her eyes lingered over a strip of dark hair rising from the top of his shorts. Liquid heat rose between her thighs, but she quickly extinguished it. Scott was taken.

"That guy should watch out for skin cancer," Jake said, pulling the curtain closed.

"Where's the en suite?"

Lisa and Jake turned from the window. Belle stood in the doorway clutching a handbag adorned with gold *C*s, her sunglasses now perched on her head. Panting slightly, she wore the expression of a new arrival at the Brontë sisters' school for daughters of impoverished clergymen.

"It's a shared bathroom," Lisa said.

Belle blanched.

"They weren't fussy about that sort of

thing in the old days," Lisa shrugged. "Chamber pots and what have you."

Belle flicked the latch of her handbag in a series of compulsive clicks.

"Never mind, honey," Jake said. "We can rough it for a few days."

Lisa was about to remind them there was a perfectly good motel in town. Then she thought of Ted.

"There's some kind of wild animal downstairs," Belle said, tapping across the floor toward Jake.

"You mean Mojo?" Lisa said.

"It looks like a dingo. They eat babies, don't they?"

"How many eyes did it have?"

"I have no idea. I was too busy running."

"Aw, honey," Jake crooned, embracing Belle, which was awkward, considering she was at least six inches taller.

Lisa felt vaguely nauseous. "Maybe she's right," she said. "We did have some wildlife come inside to shelter from the fire. Killer kangaroos and things."

Belle whimpered. Jake shot Lisa a warning look.

"And Scott was bitten by a snake. He really *was*. A big brown one."

"Give it a rest, Lisa," Jake said.

"Oh well, I'll leave you two to settle in.

Come down for dinner when you're ready."

Taking refuge in the kitchen, Lisa poured herself a large glass of merlot. The only way she was going to get through the next few days was with regular doses of alcohol.

Where *was* Mojo? There was no sign of Kiwi either. She set the table and threw together a baby spinach salad with sliced orange and walnut pieces. If she'd been feeling benevolent toward Jake she'd have made his favorite roast lamb with potatoes and garlic for old time's sake. Instead, she pulled a supermarket chicken out of the fridge and broke it in pieces.

As the wine filtered through her veins, Lisa's heart softened toward Belle. At least the woman had gone to the trouble of showing up. Perhaps some music would help Belle relax. Lisa put on the radio and let Beethoven flood the room. The god of music was in one of his raucous moods, galloping across hills, laughing into the rain. Lisa drained her glass, filled another, and toasted her reflection in the window. She turned the music up, swung her glass in time with Beethoven, and laughed along with him.

"Excuse me?"

Belle stepped timidly toward the table. She was wearing a tiny black evening dress,

349

the back of which appeared to have fallen out. Her hair swung glamorously over one shoulder.

Lisa froze with her glass in the air.

"I thought it was formal."

"What?"

"Dinner in a manor house."

"Oh. There's a dining room somewhere, but I haven't got round to setting it up. It's full of boxes."

Belle looked crestfallen.

"I could get changed if you like, but it's only chicken salad. I *could* make an apple crumble. . . ."

"I'm on a diet," Belle said.

"So am I."

At last some common ground, aside from shared knowledge of the wart on the underside of Jake's — Lisa quickly erased the mental image.

Lisa dug out a pair of candles from a drawer and stuffed them into Mexican pottery holders. She thought about lighting them, but naked flames had lost their allure lately.

"What are you two girls talking about?" Jake said, rubbing his hands together as he strode into the room. "I could feel my ears burning up there."

"It's not all about you," Lisa mumbled,

taking a surreptitious gulp.

"God, you look beautiful!" he exclaimed.

Belle flicked her hair and tittered.

"Wine, anyone?" Lisa said, spilling what was left into glasses.

Jake radiated disapproval — he hated it when she got tipsy, which was almost never. "Would you mind turning the music down?" he shouted.

As Beethoven faded into the background there was a tap on the back door. Assuming master of the house status, Jake padded over the bluestone and reached for the handle. The door burst open to an outrageous squawk. A flurry of white feathers swooped over their heads and circled the kitchen with clumsy flaps. Kiwi was flying!

"It's a vulture!" Belle yelled.

A small yowling lion exploded into the room, hot on the bird's tail feathers. Mojo pranced onto a chair and leaped up at Kiwi.

"There it is!" Belle wailed at Mojo. "That's the . . . the thing!"

Screeching, Belle knocked the chair over. Mojo sailed through the air, narrowly avoiding collision with the cockatoo. As Kiwi attempted a second circuit, Belle ran from the room. Jake was about to follow, until he saw an imposing silhouette filling the doorframe.

Scott had mercifully managed to put on a shirt, though he'd forgotten to do up the buttons. "Great, isn't it?" Scott beamed up at Kiwi. "I taught her to fly."

"You did?" Jake asked.

"Yeah, we've been practicing around the orchard. But she can't land yet."

"She can't *land*?!" Lisa was incredulous. "Why did you let her in here?"

"I didn't." Scott shrugged. "I thought you'd want to see. . . . She let herself in."

Kiwi flapped over the table and, rapidly losing altitude, toppled the candles.

"She'll wear herself out soon," Scott added.

Kiwi circled her favorite chair, lowered her claws and attempted landing. The chair clattered backwards onto the floor. The parrot flapped frantically to regain height.

Mojo sat on his haunches and watched with a combination of admiration and concern as Kiwi rallied — only to collide with the pantry door.

Lisa cried out as the parrot slid to the floor. The bird lay at her feet. Kiwi's eyes were closed, her beak slightly open, her yellow crest frozen in the shape of a smile. She was lifeless.

Mojo trotted forward and examined the prone parrot. With a shielded paw, he patted the bird's head and licked her chest with slow, loving strokes.

To Lisa's astonishment, Kiwi's wrinkled eyelids slid open to reveal shining crimson eyes. The cockatoo rubbed her beak against Mojo's forehead, as if to say thanks.

"You should put those guys on YouTube," Jake said.

Lisa felt weak with joy when Kiwi rolled over and regained her footing. The bird shook her head and preened her feathers as if she were as surprised as anyone else that she was still alive. After taking a moment to regain her senses, the cockatoo lumbered out the door to the garden with Mojo trotting after her.

Silence settled over the kitchen, apart from the radio music, which had morphed into Mozart. Lisa picked up the two chairs and straightened the candleholders.

"Pleased to meet you," Jake said, extending a hand and dousing Scott with alpha-male charm.

"Welcome to Tumbledown," Scott replied.

Jake's eyebrows twitched with confusion.

CHAPTER 30

The arrivals hall was frantic. Throngs of people pressed against the barrier and waited for the automatic doors to open, presenting loved ones like game-show prizes.

Lisa stood at the back of the crowd near the café. Maybe she'd been living in the country too long, but there were too many people squeezed in too close for her liking. Her heart started doing a butterfly dance, the excitement at the prospect of seeing Portia again tempered by anxiety.

She ordered two takeaway coffees and passed one to Zack, who badly needed to pull his jeans up. The coffee trembled in its paper cup. Her hands were damp. Maybe she had a new phobia.

If she kept hovering at the back of the crowd, Portia would never see her, so, breathing in, she plunged into the human stew. Portia was taking forever to get through customs. It wasn't the first time. Customs officers nearly always pulled Portia out of the line for interrogation, probably because she was young and pretty.

Nearly an hour later, Lisa's phone vibrated with a text. *Where r u?*

At the barrier on the right as you come through the doors. Can't wait! Where r u?

Outside by taxi stand. Been here 4eva.

Zack trailed after her toward the taxi rank, where a lofty bedouin was leaning against a pole. The figure waved and clopped toward them, trailing scarves.

"Darling girl!" Lisa cried, kissing her daughter's angular cheeks and drinking in a perfume that smelled like aftershave.

Portia didn't seem surprised to be greeted by a cameraman. She flashed Zack a professional smile. In an uncharacteristic act of chivalry, Zack loaded her bags on a trolley and wheeled them to the car.

Lisa wasted no time starting her two-week fattening-up campaign. Halfway to Castlemaine she turned off to Macedon and pulled up at a café.

As always happened when she was out with Portia, a waiter was at their table in seconds and smiling beguilingly.

"Mmmmm, the chocolate forest cake looks good," Lisa said, perusing the menu for calorie-laden fodder.

"Yummy!" Portia chimed in.

Portia listened ravenously while Lisa ordered cake with cream and ice cream on the side. Zack asked for a meat pie with tomato sauce.

"And *I'll* have a small green salad, no dressing," Portia added.

Lisa prickled with annoyance. "Aren't we sharing the cake?"

"Yes, of course," Portia said. "I'm just so hungry I'm having a main course as well."

The waiter returned minutes later and placed the salad in front of Portia with a flourish. It was big enough to fill a grasshopper. Portia bedazzled him with a smile.

"Sorry, guys," the waiter said, pulling himself together to look at Lisa and Zack. "I forgot what you ordered."

After some time, he reappeared with the pie and a mountainous wedge of chocolate rising from a lake of cream. Two breasts of ice cream rested either side of the cake, along with three token strawberries. Though Lisa had asked for three spoons, Portia was engrossed with her bowl of leaves, psyching herself up to spear a spinach leaf. Zack made quick work of his pie. Lisa was grateful he was there to help her plow through the cake.

"So what are you wearing to the wedding?" Lisa asked, casting about for neutral ground.

"I found a fantastic dress in a charity shop," Portia said, jiggling her leg.

It was a new thing, the leg jiggling. Maybe she was short of magnesium.

"Wouldn't you rather wear a new outfit? We could go shopping together."

Portia shot her a withering look. Lisa swallowed another lump of cake.

"You don't get it, Mom. The whole point of fashion right now is to look like you've just had sex."

Zack scooped his spoon around the plate to collect the last vestiges of cream.

"*Really?* In my day . . ." Lisa stopped herself right there. "What about your hair?"

"Same thing. Messed up is good."

Lisa ordered a skinny cappuccino. Zack drained a mug of hot chocolate and four marshmallows before disappearing to the bathroom.

"What happened to that nice boy you were seeing. Charlie, was it?" Lisa asked quietly.

"Charlie who?"

"I thought you were serious for a while."

Portia stabbed a tomato and jiggled her leg so violently Lisa wondered if she should

357

say something about it. "We didn't hold hands or anything." Portia's tone was impatient.

Lisa was certain Portia had slept with Charlie several times.

"I mean you can have sex with as many friends as you like," Portia continued. "But holding hands . . . That's commitment." She raised a glass of mineral water. A scarlet Care Bear on the underside of her wrist flashed a menacing grin. Two weeks was beginning to look like the limit for both of them.

For the rest of the trip, Lisa was too hot with annoyance to bother with conversation. She let the countryside unravel under violent blue sky while Zack and Portia prattled about film school and the perils of Hollywood. Lisa had to bite her lip when they agreed they'd rather be famous than rich. She feared the young's obsession with celebrity. From her own experiences of a *very* minor version of recognition, she knew the concept was overrated.

Her thoughts drifted to *Three Sisters: Emily.* She hadn't heard a word from her publisher, even though Vanessa surely had read the manuscript by now. Maybe something was wrong. Lisa pictured Vanessa in front of her computer piecing together a tactful e-mail telling Lisa it was rubbish. If the book was rejected her finances would be stuffed.

"Wow!" Portia said as they approached the manor's blackened gates. "That's some barbecue you had."

As they turned into the driveway, a tall stepladder reared over the windscreen. Lisa spun the wheel, narrowly avoiding crashing into the ladder. Ron waved at her from his perilous position on the second to top rung. On the ground beneath him, Ted was holding what appeared to be a sheet.

Portia leaped out of the backseat into her brother's arms. Seeing her two children together again, Lisa felt momentarily complete.

"What do you reckon?" Ted asked, flourishing the sheet. Decorating the driveway with bed linen was beyond fanciful, but it was his wedding.

Ted bundled Portia back into the car. As they rounded the bend, Lisa saw two figures sitting on the veranda. Kiwi was perched on the balustrade, presiding like Judge Judy over the short bald man and the giant in work boots.

Mojo was wedged between the men with his pompom head on Scott's lap. The cat opened his eye, offered a welcome squeak, and closed it again. Lisa was relieved Scott's shorts finished halfway down his thighs and his T-shirt was devoid of sci-fi creatures.

Portia was too stoned with jet lag to take in much of her surroundings, anyway. Climbing the steps, she offered a cheek to her father. "Thanks for the upgrade, Dad. Economy looked like a zoo." Then, flashing the dismissive smile reserved for anyone over thirty, Portia disappeared inside.

The men rose politely, but Zack insisted on carrying her bags. The young man seemed to have suddenly developed biceps.

"Second on the left upstairs," Lisa called after them.

Jake leaned back in the sofa and put his hands behind his head, revealing damp shadows under his arms. "Scott here's been telling me about life in the outback," he said with the ease of a prince who'd been passing the morning with a peasant.

"This is hardly the outback," Lisa said. "Has Belle recovered from last night?"

She knew Belle had survived the animal invasion from the state of the bathroom. The vanity was awash with cosmetics derived at legendary expense from the fetuses of endangered sea mammals.

"She's gone into town for a facial, or whatever they do Down Under. Guess she'll be having a clay-painting ceremony with the natives."

"Sounds more like the Peninsula Spa in New York." Lisa was aware her defensiveness was a sign of insecurity.

Scott cleared his throat and spread his legs further apart than necessary. "Young Jake here's interested in doing a spot of rock climbing. Thought we might head over to the Grampians."

Mojo flopped to the floor and sashayed inside with a swish of his tail.

Jake hadn't climbed a boulder in his life, not even Rockefeller Center with the aid of an elevator. Besides, if he took off with Scott on a suicide mission to the Grampians, Lisa might be stranded overnight with Miss Husband Stealer. "What about Belle?"

"Oh, she wants to have a girls' day out with Portia," Jake replied. "Shopping in the city."

Lisa fumed. "But I hardly ever *see* Portia! We're here for her brother's wedding . . . not some extreme shopping orgy."

Scott stood up and brushed imaginary crumbs off his thighs. "Look, I'm not that into rappelling," he said, stroking the cockatoo's head. "I've only done it a couple of times. I've got some beer in the ute. Want one, mate?"

Jake nodded. As Scott sauntered off, Jake patted the sofa, inviting Lisa to sit next to him. "I've been wanting to have a word with you," Jake said in a confessional tone. "Belle feels you treat her like a dumb blonde. . . ."

"I do?"

"She *has* got an MBA, you know."

"I'm not surprised. She's far smarter than me."

"Her family came from Russia with crumbs in their pockets. They had to fight for everything."

"Like other people's husbands?"

Jake shook his head, as if she'd just cursed over his mother's grave.

Scott trudged back up the path carrying a slab of gold cans.

Jake cleared his throat. "Scottie's done a great job here. I'm getting him to do some plans for a roof garden for me."

"Yeah, but my printer's stuffed," Scott said, opening a can with a hiss and passing it to Jake.

Jake accepted the offering and bowed, as if taking part in a native ritual. He took a tentative sip.

Scott tore open a can for himself. It glinted in the sun as he raised it to his lips. Either Scott was being uncharacteristically sensitive or . . . "By the way, I've drawn up some thoughts for your driveway," he said to Lisa. "Nothing elaborate."

"That'd be great," she lied. The truth was, she'd have to call a halt to Scott's grand designs, at least until she had the thumbs-up from Vanessa.

"If you come over to my place tomorrow evening I can make any changes you want onscreen."

"Yes, but . . ." The wedding was less than a week away, and the house was overflowing with high-maintenance guests.

"Bring your daughter along."

The cockatoo ran her beak over Scott's hand, tickling him with her gray tongue.

Well, it would be a change of scenery. And a chance to tell Scott to put the brakes on.

CHAPTER 31

Portia wandered through the ashes of the servants' quarters in a translucent nightgown, her expression flickering from longing to despair. With her hair spilling over her shoulders, she reminded Lisa of a Pre-Raphaelite painting.

"Shouldn't you be wearing shoes?"

Portia appeared not to hear. She bowed and picked up a piece of charred wood.

"Now turn your head slowly toward the sunset," Zack called from behind his camera. "That's it! Good . . ."

"Sorry to interrupt, but we have an appointment."

"Mo-om! Can't you see we're busy?"

Lisa should've known Portia would invent an excuse. The child belonged to a generation that had no curiosity beyond the mirror.

Yellow light shone from the kitchen. James was putting on an evening meal for every-

364

one. The advantages of a gourmet-chef son-in-law were greater than Lisa had first appreciated. She told him she wouldn't be away for long. He smiled and said not to hurry back. He'd leave something in the fridge.

Lisa unfolded the scrap of paper Scott had scribbled directions on, and climbed into the car. Soon Dino was humming along a ridgeline as the blue hills across the valley darkened to purple. A scarlet flash of rosellas streaked across the sky. She turned off the main road and plunged down an unpaved track. Coiling through a eucalypt forest, she opened the window and savored the air. It carried her back to childhood, her father offering her a spoon of cough mixture, assuring her she'd feel better soon.

She caught a glimpse of the river, threading like silver ribbon through the trees, then a spiral of smoke rising from what was presumably Scott's place. She wondered how she'd tell him that, with the publication of her book up in the air, her dream of keeping the manor was fast becoming a fantasy, that she'd probably have to pack up and leave after Ted's wedding.

Nestled deeply in the landscape, Scott's man cave was made of slabs of river rock, each one slotting into the next, as if fulfilling their original purpose. A wood-shingle roof sloped up to a chimney made of smaller, rounder stones.

Lisa pulled into the open space in front of the house. Gathering up her handbag, she stepped into the evening air. Somewhere below, the river gushed. A broad ramp lined with lights led her to a front door — the place must've been designed with Todd's wheelchair in mind. She tapped on the roughly hewn hardwood, and it glided open. Somewhere inside the house Tom Waits was barking "Burma Shave."

"Come through!"

Lisa stepped into a room oozing the scent of untreated cedar. She was surprised to see an entire corner lined with books, though at a rough glance most were about garden design or wildlife. A photo of Todd as a round-faced baby beamed down from a shelf. Next to it was a more recent one of him in a wheelchair, laughing with friends at what looked like a birthday party.

Flames flickered in a broad fireplace made of the same river stone as the outside chimney. A dark suede sofa sprawled across a floor scattered with animal hides. A stainless-steel standard lamp cast a pool of light over a coffee table.

Scott stood in the kitchen. He was wearing an open-neck shirt, olive green to match his eyes, and shorts that finished just above his knees. Formal attire, by his standards. She watched him slicing cheese, arranging it on a plate with green grapes.

"Hope your daughter likes Brie."

"She's not here."

Scott looked up sharply. "Ah well . . . do *you*?"

"Love it."

"You're wearing that dress," he said, pouring red wine into two glasses.

"My track pants were in the wash."

It was true. She hadn't gone out of her way to look feminine. Still, she couldn't wear the flowery dress without heeled sandals, which probably were her most glamorous shoes. The makeup and earrings had been an afterthought.

He offered her a glass.

"Beautiful place you have here," she said, flinging her handbag on the sofa and wandering over to a set of sliding doors. They opened onto a vast deck overlooking the river. Even in the fading light the view was spectacular.

"Thanks. I finished it a few months ago. Helped me sort a few things out."

"There's something I need to tell you," she said.

He was suddenly standing next to her, smelling of soap, shower fresh. She glanced down at his bare feet planted on the wooden floor. The fact he hadn't shaved for a day or so only enhanced his allure.

"You know what happened in the medical center . . ." he said, softly clinking her glass.

"You were in shock."

"That may be, but I meant what I said. I think you're amazing."

"But what about Juliet?"

Confusion flickered across his face.

"Aren't you two an item?"

He shook his head and laughed. "She's my *cousin*! First cousin, at that. *And* she's practically engaged to Jacko the vet."

Lisa wasn't sure if she was delighted or appalled. "You must have thousands of women running around after you," she said, sipping her wine. It wasn't a bad merlot.

"Haven't you heard of the woman drought in rural Australia?" he asked with a twinkle.

"Come *on*!"

"Serious," he said, raising one hand and a wineglass in surrender. "You know that TV show *The Farmer Wants a Wife*? It's all blokes looking for women, not the other way around. What's that thing you wanted to say?"

She drew a breath and took a gulp of

wine. "It's just, with the fire . . . and I think my publisher's going to turn down my book so I'm not sure . . ."

Scott ran his fingers down the stem of his wineglass. "I know I've been pretty stupid a few times," he muttered. "But Todd has to come first. . . ."

Lisa was shaken out of her anxiety and self-pity. The challenges Scott and Beverley had to face were far greater. "Why didn't you tell me about Todd?" she asked.

"I *did*!" he stepped back, defensive.

"You never told me he's disabled. There's nothing wrong with that, you know."

Tom Waits reached the poignant part in the song when they pull the girl from the car wreckage and she's still wearing her shades. It got Lisa every time.

Scott's head drooped. A weight seemed to bear down on those huge shoulders, so he could barely stand straight. "Matter of fact there is," he mumbled.

The room fell silent. Somewhere outside an owl cried.

"What do you mean?"

"I was always busy with work. But I used to try and do stuff with Todd. A couple of years ago I took him up in the hills on a quad bike."

Lisa felt a shadow of dread.

"He was fine back then. Perfectly normal kid. Amazing on the footie field. We'd been on the bike before. . . . Only this time he wanted to drive." Scott's voice cracked. He rubbed a hand over his chin. "He was fourteen. I learned to drive a truck at that age. So I sat behind and let him steer. He was doing great. Then he accelerated up this ridge. . . ."

Lisa felt her mouth form a soft O.

"The bloody thing rolled on top of us." Scott's eyes darkened. "My leg was broken in three places, but Todd was much worse. We were out of phone contact. I had to leave him there and crawl to the nearest farm."

An ache of sadness ran through her body. She lowered her wineglass and, turning, put it on the coffee table.

"By the time we got back in the helicopter it was nearly dark. The poor kid had been lying stuck under that thing for seven hours. I went over to him. He was white as a statue. He wasn't moving. I thought he was . . ." Scott swallowed hard.

Lisa stepped toward him and rested her hands on his bookshelf shoulders.

"Then I knelt down and stroked his cheek. He opened his eyes. He just looked up at me and smiled."

The house was silent apart from the

distant roar of the river. Somewhere outside an owl hooted.

Scott swiped his eyes with the back of his hand. "He was in so much pain. I asked how he was doing. Know what he said? 'Dad, I heard a lyrebird sing.' "

She wanted to weep.

"It's all my fault," he whispered. She could feel his chest shuddering. "He'll never walk again."

She drew him close and rocked him gently.

"Beverley's right, you know. I *am* a lousy dad."

"That's why you broke up?"

He straightened to his full height. "She has every right to blame me," he said after a long silence. "I'm going to spend the rest of my life making it up to him."

"And Beverley?"

"She's tough. Always has been. I used to play footie when I was a kid. Bev came along to all the games. We went out a couple of times, then she got pregnant. She wanted to get rid of it, but I . . ." His voice trailed off.

"You did the right thing," Lisa said, finishing his sentence. She cursed herself for the times she'd been angry about Scott's unreliability. His tendency to turn up and disappear was simply caused by his trying to be a perfect father as well as run a business. "How come you didn't tell me?" she asked quietly.

He stepped back from her and studied something in the corner of the ceiling. "I didn't want you feeling sorry for me." Icy pride flashed across his face.

"It's okay," she said. "I think you're amazing."

Scott shielded his eyes with his hand. "My son has every right to a normal life," he said, his voiced cracked with emotion. "We do all the adventure stuff, everything a teenage boy needs."

She took his hand and stroked the gleaming hairs on his wrist. "I think you're a brilliant dad. And I bet Todd knows it."

A slow smile lit Scott's face. His eyes were full of tender sadness. He tilted her chin toward his lips. As he lowered his lips toward hers, she savored the delicious sensation of her body melting into his.

His great, muscular frame was trembling. She felt the animal warmth of his skin. He ran his hand up from the small of her back, tracing the line of her zip.

She tensed. "I'd better go." She disentangled herself and cast about for her handbag.

He stood back, puzzled.

"We can't do this."

"Why not?"

"I'm not normal."

"I knew that," he said with a soft smile. "Anyone who'd buy old Tumbledown Manor . . ."

Smiling, she didn't bother to correct him this time. "Seriously. I had a mastectomy." She waited for him to recoil with revulsion.

His slid his arm back around her waist and held her steady. "Scars can be beautiful," he said after a long pause.

She felt the athletic thud of his heart, the gentle puffs of his cinnamon breath as he drew her closer. He kissed her again.

"Can I ask one thing?"

"Sure," he said.

"Can we turn out the . . . ?"

CHAPTER 32

A brush of lips on one cheek would've been an acceptable way to welcome a friend or relation to the parsonage — not that the Brontës had many of either. Deep kissing, however, would've been out of the question. As for sex outside the protection of marriage, just thinking about it would have brought on the vapors.

Charlotte was the only Brontë sister who walked down the aisle. The author of *Jane Eyre* declined the first marriage proposal she received, assuring her admirer he would find her eccentric and impractical. She was later persuaded marriage would provide "clear and defined duties," and tied the knot with her father's curate. Lisa hoped for Charlotte's sake that the bride had sailed the heights of ecstasy on her Irish honeymoon. Whatever the curate lacked in expertise, Charlotte would have made up for with her imagination.

Soon after, Charlotte was pregnant. Nausea and fainting fits developed into serious illness. Some say Charlotte was a victim of dehydration from morning sickness. Others insist she caught typhus from a household servant. Either way, Charlotte died four months pregnant on March 21, 1855. Compared to her younger sisters, she'd reached a grand old age — thirty-eight.

As for Emily and Anne, they were afflicted by a disease that had the scandalous ability to cause "heated blood." Doctors agreed tuberculosis could transform decent people into sex maniacs. Special hospitals were built to keep men and women apart. Winking, waving, and smiling were forbidden, along with provocative activities such as hair curling, face painting, and letter writing.

Emily and Anne were spared such indignities. They suffered at home, nursing each other into their graves. All the thwarted desire seething under their petticoats was channeled through their pens.

"You look different," Jake said, pouring himself a coffee next morning.

"What?"

"Have you lost weight?"

Lisa bent to shake food into two bowls on the kitchen floor. Parts of her body felt deliciously bruised.

"I've never known a bird to eat cat food," he mused, watching the cockatoo waddle across the room.

"Oh, and you didn't touch your dinner," he added. "It's still in the fridge."

It had been close to midnight by the time she'd crept up the driveway, and only Portia's window had been yellow with light. Lisa had felt like a naughty teenager as she tiptoed upstairs.

Lisa ignored Jake's comment about her untouched dinner. "Kiwi thinks she's a cat," Lisa said as she plonked a tub of butter on the table. "She wants everything Mojo gets."

The cat galloped to Kiwi's side and crunched contentedly from his bowl. Kiwi dipped her face into her dish and rolled a couple of pellets in her beak.

"Quite a sight," Jake said.

As Lisa rinsed a plate, images from the previous night looped through her head. She'd flopped on her bed, too sated and tired to shower. Besides, clomping around in the bathroom at that hour could've raised suspicions.

With Scott seeping through her pores and Mojo wrestling for a comfy spot in the curve of her knees, she'd hardly slept. She'd risen early and showered, soaping away the residues of pleasure. Then, weirdly energized, she'd embarked on a frantic round of floor mopping.

"Is that a new perfume?" Jake asked as she passed him the sugar bowl.

Did she still reek of pheromones? She shook her head and set four more places at the table. The grooms-to-be were unlikely to rise for another hour. And Portia was incapable of getting out of bed before eleven a.m.

A pale face appeared at the door. Belle glanced anxiously at the animals.

"It's okay, sweetie. They won't bite," Jake said.

Belle seemed to think otherwise. Lisa lifted the food bowls and carried them outside. Cat and parrot trailed after her like pilgrims.

"It's not the animals so much as the hygiene issue that concerns me," Belle said, settling herself at the table.

Lisa opened the fridge and reveled in the feeling of her battered backside. Deerskin burns.

"Juice, Belle?" she asked with hostessy charm.

As she poured the orange liquid into Belle's glass, she realized Jake must've felt a similar guilty pleasure after weeks of cheating on Lisa. No wonder he'd come home oozing charm.

"I mean, there's such a thing as bird flu," Belle said, wiping the rim of her glass with a tissue. "And cats get AIDS."

"Yes, but they can't pass AIDS to humans," Jake explained in a tone he'd used when helping Portia with her homework.

"Aren't you allergic to cats?" Lisa asked.

"Not so much these days," Jake replied, crunching into raspberry jam on toast.

Belle wiped her spoon and fiddled with her muesli.

"So what did you think of Scott's plans for your garden?" Jake asked.

Lisa felt her cheeks redden. The imprint of Scott's body was all over her, inside and out. They hadn't gone near his computer.

"Great."

"What's he dreamed up?"

Lisa swallowed a gulp of cold coffee. "A fishpond." She was shocked by how easy it was to tell a lie.

"What sort of fish?"

She couldn't tell if Jake was interested or suspicious. Maybe he'd heard her creaking up the stairs. "Goldfish."

"Won't the birds get them?"

"Not if there's plenty of waterweed."

Belle scrolled idly through her phone.

"So what are you two up to today?" Lisa asked, rattling in the sink.

"Well, I'm certainly not going to a local hairdresser. Have you noticed every woman in this town has the same haircut?" Belle babbled.

"Really?"

"They've all got a short-back-and-sides thing going. Like they've had head lice or something. We're going shopping in the city. I mean, what do people wear to gay weddings — sequins and feathers?"

Jake smirked. Lisa wanted to slap him. She assured them the dress code wouldn't be any different from that of a traditional wedding.

"Jake needs new socks, anyway," Belle added.

He always did have sweaty feet. Lisa was making such a commotion at the sink she didn't hear the tap on the back door.

"Scottie, my man!" Jake said, offering the visitor his hand. "We've just been talking about you."

The flash of uncertainty across Scott's eyes was quickly replaced by warmth when he saw Lisa. They bathed in a nanosecond of remembered intimacy before shielding themselves behind masks of civility.

Scott heaved what appeared to be a large

wooden pole into the kitchen. "Put this thing together this morning," he said. "Thought Kiwi might like it."

So he hadn't slept either. The pole had a base at one end and a horizontal perch and feeding bowl at the other.

"She'll *love* it!" Lisa said, beaming.

Scott placed the stand in a corner and ran a cloth over the wood. It was handsome, as far as bird poles went.

"So what's this I hear about a goldfish pond?" Jake asked.

Scott's cloth hovered. Lisa cleared her throat. "I was telling Jake about the fishpond you're planning to put in near the driveway," she said.

Silence echoed across the kitchen.

"Oh, you mean the *billabong,*" Scott said.

She could've kissed him.

"What's a bigglebong?" Belle asked.

"It's a pond that gets left behind when a river changes course. If we dig down a bit, we might find the remains of one and maybe create some wetlands."

"Fascinating," Jake said.

The thrill of deceiving Jake was tempered with caution. Scott had just told a lie as effortlessly as she had. Perhaps Lisa had been too quick to trust him.

"Yeah, I got my printer going, too," Scott

added. "The plans are in the ute if you'd like to take a look."

So there *was* a billabong. She felt weak with relief.

CHAPTER 33

The caterers, musicians, flowers, and celebrant had all been taken care of. While the
new front garden was raw, the curves of the
paths passed as sculptural, and the plant
beds were sprouting color. The pit for the
spa pool was still ugly and unlined, but it
was tucked away out of sight from the front
porch.

Around the back of the house, the orchard
was shimmering with spring growth. Rows
of fruit trees radiated like the spokes of a
bicycle wheel from the old apple tree in the
center. Towering over the others, the central
apple tree had exploded into a canopy of
green. The boys had decided to formalize
their commitment in its shade, underneath
the heart carved in the ancient trunk.

With the dismantling of the servants'
quarters complete, the Gray Army were
concentrating on the more pressing task of
putting up white banners along the drive-

way. They fluttered festively, drawing attention away from the fire-damaged parts of the property.

True to his word, Terence delivered a sheath of outfits, including shoes, for her to try on. They were all beautiful garments and most were surprisingly flattering. Lisa was about to settle for a modest gray suit when Terence persuaded her to try on what amounted to a full-length, cobalt-blue petticoat. The outer layer of silky fabric was an even brighter blue. On top of that was a free-flowing jacket that covered (hallelujah) the tops of her arms. The neckline wasn't prudish, but was high enough for her to feel comfortable bending over seated guests.

Terence coaxed her into a pair of high-heeled sandals. He smoothed the garment over her hips and asked her to turn around. Leaning into the mirror, she found the birthmark Scott had mentioned the night they were together. He was right. With a stretch of imagination it could be the reverse image of a map of Australia. The gown floated around her. She loved the color.

"Beautiful!" he said.

The word awakened shudders of recognition through her animal body.

Scott showed up early each morning to

work near the gate. With the aid of a back-hoe his efforts to uncover a billabong seemed to be paying off. Jake said it looked more like a swamp. Lisa was confident the end result would be fantastic. Scott's plans included a waterfall, footbridge, and water deep enough to spawn native fish. Since that night, there'd been no more talk about putting the garden on hold. Lisa still hadn't heard from Vanessa, but she'd given up caring. She remembered what her father used to say to her with a philosophical smile: *Something will turn up, Panda Bear.*

Scott declined offers to have lunch with everyone inside. Instead, he'd shelter in the shade of a blackened gum tree away from the house. She'd take him trays of tea and sandwiches, but they both were keen for something else. When he tried to kiss her one morning, she disentangled herself and glanced anxiously back at the house. She told him about Portia's rule. Being caught kissing in front of other people would be almost as shocking as holding hands.

There was no hope Scott's efforts were going to be anywhere near complete in time for the wedding, so Ted and the Gray Army brought in extra banners to camouflage the earthworks.

Subconsciously or otherwise, Jake tuned

in to the primal energies in the air. He bought a pair of shorts and took to rising early and jogging down the road on his weedy white legs. While Jake jogged, Belle, who was becoming increasingly petulant, disappeared on long walks, only to reappear furious and sunburned, using her phone as a fly swatter. Even with Kiwi hygienically ensconced on her new bird stand in the corner, Belle declined to appear in the kitchen for breakfast. Instead, Jake, with the humility of a toothless dog, would carry a tray laden with muesli and Stevia-drenched coffee upstairs.

Belle seemed to be talking to the office most nights, and Lisa began to wonder whether she'd been born clutching her phone. At mealtimes, Belle would arrange the machine upright in front of her as if it were a pagan altar. Any attempts at polite conversation were invariably interrupted by its shrieking or the unnerving plunk of a new text message. Clearly some kind of crisis was going on back at work — Belle's minions were calling her around the clock.

In the meantime, Lisa checked her e-mails daily, waiting to hear from Vanessa. At last, the day before the wedding, there it was. Lisa's finger hovered over the mouse. If she deleted the message unopened, then she'd never have to live with the humiliation. She drew a breath and clicked. . . . *Hi, Lisa, So sorry for the delay, but the ms. for the "new War and Peace" came in and I had to drop everything to read it. I LOVE your new book! Congratulations. Marketing thinks it'll go great guns. More soon, hugs, Vanessa xxx*

Lisa leaned back in her chair and let the relief wash over her. The hours spent chained to her computer hadn't been wasted. Going by Vanessa's enthusiasm, Lisa would have the money to pay for the garden, but to be honest, prospects of keeping the house remained unlikely.

That afternoon, James and Ted set up trestle tables in the orchard and put on a magnificent barbecue for friends and family. James's parents, Bill and Sue, had arrived with generous quantities of New Zealand sauvignon blanc. Bill's bright blue eyes were set in a face that resembled a battered cliff. Sue's dark hair was cropped short, and laughter lines radiated from her warm, hazel eyes. If they'd suffered any angst over their son's new commitment, it didn't show.

Stella, Heidi, and their friends arranged themselves around one table, while the older generation, including Maxine and Gordon, sat at another. Portia was in deep conversation with Zack. Lisa was thrilled to see her daughter not only pick up a piece of bread, but actually allow it to pass her lips.

Jake appeared with a fractious Belle. When Lisa suggested it could be a good idea to switch the phone off for a while, Belle looked at her as if Lisa had swallowed a crazy pill, and once more set her phone up in a cradle in front of her, where it blinked malevolently.

"I know you're exhausted," Lisa said.

"Tell me about it," Belle said, swigging from a glass of sauvignon blanc. "I can't wait to be married and get a decent rest having babies."

Lisa stifled a chuckle. Across the table, Jake cowered like an animal trapped in a box for research purposes. Lisa felt a ripple of pity for him. Still, she could think of no better punishment for Jake than having to spend his later years pushing a stroller, preferably one designed for triplets, around Soho.

"What's this I hear?" Portia said, appearing at her father's elbow. "I'm going to have a little half-brother or sister?"

Jake dabbed his lips with a napkin. The attention of both tables was suddenly on him. "Well, not just yet . . ." he mumbled.

"What do you mean?" Belle said in a tone

dripping with icicles.

"It's just a little early. . . ." he said, staring up at the sky. "Strange there aren't any stars out tonight. What'll we do if it rains for the service tomorrow?"

Ted assured him there was a Plan B.

"You think thirty-eight is *early* to become a mother?"

Somewhere across the valley a creature emitted a sorrowful whooping sound.

"There's no hurry," Jake said.

James's dad, Bill, rose to his feet and raised his glass. "Um, I'd just like to take this opportunity to thank . . ."

"Oh, *yeah*!? So make that forty-five by the time I start IVF!" Belle's voice was ragged with rage.

Bill sat down again.

"If you think it's been easy for me pretending to feel comfortable here with your ex-wife and her weird animals and this . . . this . . . *gay* wedding . . ." Belle was shaking.

"You have a problem with it?" Ted asked. His tone was cool and solemn, and Lisa wanted to run over and hug him.

"Everyone knows God made marriage to be sacred between man and woman," Belle announced.

"She's religious?!" Portia said, aghast.

"Republican," Jake muttered.

Now Belle was crying angry, overwrought tears. Pushing back her chair, she spun on her heel and hurled her glass into the orchard, before running sobbing into the darkness.

Thank heavens, Lisa thought, she'd talked the boys into getting plastic glasses.

"Oh, *no*!" Jake cried.

"What's the matter, Dad?" Ted asked.

"She's left her phone!"

"Never mind," Portia said, dethroning the thing and switching it off.

Jake seemed momentarily torn. But when Ted put his arm around his father's shoulders and escorted him to the young people's table, there was no argument. The gesture sparked a wider exchange of seats, making both tables intergenerational. Stella produced a guitar and called Heidi to her side. Tension dissolved as they sang "Till There Was You" in soothing harmony. Cheers erupted when James presented New Zealand's famous dessert — meringue topped with cream and kiwifruit — otherwise known as the pavlova.

"Don't you know we Aussies thought of that first?" Ted joked.

"Oh, don't you start!" James said. "Anything good that comes out of New Zealand always gets claimed by you Australians."

"That's why I'm claiming you," Ted said, kissing James on the cheek.

A cheer went up over the orchard. It was echoed by another cry in the distance — not of happiness but abject misery.

Jake jumped to his feet. "Belle!"

Lisa went inside and found the torch Ted had given her. Jake strapped it to his head and strode around the side of the house, with Lisa and the rest of the dinner guests on his heels.

The night was moonless, profoundly black. "If we spread out we should find her," Jake said, clearly forgetting he was the only one with a torch. "Belle!"

His cry was answered by a cross between a roar and a moan.

"Over there!" he said, charging into the labyrinth of Scott's paths in the front garden. They arrived at the edge of the empty spa-pool pit. Jake directed his torch into the chasm.

Belle's eyes shone wildly up at him. "Get me out of here!" she yelled. "You did this on purpose!"

"Did what?" Jake said.

"Humiliated me in front of everyone."

"Belle . . . I . . ."

"Oh, and by the way. I've got a message from the boss for you. You're fired!"

CHAPTER 34

Mojo pounced on Lisa's stomach and dug his paws into her, Thai-masseur style, as he sauntered over her chest. Lisa rolled over. Riding the sheets like a snowboarder, Mojo slid to the floor.

Lisa pulled on her kimono and followed the cat as he galloped onto the balcony, lion tail swishing. The hills were cardboard cutouts against the pale horizon. Sun cast dramatic slabs of gold across the valley, bringing life to everything it touched.

Mojo's good ear twitched, and his whiskers swiveled forward. He pushed his head between the balustrades. The cat always heard things before she did.

A pair of catering trucks rumbled through the colonnade of banners to park outside the kitchen. Ted and James would be up already, organizing chefs and waiters.

White wings flapped around the side of the house and with great effort ascended to hover over the balcony.

"C'mon, girl! You can do it!" Lisa cried, admiring Kiwi's pastel yellow underside.

The cockatoo squawked. Rotating her wings like helicopter blades, she executed a perilous landing on the balcony rail.

"Good girl!"

Once she'd gained composure, Kiwi preened herself modestly. Mojo sprang onto the rail to congratulate his friend. Then the cat escorted Lisa to the bathroom, which was pleasantly uncluttered, Belle's toiletries having disappeared overnight.

Mojo leaped into the bath and licked droplets of water from around the plughole. Lisa tore off her kimono and stood under the shower. Water streamed over her in joyous rivulets. She was startled by an unfamiliar noise — the sound of herself humming.

She pulled on a sweatshirt and pants and followed Mojo downstairs. To keep people out of the caterers' way, she set up a grazing table on the front veranda and loaded it with coffee, a mountain of croissants, and (with Portia in mind) a bowl of red delicious apples.

Portia was up surprisingly early. So, for that matter, was Zack, who'd ostensibly bunked down with Stella and Heidi in the old dining room. Zack was no longer wedded to his camera, it seemed. Lisa was silently thrilled when Portia ate the corner of a croissant as well as an apple.

Jake was nowhere to be seen.

A truck full of chairs and tables arrived, followed by a florist's van. Lisa could tell from the clattering and the happy voices that everything was under control. Mojo was desperate to investigate the delicious smells wafting from the kitchen, but she herded him outside to walk around the house. The land where the stables had stood had been designated a car park.

Around the back of the house, the orchard was being transformed. Stella and Heidi were arranging rows of white seats in a semicircle around the apple tree. Runners of red carpet created two aisles that met at a simple table in the leafy shade. Beyond the orchard, long tables were set up around a dance floor. Someone had erected a canvas awning to disguise the to-and-fro of kitchen staff. And up in a tree, Ted was hanging paper lanterns. They looked pretty, but Lisa quailed at the thought of another fire.

Reading her mind, Ted assured her they were lit by batteries, not naked flames. "There's just one thing I want to ask," he said, jumping down to earth in a shower of leaves. "Remember when I was a little boy and you'd make me call you Dearest Mother when I wanted a special favor?"

Lisa chuckled. "That was just to make up for all the times I had to pick up your Legos off the floor."

"Well, Dearest Mother, as the person who gave birth to me and cleared up my Legos, could you honor me by giving me away?"

"What about your father?"

"He hardly knows me," Ted said after a long pause.

They hugged. Lisa willed the day to slow down so she could savor every happy moment like this. But Terence had arrived with Damien the hairdresser, and Lisa was ushered upstairs.

Lisa climbed obediently into her gown and tried to be patient while Damien upgraded her looks. With layers of makeup and her hair smoothed and swept up, Lisa hardly recognized the face in the mirror. Terence riffled through her jewelry box and dug out a pair of silver, sun-shaped earrings she hadn't worn since she was a teenager. He said they'd be perfect and, oddly enough, they were.

"The cat needs a comb-up too!" Terence said, wielding a brush at Mojo. For a one-eyed feral cat, Mojo proved surprisingly vain, purring and arching his back as Terence fluffed out his socks and mane. Special attention was paid to the pouf at the end of his tail, which was tied with a white ribbon.

"That'll last five minutes," Lisa said.

But after sniffing and patting the bow a few times, Mojo approved of the adornment.

Lisa could hear cars on the driveway. The guests had started to arrive. She hurried out onto the balcony. Maxine, in a stunning jade suit and matching fascinator, was escorting Aunt Caroline, resplendent in a silver wig and vibrant yellow jacket. Gordon, bringing up the rear, had gone out of his way to wear a suit.

Their daughter, Nina, stopped them for a moment to take a photo while Dan, the colorectal surgeon, wrangled their flurry of delightful children. Lisa called out and waved to them — no wedding was complete without children. Then she squeezed into her shoes and, following the swish of Mojo's ribbon, wobbled downstairs to greet the guests.

An archway of roses had sprung up to direct people toward the orchard, and guests were now passing through it in droves — a tribe of relations from New Zealand; Juliet and her nearly fiancé, the vet; the Gray

Army and their wives. Beverley was decked out in scarlet to match the color of her husband, Bob's, complexion. "Oh, how cute," she said to Lisa. "You've brought your cat to the wedding."

Lisa smiled. "He brought himself, I'm afraid," she said as Mojo, on Sharky alert, dived into the depths of her gown and coiled around her ankles.

Underneath her hostessy smile, Lisa was anxious for the men in her life to put in an appearance. Not that Jake was officially in her life anymore, but she didn't want him hurting Ted by finding an excuse not to show. As for Scott, she wouldn't be surprised if he'd gotten cold feet. Gay weddings weren't everyone's glass of latte.

Excitement mounted. A string quartet in white ties and tails sat to one side of the apple tree and chirped out Vivaldi's *Spring*. Bees hovered above the women's hats. Lisa scanned the crowd. Most of the guests were seated. A gorgeously handsome man kissed her on the cheek. Ted looked like a duke in his dark suit and dove-gray tie. She slid a white gardenia in his buttonhole.

"It's time," Ted said, quietly leading her away from the apple tree to the end of one of the red carpets.

Lisa glanced across to the other carpet

where James stood, wearing an equally elegant suit and white gardenia. On his arm was his mother, Sue, glorious in a hot-pink dress with red roses in her hair. She and Lisa exchanged discreet waves.

As the music changed to the refined strains of Bach, the celebrant took her place in front of the table under the apple tree. Her gray hair was pulled back in a bun, and her dark blue suit looked like a uniform.

"Dorothy Thatcher?" Lisa whispered.

"There were only two celebrants in the book," Ted whispered back. "The other one's on holiday in Bali."

Lisa straightened, drew a breath, and took her young man's arm. As they were about to step forward there was a commotion at the archway. Todd moved forward on a pair of crutches. Wearing a white shirt and tie, he was every bit as tall and good-looking as his father.

Scott walked proudly beside his son and found him a seat near the back of the congregation. Then he strode over to Lisa and apologized for being late. "You've missed one important guest," he whispered. "Can you hang on a sec?"

Ted nodded and held up his hand to James as a signal to wait. Scott dashed around the side of the house, returning moments later with Kiwi, bright-eyed on her perch.

Ted burst out laughing. "You're right! How could we forget a guest of honor?"

A ripple of amusement went through the crowd as Scott put the cockatoo and her stand in pride of place under the tree. Kiwi flapped her wings and squawked appreciatively.

The music swelled. Scott returned to the back of the gathering and took his seat next to Todd. Ted and James exchanged nods. Floating on Ted's elbow, Lisa recalled the moment her son was born and how the midwife had helped her lift him out of her body; the ecstasy of holding him in her arms for the first time; the years of worry and happiness, tears and triumphs.

The only thing that kept her eyes dry was fear she might topple over Mojo, who was prancing backwards and forward after a butterfly.

As the two grooms and their mothers arrived at the altar in miraculous unison, the musicians fell silent. Expectation hung over the crowd. Lisa and Sue kissed their sons' cheeks and took their seats at the front of the gathering. Sitting beside Portia, Lisa was grateful Stella had moved to fill Jake's empty chair so there was no obvious gap.

Dorothy Thatcher turned out to be an impressive celebrant. She welcomed everyone and alluded to Ted's historic connection to the manor without, to Lisa's relief, any creepy undertones. "I suppose this is the part where I ask anyone who has any objections to this union to speak up now," she added, smiling.

Kiwi emitted a screech of alarm. There was shouting and clattering from behind the canvas awning shielding the kitchen. One hundred and fifty sets of eyes swiveled to witness the canvas bulge then tear apart to reveal a fraught-looking Jake.

"How the hell do I get out of this thing?!" he yelled, punching flaps of canvas.

Waiters bustled forward and tried to close the gaping hole with their hands. Simultaneously, a genius of improvisation appeared with a basket of clothes pegs and sealed the hole.

Jake's suit was ruffled and his hair resembled a mess of steel wool. Portia hurried to his side, brushed him down, and straightened his tie before leading him to the seat Stella had tactfully vacated.

Dorothy Thatcher adjusted her spectacles and surveyed the guests. "Are we ready to continue?"

Gazing into each other's eyes, the boys

recited the vows they'd written and memorized word for word. When Dorothy called for the ring bearers, Portia and James's sister Eleanor stood and presented their brothers with a white rose each. The grooms lifted their gold bands from inside the petals.

After they'd exchanged rings, Dorothy announced that the grooms had decided to change their names to something with a historic connection. From now on they would like to be known as Ted and James Trumperton.

Lisa was deeply moved Ted had chosen to keep her family name alive. Portia passed her a tissue.

After the ceremony, a feast was laid out on the tables, and the afternoon melted into evening in a haze of laughter and sparkling wine. Mojo disappeared, leaving a shredded white ribbon on the dance floor. When a pearly smile of a moon rose over the hills, Ted's lanterns flickered to life, casting pastel shades through the trees.

Aunt Caroline and Castlemaine's more sedate citizens settled into outdoor seats as a jazz band struck up with "It Had to Be You." Ted and James performed a circuit of the floor before inviting their mothers to dance.

"Are you happy?" Ted asked.

"One of the happiest days of my life," Lisa replied.

Ted excused himself to beckon Portia onto the floor, and Lisa made an obligatory beeline for Jake. "I had to drop Belle at the airport," he muttered. "Her flight was delayed."

Over Jake's shoulder, Lisa spotted Scott chatting with Juliet and Jacko under a cherry tree. Kiwi was perched on Todd's shoulder. The boy laughed as the cockatoo ran her beak through his hair.

Maxine appeared at Lisa's side and put a soft arm around her. "They're playing our song," she giggled.

The band was riffing on "Anything You Can Do."

"Not true!" Lisa protested.

"Well, I'm not a world-famous author," Maxine said, guiding her onto the dance floor.

"And *I* haven't managed to stay married to the same devoted husband *and* have my kids and grandchildren all in the same city."

"It's not all it's cracked up to be," Maxine said, leading Lisa into a gentle spin. "You're looking great, by the way."

"So are you."

"You're tipsy," Maxine said, breathing wine over Lisa's face.

"I'm not. *You* are."

"Sorry I was mean to you about buying this place," Maxine slurred, swaying in time to the music. "I was just worried you were taking on too much."

"It's okay. How's the townhouse I nearly bought?"

"There was something wrong with the foundation. The whole lot had to come down. And there's going to be a high-rise apartment block right next door."

"Really?"

"Yup."

"You mean, I could've had just as much trouble in Camberwell?"

Portia and Zack jerked past, shadowing each other in what Lisa could only assume were hip-hop moves.

"What's up with those two?" Maxine asked.

"Nothing. They're not holding hands."

Maxine stopped dancing and put her arms on Lisa's shoulders. "I'm so glad you came home." She fixed Lisa with a serious emerald gaze. "You have no idea how much I worried about you when you were ill."

Lisa sank into the familiar fold of Max-

403

ine's neck. Maxine's skin was looser than when they were girls, but it felt softer, wiser, more forgiving. "Thank you," Lisa whispered. "I love you to bits."

Maxine straightened and set her jaw. She wasn't a fan of soppiness. "You know how it is," she said matter-of-factly. "You'll always be my little sister."

As they stood swaying gently together in the soft light, it occurred to Lisa that, of all the people present, no one knew her better than Maxine. Those same green eyes had peered over the edge of her bassinette. Though Maxine had played merciless tricks on her through childhood, Lisa was deeply grateful they'd both lived long enough to accept all their differences. To forgive real and imagined hurts — and acknowledge the love between them — was all that mattered now.

But her shoes were killing her. She eased them off and kicked them away. They scuttled across the floor to land, like shipwreck victims, in front of a pair of size-thirteen lace-up boots.

"Was that an invitation to butt in?" Scott asked, his smile beaming through to her core.

Lisa could feel Maxine assessing the situation with sisterly accuracy. With a knowing smile, Maxine stepped back and dissolved into the whirl of dancers.

"Great wedding," Scott said as he cradled her hand in his and pressed her gently against his body. "You look *stunning.*"

Lisa tried to persuade herself he was having no physical effect on her.

"Is Todd okay?"

"See for yourself," he said, nodding over her shoulder.

To her delight, Todd was on the dance floor with James's sister Eleanor. Supporting each other by the elbows, they swayed in time with the music. Todd's sticks were resting on a chair. Lisa had never seen him so animated.

"Is he getting better?" she asked, hopeful.

"He's got a new doctor," Scott said, drawing her closer. "She thinks there's a chance he might walk."

"That's *wonderful!*" Lisa could feel his breath on her ear. If she turned her face, they would sink into a kiss. "Please," she muttered, fighting every instinct in her body. "Not here."

Scott released his hold and let space expand between them. "Bit of a raver, your Aunt Caroline," he remarked as the old girl and Gordon tripped by in a steady foxtrot.

A pale hand tapped Scott's shoulder.

"This one's for the parents of the groom, I believe," Jake shouted more loudly than the music's volume warranted.

Scott dutifully released his hold and backed away.

Jake had never liked dancing. He steered her sideways, working her right arm like a pump. "She's not very happy," he shouted.

"Who?"

"Belle."

"Oh."

"She pretty much called it off."

The dance was mercifully near its end. Lisa thanked him and, feigning exhaustion, went over to sit with Portia and Zack.

"How's the documentary coming along?" she asked.

Zack's smile broadened. "Do you want the good or the bad news?" he asked.

Lisa always preferred to get bad news over and done with.

"There was a technical glitch with the camera. My fault, really. I forgot to turn the sound on."

"Oh, Zack!"

"I was on deadline to get the project in, and it was too late to start anything else. So I turned it into a silent film."

"You should see it, Mom!" Portia enthused. "It's real art-house."

406

Lisa tried to maintain a bright, encouraging expression, but, really, it was a disaster.

"Yeah, so I got it in on time and . . ."

"He won a medal!" Portia interrupted. "For best creative work of the year. And . . ."

"It's okay. You don't have to tell everyone," Zack muttered through a fringe of modesty.

"It's going to be on TV."

"Only on some Sunday-afternoon arts program," Zack said, shrugging.

"*And* he's got funding to make a short film."

"Zack, that's fantastic!" Lisa said. "Congratulations."

Portia stood up and kissed Zack on the cheek. As she led him onto the dance floor, Lisa noticed something momentous was taking place — they were holding hands.

CHAPTER 35

Pink ribbons fluttered from the Kombi van's side mirrors. Portia was spray-painting JUST MARRIED in big, loopy letters on the rear window while Zack tied tin cans to the tow bar. They scurried away, laughing, as the grooms appeared on the porch.

"Get thee to a nunnery!" Ted called after his sister. He'd changed out of his formal suit into a pale linen shirt. James was wearing a check shirt. It was no secret they were catching the ferry to Tasmania for their honeymoon. James was keen to visit the famous modern art gallery in Hobart.

Ted and James wrapped Lisa in their arms and kissed her cheeks. "Thanks for the best wedding in the world!" Ted said.

"My pleasure," she replied. "You did all the work."

Jake hurried down the front steps to shake hands with his son and new son-in-law. Then, after embraces and kisses all around, the happily married couple climbed into the Kombi van. As they rattled down the drive in a flurry of ribbons and tin cans, Lisa's lips trembled. It was the best wedding she'd ever been to, including her own.

Guests were reluctant to say good-bye and retreat to their houses and motel rooms. As people began to leave, the band packed up their instruments while waiters cleared tables. Everyone agreed the wedding had been a cracking success. As well as dancing with James's dad, the Gray Army, and half of Castlemaine, Lisa had managed to sneak in a couple of extra waltzes with Scott.

A few partygoers lingered, sitting on the steps of the front veranda. Stella brought out a chair for Todd. Scott helped Heidi carry out plastic seats for those whose backsides were too soft or elderly to sit on concrete. He then joined Jake on the steps to continue their bromance.

Maxine's attempts to lure Aunt Caroline back into her Golf had failed. The old girl was holding court on the sofa. Wedged between Maxine, Gordon, and Dorothy Thatcher, Aunt Caroline was nattering on about being on the royal yacht *Britannia* again. "As for that Colonel Gaddafi, my, he was a tiger between the sheets!" she announced. It was sad to witness the decline of a once-intelligent woman into gaga land.

Lisa placed a cup of treacle-colored tea at her aunt's feet, but the old woman kicked it away, demanding a glass of port instead. At that point Maxine took Lisa aside and begged her not to give Aunt Caroline any more alcohol or Maxine would never get her home.

When Lisa returned from the kitchen to inform her aunt she was out of port, the old woman was stunned into momentary silence. Ron came to the rescue, saying he might have a bottle of dessert wine in the back of his van.

He returned from the car park carrying a brown paper bag.

"That's my lad!" Aunt Caroline whooped.

The liquid tumbled into her glass and down her leathery old throat at a startling rate. After her third or fourth glass, the group was reduced to awed silence.

Aunt Caroline's cheeks turned crimson. Her eyes took on an alarming sheen. "Come on, you lot!" she announced. "How about a sing-along?" She launched into a rendition of "Roll Out the Barrel," using her glass as a baton. Stella and Heidi swung their champagne flutes in time and sang along. They were joined by Ron and Gordon, with Dorothy Thatcher singing the descant. Maxine was dug in the ribs until she, too, sur-rendered and sang along. Todd smiled and nodded obligingly in time.

"Sing *boom* ta-ra-ra!" Aunt Caroline warbled. "Wait a minute . . . STOP!" The old woman pointed a manicured claw at Scott and Jake, who were sitting on the bot-tom step, engrossed in quiet conversation. "Don't you boys know how to have fun?" she said, accusingly. "Come here immedi-ately."

Scott loosened his tie.

"Not you," she snapped. "The little one."

Jake reddened, stood up, and dusted down the back of his pants.

"Come here, my boy," Aunt Caroline com-manded.

Maxine appeared about to intervene, but when she saw how humiliated Jake looked, she stopped.

"Actually, I was about to go to the bath-room," he mumbled.

"Nonsense!" Aunt Caroline took a walking stick from the floor and waved it menac-ingly. "Up you come."

Jake ran a hand through his hair. He shrugged at the audience and made his way up the steps.

"No need to be shy." Aunt Caroline looked like a shark about to snaffle a shrimp. "Now come here!" The old woman seized Jake around the thighs and pulled him down.

He cried out as he toppled onto her lap. The sofa squeaked and groaned under the extra weight. Maxine tried to scramble to her feet, but the seat lurched like a sinking ship. With a tremendous crack it snapped in the middle and, in a flurry of shouts and dust, collapsed.

Lisa ran forward, grabbed her aunt, and yanked her out of the wreckage. The old woman's wig had slipped sideways.

"Are you all right, Aunt Caroline?" she asked, lowering the nonagenarian onto a plastic chair.

"Fine, perfectly fine."

Lisa retrieved her aunt's walking stick and handbag and placed them under her seat.

Dorothy Thatcher, Ron, and Maxine seemed shocked rather than injured. Worst off was Gordon, who'd softened the old woman's fall. He was on his knees, reaching for support from the balustrade.

The sofa resembled a dead animal sprawled on the veranda, vomiting rusty springs and horsehair. From behind a fold of rotting fabric, Lisa saw what looked like a silvery chain. She bent down and tugged it. Attached to the chain was a heart-shaped locket. The silver case was blackened with age, yet the engraving was still visible. Roses were etched around the outer edge of the heart to frame a pair of letters that were intertwined. They were difficult to decipher, as if written in code.

"Who were A and M?" Lisa asked slowly.

Aunt Caroline let out a cry and lurched forward.

"She's having a turn!" Maxine said. "Where's her inhaler?"

"H-h-handbag," Aunt Caroline gasped.

"Gordon!" Maxine barked. "Get her handbag."

"Where is it?" Gordon asked.

Aunt Caroline raised a vein-roped hand and pointed between her legs.

"I can't go in *there*!" he said.

Exasperated, Maxine dived under Aunt Caroline's skirt and retrieved the handbag. The old girl grabbed the inhaler, flicked the lid off, and sucked for all she was worth.

As Aunt Caroline's lungs resumed normal service, Lisa turned her attention back to the locket. "I wonder if it can be opened?"

Aunt Caroline lunged and grabbed the chain. Lisa refused to let go. The old woman summoned all her energy and gave a sharp tug.

The links of the chain stretched, then broke, sending the locket spinning through

413

the air. Lisa cried out as it clattered onto the floor. The impact split the silver heart in two. As she bent to pick up the first half she saw it contained an old sepia photo. The man's face was long and sensitive, the eyes hooded and sad. "It's Alexander, our grandfather!" Lisa cried.

The other half of the locket had skidded under Todd's chair. Lisa crawled over the tiles toward it, but Aunt Caroline's stick blocked her path. "I doubt it's even sterling silver," the old woman said imperiously. "Not worth your trouble."

Lisa pushed the walking stick aside and seized the piece of silver. Standing up, she dusted it off. Inserted in the locket segment was a sepia photo to match the one of her grandfather.

It was of an Aboriginal woman and a baby. Alexander and a black woman? And who was the baby?

Lisa's reverie of shock and fascination was interrupted by the irritating bleep of Maxine's punching numbers into her phone and shouting. "Hello? Emergency services? We need an ambulance. Fast."

CHAPTER 36

Aunt Caroline had suffered a restless night, but she'd stabilized, the nurse said. Everything was being done to keep her comfortable, she assured them.

"I don't like the sound of that," Maxine muttered as they followed the nurse down the gleaming corridor.

The old woman was as white as her pillow, her face chiseled, her hair flattened like seaweed. Her eyes blazed with unworldly intensity over the oxygen tubes in her nostrils. She smiled at the paper sheath of flowers Lisa was holding, but when she saw what they were, her mouth settled in a line.

"I'm sorry," Lisa said. "I know you hate carnations, but it's all they've got in the hospital shop. They smell nice."

"How are you?" Maxine asked.

"Terrible," the old woman rasped. "Some Greek woman across the hall was shouting all night."

Maxine took the flowers away to find a vase.

"So you've come to badger me," Aunt Caroline said.

"Of course not."

"I suppose you were bound to find out sooner or later. This town's full of snoops like that celebrant woman, Dorothy Whatchamacallit."

Lisa took the old woman's hand. It was waxy and cool. Aunt Caroline drifted off. Her lungs labored to empty and fill themselves.

When Maxine returned with the vase of flowers, Aunt Caroline jolted awake. "Where was I? That's right." She breathed in, focusing on a spot on the ceiling. "Your grandfather Alexander was a dashing young man. All the ladies loved him. Except his tastes were . . . how do you say . . . exotic. . . ."

Aunt Caroline was drifting off again. Lisa raised a paper cup of water to her aunt's cracked lips. The old woman gulped like someone who'd found an oasis in a desert.

When she'd finished drinking, she raised her hand, her nails glistening scarlet. "He became involved with a servant girl at the manor. Maggie, she was called. The silly fool went and got herself pregnant. Alexander wanted to marry her, but it simply wasn't done." Aunt Caroline drew a ragged breath.

Lisa plumped her aunt's pillows to make her breathing more comfortable. "Look, you don't have to tell us this," Lisa said gently. "Just concentrate on getting better."

The old woman snorted. "I'm ready to go over the border."

Maxine and Lisa exchanged glances. "Shall I call the doctor?" Maxine asked.

"Keep that idiot away from me. He can go back to Pakistan."

Lisa threw Maxine a look of horror.

"Tell us what to do, Aunt Caroline," Maxine said in a soothing voice.

"Shut up and listen," Aunt Caroline snapped. "My grandparents threw her out, of course. There was nothing else for it. I mean, it's not as if those people had any understanding . . ."

Lisa cringed.

Aunt Caroline turned to gaze out the window. Boys were kicking a football around on a stretch of grass. Assuming the scandalous story was over, Lisa smoothed the hospital sheets.

But the old woman grabbed Lisa's hand and rallied. "My grandparents threw a society ball to take Alexander's mind off things," she croaked. "They wanted to marry him off to a judge's daughter. It was the biggest ball of the season. You can imagine what it was like. Horses and carriages trotting down that driveway. The ballroom full of beautiful gowns . . ." The old woman's lips settled in a faint smile. "The Trumpertons always thought themselves a cut above the rest," she continued. "Turned out the servant girl came from an important family, too. She was the daughter of some chief."

"You mean Elder?" Maxine said.

"That's it. Anyway, when he found out what'd happened to his daughter, he decided to visit the Trumpertons."

Aunt Caroline's legs thrashed under the sheet. Lisa stroked her forehead, trying to soothe her, but the old woman pushed Lisa's hand aside.

"On the night of the ball, the Elder and his people assembled in the garden in front of the house. Maggie stood with them holding her baby. Grandfather was highly embarrassed, of course. He shouted at them to go away."

"What did they do?" Lisa asked.

"They sang."

"Sang?"

"It drove Alexander's father mad. He set the dogs on them, but they didn't run, so

418

the dogs weren't interested. All Castlemaine society was watching and laughing at him. The way he saw it he had no option but to . . ." Aunt Caroline's voice faded. Her eyes drooped.

Across the corridor, horses were galloping to the finish line on a television screen.

"Do you think we should let her rest?" Lisa asked Maxine.

The old woman's eyes snapped open. "I'll have time for that soon enough. . . . Where was I? That's right. Alexander's father took his shotgun from the library. He marched Maggie's father into the stables."

"My God!" Maxine gasped.

"A single shot it was, through the temples."

"Our great-grandfather was a *murderer*?"

"They didn't call it that in those days," Aunt Caroline said with a wave of her hand. "Not when those people were involved."

Lisa and Maxine exchanged looks.

"Surely there was retribution of some kind?" Lisa asked.

"The servants' quarters went up in flames next day. Nobody was hurt."

"Was our great-grandfather arrested?"

"He was never charged, but the scandal affected their business. They lost their money and left for New Zealand. That's where Alexander met my mother, your grandmother Geraldine." Aunt Caroline slumped back against the pillows. The old woman's eyes rolled back under half-closed lids.

"So what happened to the baby?" Lisa asked.

The ancient face turned to her. "Try asking those people in the house across the road from you," she whispered.

"You mean *Mrs. Wright*?"

Aunt Caroline nodded. "Shameful business. I tried to keep you away."

"You mean Mrs. Wright was Maggie's baby?"

"No, not her," Aunt Caroline gasped. "There was a boy. A Trumperton from the wrong side of the doona."

The old woman shuddered violently. A jumble of sounds gurgled from the back of her throat.

"She's trying to say something," said Maxine.

"What is it?" Lisa asked, bending close to the withered lips.

"Next time, bring champagne. Make sure it's French."

Aunt Caroline's chest rattled. Life drained from her eyes.

Chapter 37

Kiwi fixed Lisa with a ruby eye as she wandered into the kitchen, Mojo coiling around her ankles. Lifting a muesli packet off the shelf, Lisa considered the unpredictability of life. Years could pass, sometimes decades, in a rut of routine. Changes were slow and subtle enough to be barely noticeable. Children grew slightly taller, facial lines a little deeper. It was easy to be lulled into a false sense of security, boredom even, and allow yourself to settle like oatmeal grains inside a muesli packet.

Then someone — or some*thing* — picks it all up and gives it a damn good shake. Seeds that were sitting at the bottom of the packet suddenly get thrust to the surface. Raisins collide with nuts. Oatmeal spills over the floor. People get divorced and change countries.

As she watched the muesli tumble into the bowl, her phone bleeped with a text from Maxine: *OMG! A.C. left a note @ retire-ment home demanding cardboard coffin.*

Maxine was in her element, organizing the life out of their aunt's funeral.

Was she an environmentalist? Lisa typed.

No. A cheapskate. Am upgrading to veneer.

Portia glided into the kitchen, her hair gleaming like spun gold. "This new shampoo's great, Mom. Where did you get it?"

"Belle left it here."

Portia opened the fridge and pulled out a plate of leftover lasagna. Lisa tensed — the child was actually going to eat! Excitement flattened to disappointment as Portia tore off a corner of pasta and fed it to Kiwi.

"Can we go see the old people across the road?"

Lisa regretted sharing Aunt Caroline's revelations about the murder with Portia the night before. Now Portia was bursting with curiosity.

Lisa hadn't been near the Wrights' house since the fire. Workmen's vehicles had been parked outside the cottage for some weeks. The roar of chainsaws had gradually morphed into the buzz of saws and the tap of hammers. The old Holden was back in their driveway, but Lisa was nervous about rocking up.

"I'm not sure they want to see us."

Kiwi tugged another square of pasta from Portia's hand.

"Only one way to find out," Portia said.

It was unlike Portia to take interest in anyone outside her generation, so Lisa put on a sunhat and tossed another across the table. Portia inspected it briefly and cast it aside with a smirk. Cancer Council protection was painfully uncool.

Lisa maintained a slow jog to keep up with her daughter's lolloping stride as they crossed the road. A magpie warbled at the top of the Wrights' dirt drive, the bird's black-and-white plumage contrasting with the flush of red flowers on the bottlebrush tree, a miraculous survivor of the fire.

One for sorrow . . . Lisa wasn't superstitious, but it was impossible not to search for the second magpie. She couldn't remember when her father had first recited the rhyme to her. No doubt Alexander had taught it to him the way she'd passed it on to her kids.

"There it is!" Portia cried, pointing out the magpie's mate strutting through the undergrowth. "Two for joy."

Lisa stopped looking for any more magpies. *Three for a letter* didn't make sense. Unless you counted e-mails.

As she and Portia walked through the corridor of blackened tree trunks, Lisa was impressed by the vigorous new growth sprouting from branches. Clumps of green were springing to life on the ground. The Australian bush had much to teach human beings about resilience.

The Wrights' cottage was freshly painted in an apricot shade with a green trim under the windows. A new corrugated iron roof glinted in the sun. Weeds and a few tufts of grass fought through scorched earth that had once been lawn. Lisa glanced around the side of the house. The concrete gnome was still chortling into his pipe under the birdbath, but the tip of his hat was missing. He must've lost it when she'd hurled him through the window.

Mrs. Wright opened the front door. A floral apron encased her tiny, stooped body. White hair frothed around dark brown eyes that flickered with confusion. Lisa felt her cheeks redden. She felt like a little girl trick-or-treating at the wrong doorstep.

The old woman's face softened and beamed with recognition. "Oh, it's you!" she said. "Come on in." Leaning on her walking stick she beckoned them up the steps.

Portia and Lisa followed her into the front hallway.

"I can't thank you enough," the old woman said, taking Lisa's hand and gazing into her eyes.

It occurred to Lisa that only old people and babies could light up spaces with smiles that were incandescent. Perhaps those living close to life's extremities experience each moment with full awareness and intensity. Overcome with shyness, Lisa mumbled that they had to be going soon.

"But you're just in time for a cuppa," her neighbor insisted. "And please. Call me Aunty May."

Lisa and Portia removed their shoes and trod reverently down the hall. The house smelled of fresh paint and lavender. Lisa glanced into the bedroom. Net curtains shifted in a breeze. A 1950s wedding photo presided over a candlewick bedspread. A battalion of pill bottles stood to attention on the dresser. Without the clutter of boxes and old junk the bedroom seemed almost stark.

In the kitchen at the end of the hall, Mr. Wright sat hunched over a Formica table peering at the horseracing page of the *Herald Sun* through a magnifying glass.

"This is the young lady who saved our lives," Aunty May shouted.

He raised himself to a semistanding position and offered a hand wrinkled as brown paper. Lisa shook it and smiled into the oil pools of his eyes. He creaked back onto his chair and raised his magnifying glass.

"Never mind him; he's deaf," Aunty May said. "Do you like living here?"

"I've had my ups and downs, but I love it."

Aunty May hobbled to the sink and filled the kettle, while Portia admired photos of dark-haired children on the window ledge.

"I hear we have a few things in common," Lisa said, clearing her throat.

"What's that, dear?"

"Trumperton Manor."

"Oh, that," Aunty May said, easing herself onto a chair. "We were happy there, but the garden got too much for us, and I couldn't handle the stairs anymore. . . ." The old woman's voice trailed off.

"I know what happened," Lisa said, digging into her pocket and retrieving the pieces of locket.

"My grandfather, Alexander," Lisa said, offering Aunty May the photo.

The old woman nodded politely, as if someone were showing her a scarf she'd knitted. Lisa produced the second half of the locket.

"Do you know who this is?"

Aunty May pointed at her glasses on top of the fridge. Portia reached for them and passed them over. As the old woman perched them on her nose and studied the photo of the woman and child, she lurched forward. She let out a cry so weak and cracked with emotion, Lisa thought Aunty May might collapse.

Mr. Wright glanced up at his wife and assessed the situation. "Women's business," he lisped through stumps of yellow teeth. He raised the magnifying glass and resumed his interest in tomorrow's race.

"That's my mother, Maggie," Aunty May said, after she'd regained her composure.

"Your *mother*?" Lisa said.

The old woman took a handkerchief from the pocket of her apron and dabbed her eyes.

"Then who's the baby?"

The old woman removed her glasses and rested them on the table. "That's my half-brother, George," she said. "A lovely boy. He died of TB when he was sixteen."

Lisa struggled to absorb the connection between herself, this woman, and her own daughter standing solemn and white as milk next to the refrigerator. Lisa's brain felt limp as a sponge.

"So you need to hear the story?" Aunty

May said. Her tone was flat and grave.

Lisa nodded.

Aunty May raised a wrinkled hand and pointed at the two kitchen chairs that were free. "Mind that one," she said as Portia took a seat. "It wobbles."

Portia and Lisa exchanged glances while Aunty May put her glasses back on and gazed at the photo of the woman and the child in the locket. "People said my mother, Maggie, was heartbroken when things went bad at the manor. She got very sick. After Alexander left for New Zealand she kept going back there at night. Some thought she was a ghost. . . ."

Nausea churned Lisa's stomach.

Aunty May curled the locket inside her hand and gripped it. "But she was strong. And she loved little George. After a while she started to get better. She met a good man called Bazza. He worked in the brewery. They married and had five kids, including me."

Lisa felt overwhelming relief that Maggie's story had some happiness in it.

"Nobody wanted to live in the manor after what went on there. There were no cars in those days, and it was miles from anywhere. It was derelict for a while. In the end, Mum and Bazza bought it for a song and moved in with us kids. When Mum died she left the place to me."

Lisa's family tree was beginning to look more like a monkey puzzle than a straightforward pine.

"So Alexander was your half-brother's father?" Lisa said, slowly piecing the branches together.

The old woman turned the locket in her hand. The sadness of the past weighed heavily in the room. Lisa slid onto her knees and put her arms around Aunty May's fragile waist. "I feel terrible for what my ancestors did to yours," Lisa whispered. "My great-grandfather committed a brutal murder. You must feel outraged he was never punished. I'm so sorry. . . ."

Aunty May rested her hand on Lisa's shoulder. The old woman's eyes clouded. "There are tears in every family," she said, patting Lisa's back in a gentle, soothing rhythm. "Let go of the past. We're family now."

The two women wept quietly together.

CHAPTER 38

Shoals of BMWs pulled up outside St. John's Toorak. Lisa stood at the doorway and watched Melbourne's great and good spill down the aisle into the pews. It was an important occasion, but she couldn't wait for it to be over so she could get back to Castlemaine. Scott had asked her out for dinner. Her nostrils flared at the thought of his wearing that aftershave, the one he swore was just soap. Then she felt guilty.

The coffin was smothered in red roses. On top of the narrow end, where Aunt Caroline's feet lay inside their Christian Dior shoes, sat a framed photo that couldn't have been taken later than 1933. The subject's gaze was dreamy and focused slightly off camera, as if she might be recalling a flirtation with an Arab sheik. Aunt Caroline's lips were vermillion, her eyebrows thin and arched. There was no doubt she'd been a beauty, but one with a crafty glint in her eyes.

As the organ swelled in spooky harmonies, Lisa looked for somewhere to sit. She spotted Maxine sitting in the front row, wearing something purple and a black pillbox hat sprouting a peacock feather. The plume dipped and teased Gordon, who was sweating quietly in a suit. Their son, Andrew, fresh from Silicon Valley, sat next to him, alongside Nina and her colorectal surgeon. The grandchildren, dressed in the latest Jacadi outfits, vandalized prayer books while their mother studied her phone.

Sweltering in her interview suit from New York, Lisa noticed an empty pew near the back of the church. Telepathic as usual, her sister turned and flashed a look. Maxine pointed at the pew behind her and beckoned.

"I'm pleased I could make it," Jake whispered as they took their seats. "It was great timing."

"Stop saying that!" she hissed. She wished Jake hadn't felt the need to put on a charade of family togetherness.

Ted and James slid along the pew to sit next to them. "So good of you to cut your honeymoon short," she whispered.

"It was nothing," Ted replied, squeezing

her hand.

As the congregation stood to bleat "The Lord's My Shepherd," Portia skittered down the aisle and slid in next to James. "Sorry!" she mouthed. "We had a few technological hitches."

Portia was wearing a tiara made of small blue stones and sparkles that might have been diamonds. "I found it in Aunt Caroline's dresser," she said, patting the ornament into her hair. "Can I keep it?"

"You'll have to ask Aunt Maxine."

Lisa wished she'd had more time with Portia after they'd visited Aunty May. Lisa wanted to make some sense of their family history with her. But Zack had been waiting at the end of the Wrights' driveway, ready to whisk Portia back into the city to put together the slide show for the funeral.

The vicar cleared his throat and droned on about being here today to celebrate the life of Caroline Agnes Trumperton . . . hostess, patron of the arts. . . .

Gordon stood up and read the eulogy Maxine had written. He ran a finger around his collar, and his face was red and mottled like salami. His voice trembled with nerves as he spoke of the dutiful aunt who was an excellent gardener and who always attended the children's school plays. The congregation was lulled into semiconsciousness. Aunt Caroline's life had been as boring as everyone expected.

Then Zack appeared at the side of the altar, where a large screen had been set up. His laptop oozed Cole Porter songs while an assortment of images lit up the church: Aunt Caroline smiling over a cup of tea with the Queen, smoking a cigar with Castro, astride a camel alongside a dashing young Gaddafi.

No wonder Aunt Caroline had found the nursing home on the quiet side! "Amazing!" Lisa whispered to Portia. "Where did you get them?"

"From a box in the back of her wardrobe. There was one of her with someone who looked like Mussolini, but we thought we'd better leave it out."

The wake was conducted in the church hall in accordance with Aunt Caroline's orders. The tea was Lapsang souchong, and the cucumber in the sandwiches was crisp enough to pose a danger to dental work.

Lisa watched Portia float past the butterfly cakes and lemon slices without landing on a single calorie. Lisa tried to make conversation with a retired admiral to whom Aunt Caroline was rumored to have once been engaged, but images of Scott kept dancing across her brain. The little crossover tooth that stopped his smile from being perfect, the scar above his eyebrow, the hair on the back of his hands . . . He was going to pick her up just before seven. She'd have at least an hour to shower and get ready.

She noticed the more elderly mourners were aiming their walkers at the door. Jake was in a corner chatting up a towering blonde. "Do you think we can go?" Lisa asked, tapping his shoulder.

He glanced at his watch. "Bit early, isn't it?"

"I have to get back to . . . feed the cat."

"That thing can look after itself."

Lisa smiled at the blonde, who was older than she'd seemed from across the room. Jake's taste was improving.

"There's the bird, too."

"Honestly, Lisa, I think we should stay on another hour."

Since when had he become Mr. Etiquette?

"It's okay, Mom," Portia said, appearing at her elbow. "I'll come home with you. Dad can catch a lift with the husbands."

"What about Zack?" Portia and Zack were practically a salt and pepper set these days.

"He's dropping the screen back at his friend's place, then he's catching a lift to Castlemaine with the others. He's never been to a post-wake wake before."

Lisa could hardly believe it. An entire ninety minutes alone in the car with her daughter.

Maxine was engrossed in conversation with the incoming president of the Melbourne Club. The timing was impeccable. Lisa hurried across the room, kissed Maxine on the cheek, and said good-bye.

"But wait!" Maxine said, purple fingernails glistening on Lisa's forearm. "Aren't you coming to the lawyer's office?"

"Whatever for?"

"We *are* her closest relatives."

Aunt Caroline had lived like a pauper. She'd spent the past thirty years collecting string and used wrapping paper. Every Christmas, she had sent Lisa and Maxine each a five-dollar note inside a card. Lisa couldn't face the thought of sitting in a lawyer's office arguing over the old girl's pressed-flower collection.

Instead, she fired up Dino and headed down the motorway. Portia plugged white wires into her ears and drifted off into a hypnotic state. It wasn't shaping up to be the mother-daughter time Lisa had been hoping for. "What are you listening to?" Lisa shouted.

"Nothing."

"Are they new?"

"You wouldn't know them."

Lisa felt the familiar thud of Portia's pulling up the draw-bridge. She turned off at Macedon and parked outside Sitka Café.

"What are we stopping for?" Portia asked.

"You didn't eat much earlier. I thought we'd have afternoon tea."

Portia rolled her eyes. "I'm not going in there."

"Why not?"

The tiara twinkled defiantly. "Because you'll force-feed me like one of those geese in France. Because you're *obsessed* with *food*!"

"Me?!" Lisa hadn't heard anything more ridiculous in her life. Though on second thought, she was the one with the stash of protein bars and special treats for when she couldn't diet anymore, the one who couldn't write a sex scene without eating truckloads of chocolate. "I just worry about you."

Portia seized the door handle. "You don't have to *worry* about me," she said in a voice steeped in sarcasm.

"But . . ."

"You don't understand."

Lisa fizzed with frustration.

"I'm not your little girl anymore!"

The words sliced through Lisa with the

cruel accuracy of surgical lasers.

Portia flung the door open and stormed down the empty street.

Lisa was left momentarily breathless. Gum trees flailed against a pale sky. An exhausted sun was drifting down toward the hills. She started up the engine. As she trailed after the wild, weightless string puppet running into the distance, a vision of Emily Brontë's coffin swam in Lisa's head. Undiagnosed anorexia had surely contributed to her early death.

Portia turned a corner. Lisa followed and curb-crawled alongside her. Portia stopped outside a house with a white picket fence and a statue of the Virgin Mary in the window. Portia's face was pale and wet with tears, her hands clawed with anguish.

Lisa climbed out of the car and stood on the street. The women assessed each other across the gulf of a generation.

"I know you're grown up," Lisa said in a calm, even voice. She was intrigued to hear the words come from her own mouth, but the truth was, Portia was right. Part of Lisa had refused to accept that her daughter was an adult, independent in every way (except financially, Lisa would have liked to point out — not even an ant could survive on part-time waitressing and unpaid acting work, so Lisa and Jake were always topping up Portia's account). "Can we talk?" Lisa asked.

"You wouldn't understand," Portia said, as remote and untouchable as an ice queen.

Lisa was beginning to think "understand" was an overrated word. Even empathy was a challenge. Portia was treating Lisa as if she'd always be there, like the sea. Lisa wanted to grab Portia and tell her she was fragile, too. That if life had any kindness in it at all, she, Lisa, would be dead and gone long before her daughter.

Portia crossed her arms and stared up at a dragon-shaped cloud. Her lower lip quivered. Lisa stepped on the footpath and reached out for her.

"You don't know how hard I'm trying." Portia's voice trailed away.

"To do what?"

"Be beautiful . . . clever."

"But you *are*!"

Portia shook her head. "No, I'm not! I want to be . . . perfect."

Lisa glanced sideways at the statue of the Virgin Mary, her hands clasped in prayer. "Only Allah is perfect," she said, aching for her daughter's pain. Lisa's father had once taken her to a shop where Persian rugs hung from the walls, transforming the place into a grotto of jeweled color. His eyes had blazed as he explained how every knot had been tied by hand, making every rug unique. "They put a deliberate mistake in every rug, Panda Bear. See?" He'd run his hand over a crimson runner covered with flowers and diamond shapes. "If this pattern was regular there'd be a diamond on this side to match the one over there, but the rug maker left it out on purpose, as a reminder that only Allah is perfect."

"I'm so fat," Portia mumbled.

"Have you looked in the mirror lately? Your legs are like pins."

Portia's eyes flashed with rage. "Why do you always *do* that?!" she yelled, tears streaming down her cheeks.

"Do what?"

"Comment on how I look."

"When I was little and even fatter, you used to tell me I was beautiful every day," she sobbed. "You don't say that to me anymore, but everyone else does." Portia crumpled like a sparrow into Lisa's arms.

As she gently rocked her daughter, Lisa's confusion tumbled into a crevasse of sorrow. The Virgin Mary, the ultimate mother, knew a thing or two about the painful aspects of parenting. The statue's eyes were raised to heaven. "Darling daughter. I love you so much."

"I love you too," Portia whispered.

Lisa gulped back tears. It had been years since Portia had last delivered those precious words to her.

"I know what you're going to say," Portia said, wiping her eyes and adjusting her tiara.

"You do?"

"You think I need professional help."

A flock of galahs swooped over their heads.

Lisa drew a breath. "Do you think that's what you need?"

Portia wrapped a tangle of arms around Lisa and convulsed into her neck.

"Would you like me to come back to the States and help you find someone?"

"I'm not going back!" Portia wailed. "I'm staying here!"

"What? Wait," Lisa said, taking Portia by the shoulders.

"I'm moving in with Zack. We're starting up a theater company in the city," Portia said, rubbing her eyes. "And I've found a counselor."

As they walked back to the car arm in arm, Lisa was both overjoyed and chastened. She was elated Portia was staying in Australia and ashamed she'd misread her daughter for so long. Portia was more grown-up than Lisa had realized.

Chapter 39

It was a date. Even Scott had called it that. Lisa had heard him make the booking for seven p.m. at one of Castlemaine's smartest restaurants, the Public Inn. She was running late. By the time she and Portia arrived back at the manor, Lisa's nerves were frazzled. On the road from Castlemaine, she'd had to swerve to avoid a human-sized kangaroo that had sprung out in front of the car with supreme nonchalance.

While Portia disappeared into her room, Lisa dashed upstairs. She tore off her funeral clothes, dived into the shower, and slipped into her lucky floral dress, over which she threw an aqua shawl. By the time she was spruced up and sitting on the porch steps it was 6:40. Mojo, his ginger mane still fluffy from his wedding hairdo, sprang onto her lap. He butted his head into the palm of her hand and purred.

A coil of dust made its way along the main

441

road. Her throat turned to parchment as a pair of headlights glided down the driveway.

But it wasn't Scott's ute. Ted and James climbed out of the Kombi with Zack and Jake close on their heels.

"Hey, gorgeous!" Jake said, lumbering up the steps in his funeral suit. "Going somewhere special?"

She tightened the shawl around her shoulders and studied the hills. Zack sprinted past on the way to Portia's room.

"There's lasagna in the fridge!" she called after him.

Jake shrugged and followed the others inside.

Lisa checked her phone. Five to seven. Scott was bound to arrive any minute. She watched a line of ants crawl out of a crack between some bricks. The next owner would have to fix that.

At seven fifteen she dialed Scott's number and was put straight through to his cheerful drawl on voice mail. She pictured wineglasses gleaming at the empty table, a waiter checking his watch.

The ants were smaller and browner than usual. Maybe they belonged to a different colony.

Ten minutes later she sent a text. No reply.

A familiar figure appeared on the porch.

"Is this seat taken?" Jake asked, lowering himself onto the step beside her.

Maybe it was the comforting click of his knee as he sat down, or the fact she was exasperated with Scott, but she was grateful for the ease of her ex-husband's presence.

"The boys are hoeing into that lasagna," he said, undoing his tie and stowing it in his pocket. "You look like you deserve something more upmarket."

She ran her hand over the arch of Mojo's spine. Jake was on a charm offensive.

"What say we head into town?" he asked, undoing his top button. He always did look good in a plain white shirt.

The Public Inn was bustling, but a spare table for two had miraculously come free because of a no-show. They followed a sunburned young waiter to an intimate spot in the corner. Lisa snuggled into the padded seat against the wall while Jake took the chair facing her.

"Best view in the house," he said, fixing her with a dazzling smile.

For once Lisa couldn't think of a smart retort.

"Great spot here," he said, scanning the wine list. "What do you say to a little French champagne?"

He hadn't bought the real stuff for years. "I thought you liked prosecco?"

"I do, but tonight's got a special feel to it, don't you think?"

She was tempted, but, for all she knew, Jake was expecting to go dutch.

"Prosecco's fine," she said.

He didn't put up a fight. She ordered duck while he went for the usual steak.

"To us," he said, raising his glass and clicking it against hers.

Her attention drifted sideways to the young couple next to them. She couldn't remember how it felt to be that much in love.

The waiter placed a basket of bread and a dish of olive oil on their table.

"I was just wondering . . ." Jake continued. "I mean, don't you miss our old life?"

"What parts of it?" She was tempted to ask if he was referring to the cheating, the rejection — or both.

"Oh, I dunno . . . a Broadway show whenever we felt like it, the galleries and Lincoln Center . . ."

Something inside her chest softened. Jake still knew exactly where her buttons were located and how to push them. She noticed with approval that his temples were fading back to their natural gray.

"And our favorite restaurant," he said, slipping into nostalgia like a warm bath. "You know, the one Anthony Bourdain set up?"

"Les Halles."

"Yeah, that's it. And we have great friends."

The bread was too good to resist. She took a slice and tore it apart. It was still warm from the oven. "You mean *had*," she said.

Jake refused to rise to the bait. "You know, I've learned a lot coming out here," he said, dunking his bread thoughtfully.

"Such as?"

Jake dabbed his lips with a napkin and leaned toward her. "There's nothing like shared history."

That was her old line. She resisted the urge to giggle. "So Belle dumped you."

Jake sprang backwards and raised his hands in denial. "I swear!"

"Come on. She dumped you."

The waiter lowered a plate of sweet-smelling duck in front of her.

"I ended it," Jake said, flattening his napkin in his lap. "And d'you want to know why?"

The waiter leaned forward so as not to miss a word.

"I never realized what a good marriage

you and I had," he said as the waiter released a confetti of black pepper over Jake's
steak.

Corkscrews of steam rose from Lisa's
plate. She waited for the waiter to leave.
"Jake, we're *divorced.*"

He rested his knife on the side of his plate.
"There's not a day goes by I don't regret
what happened, Lisa."

"But you left me!"

"You know how sexually aggressive these
younger women are," he said, glancing
sideways. "She chased me."

Lisa swallowed a gulp of prosecco. "You
want us to get back *together*?" The lines
across his forehead had deepened lately.
He'd given up on the boyish grin. The new,
deflated Jake wasn't without allure.

"We can't just wipe out twenty-three years
of marriage," he said, fixing her with eyes
like melted chocolate.

Lisa took a mouthful of duck. The flavor
was edged with spice.

"My life's a mess without you," he went
on. "I can't sleep. I can hardly breathe."

"That's the dust in the air out here."

He winced as if she'd stabbed him with a
needle. "Don't you miss me?" he asked after
a pause.

She glanced around for the waiter. He was

safely out of earshot. Somewhere in the background, Diana Krall crooned about having someone under her skin. It was true Lisa *did* miss Jake — well, aspects of him. He wasn't a bad man. Besides, he was the only person on earth who claimed to need her. To be needed was something, especially, as Maxine would say, at Lisa's age.

"You know I've always loved you," he said, cradling her fingers.

Her back straightened against the wall. "In the having or desiring way?" she asked. She waited for him to accuse her of being acidic, but he ignored her tone.

"Both ways, Lisa," he said, reaching into the breast pocket of his jacket and retrieving a wad of paper. "Two first-class tickets to New York," he said, unfolding the airline printout and flattening it on the table. "Leaving Friday."

She was stunned into silence. The trees in Central Park would be turning red and gold about now. Ice skaters would be twirling under the statue at Rockefeller Center. The first snowfall would be only weeks away. "But the kids . . ."

"They're getting on with their own lives. We can come back and visit as often as you like."

"And my animals?"

"We could find a pet-friendly apartment."

He had to be serious if he was offering to live with a cat and a cockatoo. "What about Trumperton Manor?"

"C'mon, Lisa. You've had a hell of a time with that old dump."

He was right. The house had pushed her to her limits. She'd have to call Beverley and put it on the market soon.

"I'll take a year off before I start looking for another job," he added. "We'll take that cruise around Norway you've always talked about."

Lisa pictured mountains rising from a fjord, and a steward folding down the sheets on a king-sized bed and placing a chocolate on her pillow.

"I'll never let you down again," he said, raising her hand and pressing it earnestly to his lips. "I worship you, darling. Let's stop off in Fiji and get married again."

A shadow reached across the table. The waiter should've been trained to be more discreet about eavesdropping on people's private conversations.

"Everything's fine, thanks," Jake muttered with a wave.

Except it wasn't the waiter standing over them to ask how their meals were. It was Scott. Freshly showered in a pale, open-necked shirt, he stared down at them. He was white as shaving cream.

Lisa's mouth dropped open. Scott turned on his heels. Crashing past tables like some distraught fairy-tale giant, he lumbered out onto the street.

Lisa disentangled her hand from Jake's. She stood up and pushed her way past startled diners to the restaurant door. Warm night air stroked her cheeks as she stood at the entrance and scanned the street.

An engine sputtered to life. Scott's ute pulled out from a parking space. She waved her arms and shouted. The ute's taillights glowed like a pair of dragon's eyes as Scott roared off into the dark.

CHAPTER 40

A heat wave sailed in from the desert that night. Lisa tried to sleep, but her body felt heavy and sticky like Play-Doh. She thrashed her sheets onto the floor.

Roasting inside his new fur coat, Mojo watched over her from the end of the bed. Sometime after midnight, she felt him thump on the floor and creep away. She checked her phone. Nothing from Scott.

Not long after, she heard an unmistakable tapping on her bedroom door. Jake. She toyed with the idea of letting him in, but it would be the same old routine — unless Belle had taught him some new tricks. A vision of the first-class air tickets to New York hovered over the bed like a delectable pastry. Maybe, with counseling, she'd learn to trust him again. They could talk about it in the morning. She screwed her earplugs in deeper and rolled over.

Soon after dawn, she slipped into her

kimono and flung the balcony doors open. A hot breeze licked over her. She slammed the doors and pulled the curtains, before bundling up the sheets and smoothing fresh, cool ones onto the bed.

Downstairs, a note from Portia sat under a glass on the kitchen table.

Gone 2 Melbourne with Zack. He's got air-con xxxx.

Kiwi flapped on her perch and squawked to be let outside. The cockatoo sailed out the door to the orchard as if it were perfectly normal to take to the skies in forty-degree heat. Meanwhile, Mojo lay as stiff and life-less as a museum specimen on the flag-stones.

Lisa's throat was parched, and her eyes felt like poached eggs after the pan had boiled dry. Yet the day had barely started. She filled a glass of water.

"You're looking lovely," Jake said, sud-denly appearing at her elbow.

She sensed him leaning toward her and on his toes for a kiss. She raised the glass to her lips. It was the perfect barrier.

Freshly shaved, Jake smelled of moss and was wearing a black T-shirt with STAY CLASSY across the front. "Look what I found," he said, turning their old photo album in his hand.

Jake made plunger coffee for them both and carried it on a tray out to the veranda. The sofa was still lying on its side like a dead animal. He sat on the top of the steps and beckoned her to join him. Side by side they pored over the album, chuckling at the sight of their younger selves radiating desire under the Fijian sun. His thigh pressed against hers, almost imperceptibly to begin with. When the pressure became more insistent, she eased away from him. Then he rested his hand on her lap as they cooed over Ted's baby photos. She lifted his hand and gently placed it on his knee as they oohed over Portia in a pram.

"I meant what I said last night," Jake said, closing the book and leaning toward her lips. "Lisa, will you remarry me?"

They were interrupted by the thrumming of tires on the driveway.

"Jeeezuz!" he groaned.

A lime-green Golf trundled to a halt in front of them. Maxine emerged wearing a red paisley caftan and a broad-brimmed hat to match.

"Look what the wind blew in!" Lisa said.

"Isn't this heat awful?" Maxine said, tearing off her sunglasses and striding up the steps. "I've been watching your temperatures. Always two degrees hotter out here." She stopped on the second step and stiffened. "What's *he* doing here?"

Animosity hovered like gun smoke between the two.

"Just extending my stay a little," Jake said. Lisa invited Maxine into Alexander's room while Jake scurried away to make another plunger of coffee.

"That has to have been the most exhausting funeral I've ever been to," Maxine said, staring into her compact mirror and shaping her mouth into a scarlet wound.

"Aunt Caroline would have approved."

Maxine lowered herself into an armchair while Jake appeared with coffee and biscuits. "Guess you'll be going ahead with the spa pool and everything now," she said.

Jake took a mug and perched on the ottoman under the window.

"Pigs would sprout feathers," Lisa said, taking a wistful chomp of a Tim Tam.

Maxine straightened in her chair. "Didn't you tell her?" she hissed at Jake.

Jake shifted uncomfortably.

"About what?" Lisa asked.

"Our session at the lawyer's office," Maxine said, flashing a lightning bolt of rage at Jake. "His lordship here pushed his way in.

453

I tried to stop him, but he convinced the lawyer he was representing you and the kids."

Jake crossed his ankles and shrugged. "I only did it because you were rushing back to Castlemaine with your pants on fire," he said to Lisa.

Maxine bristled like an echidna. "Tell her!"

Jake took a handkerchief from his trouser pocket and wiped his neck. "Turns out your Aunt Caroline was loaded," he said.

An image of Aunt Caroline's wrapping Christmas presents in last year's paper sprang to Lisa's mind. "But she collected rubber bands," Lisa said.

"Go on," Maxine said, dangerously close to pouncing on Jake and throttling him.

Jake cleared his throat. "Apparently some old earl was very 'fond' of her back in the thirties," he said. "He left her a fortune."

Lisa licked the chocolate off her thumb. "Good on her. She was a master of secrets. Or, in this case, a mistress . . ."

"Really, Lisa, you can be so naïve!" Maxine slammed her mug on the table. "Aunt Caroline never spent the dosh. She kept it in her post-office savings account. And now she's left it to us."

"You and me . . . ?" Lisa asked carefully,

in case the "us" meant just Maxine and Gordon.

"We're wealthy now," Maxine said. "You and I can do what we bloody like."

Lisa sank into a long silence.

"And while we're here, you can tell her your other news," Maxine said finally, fixing Jake with a lethal glare.

Jake arranged his hands in the prayer position and sandwiched them between his knees. "I've been meaning to tell you, my investments — I mean *our* investments — in the Tongan quinoa industry went down the toilet. On top of everything else, well . . ."

"Tell her!" Maxine snapped.

Jake shifted his weight on his buttocks. "I had to file for bankruptcy."

Maxine pursed her lips with satisfaction. "I sat next to that little floozy of his the night before the wedding," Maxine said. "She told me everything."

Lisa felt giddy with shock. Jake had his faults, but he'd always been sensible with money. "You lost everything?" she asked him.

He nodded and stared down at his lap.

Why had he bought first-class tickets when he was on the bones of his backside? The pieces began to turn and click together like glass inside a kaleidoscope. "So the only reason you were so keen for us to get back together was because Aunt Caroline left me a pile of dough?"

He stood up, brushed his trousers down, and headed for the door. But his exit was blocked by a mass of vegetation. An enormous bush of red bottlebrush and orange eucalyptus flowers filled the doorframe.

Visible below the outrageous bouquet was a pair of well-worn work boots, size thirteen.

CHAPTER 41

Lisa glanced up from her computer. Her study no longer smelled of paint. With its dark-green walls lined with books and Polynesian masks, it felt like home. The photos of Alexander with his Castlemaine love and their baby gazed down on her. Since she'd had the images enlarged and repaired, the affection between the couple beamed across the decades. Aunty May was thrilled with the copies Lisa had given her.

Working on *Three Sisters: Anne* had been a breeze, and the last chapter practically wrote itself. Anne was in love with Harold, the good-hearted farmer whose son was confined to a wheelchair. Harold had even mentioned the *m* word. But after all she'd been through, Anne couldn't face the thought of getting married. Or even, as Harold put it, "shacking up for a bit." Anne suggested it might be more romantic if they maintained the status quo, living separately and staying over at each other's houses now and then. Harold was about to agree when Lisa heard a voice calling from down in the garden.

Mojo grumbled and rolled off her lap. Lisa stood and opened the window. Across the valley, the sun was sinking into the hills. Clouds were blushing red. The angular silhouette of the pergola rose against the sky. Its rust-colored frame was taller, more modern, than it had appeared on the plans. The sight of Scott's panther-like body still made her breath catch at the back of her throat. Holding a hose in one hand, he waved up at her. "Come on down! It's nearly full."

It had been his idea to divide the pool into two sections. When hot wind ripped in from the desert, the cool, deep plunge pool would be a godsend. On chilly nights, when the sky became a jewel box of stars, the smaller, heated spa would be irresistible.

Lisa watched Scott toss the hose aside and tear off his shirt. He launched into the plunge pool, creating a fountain of diamonds.

Mojo galloped ahead as she hurried to her room, then eyed her curiously as she pulled on her swimming costume and self-consciously draped a towel over her thighs.

As she made her way downstairs the cat charged outside and galloped along the paths. He skidded to a halt when he reached the edge of the pool. Sitting on his haunches, he dipped a tentative paw in the water and shuddered.

She dropped her towel on the tiles and lowered herself into the cool water. It was deeper than it looked. Scott dived under and tugged her leg. She squealed and kicked him off.

"It'll take a couple of hours for the spa to heat up," he said, shaking droplets off his hair. "We could try it later on, when it's dark. . . ." In a couple of over-arm strokes he was at her side. His shoulder muscles glistened. "Two weeks," he said.

"What?"

"That's what I gave you when you moved here."

She drew a breath and sank through the silky depths till her toes touched the concrete floor. She filled her mouth with water, pushed herself to the surface, and squirted his face.

"Honestly!" he laughed. "How was a stuck-up New York writer lady going to survive out here?"

"Stuck-up?!"

"C'mon. You were fancy as hell. . . .

Per*gola*, *pergola*."

"Thanks a lot."

She heaved herself up onto the edge of the pool and reached for her towel. Droplets sparkled on her arms. Across the valley, trees glowed gold with autumn. Scott rose effortlessly out of the water, pulled her to her feet, and wrapped her in his arms.

The night after the funeral she'd been ready to dump him. She'd been too engrossed in her own agenda to imagine what might be happening at Scott's place. Around the time Lisa was slipping into her lucky dress, Todd had tried to walk without help and had taken a nasty tumble. Scott had driven him to Accident and Emergency. He'd tried to call Lisa, but his phone had been out of juice.

Any offense she'd taken had evaporated. If Scott was to be part of her life, Todd would be included without question. The young man was a regular visitor to the manor, where he was a huge hit with Mojo and Kiwi. Lisa was fond of him, too. His campaign to walk again was surprising the medical profession. He'd actually managed to take a few steps alone.

Seeing more of Todd involved arranging pick-ups and drop-offs with Beverley. While she and Lisa would never be soul mates,

Lisa had learned to respect Beverley's chutzpah, along with her pink boots and rhinestones.

As Lisa and Scott strolled hand in hand toward the house, a pair of white wings sailed off the upstairs balcony and swished steadily toward them.

"Incoming!" Scott warned, releasing her hand and rearranging his towel over his neck. As the bird approached, she extended her gray claws toward Scott's shoulders. The landing would've been perfect if she hadn't nearly toppled down his back.

"C'mon you!" Lisa said, scooping Mojo up to nuzzle his soft face.

The cat squirmed out of her grasp and dropped to the ground. Some things never changed.

Kiwi teetered like a drunk while Scott bent and ran his hand over Mojo's back. The ginger lion cat arched with pleasure.

With its crisp white shutters and shining windows, Trumperton Manor was hardly recognizable as the house she'd first seen. Now that the stables and the servants' quarters were gone, it was released from its painful history and ready to begin a new phase. A new sign had sprouted from the flowerbed beside the front steps. Carefully carved and painted by Scott, it read TUM-

461

BLEDOWN MANOR.

Aunt Caroline's windfall couldn't have come at a better time. It allowed Lisa to settle her debts as well as finish the renovations and landscaping. True to form, Maxine had spent her share of the inheritance on a beach house at Portsea on the peninsula.

Lisa was in no hurry for Ted to finish drawing up plans for the new stables. He and James visited nearly every weekend, but there was plenty of room for them to stay in the house as it was.

Portia's counseling sessions were going well. Her weight was improving. The play she'd written with Zack, *Care Bear Killer,* was in the final stages of rehearsal. Lisa had swapped with another volunteer at Juliet's animal rescue center so she and Scott could drive into the city for opening night.

The billabong and wetlands were attracting birdlife Aunty May said she hadn't seen since she was a girl. Lisa loved the way the water surface turned silver at dusk.

Now, as Scott and Lisa climbed the steps to the veranda, pink clouds streaked across the sky. The horizon melted to amber. Pulling her towel tighter around her, Lisa made a beeline for the sofa. Scott had done a reasonable job fixing it, but it was still hard on the backside. Once she was settled, Mojo sprang onto her lap. Kiwi took that as a cue to take up her position on the balustrade.

Scott pointed at his toolbox, which he'd left on the sofa beside her. "Upgraded my screwdrivers," he beamed. "Thought you'd like to take a look."

Really, he could be a dope sometimes. As if she cared about screwdrivers.

"Go on," he nodded. "Take a look."

Preparing to feign enthusiasm, she flicked the lock and opened the lid. Inside were two crystal flutes and a bottle of champagne. "French?" she gasped, lifting the bottle and reading the label.

"I figured you deserve the real McCoy," he said, taking the bottle from her hand and easing the cork with a muted pop.

As he filled her glass, a shaft of sunlight shot the liquid through with gold. She watched the tiny bubbles stream to the surface.

A kangaroo bounded toward purple hills as she savored the eucalyptus-laden air. Trumperton Manor and its land were in her veins. She belonged.

Scott grinned and raised his glass. "Here's to the new Duchess of Trumperton Manor." She chuckled and assured him she was no aristocrat.

They clinked glasses, then Lisa took a sip. "To Tumbledown Manor!" she said.

ACKNOWLEDGMENTS

When I was growing up in New Zealand, Dad often spoke of Ferndale Manor in country Australia. His mother had lived there as a young woman. His eyes would shine as he regaled us with stories of society balls, garden parties, and an unspecified tragedy that happened in the stables. In a pre-Internet era, there was no hope of finding out how much he was making up. The manor house, if it existed at all, was across more than a thousand miles of sea, on the outskirts of a town called Castlemaine.

I thought Dad was fantasizing, until the day he unearthed a pile of motley sepia photos. Ferndale Manor was indeed a magnificent building. In one photo my grandmother, a pretty young woman in a long gown and hat, stands outside the gates. Her pose is demure. She seems to be looking down at something in her hands — a small book, perhaps. Her top-hatted brother is bolt upright astride a nearby horse. There's something defiant in the way he meets the camera's gaze. Inside the gates, farther down the driveway, an older woman dressed in black watches over the scene. She seems wary, as if she expects her adult children to run off and do something scurrilous.

The photo still fascinates me. I'd love to breathe the same air as those three ancestors just for a few moments. Their lives weren't short of drama. It wasn't long after the photo was taken that they lost all their money and fled to humbler conditions in New Zealand.

Life has ways of looping back on itself. Many years after Dad died, I found myself living in Melbourne, just a ninety-minute drive from Castlemaine. Ferndale Manor isn't at all tumbledown, by the way. It has been lovingly restored. The gateposts are just as they were in Dad's old photo. Once, when we cheekily knocked on the door, the owner was generous enough to show us around. The upstairs ballroom was stunning. I was deeply touched when she showed us a piece of original wallpaper. She confirmed a tragedy had taken place in the stables, a suicide.

Though I love traveling, particularly to

the United States, I often feel the pull of Castlemaine. After one trip away, I asked my husband, Philip, to drive me out there. The car rattled down a dirt road, and suddenly we saw the old house basking in the afternoon sun. Overcome with a sense of longing, I told Philip it was just as well the place wasn't on the market. I'd want to buy it immediately. In that moment, Lisa's story was born.

Around the time I was inspired to write about Lisa buying back her heritage, several women friends were facing horrendous midlife challenges. Husbands were walking out, teenagers were playing up. Others were physically unwell, losing jobs they'd devoted their lives to — or enduring painful combinations of the above. I wept with them and wondered how on earth they'd get through.

There are no road maps for the second half of life. It's no wonder when just a hundred years ago, the average life span was forty years. A woman of fifty was expected to wear her hair in a bun and rock her days away — in a chair, not at a Bruce Springsteen concert.

I'm happy to report that a few years after their midlife catastrophes, my women friends are flourishing. It wasn't always easy for them, but transformation is never straightforward. Just look at a butterfly struggling to shed its chrysalis. These days, most of my friends are actually grateful circumstances forced them to reinvent themselves. They've done it with tremendous style, I might add.

Tumbledown Manor is my homage to these women. I'd like to think the book might also give hope to others. With laughter, imagination, and dollops of courage the second half of life can be a joyous flight.

My brilliant editor, Michaela Hamilton, deserves a medal for wading through my first attempt at fiction and letting me know where I was going wrong. She's also responsible for the country dance scene in *Tumbledown Manor.* When I was in New York, she took me to a glorious contra dance in the basement of a church in Chelsea. There's no better way to burn calories. A few weeks later in Castlemaine, I discovered traditional dancing is pretty much the same there — except this time there were no bearded men in ball gowns.

I'd also like to thank Philip, my family, and friends. You are my moon and stars.

ABOUT THE AUTHOR

Helen Brown was born and brought up in New Zealand, where she first worked as a journalist, TV presenter, and scriptwriter. A multi-award-winning columnist, Helen now lives in Melbourne, Australia, with her family and feline, the internationally beloved Jonah. *Cleo* rose to the top of the bestseller lists in its first weeks in the United States, United Kingdom, New Zealand, France, and Australia, and has been translated into more than sixteen languages. *Cats & Daughters* further increased her audience with publications in six countries. *Tumbledown Manor,* already a bestseller in Australia/New Zealand and in Germany, shows her storytelling talents at their best. You can visit Helen Brown at www.helenbrown.com and follow her on Facebook.

The employees of Thorndike Press hope you have enjoyed this Large Print book. All our Thorndike, Wheeler, and Kennebec Large Print titles are designed for easy reading, and all our books are made to last. Other Thorndike Press Large Print books are available at your library, through selected bookstores, or directly from us.

For information about titles, please call:
  (800) 223-1244

or visit our Web site at:
  http://gale.cengage.com/thorndike

To share your comments, please write:
  Publisher
  Thorndike Press
  10 Water St., Suite 310
  Waterville, ME 04901